Her Dark Curiosity

Also by Megan Shepherd:

THE MADMAN'S DAUGHTER

HER
DARK
CURIOSITY

A Madman's Daughter Novel

MEGAN SHEPHERD

BALZER + BRAY

An Imprint of HarperCollins*Publishers*

Balzer + Bray is an imprint of HarperCollins Publishers.

Her Dark Curiosity
Copyright © 2014 by Megan Shepherd
All rights reserved. Printed in the United States of America.
No part of this book may be used or reproduced in any manner whatsoever
without written permission except in the case of brief quotations embodied
in critical articles and reviews. For information address HarperCollins Children's
Books, a division of HarperCollins Publishers, 10 East 53rd Street,
New York, NY 10022.
www.epicreads.com

ISBN 978-0-06-212805-8 (trade bdg.)
ISBN 978-0-06-232653-9 (international edition)

Typography by Alison Klapthor
13 14 15 16 17 LP/RRDH 10 9 8 7 6 5 4 3 2 1
❖
First Edition

To Peggy and Tim,
for a childhood filled with books & love

ONE

THE AIR IN MY crumbling attic chamber smelled of roses and formaldehyde.

Beyond the frosted windowpanes, the rooftops of Shoreditch stretched toward the east in sharp angles still marked with yesterday's snow, as chimney stacks pumped smoke into an already foggy sky. On nights like these, I never knew what dangers might lurk in the streets. Yesterday morning a flower girl around my age was found frozen on the corner below. I hadn't known her aside from glimpses in the street, one girl on her own nodding to another, but now her dark, pretty eyes would never again meet mine in the lamplight. The newspapers said nothing of her death—just one of dozens on such a cold night. I'd learned of it in slips and whispers when I made my usual rounds to the flower stalls and butcher stands. They told me she'd tried to stuff flowers between the layers of her meager clothing for warmth. The flowers had frozen too.

I pulled my patchwork quilt tighter around my

shoulders, shivering at the thought. After all, a threadbare scrap of fabric wasn't much more than crumpled flowers.

Winter in London could be a deadly time.

And yet, as I studied the street below where children trailed a chestnut roaster hoping for fallen nuts, I couldn't help but feel there was something about the narrow streets that whispered of a certain familiarity, a sense of safety despite the rough neighborhood. The tavern owner across the street came out to hang a sparse holly wreath on her paint-flecked door, getting ready for Christmas in a few weeks. My thoughts drifted backward to memories of mincemeat pies and presents under a fir tree, but my smile soon faded, along with the fond remembrances. What good would presents do me now, when death might be just around the corner?

I returned to my worktable. The attic I let was small, a narrow bed and a cabinet missing a drawer arranged around an ancient woodstove that groaned into the night. My shabby worktable was divided in two halves; the right-hand side contained half a dozen twisted rosebushes in various states of being grafted. A flower shop in Covent Garden paid me to alter these bushes so that the same plant would produce both red and white flowers. The meager profit I made helped pay for the rent and the medical supplies on the left side of the table: a syringe from my previous day's treatment, a package wrapped in butcher paper, and scrawled notes about the healing properties of hibiscus flowers.

I took my seat, letting the patchwork quilt pool onto the floor, and reached for one of the glass vials. Father had developed this serum for me when I'd been a baby, and until recently it had kept the worst of my symptoms at bay. Over the past few months, however, all that had begun to change, and I was growing more ill: muscle spasms, followed by a deep-seated ache in my joints, and a vertigo that left my vision dulled. The instant I touched the vial, my hand clenched with a sharp tremor, and the small container slid from my fingers and shattered on the floor.

"Blast!" I said, hugging my quaking hand to my chest. This was how the fits always began.

As flickering shadows from my lamp threw beast-like shapes on the roof, I cleaned the broken glass and then unwrapped the butcher's package and smoothed down the edges. The smell of meat filled the air, ironlike, only just beginning to rot. My head started to spin from the odor. I lifted one of the pancreases. The organ was the size of my fist, a light fleshy color, shriveled into deep wrinkles. The cow must have been killed yesterday, maybe the day before.

Its death might mean my life. I'd been born with a spinal deformity that would have been fatal, if my father hadn't been London's most gifted surgeon. He'd corrected my spine, though the operation resulted in a scar down the length of my back and several missing organs that he'd been able to substitute in his desperation with those of a fawn. My body had never quite accepted the foreign tissue, resulting in the tremors, dizziness, and need for daily injections.

I wasn't certain why the serum was failing now. Perhaps I was becoming immune, or the raw ingredients had altered, or perhaps now that I was growing from child to woman, my body's composition was changing, too. I'd out-grown his serum just as I had my childish respect for him. His serum had only ever been temporary anyway, lasting a day or two at most. Now I was determined to create something even better: a permanent cure.

The pancreas's puckered flesh yielded under my scalpel's sharpened blade, separating like butter. It required but three simple incisions. One down the length. One to expose the glycogen sac. Another to slice the sac free and extract it.

I slid over the tray clinking with glass vials, along with the crushed herbs I'd already mixed with powders from the chemists'. This work had a way of absorbing me, and I scarcely realized how the afternoon was passing, or how cold the air seeping through the window was growing. At last I finished this latest batch of serum and waited impatiently to see if the various ingredients would hold. In order to be effective, the disparate parts would need to maintain cohesion for at least a full minute. I waited, and yet after only ten seconds the serum split apart like a bloated eel left too long in the sun.

Blast.

It had failed, just like all the times before.

Frustrated, I pushed my chair back and paced in front of the twisted rosebushes. How much longer could I go on like this, getting worse, without a cure? A few more months? Weeks? A log cracked in the woodstove, sending hot light licking at the stove's iron door. The flames flickered like those of another fire long ago, my last night on the island. I had been desperate then, too.

Montgomery stood on the dock, the laboratory where he'd helped Father with his gruesome work blazing behind him. Waves lapped at the dinghy I crouched in, waiting for him to join me. We'd sail to London, put the island behind us, start a new life together. And yet Montgomery remained on the dock, let go of the rope, and pushed me out to sea.

But we belong together, *I had said.*

I belong with the island, *he'd replied.*

A church bell rang outside, six chimes, and a glance at the window told me night had settled quickly. I was late again, reliving memories I'd sooner forget. I grabbed my coat and threw open the door, dashing down four rickety flights of stairs until I was outside with the wind pushing at my face and the cold night open before me.

I stuck to the well-traveled, gaslit thoroughfares. It wasn't the fastest route to Highbury, but I didn't dare take the shortcuts through the alleyways. Men lurked there, men so much larger than a slip of a girl.

I turned north on Chancery Lane, which was busy at all hours with people loitering between pubs, and I hugged my coat tighter, keeping my eyes low and my hood pulled high. Even so, I got plenty of stares. Not many young ladies went out alone after dark.

In such chaos, London felt much like Father's island. The beasts that lurked here just had less fur and walked more upright. The towering buildings seemed taller each day, as though they'd taken root in the oil and muck beneath the street's surface. The noise and the smoke and the thousand different smells felt suffocating. Too closely packed. Ragged little children reached out like thorny vines. It felt as if eyes were always watching, and they *were*—from upstairs windows, from dark alleys, from beneath the low brims of wool caps hiding all manner of dark thoughts.

As soon as I could, I escaped the crowd onto a street that took me to the north section of Highbury. From there it wasn't too far to Dumbarton Street, where the lanes were wide and paved with granite blocks, swept clean of all the refuse found in the lesser neighborhoods. The houses grew from stately to palatial as my boots echoed on the sidewalk. Twelve-foot-high Christmas trees studded with tiny candles shone behind tall windows, and heavy fir garlands framed every doorway.

I paused to lift the latch of the low iron gate surrounding the last house on the corner. The townhouse was three stories of limestone facade with a sloping mansard roof that gave it a stately air, as though it had quietly withstood regime changes and plague outbreaks without blinking an eye. It was on the quiet end of Dumbarton, not the grandest house by far, despite the fact that its owner was one of London's wealthiest academics. I dusted off my coat and ran my fingers through my hair before ringing the doorbell.

The door was opened by an old man dressed in a three-piece black suit who might look stern if not for the deep wrinkles around the corners of his eyes, which betrayed his inclination to smile in a charmingly crooked way—a habit he gave in to now.

"Juliet," he said, "I was starting to worry. How was your visit with Lucy?"

I smiled, the only way I knew to hide my guilt, and pulled off my gloves. "You know Lucy, she could chatter away for hours. Sorry I'm a bit late." I kissed his cheek as if that would make up for the lie, and he kindly helped me out of my coat.

"Welcome home, my dear," he said.

TWO

PROFESSOR VICTOR VON STEIN had been a colleague of my father's—and the man who turned him in to the police ten years ago for crimes of ethical transgression. The professor's betrayal of their friendship might have bothered me when I was younger and still had respect for my father, but now I thought he'd done the world—and me—a favor. I owed him even more because, for the last six months, he'd been my legal guardian.

When I'd left Father's island, I'd followed Montgomery's instructions to find a Polynesian shipping lane and, after nearly three scorched weeks in the dinghy, was picked up by traders bound for Cape Town. From there, the expensive trinkets Montgomery had packed bought me passage to Dakar, and on to Lisbon. I'd gotten sick on the last leg of the voyage, and by the time I reached London was little more than a skeleton, raving about monsters and madmen. I must have said my friend Lucy's name, because one of the nurses had summoned her, and she'd taken care of me, but my good fortune ended there. One of the doctors was an old acquaintance from King's College by the name of Hastings. A year ago he'd tried to have his way with me and I'd slit his wrist. As soon as he learned I'd returned, he'd had me thrown in jail, which was where Professor von Stein had found me.

Lucy Radcliffe told me your circumstances, he had said. *Is it true what you did to this doctor?*

He needn't have asked. The scar at the base of Dr. Hasting's wrist matched my old mortar scraper exactly.

It is, I'd said, *but I had no choice. I'd do it again.*

The professor had studied me closely with the observant eyes of a scientist, and then demanded I be released into his custody and the charges dropped. Hastings didn't dare argue against someone so highly respected. The next day, I went from a dirty prison cell to a lady's bedroom with silk sheets and a roaring fire.

Why are you doing this? I had asked him.

Because I failed to stop your father until it was too late, he'd replied. *It isn't too late for you, Miss Moreau, not yet.*

Now, sitting at the formal dining table with a forest of polished silver candlesticks between us, I secretly kicked off my slippers and curled my toes in the thick Oriental rug, glad to put that old life behind me.

"An invitation arrived today," the professor said from his place opposite me. The hint of an accent betrayed that he'd grown up in Scotland, though his family's Germanic ancestry was evident in his fair hair and deep-set eyes. A fire crackled in the hearth behind him, not quite warm enough to chase the cold that snuck through the cracks in the dining room windows.

"It's for a holiday masquerade at the Radcliffes'," he continued, removing a pair of thin wire-rimmed spectacles from his pocket, along with the invitation. "It's set for two weeks from today. Mr. Radcliffe included a personal note saying how much Lucy would like you there."

"I find that rather ironic," I said, buttering my roll with the hint of a smile, "since last year the man would have thrown me into the streets if I'd dared set foot in his house. He's changed his tune now that I'm under your roof. I think it's *you* he's trying to win over, Professor."

The professor chuckled. Like me, he was a person of simple tastes. He wanted only a comfortable home with a warm fire on a winter night, a cook who could prepare a decent coq au vin, and a library full of words he could surround himself with in his old age. I was quite certain the last thing he wanted was a seventeen-year-old girl who slunk around and jumped at shadows, but he never once showed me anything but kindness.

"I fear you're right," he said. "Radcliffe has been trying to ingratiate himself with me for months, badgering me to join the King's Club. He says they're investing in the horseless carriage now, of all things. He's a railroad man, you know, probably making a fortune shipping all those automobile parts to the coast and arranging transport from there to the Continent." He let out a wheezing snort. "Greedy old blowhards, the lot of them."

The cuckoo clock chimed in the hallway, making me jump. The professor's house was filled with old heirlooms:

china dinner plates, watery portraits of stiff-backed lords and ladies whose nameplates had been lost to time, and that blasted clock that went off at all hours.

"The King's Club?" I asked. "I've seen their crest in the hallways at King's College."

"Aye," he said, buttering his bread with a certain ferocity. "An association of university academics and other professionals in London. It's been around for generations, claiming to contribute to charitable organizations—there's an orphanage somewhere they fund." He finished buttering his roll and took a healthy bite, closing his eyes to savor the taste. He swallowed it down with a sip of sherry.

"I was a member long ago, when I was young and foolish," he continued. "That's where I met your father. We soon found it nothing more than an excuse for aging old men to sit around posturing about politics and getting drunk on gin, and neither of us ever went back. Radcliffe's a fool if he thinks they can woo me again."

I smiled quietly. Sometimes, I was surprised the professor and I weren't related by blood, because we seemed to share what I considered a healthy distrust of other people's motives.

"What do you say?" he asked. "Would you like to make an appearance at the masquerade?" He gave that slightly crooked smile again.

"If you like." I shifted again as the lace lining of my underskirt itched my bare legs like the devil. I'd never understand why the rich insisted on being so damned uncomfortable all the time.

"Good heavens, no. I haven't danced in twenty years. But Elizabeth should arrive by then, unless there's more snow on the road from Inverness, and I've no doubt we shall be able to wrangle her into a ball gown. She used to be quite the elegant dancer, as I recall."

The professor stowed his glasses in his vest pocket. Elizabeth was his niece, an educated woman in her mid-thirties who lived on their family estate in northern Scotland and served the surrounding rural area as a doctor—an occupation a woman would only be permitted to do in such a remote locale. I'd met her as a child, when she was barely older than I was now, and I remember beautiful blond hair that drove men wild, but a shrewdness that left them uneasy.

"You know how the holidays are," he continued, "all these invitations to teas and concerts. I'd be a sorry escort for you."

"I very much doubt that, Professor."

While he went on talking about Elizabeth's Christmas visit, I dug my fork beneath my dress and scratched my skin beneath the itchy fabric. It was a tiny bit of relief, and I tried to work it under my corset, when the professor cocked his head.

"Is something the matter?"

Guiltily, I slid the fork into my lap and sat straighter. "No, sir."

"You seem uncomfortable."

I looked into my lap, ashamed. He'd been so kind to take me in, the least I could do was try to be a proper lady. It surely wasn't right that I felt more comfortable wrapped in a threadbare quilt in my attic workshop than in his grand townhouse. The professor didn't know about the attic, and only knew a very limited account of what had happened to me over the past year. I had told him that the previous autumn I'd stumbled upon my family's former servant, Montgomery, who had told me that my father was alive and living in banishment on an island, to which he took me. I'd lied to the professor and said Father was ill and passed away from tuberculosis. I had claimed that the disease had decimated the island's native population and I'd fled, eventually making my way back to London.

I had said nothing of Father's beast-men. Nothing of Father's continued experimentation. Nothing of how I'd fallen in love with Montgomery and thought my affections returned, until he'd betrayed me. Nothing of Edward Prince, either, the castaway I'd befriended, only to learn he was Father's most successful experiment, a young man created from a handful of animal parts chemically transmuted using human blood. A boy who had loved me despite the secret he kept carefully hidden, that a darker half—a Beast—lived within his skin and took control of his body at times, murdering the other beast-men who had once been such gentle souls. Edward was dead now, his body consumed in the same fire that had taken my father. That didn't mean, however, that I'd ever managed to forget him.

By the time I looked up, I found the professor's attention had strayed to his newspaper. I returned to my baked hen, stabbing it with my fork. Why hadn't I seen Edward's secret? Why had I been so naïve? My thoughts drifted to the past until the professor let out a little exclamation of surprise at something he read.

"Good lord, there's been a murder."

My fork hovered over my plate. "It must have been someone important if it's reported on the front page."

"Indeed, and unfortunately, I knew the man. A Mr. Daniel Penderwick, solicitor for Queensbridge Bank."

The name sounded vaguely familiar. "Not a friend of yours, I hope."

The professor seemed absorbed by the article. "A friend? No, I'd hardly call him a friend. Only an acquaintance, and a black one at that, though I'd never wish anything so terrible upon the man as murder. He was the bank solicitor who took away your family's fortune all those years ago. Made a career of that dismal work."

Uneasiness stirred at the mention of those darker times. "Have they caught his murderer?"

"No. It says here they've no suspects at all. He was found dead from knife wounds in Whitechapel, and the only clue is a flower left behind." He gave me a concerned glance above his spectacles, then folded the paper and tossed it to the side table. "Murder is hardly proper dinner conversation. Forgive me for mentioning it."

I swallowed, still toying with the fork. The professor was always worried that whenever an unpleasant topic of conversation arose, I'd think of my father and be plagued by nightmares. He needn't have worried. They plagued me regardless.

After all, I had helped kill Father.

When I looked up, the professor was studying me, the laugh lines around his eyes turned down for once. "If you ever need to discuss what happened while you were gone . . ." He shifted, nearly as uncomfortable with such conversations as I. "I knew your father well. If you need to resolve your feelings for him . . ." He sighed and rubbed his wrinkles.

I wanted to tell him how much I appreciated his efforts, but that he would never understand what had happened to me. No one would. I remembered it as if it had happened only moments ago. Father's laboratory burning, him locked inside, the blood-red paint bubbling on the tin door. I feared he would escape the laboratory, leave the island, and continue experimenting somewhere else. I'd had no choice but to open the door. A crack, that was all it had taken, to let Jaguar—one of my father's creations—slip inside and slice him apart.

I smiled at the professor. "I'm fine. Really."

"Elizabeth is better with this sort of thing. You'll feel more comfortable with another woman in the house, someone to speak with freely. What would a wrinkled old man know about a girl's feelings? You're probably in love with some boy and wondering what earrings to wear to catch his eye."

He was only teasing now, and it made me laugh. "You know me better than that."

"Do I? Yes, I suppose so." He gave his off-balance smile.

It wasn't my way to be tender with people, but the professor was an old curmudgeon with a kind heart, and he'd done so much for me. Kept me from prison. Given me elegant clothes, kept me fed on French cuisine, and done his best to be the father figure I should have had.

On impulse I went to his end of the table, where I wrapped my arms around his shoulders and kissed his balding head. He patted my arm a little awkwardly, not used to me showing such emotion.

"Thank you," I said. "For all you've done for me."

He cleared his throat a little awkwardly. "It's been my pleasure, my dear," he said.

After dinner I climbed the stairs, jumping as the cuckoo clock sprang to life in the hallway. I considered ripping the loud-mouthed wooden bird out of its machinery, but the professor adored the old thing and patted the bird lovingly each night before bed. It was silly for him to be so sentimental over an old heirloom, but we all have our weaknesses.

I went to my room, where I locked the door and took out the silver fork I'd stolen from the dinner table, pressing my finter against the sharp tines. The professor had set up accounts at the finer stores in town for me, but what I needed was cash—paper money for my secret attic's rent, for the equipment and ingredients for my serums, and grafting roses only paid so much. I stared at the fork, regretting the need to steal from the man who'd given me a life again. But as I looked out the window at the dark sky and saw the snow falling in gentle flakes, flashing when hit by the lights of a passing carriage, I told myself I was desperate.

And desperation could lead a person to things one might never do otherwise.

THREE

THAT NIGHT, LIKE MOST nights, I lay in my sprawling bed, staring at the ceiling, and trying desperately not to think about Montgomery.

It never worked.

When I had moved into the professor's home, he had wallpapered my bedroom ceiling in a dusky pale rose print. Now, my eyes found hidden shapes among the soft buds, remembering the boy who would never give me flowers again.

"He loves me," I whispered to nothing and to no one, counting the petals. "He loves me not."

When I'd been a girl of seven and he a boy of nine, he'd once accompanied us to our relatives' country estate. One morning after Mother and Father had gotten in a terrible row, I'd found a small bouquet of Queen Anne's lace on my dresser. I'd never had the courage to ask Montgomery if he'd left them. When Mother found the flowers, she tossed them out the window.

Weeds, she had said.

Years later, he'd given me flowers on the island, when we were no longer children and he'd outgrown his shyness. He'd won my affection, but his betrayal had left my heart dashed against the rocks, broken and bleeding.

"He loves me, he loves me not," I whispered. "He'll forget me, he'll forget me not. He'll find me, he'll find me not...."

I sighed, letting the sounds of my whispers float up to the rose-colored wallpaper. I rolled over, burying my face in my pillow.

You must stop with such childish games, I told myself, as the place beneath my left rib began to ache.

THE NEXT MORNING THE professor took me to the weekly flower show at the Royal Botanical Gardens, held in the palatial glass-and-steel greenhouse known as the Palm House, where I found myself surrounded by ranunculus and orchids and spiderlike lilies, and where the only things more ostentatious than the flowers were the dozens of fine ladies sweating in their winter coats. A year ago I'd never thought I would find myself wearing elegant clothes once more, amid ladies whose perfume rivaled the flowers, who tittered about my past behind my back but wouldn't dare say anything to my face.

It was shocking how much one's fate could twist in a single year.

The professor, who I was quite certain wished to be anywhere but in a sweaty greenhouse surrounded by ladies, wandered off to inspect the mechanical system that opened the upper windows, leaving me alone to the sly looks and catty whispers of the other ladies.

. . . used to work as a maid . . .

. . . father dead, you know, mother turned to pleasing men for money . . .

. . . pretty enough, but something off about her . . .

Through a forest of towering lilies, a woman in the next aisle caught my eye. For a moment she looked like my mother, though Mother's hair had been darker, and she'd been thinner in the face. It was more the way this woman hung on the arm of a much older white-haired man, dressed finely with a silver-handled cane. The woman wore no wedding ring—so the man was her lover, not her husband.

The couple paused, and the woman stopped to admire the lilies. I was about to leave when I overheard her say, "Buy me one, won't you, Sir Danvers?"

Sir Danvers. I gave him another look, discreetly, studying the expensive cane, the bones of his face. Yes, it was he. Sir Danvers Carew, Member of Parliament, a popular lord and landowner—and one of the men who used to keep my mother as his mistress. He'd seemed kind, like his reputation, until he turned to drink. He had once knocked Mother around the living room, then struck my leg with that same cane when I'd tried to stop him. I hadn't thought of him in years, and yet now my shin ached with phantom pain from that day.

I turned away sharply, though there was no danger of him recognizing me. Back then I'd been the skinny child of a mistress he hadn't kept but a few weeks, and now I was one of the elegant young ladies come to admire hothouse flowers in winter.

"May I show you these lilies, miss?" a vendor across the aisle said. I turned my head, still a bit dazed by the memories. "They're a new hybrid I developed myself," she continued. "I cross-pollinated them with Bourgogne lilies from France."

Eager to be away from Sir Danvers, I pretended to admire the flowers. The blooms were beautiful, but the hybridization had made the stems too thick. They would have done better crossed with Camden lilies to keep the stems strong but delicate. I didn't dare start talking aloud about splicing and hybridization, though—I'd have sounded too much like Father.

I swallowed. "They're beautiful."

"There you are!" called a voice at my side. Lucy came tripping along the steam grates in a tight green velvet suit, fanning her face. "I've been up and down every hall looking for you. Oh, this blasted heat." With her free hand she dabbed a handkerchief at the sweat on her forehead. Beneath our feet, the boilers churned out another blast of steam that rose as in a Turkish bath. I inhaled deeply, letting it seep into my pores. I felt healthier here, in the tropical warmth, where the symptoms of my illness never seemed quite as bad.

Lucy glanced rather disdainfully at a bucket of mangled daisies with broken stems. "Good lord. It looks as though someone pruned those flowers with a butter knife."

"It isn't about the sharpness of the blade," I said. "It's

about the hand that holds it."

"Well, if you ask me, that hand isn't anything special either. Must we come here every week? What do I care for flowers, unless a young man is giving them to me?"

I smiled. "Which dashing young man would that be? You seem to have quite a few these days."

Her powdered cheeks grew pinker as she brushed by a display of orchids, absently knocking their petals to the floor. "Papa prefers John Newcastle, of course, and I know he's handsome and a self-made man and all that, but he's so *boring*. And then there's Henry, and my goodness, I simply can't abide him. He's from Finland, you know, which might as well be the end of the earth. He hadn't even seen an automobile until one practically ran him over in Wickham Park."

As I watched her carelessly knock over an entire plant, I said, "For a boy you keep claiming to dislike, you certainly seem to dwell on him."

She gasped with indignation and rattled on more about her other suitors, but I only half listened. I'd heard all this before, time and time again, different young men depending on the week. I nodded absently while I stooped to clean up the flowers she'd knocked over.

"Really, Juliet," Lucy said in exasperation. "You must remember you're not a maid anymore."

I paused. She was right. I lived with a wealthy guardian now and was back in good social standing. Seeing Sir Danvers and remembering my mother's fall from grace had made me relive my former shame all over again. At the far end of the aisle, Sir Danvers and his mistress admired some orchids. He tapped the cane on the steel grates at his feet, sending vibrations all the way to where we stood. I had the sudden urge to stride over, snatch the cane from his hand, and slam the silver tip into his shin, as he had once done to mine. For a man his age, it wouldn't take much force to shatter the bone.

My hands itched for that cane. More tittering laughter came from behind me, cruel and high-pitched, and I imagined the flower show ladies whispering among themselves.

. . . violent tendencies . . .

. . . well, with a father like hers . . .

Itch, itch, itch. But I forced myself to turn away. The professor wanted to prove I could be a respectable young lady despite who my father had been. The only problem was, being respectable wasn't nearly as second nature as I had thought it would be.

I turned my back on them, facing the frost-covered wall of the greenhouse, beyond which I could make out the shadowy shapes of falling snow. As I watched, a black police carriage pulled up outside. My breath froze. Ever since Scotland Yard officers had arrested me in response to Dr. Hastings's accusations, I'd been jumpy around policemen.

All that is behind you, I reassured myself.

But the carriage stopped, and a handsome officer perhaps ten years my senior climbed out, and through the glass panes dripping with condensation, he looked directly at me.

I TURNED TOWARD THE sprays of ferns, Sir Danvers forgotten, thoughts racing. If this had been Father's island, I could have disappeared into those vines with silent steps I'd learned from his beast-men. But large as the greenhouse was, the police would find me in minutes.

Lucy gave me a strange look, dabbing at her brow. "Whatever's the matter with you?"

"The police are here," I whispered. I jerked my chin toward the door at the far end of the palm court, where the groan of the heavy iron door sounded. I should get away from Lucy. It would only humiliate her to have her friend arrested so publicly.

I started for the door to intercept him, but Lucy grabbed my arm. "The police? Oh, don't tell me you're still afraid of the police. That was ages ago, and everything was sorted out. And look at you; you'd look like royalty if you'd just stop slouching so much. Only criminals slouch."

My heart pounded harder as the officer appeared through the vines that draped from the catwalk above. He was a tall man with a sweep of chestnut hair that matched Lucy's, and he walked with the confidence of the upper classes. Not a beat patrol officer, then. They'd sent someone important for me—how thoughtful. He was dressed in a fine dark suit with an old-fashioned copper bulletproof breastplate beneath his cravat, and a pistol at his hip.

My muscles twitched, urging me to flee, but Lucy's arm still held me.

"Oh, him?" She sighed. "You've nothing to worry about. He's not here for *you*. Papa must have sent him to collect me."

I looked between the officer and Lucy, still not

understanding. "What do you mean?"

"That's John Newcastle, the suitor Papa's so fond of," she said. "I was just telling you about him. Weren't you listening? Really, Juliet."

I stared at her. "You didn't say he was a police officer!"

"He isn't a police officer," she said, fluffing her hair where the humidity had made it go flat. "He's an inspector. Scotland Yard's *top* inspector." Her voice dropped to a mutter. "He's rather fond of telling me how important he is, not to mention handsome. He'd marry himself, I do believe, if he could."

"Lucy—" I started, but Inspector Newcastle reached us then and gave us a dashing smile, his eyes only darting to me in a perfunctory manner before settling on Lucy.

"Lucy, darling." He bent forward to kiss her cheek, which left a glistening mark that she dabbed at with the handkerchief.

"Papa sent you, I presume?"

"He invited me to supper, and I offered to come collect you."

She pounced on my arm again. "John, this is my friend Juliet Moreau. Oh, Juliet, I've a fine idea. Go ask the professor if you can join us for a bite to eat." Her insistent wink told me she didn't want to spend an extra moment alone with her suitor.

"Yes, you're welcome to join us, Miss Moreau." He extended his hand to take mine, but as soon as my fingers were in his, his hand tightened. "Have we met before? Your name sounds somewhat familiar."

I glanced at Lucy. "I don't believe so, Inspector. I think I would remember." I extracted my fingers from his grasp, wishing I could just as easily remove his suspicions about my name from his thoughts. I nodded my chin toward his copper breastplate. "What an unusual piece. Is it an antique?"

"Why, yes," he said, clearly pleased. "It belonged to my grandfather. A lieutenant in the Crimean War. Kept him alive despite five bullets and a gunpowder explosion. I try to be a modern man, and we have better protective garments these days, but a little sentimental superstition can be healthy, don't you think?" He tapped his breastplate good-naturedly.

I smiled, relieved I'd managed to distract him from my name.

Lucy slid her arm into mine and said, "Juliet's quite a tragic case, I'm afraid. Both parents dead, left penniless. She even had to *work* at one point."

She started to lead me toward the door, but I pulled away a little too fast. I had errands to run before returning home, errands I had to keep secret.

"Thank you for the offer, but I've plans with the professor. It was a pleasure meeting you, Inspector. I'll see you soon, Lucy."

I ducked away from them and found the professor amid the crowd, still engrossed by the rusted mechanics of the greenhouse. He smiled warmly when he saw me.

"I wondered if you'd mind if I had a bite to eat with Lucy," I said.

"Well, certainly," he said, eyes twinkling. Now he

could go home to his books and a thick slice of Mary's gingerbread cake. I kissed him on the cheek and hurried through the tunnel of palms to the doorway, where I could at last be on my own. I took one last breath of the thick, warm air, before pushing the heavy door open and bracing for the cold.

A swirling gust of snow ruffled my velvet skirts. The botanical garden's ice-covered lake spread in front of me, the water sprite fountain in the center now frozen under a waterfall of ice.

I'd get an earful from Lucy later. She wouldn't like that I'd left her to fend off John Newcastle's kisses alone. But just being around the police—even a well-mannered inspector—made me nervous.

And I had my errands to run.

I drew my fur-lined coat around my neck and waited behind the frozen skeleton of an azalea for Inspector Newcastle and Lucy to leave. They climbed into the black carriage amid pleasantries I couldn't make out, save for a single curse from Lucy when her skirt caught on the curb. I smiled at her impropriety as their carriage rolled away over the cobblestone.

Pulling my coat tighter, I made my way toward Covent Garden. The sun was already heading for the horizon, so I slipped into an alleyway that would cut my walk by half. The alley was quiet, save for a pair of cats chasing each other through abandoned crates.

Ahead of me a short young man approached from the opposite direction, cap pulled low over his brow so his face was hidden in shadows. As our paths grew closer, he took his time looking me up and down, giving me gooseflesh. He wasn't wearing gloves, and I noticed that he was missing his middle finger—a difficult detail to ignore. I stiffened. The only reason an otherwise warmly dressed man wouldn't wear gloves on a day this cold was if he planned on needing his dexterity for something.

I stepped into the street to pass him with a wide berth, but he spun around and walked alongside me. The hair on the back of my neck rose. I forced myself to keep walking, hoping he'd just doubled back on some forgotten errand, even though I knew it was too late for wishes. I glanced at my boot, where a knife was hidden—a trick I'd learned from Montgomery.

"Spare a coin, miss?" the man asked, suddenly right at my side, in a voice that seemed unnaturally deep. His bare fingers reached out, the missing middle finger leaving an unnatural vacancy.

I jerked away. "Sorry, no."

"With those fine buttons? Come on, miss. Just a coin. It isn't safe out here, alone on the streets. Not safe for a girl at all."

I saw his arm twitch a second before he grabbed my coat. I ducked out of his grasp and pulled the knife from my boot, then shoved him against the curb at the right angle for his ankles to catch. It threw him off-balance and he fell. I collapsed on top of him, knee digging into the soft center of his chest, knife at his throat, as I checked the alley to make certain we were alone.

His cap fell back, and I started as shoulder-length red hair tumbled out around a pretty face. A girl younger than me, disguised as a man, which explained the put-on deep voice. That was good—a girl I could scare off. A man I might have had to inflict some damage upon.

"I know it isn't safe," I hissed. "What do you think *knives* are for?"

I pressed the knife closer against her neck, watching the flesh wrinkle beneath it. Her eyes went wide.

"I didn't mean nothing!" she said, voice substantially higher now. "Please, miss, I swear, I just wanted them buttons!"

I narrowed my eyes at her, digging my knee deeper until I felt a rib, and then gave an extra jab before climbing off her.

I jerked my chin toward the opposite street. "Go on," I said. "And next time put some lampblack on your chin to look like a beard, and for god's sakes wear gloves; your bare hands gave you away instantly."

She scrambled to her feet, brushing the muck off her clothes, and stumbled away at a run. I sheathed the knife in the boot holster, then wiped a trembling hand over my face, breathing some life back into my cold hands.

I took off at a brisk walk, still shaken, the afternoon clouds overhead the only witness to the incident I couldn't forget fast enough, until at last I saw the shining lights of Covent Garden.

FOUR

THE MARKET WAS FILLED at all hours with a vast range of people, and I gladly plunged into the safety of their midst. Ladies in fine dresses shopped for Christmas presents, scullery maids swarmed past the wrinkle-faced vegetable women, tailors and seamstresses haggled in the textile quarter. My fine coat and boots caused no one to give me a second glance, until I slipped into the meat section of the market. Few fine young ladies could stomach these narrow passageways. Eels as long as my arm twitched on hooks above lambs' glassy dead eyes, and stray cats licked up the salty blood pooling on the floor. By the time I reached Joyce's Choice Meats, I was getting nothing but strange looks.

Jack Joyce, however, tipped his hat to me.

Joyce, an Irish ex-boxer who'd turned to the meat trade in his old age, cracked a broken-toothed grin as I approached. His previous profession had left him not only minus a few teeth but with a permanent squint eye that never seemed to be looking in the same direction as the other. A small black dog with a white spot on his chest and notable only in his ugliness, wagged his tail.

"Hello, Joyce," I said, and then knelt to scratch the dog's bony head. In general, I did my best to stay away from animals. They only reminded me of the dark experimentation Father had done. That was why I limited myself to plants. Roses couldn't kill, or maim, or betray.

"And hello to you too, boy." I picked up the dog, though he was heavy in my arms. "He's put on a pound or two, I believe."

"Aye. Soon enough he'll be fatter than a queen's lapdog, if you keep buying him scraps. And just as lazy." Joyce took his knobby old hands away from his fire and dug around behind the counter until he came back with some chicken bones that he tossed to the dog.

Technically, the dog was mine. He'd started following me around town ever since I'd first come to Joyce's Meats six months ago. It was the meat in my pocket he smelled, and the only way I could get him to keep from trailing at my heels was to pay Joyce to keep him well-fed on scraps, a task that despite his grumbling, I suspected, the old boxer rather enjoyed.

"Let's see," Joyce said, digging around beneath the counter. He came up with a package wrapped in butcher paper and tied with twine. "Here's your order. Two pancreases, one liver. Couldn't get my hands on the deer heart you wanted. I should have it next week."

"That's fine," I said, slipping the package into my pocket. Just being here stirred the bones of my hands from their slumber, made them remember what Father had done to me. I flexed them, hoping to hold off the symptoms of another fit.

The dog finished his chicken bone and barked at Joyce, who stooped down on his bad knee and scratched the dog's head. "When are you going to give this ugly fellow a name already?" he asked.

I leaned against the counter, watching the dog thumping his tail. "He isn't *my* dog."

"Don't think he understands that."

"My guardian wouldn't care much for a stray in his house. I fear I'm already uncivilized enough for him." I didn't mention how the last dog I'd named, a puppy called Crusoe, had died under Father's scalpel. The thought made my stiff hands ache more, and I pushed them into my coat pockets.

Joyce grinned. "Aw, you could use a companion. Keep him in a back garden. How about Romeo, eh? Romeo and Juliet, you were made for one another."

"I was made for a flea-ridden stray?" I couldn't help but laugh. "Well, perhaps you're right. Though in any case, Romeo doesn't suit him. Who's that boxer you're always talking about? The underdog. That mutt's an underdog, if I've ever seen one."

"Mike Sharkey," Joyce said. "Pride of Ireland. He beat that big Turkish bloke four to one. What do you say, fella? Are you a Sharkey?"

I watched Joyce pet him and scratch beneath his chin.

Joyce had always been friendly with me, and never once asked what a well-dressed young woman wanted with so many animal organs.

"Hope you're taking care out there, miss, walking around town on your own, especially this late in the afternoon. It'll be dark soon. You've heard about the murders, I wager?"

"Which murders? This is London. There are a dozen murders every day."

His eyes went serious beneath his brow. "Didn't read the morning paper, did you?" He rooted around in the stack of old newspapers he used to wrap cuts of meat and slapped one down on the table.

"A MASS MURDERER IN THE MAKING?" the headline read.

"Three murders in the last two days," Joyce said. "Scotland Yard says they're connected; the murderer leaves his mark at each crime scene. It's all anyone's been talking about. They're calling him the Wolf of Whitechapel on account of how he claws up the bodies. One of them had a purse on him and a gold watch, but the murderer didn't touch it. Wasn't interested in anything but tearing that man apart like an animal."

Like an animal.

The twist in my gut grew to a desperate squeeze, and I had to lean on the counter to catch my breath. *Like an animal*, that's how Edward had killed his victims. Ripped their hearts out with six-inch claws.

My hand slid to my chest, pressing against the hard

whalebone corset. On the island, I'd seen a woman with her jaw ripped off. Buzzing flies. A blood-stained tarpaulin. Mauled, like all the others.

To this day, even so long after his death, my heart wrenched to think that Edward had killed so many of the islanders. He had seemed such an innocent young man, and yet beneath his skin lurked a monster.

A monster created by my father.

"Christ, didn't mean to frighten you, miss. I forget you're a proper lady sometimes."

"It's quite all right, Joyce," I said with a shaky smile.

I started to pick up the package to go when he said, "You just be careful, miss. Flowers dipped in blood, that's his mark. That's how they know the bodies are connected."

I slowly turned back to him. The professor had said that a flower had been found beside the body of that terrible solicitor, Daniel Penderwick, who had taken my family's fortune on behalf of the bank. Shocked that I had been acquainted with the first victim of what the police thought might be a mass murderer, I pointed toward the paper. "On second thought, do you mind if I read that article?"

He passed me the newspaper and I pored over it carefully. There was Penderwick's name, listed as the Wolf of Whitechapel's first victim. A second victim had been found last night, torn apart with violent wounds, and a white flower left nearby. The victim's name made me start.

Annie Benton.

A creeping feeling began in my ankles, making my toes curl. Annie Benton had been my roommate when I worked as a maid at King's College. She'd had a bad habit of digging through my belongings. A few months ago she'd gotten back in touch with me under the pretense of friendship, but had then stolen my mother's small diamond ring—the only thing I had left of her.

I leaned against the butcher's stand to steady myself. If I'd read Annie's name in any other context, I would have been seething with anger, but the thought of her murdered by such violent means left me feeling strangely hollow and out of place, as though time was moving backward.

Was it coincidence that I'd known two of the victims?

"These are the only murders? Annie Benton and Penderwick?"

"Rumors of another one found just an hour ago. Unidentified body—so they claim," Joyce said. "I'd like to think there won't be more, but Scotland Yard don't have much to go on."

The creeping sensation ran up the backs of my legs. My vision started to go foggy as blood pooled in my extremities. I gripped the butcher's stand harder and accidentally brushed against one of the glassy-eyed pig's heads. I jumped and cried out.

"You feeling all right, lass?"

"Yes," I stuttered. "Here—some coins for this package, and to keep the dog fed. I should go."

"I'll see you next week for the usual order?"

I nodded before leaving, still clutching Joyce's newspaper, along with the meat. It wasn't until I was halfway to Highbury, and the sun had dipped behind the skyline, that I realized I'd taken the wrong road.

I'd wandered into the seedy end of Whitshire, where rats outnumbered the people ten to one and more gaslights were broken than not. The hair rose on the back of my neck, reminding me of my altercation with the girl thief earlier. I'd been lucky that time to escape unharmed. I might not be lucky again.

I took a deep breath as I mentally worked out a map for the direction I needed to go to get me back to a well-lit street. I hurried past a dress shop full of headless mannequins, taking care to avoid the open street, but a foggy feeling crept upon me.

Stay near the lampposts, I told myself. *Stay near the light.*

I turned the corner onto a shadowy street with only a single lamp glowing at the far end, and my heartbeat sped. After a few minutes I felt the neck-tingling sensation that I was being followed, and considered reaching for the knife in my boot. But as I strained my ears, I made out only the sound of little footsteps that stopped when I stopped, and when I whirled around to face my pursuer, the little black dog was behind me. He wagged his tail.

"Oh, Sharkey," I gasped. He ran over and I gave him a good scratch. "You weren't supposed to follow me! I haven't time to take you back to the market now—I'll be late getting home as is." I sighed. "Well, come on."

It was a quiet evening, save for the wind that ruffled the strands of hair that had come loose from my braid. I hurried through the streets with Sharkey at my heels, though

I hadn't a clue how I'd explain him to the professor. Lock him in the garden, perhaps, until morning. It was impossible to think about anything but the murders, until I nearly stepped on a white flower on the ground in front of me.

I stopped.

A flower itself was rare enough in winter. I knew all too well how much care and tending they needed to stay as fresh as this one was. It lay all by itself on a patch of sidewalk wiped of snow as though someone had left it for me, creamy white petals radiating from a gold center, a delicate stem no thicker than a bootlace.

A tropical flower.

There was a rustle in the alleyway to my side—a rat, no doubt—and the dog took off after it. I knelt in front of the flower. Five petals, not unlike the ones that had grown on Father's island. Montgomery had picked one, once, from the garden wall and tucked it behind my ear. The memory of Montgomery made the place around my rib throb with familiar hurt.

He loves me, he loves me not. . . .

My heart twisted at the memory, and I turned to go. I should get home, before I was late for supper and the professor grew suspicious. But the flower was so beautiful, delicate as a whisper there in the snow, that I couldn't leave it.

I pulled off a glove and reached down to pick it up.

As soon as I did, I knew something was wrong. My bare fingers touched a wet substance beneath the flower. I held my fingers up to the faint light from the lamppost.

Blood.

Blood spotted the back of the flower, as though it had been pressed into a pool of it. It was still fresh.

FIVE

FLOWERS DIPPED IN BLOOD, Joyce's voice echoed. *That's his mark.*

In a blind panic I stumbled to my feet, screaming for Sharkey. His little face peeked out from the alleyway.

"Come here, boy!" I cried.

He took a few shaky steps toward me, and my eyes went to the tracks he left in the snow.

His paw prints were bloody.

"Sharkey!" I raced toward him, scooping him up and checking his feet, his legs, his body for cuts, but it wasn't his blood in the snow, and I set him back down. *Whose blood was it?* He must have tracked the blood from within the alleyway, and whatever he'd seen or smelled in there now made him shiver and bury his snout in the fold of my arm.

The light was dark, and I fumbled for a matchbox in my coat pocket. I knew I shouldn't look, and yet it was impossible not to. I lit a match and took a step deeper into the alleyway, then another, and another, despite my every sense screaming to turn away. The match light caught on a dark pile of rags in the corner, splashed with blood that smelled sharp in the crisp air. A pale hand lay beneath the pile, missing a middle finger, heavily bruised as though it had been trampled.

I jolted with recognition—the girl who tried to steal my silver buttons not but an hour ago, now trampled and bleeding. Murdered.

I took in the crime scene in flashes of the flickering match, my mind whirling as I stumbled closer, then away, then closer yet again, my instincts caught in a frantic fight-or-flight, curiosity winning in the struggle. I could only see tears in her men's clothing, smell the blood. In my delirium, it brought back too many memories from the island.

A crack of ice sounded behind me. I gasped, afraid I wasn't alone, and broke into a frantic run with Sharkey at my heels. I raced through the snow, ignoring the burn in my lungs. Sweat poured down my back like oozing fear, and my strangled breath grew shallower the farther I ran, past the row of closed doors, past the dress shop with headless mannequins, into the wider street where lights shone like beacons of safety.

I collapsed in the doorway of a closed bakery and glanced behind to make sure I wasn't being followed by anyone other than Sharkey, who trotted up beside me. Visions of the girl thief's body haunted me. Steam still rising from the body, signaling a fresh kill. The murderer must have been there moments before—the murderer Scotland Yard was so desperately hunting. The man who had killed Daniel Penderwick. Annie Benton. An unnamed victim.

And now one more.

The wind blew cold enough to make my teeth ache. A rusty hinge groaned, and I jumped back into a run. It all threatened to overwhelm me—the thief's body curled in the snow, the bloody flower—and I had to choke back a sob. At last I reached the church on the corner and turned onto Dumbarton Street, where I slowed to a jittery walk. Sharkey trotted beside me, still shivering. I picked him up and wrapped him in the folds of my coat as best I could, mindless of the blood getting on the fabric.

It wasn't easy to climb the professor's garden trellis with the dog tucked inside my coat, but I managed. The window had a keyed lock, but I had broken through that my second night in the house. Hydrochloric acid was easy to get from the chemist's, and it dissolved iron even in small doses. After that it had been a simple matter of replacing it with a similar lock to which I held the key.

I eased the window up as quietly as I could and climbed inside. I wiped Sharkey's paws with a handkerchief before setting him on the rug, then tore off my coat and stripped out of my dress and corset and all the trappings I was made to wear, leaving them pooled in the corner of the room.

Tomorrow I'd hide the bloody clothes from the maid.

Tomorrow I'd see things clearly again.

Today, though, all I could manage was to dress in fresh clothes and grab another coat, then climb back out of my window and return to the front door so the professor wouldn't suspect anything was wrong. I smoothed my hair back, checking my hands one last time for flecks of blood, and then pressed a trembling finger against the door chime.

An eternity passed before Mary answered, drying her hands on a cotton towel, her face flushed from the kitchen fire. She had the smell of ginger on her and a streak of rust-colored cinnamon across her apron, but all I could think of was blood, and my stomach lurched.

"Evening, miss." She barely glanced at me as she brushed away the streak of cinnamon. I had to force my body to step into the foyer. Close the door behind me. Lock it tight.

From the dining room came a half-strangled sound like a cat dying, and my nerves flared to life again. I should tell someone about the body. I must. And yet the police would have certainly found her by now. If I said anything, there would be questions: why was I in such a rough neighborhood, not at tea with Lucy where I belonged. . . .

Mary sighed as another mechanical shriek came from the dining room. "It's that clock of his," she whispered. "Broke this morning while you were out, and he's gotten it into his head to fix it himself." Another strangled cry of the wood bird sounded. "Maybe *you* can convince him to take it to the clockmaker." She sniffed the air suddenly. "The gingerbread!"

As she fled to the kitchen, I undid the buttons of my coat, glancing up the stairs toward my bedroom where the little dog was hidden from the world along with the blood-stained coat. My fingers felt stiff, my limbs like wood. I entered the dining room like a ghost, and I must have looked the same, but the professor was so occupied by the broken clock that he didn't do more than glance at me as I sank onto one of the straight-backed dining chairs at the table.

I wanted to rest my head in my hands. I wanted to tell him everything.

"Blast these tiny parts," he muttered, holding up a spring no larger than his fingernail. "They were made for nimbler fingers."

The wooden clock sat upright on the table, its insides laid out as the professor performed his mechanical autopsy. He hadn't practiced surgery in over a decade, but his skill was apparent in the way he cataloged the clock's parts, testing each one methodically for faults. I kept my hands clasped under the table, my mind still too numb for words.

Mary brought out a plate of gingerbread cut into star shapes, warning us not to eat too many and ruin our appetites, though that hardly stopped the professor. I couldn't yet face returning to my room, to the dog who had trod in a dead girl's blood, and to the stains on my coat. Besides, watching the professor work calmed me. He was careful and attentive, but he paused for bites of cake. So unlike my father, who had been so serious. So unlike me, too.

I stayed up quite late to avoid the secrets stashed in my bedroom, long after Mary left for the day and the professor retired to bed. Then, by the light of a lantern, I worked on the clock myself, using an old book of mechanics to repair the broken gears that were too small for the professor's arthritic old fingers. At last I replaced the final screw and closed the clock's wooden door. When the professor woke in the morning, it would be to the god-awful squawk of that blasted bird he loved so much. It wasn't much to repay his kindness, but it was something.

At last I climbed the stairs with weary limbs and closed myself in my bedroom. The fire had long since gone out. When I called Sharkey, he came out from under the bed, blinking, and something broke inside me.

I grabbed him and slid between the covers, my body wracked in shivers, and pulled the little dog against me. We shivered together under the expensive duvets and sheets, neither of us belonging in so fine a house.

There was no sleep for me that night. I tried to picture the alleyway again, to remember exactly what the thief girl's wounds had looked like, but the match light had been so faint, and my fear had been a distorting lens. Certainly it wasn't strange that a girl who'd tried to rob me had later ended up dead. She was a criminal, after all, and she'd been in a dangerous neighborhood. Maybe she'd tried to pick the wrong pocket, or gotten in a brawl, or someone had found out there wasn't a man's body under that clothing.

I let these dangerous thoughts unfurl in my head, exploring them cautiously, feeling their weight. After some time, when I was certain the professor was fast asleep, I climbed out of my warm bed where the little dog snored softly, and relit the fire. Once it crackled to life, I knelt by my pile of crumpled clothes, ready to burn them. I could smell the blood on them, along with something more fragrant—pollen.

I dug through until I found the flower. Why had I kept it? I should have thrown it to the street, but for some reason

I'd slipped it in my coat pocket instead.

I could still get rid of it. Burn it in the fire. Throw it out the window.

Instead, I kept the flower separate and burned my bloody coat and dress. With trembling fingers, I carefully placed the flower within the pages of my journal. I don't know what instinct made me keep such a bloody memento of a murderer. Call it sentimentality. Call it curiosity.

Just don't call it madness.

SIX

IN THE MORNING, THE previous day's adventures seemed as unreal as nightmares, and yet the flower pressed within my journal was real enough, as was the sleeping dog beside me.

All trace of my bloody coat had burned in the fireplace except for the silver buttons, which I slipped into my pocket. I wasn't looking forward to telling the professor I'd need a new one. I pulled out Jack Joyce's newspaper and reread the article again. The familiar names of the victims stared at me from the page, as did another name—Inspector John Newcastle. Lucy's ambitious young suitor had been chosen to lead the investigation into the Wolf of Whitechapel, and I wasn't certain whether this news was welcome or not; as much as I loathed the idea of seeking information from the police, Inspector Newcastle might be able to give me more clues about the murderer and his victims. But how could I possibly explain my interest to the inspector? Well-bred seventeen-year-old girls weren't fascinated by murder suspects, as a rule. If I said three of the four victims had personally wronged me, I'd become the prime suspect.

My fingers clenched the newsprint. If only Montgomery were here, he'd know what to do. He had always been better than me at these things: investigating, tracking, *lying*. For the longest time I'd thought him a terrible liar, and yet in the end, he'd fooled me well enough. I could still remember his voice: *You shouldn't have anything to do with me. I'm guilty of so many crimes.* He'd warned me plain as day, and yet I'd still fallen in love with him, believed we had a future . . . and now here I was, alone with ink-stained fingers, only a dog for company and an old man who didn't begin to know the truth about me.

I skipped over Inspector Newcastle's name and let my gaze linger on the last line of the article, a line that I'd barely glanced at in my hurry yesterday: "The bodies are being kept in King's College of Medical Research until autopsies can be performed to shed light on the exact nature of the deaths."

King's College—I knew those dark hallways only too well. I'd scrubbed blood from the mortar there, dusted cobwebs from between skeletons' bones. That was where Dr. Hastings had decided a simple cleaning girl wouldn't dare refuse his sexual advances, and I'd slit his wrist. I still remembered the crimson color of his blood on the tile.

The last thing I wanted to do was return to those hallways.

And yet the bodies there called to me, promising to tell me the answers buried within their cold flesh.

It was a call I couldn't resist.

I DRESSED AND CAME downstairs with a lie prepared about needing to do some Christmas shopping in the market. To my surprise, I heard sounds of arguing and found the professor in the library with a visitor, a stout man with stiff waxed hair and thick glasses whose face froze when he saw me standing in the doorway.

"Ah, Juliet, you're awake," the professor said, rising to his feet. His mouth was still tense from their argument, but he forced a smile as he pulled me into the hallway.

"Who's that man?" I asked, trying to peek around his shoulder.

"Isambard Lessing. A historian, one of the King's Club men. No need to concern yourself with him; he's here to inquire about some old journals and family heirlooms. Did you need something?"

"I was thinking of going shopping. This close to Christmas—"

"Yes, yes, a fine idea," he said, herding me toward the stairs. He fumbled in his pocket for some bank notes and pressed them into my hand. "I'll see you back here for supper."

I muttered a silent prayer of thanks that he was distracted and wasted no time hurrying from the house with Sharkey. I took the dog to the market and firmly deposited him with Joyce, so by the time I got to King's College— wearing an old apron over my fashionable red dress—classes were already in session for the morning. I entered through the main double doors into the glistening hallway with polished wood-inlay floors and wall sconces bearing electric lights. My boots echoed loudly in the empty hallways. I'd never felt comfortable on this main floor, the realm of academics and well-off students from good families. Grainy photographs lined the walls showing the illustrious history of the university and its construction. One brass frame bore the crest of the King's Club with the motto underneath: *Ex scientia vera.* From knowledge, truth. I thought of stiff Isambard Lessing and his red face. I paused to look at the date on the frame's inscription.

1875. Four years before I was born. The photograph documented the King's Club membership at the time, two lines of a dozen male faces wearing long robes and serious expressions. Lucy's railroad magnate father, Mr. Radcliffe, was among them, his beard much shorter, standing next to a stout man I recognized as Isambard Lessing himself, and with a shudder I recognized a young Dr. Hastings. I also found the professor's face among them, decades younger but with the same wire-rim glasses and a hint of a smile on an otherwise stern face. On his left was a young man whose face I knew all too well—my father.

I shifted in my stiff clothing. The professor had mentioned they'd met in the King's Club, so perhaps I shouldn't have been surprised. In the photograph Father had dark hair cut in the fashion of the time, and his eyes were alert and focused, so unlike his wild-eyed, gray-haired visage I had known more recently. The face in the photograph was the face I knew from my earliest memories, when I'd idolized him, before madness and ambition had claimed him.

I tore myself away from the old photograph and hurried for the stairs to the basement, where I felt instantly more at ease. The morning cleaning crew was already hard at work scouring the stairs leading to the basement hallways. I recognized my old boss, Mrs. Bell, as her rounded body stooped to scrub the treading. A woman who used to watch out for me when no one else did. When she stood to refill her bucket, I grabbed her hand and pulled her around the corner.

"Mercy!" she cried, putting a hand over her heart. "Juliet Moreau, is that you? My, but you gave me a fright."

"I'm sorry, Mrs. Bell. I wondered if I might ask you a favor."

"You aren't wanting your old job back, I hope," she said, then cocked her head at the fine dress beneath my apron. "No, I suppose not. . . ."

"It isn't about that. As a matter of fact, I've had a change in fortune, and it's only right for me to share." I fished in my pocket for the silver buttons and pressed them into her hand before she could object. "I just need to know if you've already cleaned the hallways on the east side."

The buttons jangled in her callused hand. "Heading there next, right after we finish these stairs."

I bit my lip, glancing at the two other cleaning girls. "Could you start on the west side instead? It's a long story . . . a student friend of mine thinks he might have dropped some cufflinks there and I'd like to look for them."

She gave me a stern look, and I half expected her to ask what the real story was, but luckily for me she just threw her hand toward the hallways.

"Have at it, girl."

I started past the steps, where a rail-thin cleaning girl was polishing the brass handrail. Her basket sat beside her, filled with a collection of cleaning tools that were all quite familiar to me. How many hours had I spent on hands and knees on this very floor, sleeves hitched above my elbows, scrubbing so hard my knuckles bled? What a lonely life that had been, with only my memories to keep me company. How easily I could be back there if not for the professor.

The skinny girl turned around when she saw me staring at her basket. Her eyes went to the dirty apron that didn't quite match my fine dress—an incongruity only the poor would notice.

"Can I help you . . . miss?" she asked.

"Oh no," I said quickly. "I'm sorry. My mind was wandering."

She nodded, still looking at me strangely, then returned to work. Once her back was turned, I bent down to pretend to lace my boots and secretly grabbed one of the brushes out of her basket, a soft-bristled one meant for cleaning fabric. If I ran into anyone here, I might need it as disguise. I hid it in my apron and hurried down the stairs into the basement.

The electric lights were on, buzzing and clicking, spilling artificial light over the tiles. Fresh sawdust had been sprinkled on them to soak up any blood fallen from patients or bodies. I wound my way down another corridor and paused at the closed door to the storage rooms where they kept cadavers for autopsies.

I peeked through the keyhole to make sure the room was empty. Unwanted memories returned of a night a year ago when Lucy and I had come here on a dare, only to stumble upon medical students dissecting a live rabbit. My arm twitched, just as that rabbit's hind leg had, and I clamped a hand over my arm to keep it calm, hoping the rest of my illness's symptoms wouldn't soon follow. Through the keyhole, I spied cold tables draped with clothes.

Voices came down the hall, making me jump.

"Old coot doesn't know his head from a hole in the ground," one said.

Whoever they were, their footsteps were headed my way. I pulled the soft-bristled brush out and stooped to hands and knees on the sawdust-covered floor just as two medical students rounded the corner.

"You can't expect him to—" The one speaking paused when he saw me, but then continued. "You can't expect him to graduate you when *he* couldn't even pass the exams." The two students stepped over my arm as I pretended to scour the floor. One glanced back briefly, but I made sure to keep my face toward the ground. Cleaning girls weren't worth anything to boys like them except a quick glance to see if they were pretty.

They neared the corner and I started to let out my held breath, until I heard a third voice behind them, clearly belonging to an older man.

"Bentley! Filmore! Stop right there."

My spine turned to ice. I knew that voice, even without

looking at its owner. Dr. Hastings—the professor who had attacked me last year and caused me to flee London. I fought the urge to panic and forced my hand to move rhythmically over the tiles, pretending to clean the mortar with a useless soft-bristled brush. As his footsteps neared, I cringed.

"Yes, Doctor?" one of the boys said, considerably more polite now.

Dr. Hastings came to stand beside me. I glimpsed his silver-tipped shoes before quickly looking away.

Focus on the tiles. Focus on the tiles. Focus on the—

"Don't think I don't know about those pranks you've been pulling. It's one thing for boys to have a bit of fun, but quite another to chase me down Wiltshire at night. I nearly broke a shoelace."

"It wasn't us, Doctor, I swear!" one of them sniveled.

I didn't worry about being recognized by most professors here—they never bothered to glance at the cleaning crew. But Dr. Hastings had always been different. I think he liked to think of us on our hands and knees, cleaning up the messes he made. If he found me here now, he could do anything to me and not a soul would ever know.

I swallowed, wondering if I could crawl backward and scoot away. But to my relief, the two students had his entire attention. He stepped around me and started after them down the hall, chastising them about schoolboy pranks. The moment they were around the corner I leaped up, shoved the brush into my apron pocket, and snuck into the autopsy room.

I waited ten seconds, twenty, a minute, and heard no

more voices. A shiver ran down my back as I found a switch on the wall. The artificial electric light snapped to life, bathing the room in a garish glow so much starker than the hurricane lamps my father used in his laboratory.

Eight tables lined the walls, four of which were occupied with cadavers. Each body was covered with a heavy cloth. One was large, over six and a half feet tall—that had to be Daniel Penderwick, the solicitor. In my memory he'd been tall as the devil himself, with just as black a heart. I lifted the cloth and looked at his pale, dead body. His naked chest was gutted open with slash marks now drained of blood. The wounds pulled me to them. They whispered truths—memories—I wasn't certain I wanted to ever recall.

I approached the next body cautiously, uncertain who I'd find beneath the heavy cloth. Annie's body would be here, as well as the thief girl's. But what of the unidentified one? Would it be familiar to me, like the others? Could I still call it all a coincidence if it was?

I pulled back the next cloth with stilled breath and looked upon the body of the thief. Red hair matted in blood, body bruised from a man's heavy boot that must have trampled her. At the time I had thought her my age, but she looked far younger in death. Thirteen, maybe fourteen. A missing finger was nothing compared to the missing heart now torn from her chest. More blood drained away from my face.

I went to the next table, shakily leaning over the cloth. I could tell from the shape it was another young woman. Annie—or what if it wasn't? What if it was Lucy's cold body, or our maid Mary, or someone else dear to me who never deserved *this*?

Dread scratched its tiny claws at me but the urge to know was stronger, and I pulled back the cloth. Annie Benton, though I was hardly relieved. She hadn't deserved this. Her light brown hair and fair skin looked so much paler in death. Years ago she'd slept in the bed next to mine, and we'd eaten porridge together at breakfast, and each evening we'd scrubbed our single change of clothes in the boarding-house's laundry room. She'd shared her soap with me once.

It was hard to concentrate on anything besides the gaping wounds in her chest, almost perfectly slicing her in the middle. The cuts were jagged, furious, nearly beautiful in their destruction, like all the others. Whoever had made them had done so with a passion for violence. Perhaps I should have looked away, but I didn't.

Eventually I moved on to the last body. The unnamed victim. My instincts urged me not to look in case it was someone dear to me, yet somehow my feet took me there, winding around the bare cadavers, their lifeless eyes watching me. I drew the cloth back and jerked in surprise. My heart stampeded in my chest. I collided with the table behind me, brushing against Daniel Penderwick's cold, dead hand.

I recognized the fourth body.

It was the old white-haired man from the flower show, Sir Danvers Carew, the beloved member of Parliament who had once abused my mother and me. I'd seen him only days ago, and now . . . *dead*. I closed a hand over my mouth as my mind crawled over his pale face, his bloodstained skin, trying to understand. He had the same slash marks on his chest, and bruises all over his body, made with some blunt sharp object. *Like a cane.* No wonder the paper had declined to name him. Such an important man, surely his family would prefer not to be associated with a mass murderer. It hardly mattered. He was dead either way.

Four. I knew all four victims.

And in turn, I realized, I had been victim to each of them.

The idea made me step away from the bodies, back pressed against the cold metal door. It didn't matter how I tried to explain it—nothing about it felt right. Four deaths, four people who had wronged me.

Almost as though . . .

I hesitated, telling myself I might possibly be going mad.

. . . almost as though someone was watching out for me.

I shivered uncontrollably, as the bones in my hands and arms shifted and popped, threatening another fit.

A premonition that had been growing now gripped me hard, as my mind flashed back to all the bodies on the island. Alice, Father's sweet maid, dripping blood from dead feet. A beast-woman separated from her jaw. Those wounds, as well, had been lovingly made by a monster.

By Edward.

Edward is dead, I told myself. *The dead don't come back.*

And yet the fear kept squeezing my heart, trying to get me to believe in the impossible. My head was already aching. Soon I'd grow faint. In a desperate fury, I decided the only thing that would calm my mind would be to prove scientifically that the wounds were different and therefore couldn't have been made by Edward. On the island, I had read and memorized meticulous autopsy reports from Father's files for all of Edward's victims. Eleven and a half inches long, one inch apart, and two inches deep.

I pulled out a thread from my pocket and measured the length of Annie's cuts, the spacing between them, even gently pulled apart the wounds to measure the depth. I repeated the process on all four bodies.

They were all the same: eleven and a half inches long, one inch apart, and two inches deep.

I stumbled back against the empty table, stunned. The thread slipped from my fingers, along with a spool of my sanity.

The murderer was the same. Somehow, even though I'd thought him dead, there was no doubt.

Edward had done this.

SEVEN

I FELT LIKE THE room was turning upside down. My legs threatened to give out. I curled my fingers around the table's edge as though it could keep me from floating to the ceiling.

Edward Prince was alive, and here was my proof.

Against all odds he must have survived the fire and come to London—why? If it was only victims he was after, he needn't have traveled half the world. But his victims were all very specific. Connected. All people who had at one point in my life wronged me.

My mind slipped and slid back to the island, and the castaway with the gold-flecked eyes.

We belong together, he had said. *We're the same.*

Was that why he had returned, as part of a grotesquely misguided attempt to protect me and win me over? Or was he sending me some sort of threat after I'd spurned his advances?

I paced, hands kitting together, among the cadavers.

How did he even know about Annie stealing the ring? No one knew about that except Lucy, unless Annie had told someone. . . .

Hands trembling, I managed to pull the cover back over Annie's face, and the rest of the bodies. I stumbled into the hallway outside, eyes closed, drawing in a deep breath. The hallways here always had the usual smell of chemicals, along with some traces of lingering cologne from whichever gentleman doctor had last been here.

I couldn't shake this new information: *He's alive. Alive. Alive.*

Footsteps came from down the hall, and I spun, expecting to find Edward's yellow eyes in the shadows. Heart pounding, I hurried for the stairs, away from these bodies and what they meant. I threw a glance over my shoulder as I turned the corner and nearly collided with a man coming into the hallway from a side door.

Not just any man. Inspector John Newcastle.

My heart shot to my throat. "Excuse me," I said in a rush, keeping my head down with the hope that he wouldn't recognize me. But his hand held my elbow, and he frowned as if trying to place me.

"Miss . . . Moreau, isn't it? Lucy's friend. What on earth are you doing down here?"

"Nothing, Inspector," I stuttered. "Visiting some old friends."

His eyebrow rose with a touch of irony as he glanced at the cadaver storage room door behind me. "You keep strange company for friends, Miss Moreau."

"Oh no, that isn't what I meant. I used to work on this cleaning crew last year, before the professor took me in. I hadn't seen them in a year, so . . ." I swallowed, watching as his eyes followed my footsteps in the sawdust-covered floor to the storage room. My footsteps contradicted me. He'd know I'd been in there with the bodies.

My heart pounded. He could so easily make trouble for me, being down here where I wasn't supposed to be, snooping around bodies. The professor's guardianship could protect me only so far.

"I came to check on the autopsy report for the latest victim of the Wolf of Whitechapel," he said. "But I would be happy to escort you back to the main floor."

I sighed in relief. "That's not necessary. I know my way. And I really must be going." I smiled as graciously as I could and turned away, heart pounding, feet unsteady on the tile floor. All I could think of was Edward. All I could feel was a thousand tangled emotions.

"Wait, Miss Moreau."

My eyes fell closed, only for an instant. I turned around with another shaky smile. The inspector wasn't smiling now, as he dropped his voice to a whisper.

"After I met you, I looked up your name. I'm protective of Lucy, you understand, and your name sounded so familiar. I found a police report. . . ." He glanced down the hallway, making sure we were alone. My instincts jumped to attention. A dozen scenarios flashed through my head of what I'd do if he tried to arrest me. All of them ended poorly for me.

"It was self-defense," I said firmly. "Dr. Hastings attacked me. I was a cleaning girl then; no one would believe me—"

He dismissed that with a wave. "None of that interests me. I've no doubt it was Hastings's fault—it isn't the first incident of this sort with his name on it. No, Miss Moreau, the reason I recalled your name was because of your father's crimes, not your own."

My body froze, afraid to take a single breath.

At my silence, he continued. "I was young at the time, in college training to be an investigator. The case was quite notorious. I went back and read the file on your father, and it seems the case was never closed. He fled England, and no one heard from him again. I hate to leave this sort of thing open, if we can file it away as a solved case. Your assistance, Miss Moreau, would be invaluable to our efforts."

I stared at him, speechless. After I'd been hiding from the police for the last year, now they were coming to me for *help*? I might have laughed, if I hadn't feared sounding like a madwoman.

"I assure you, you can trust me," he continued. "We'll handle the information in the most sensitive manner. It isn't my intention to cause a sensation, just to solve a long-standing case. It would be a feather in my cap, you see, even lead to a promotion. Together with this Wolf of Whitechapel case, I would be made head of the entire division. Which means I'd be better suited to care for Lucy."

"Care for Lucy?"

He smiled boyishly. "It isn't official, of course. I

haven't yet asked her father for her hand in marriage, but I know he'll give me permission. Any day now, expect to get the news of our engagement."

There was something undeniably tender about the way he said it. I was quite certain Lucy had no idea the inspector's intentions were this immediate. My head whirled with the idea of Lucy wed, and Newcastle wanting me to help solve my own father's case, and among it all, Edward. *Alive.*

Mrs. Bell rounded the corner and stopped short when she saw us. "Can I help you, sir?"

I took the opportunity to step away from Inspector Newcastle. "I'm sorry, Inspector," I said quickly. "There's nothing I can help you with. I've heard rumors that my father is dead—I might trust those, if I were you."

Before he could respond, I bade farewell to him and Mrs. Bell, and hurried from the hallways where the electric lights still clicked and sputtered, as if warning me to never come back.

EIGHT

As soon as I left King's College, I rounded the edge of the building and slumped against the rough brick wall, fighting to calm my erratic heartbeat. The day was clear but bitingly cold. My coat hung open, my hands bare, yet I didn't reach for my gloves nor do up my buttons. I couldn't. All I could manage was to slide down the brick wall to the frozen grass and let the cold seep up from the ground into me.

Edward was back from the dead.

If he truly was alive, if he had done this, then he must have been following me for some time. My mind searched through the past few weeks and months, trying to remember if I'd felt like I was being followed. But that was just it—one *always* felt followed in this city. Always felt eyes, always heard footsteps.

A flock of ravens alighted in the central courtyard, and my head whirled around. Was he following me even *now*? So many places to hide: behind those skeletal trees, on the rooftop of a nearby building . . .

I hugged my knees tight, not daring to close my eyes. If he knew about Annie stealing my mother's ring, what else did he know? Did he know about my secret workshop and my growing illness? Did he know how I was stealing from the professor? Did he know that back on the island I'd opened the laboratory door so Jaguar could kill my father?

It terrified me that Edward might know all my secrets. If he chose to, he could expose me. Hurt me for how I'd hurt him when I'd rejected his affections. People loved a good gruesome rumor. If he revealed that the vilified Dr. Moreau's daughter had murdered her own father, this city's gossip mills would devour me alive.

I ran numb fingers over my face, thinking. Edward was tied up in all those secrets too. Exposing my secrets would also expose his own—his unnatural origin and his inclination to kill. No, the more I thought about it, the more I was certain it wasn't my secrets he was after.

Maybe it was my life.

A tingling started deep in my spine. For all I knew, I could be Edward's next target. He could merely be toying with me, killing those who had wronged me to create a false sense of safety before he struck. After all, I'd rejected his love and then left him for dead. I could hardly expect him to do anything logically. How much control did Edward really have over himself? Where was the line between Beast and man?

Yet if Edward had wanted to kill me, there were far more effective ways. I'd given him a thousand opportunities to strike as I slunk along Shoreditch at night on my way to my secret workshop. And I might have left him for dead, but I'd prevented Montgomery from slitting his throat. I had given him a chance.

So what were these bodies supposed to tell me? If he meant me no harm, why hide behind such macabre gestures of affection?

It's different with you, Juliet, Edward had said. *We belong together.*

He'd been wounded before he'd been able to explain what he meant by that plea for help. As I leaned against the brick wall, body ravaged by too many emotions, I wondered if Edward Prince had come back to London with that in mind. Not to destroy my life with rumors, not to claw out my heart, but to confess his love once more.

A hundred uncertainties twisted at my heart. The question was, Who else had to die first? Who else had wronged me? *I could give him a list*, I thought blackly, *starting with Dr. Hastings*. But I immediately regretted such thoughts. Edeard was the murderer, not me. The truth was, he had to be learning about all these people from somewhere. No one knew about Annie stealing that ring except for Lucy. Perhaps she told someone; perhaps Lucy wrote it in a journal that he'd found.

Could he be following *Lucy*, too?

Before I knew it, my feet were racing along the streets toward Lucy's neighborhood, throwing glances over my shoulder. I didn't dare involve her in any of this, and yet I needed to make sure she was safe. Edward could be *anywhere*. I made my way toward her house in the finest part of town, where the muddy snow had been cleared from the streets. Every manor was stately here, even finer than in the professor's neighborhood, and each home was decorated for the holidays with mistletoe over the entryway.

Lucy's family's mansion was impossible to miss, a four-story red-brick palace on the most prominent corner, by far the grandest house in Belgravia. A wall of perfectly trimmed hedges designed to keep the riffraff out circled the rounded brick turrets. An iron gate opened onto the front walk to the imposing entryway topped with a holiday garland that smelled of pine.

I paused by the gate, casting another cautious glance over my shoulder. The smell took me back to my childhood, when I used to come here for parties. We'd had the most beautiful carriage then. I remembered soft lace curtains and peach upholstery. Montgomery would sit up front with the driver, learning his duties as groomsman, while Mother and Father and I rode in silence in the back until we pulled up at this very gate. Montgomery would take my hand—never meeting my eyes, as a proper young groomsman—and help me down from the carriage. The place beneath my left rib throbbed again at the memory.

A door slammed and a maid appeared in an upstairs window with a rug and duster. I started to pull my hood over my hair and duck away, but I reminded myself that I was once again welcome in this house. The Radcliffes had forbidden Lucy to see me after Father's scandal, but now that I was ward of the illustrious Professor von Stein, they had no problem smiling at me like nothing had happened. I approached the front door and knocked.

Clara, the maid, answered the door while wiping her hands on a rag. Her face lit up when she saw me. "Miss Juliet! What a treat—we haven't seen you around here much." She paused. "You looked like you've seen a ghost, miss. Are you ill?"

I shook my head, though she was closer to the truth than she could imagine. "Is Lucy home?"

"She's in the salon with her aunt. Shall I tell her you're here?"

I hesitated. My heart thumped with the need to make certain Lucy was safe. But with her aunt in the room, I wouldn't be able to speak openly. "I didn't realize she had company. I'd really wanted to speak with her alone. If you'll just pass along the message that I came, and have her come visit as soon as she can . . ."

"Juliet!" Lucy's face appeared behind Clara, and she jerked the door open wider. Her frown accused me just as much as the finger pointing at my chest. "You're not leaving without saying hello, are you?"

Her face was so warm and full of life, after those in the basement. "If you've already got company—"

"Henry's here for tea and Aunt Edith is chaperoning. And I'm in desperate need of you, you horrid friend. After you left me alone with John, I practically had to fend him off with an umbrella to keep him from kissing me."

"I'll come back tomorrow. We'll chat then."

Lucy folded her arms across her chest. "I've told Henry so much about you that he must believe you're an imaginary friend I invented out of boredom. The least you could do is have a cup of tea with the poor man."

At the end of the alley a carriage rumbled by in the direction of Covent Garden. I should be headed there now, to get the latest gossip from Joyce about the murders and see what else I could find out about Scotland Yard's investigation. But Lucy was narrowing her eyes at me, and I said, "All right. Though I can't stay but a few minutes."

"We'll see about that. And Clara, I came to tell you I've eaten all the gingerbread cakes and we need more."

Lucy linked her arm in mine as she dragged me up the main staircase to the parlor. "Thank god the holidays will be over soon, else I'd put on a stone in weight. Oh, I'm so glad you arrived! Henry's been boring my ears off and I'm desperate for some real conversation. At least he's nice to look upon." She caught herself, and quickly added, "Though only in a certain light. Otherwise he's an ogre."

We reached the top of the stairs and I tried to brush my hair back and make myself look presentable, when all I could think about was a boy back from the dead.

We entered the parlor, a small but opulent room with a cheerful fire crackling in the ornate fireplace and tea service set out on the low table between the upholstered chairs. Lucy's aunt, a rather stiff-lipped, dried-out woman, turned when we entered, eyebrows raised at my sudden appearance. Henry was sitting on the sofa with his back to us.

Lucy brushed an errant curl back. "Aunt Edith, Henry, I'd like to introduce you to a dear friend. This is Juliet Moreau."

I dimly heard my name, but for some reason she sounded far away. Henry had turned at the sound of her voice and was staring at us. At *me*. Suddenly the room felt too small, as though the furniture was pressing in and the fire consuming all the oxygen. He stood slowly to greet us. I was vaguely aware of Lucy's aunt standing as well, her mouth moving and sound coming out, but she was no more real than a dress shop mannequin. Everything seemed equally unreal, just vague suggestions of furniture and people.

Everything, that was, except for the young man whose gold-flecked eyes met mine.

"Juliet," Lucy said, "may I introduce Mr. Henry Jakyll."

He stepped forward to shake my hand.

The faded scar on his right cheek. The face that was so achingly familiar.

The hand extended to me belonged to Edward Prince.

NINE

THE FIRE STOPPED CRACKLING. The steam froze in the air. Everything had drifted into a far-off place, shifting into a colorless world like a fading photograph.

Everything but Edward.

Jakyll, I thought. Another false name, just like the other name he'd created—Edward Prince, or rather Prince Edward, a name borrowed from the pages of Shakespeare. Edward didn't have a given name since he'd never truly been born, but made in a laboratory out of a handful of animal parts. Fox. Heron. Jackal. Of course—that was the source of his false name, a testament to his darker animal side.

The *jackal* side.

He had changed in the months since I'd seen him. Though the scar under his left eye still marred his face, his features had sharpened in a way that gave him a dramatic, brooding look. His eyes seemed a darker shade of brown—very nearly black—as did his hair. The most shocking change, however, was his size. Never a large young man, he now stood several inches above me and seemed to have put on a stone of muscle.

No wonder Lucy was so taken with him.

I gradually became aware that the room had gone silent and that Aunt Edith and Lucy stared at me expectantly. Edward's outstretched hand, no longer skeletal but strong, powerful, hiding six-inch-long claws, awaited my own.

I had to make a choice. I could scream. I could tell Lucy and her aunt everything, accuse Edward of being the Wolf of Whitechapel, throw the boiling tea in his face to blind him, and run him through with the poker.

But the hand extended to me wasn't that of a monster. Edward was split into two selves that shared the same body: one a sharp-clawed monster, the other a tortured young man who wanted nothing more than to be free from his curse. I thought of the little white flower tinged with blood I'd pressed into my journal. A gift from this young man before me, who had once loved me madly.

Well, whatever Edward had felt, it didn't matter. Everything had changed when I walked into this parlor to discover Edward had involved Lucy in this. *He* might not intend to harm her, but the Beast could have other plans.

Edward's throat constricted as he swallowed. I wondered, fleetingly, if he was as thrown off balance by seeing me as I was seeing him.

"It's a pleasure to meet you, Mr. Jakyll," I said at last.

Lucy flopped onto the sofa and reached for her tea. Aunt Edith might have greeted me; I wasn't sure. If she had, it had been brief and normal, just as though today was any other day and this was any other tea. But it wasn't any other day. And this wasn't any young man.

Clara bustled in with a tray of gingerbread cakes. "Pardon me, miss," she said with a grin, shuffling around me.

I slowly sank onto the sofa next to Lucy, feeling it first with my hands to make sure I wouldn't miss the seat. Edward sat directly across from me in a dark green velvet chair. My head couldn't reconcile his presence with Clara's smile, Lucy's carefree posture, the sunlight pouring in from the window.

None of them knew they were having tea with the Wolf of Whitechapel.

"Juliet's traveled the world as well," Lucy said to Edward, throwing her arm casually on the sofa back. "Henry's been all over, knows about practically every country in the world, but you'll have to forgive him if his customs are strange. He's from Finland, you know."

I raised an eyebrow. "Finland."

"Oh, I couldn't bear it," Aunt Edith said, brushing a crumb off her dress. "All that cold year-round."

I stared at them as though they spoke a foreign language. Lucy reached for another gingerbread cake and Aunt Edith made a disapproving cough in her throat.

My eyes trailed back to Edward. The last time I'd seen him, blood was pooling beneath his head into fresh straw. Why had I stopped Montgomery from slicing his throat? I wasn't sure, but it might have had something to do with the look on his face now, somehow innocent despite all his hands had done.

"I've heard quite a bit about you, *Henry*," I said.

The accusation was heavy in my voice, and though the ladies didn't seem to notice it, Edward did. His eyes searched mine, pleading for forgiveness. How could I forgive him for placing Lucy in danger? For making me care about him when everything had been a lie? For *murder*?

Edward stood and began to pace as though he needed to stretch his legs, but I recognized that nervous agitation. The Beast was there, lurking just below the surface. "Yes, I wondered when we might meet each other," he said quietly. "From what Lucy has said, we seem to have some interests in common."

Lucy clapped her hands. "Oh yes, I forgot to tell you! Henry was interested in something about chemistry . . . that was it, wasn't it? I told him you were much better at science than any boy I know."

Edward's haunted eyes stayed on me. They said everything his voice couldn't. He hated his dark other half—the Beast—and the terrible things it led him to do. Even now, his eyes pleaded with me for help.

I couldn't bear this, having tea with a murderer. All I could think about was the bodies in the morgue. Four people no longer breathed because of him. He'd killed people I cared about, like Alice. Innocent people. And yet, wasn't I as good as a murderer myself? Father might still be alive if I hadn't opened that door to his laboratory for Jaguar.

I clutched the sofa's arm, rubbing my thumb against the rough upholstery seam to stay connected to the present.

Outside, the sun was past its zenith.

"I should go," I choked. Lucy and her aunt looked at me, surprised. "I didn't tell the professor when I'd be home."

"No, you don't," Lucy said. "You're not running off without even touching your tea. If the professor is in need of you, I'm certain this is the first place he'll look. Oh my, Juliet, do you feel all right? You've gone pale."

Aunt Edith said something droll about her own constitution and Lucy answered back smartly, and they started arguing again.

"Drink some tea, Miss Moreau," Edward said quietly. "You'll soon feel better."

I tried to pick up the delicate cup, but it was like my hands were paws, my fingers too thick. It trembled so badly, I had to set it down.

Edward leaned on the back of the chair opposite me, his dark hair falling over his forehead. "Have you seen the hedge maze in the garden, Miss Moreau? There's a wonderful view from the window." His eyes flickered toward the sun-drenched windowpanes. It was a good ten paces from where Lucy and her aunt argued—well out of earshot. He wanted to speak in private. When I hesitated, he leaned forward, his voice dropping to a whisper. "*Please*, Juliet."

There was such tightly controlled desperation in his words that I set down my tea and glanced at Lucy. They were talking of the grand Christmas tree that would soon be delivered in preparation for the masquerade. I stood and walked to the window with unsteady steps, Edward

right behind me. It was a beautiful winter's day outside, the hedges evergreen, not a cloud in the sky.

I kept my voice at a whisper. "If you dare to hurt Lucy—"

"I won't," he said quickly, matching my hushed tone. "I would never hurt her. I have some measure of control over—"

"Henry!" Lucy called behind us. "Henry, come tell Aunt Edith how we met that day in the rain. She wants to hear, and you know I've no patience for storytelling."

His smile to her was artificial, though not unkind. "One moment, darling."

When his eyes returned to mine, the false smile had vanished. "I swear to you I mean Lucy no harm. I wouldn't ever let myself be around her if I thought the Beast might get free. I have a small measure of control over him; not enough to prevent the transformations, nor the crimes he commits, but I can delay them."

I studied the deep crease in his forehead. I'd spent weeks with Edward at sea and on Father's island, ignorant of his darker nature, and he had never hurt me, always managing to curb his other half's cravings until he could release the Beast on some other poor victim. Perhaps he did have some measure of control over his transformations, but all I could picture was the cadaver room full of bodies.

"How did you escape the island? I thought you were dead."

"The Beast is stronger than you think." His eyes were hooded, his body tense. "I'm trying to cure myself. I'm close."

Here was the Edward I knew, the young man whose eyes were like a mirror to my own. "What kind of cure?" I whispered, rubbing my own knuckles, which were already beginning to ache.

"I just need to identify one missing ingredient in the serum. I need a little more time."

"You should have come to me sooner."

"I didn't dare involve you. I've gone to great lengths to avoid direct contact with you, afraid the Beast might learn some information he could use later to harm you. I've settled for slips of news from Lucy. She cares about you a great deal. She speaks of you often." His throat tightened. "It didn't mean that I didn't want to see you. In fact, I wanted to see you quite badly."

The look in his eyes gave me pause. Nothing of the Beast's glowing yellow eyes lurked there now, though what I saw frightened me nearly as much.

Desire.

I looked away, wishing my cheeks weren't turning warm. It seemed Edward's infatuation with me hadn't lessened with the passing months.

"Meet me somewhere," I said, quick and low. "You must tell me what is going on."

He shook his head. "I don't dare. Not until I'm cured."

"I don't care what you want! People are *dying*, Edward." I darted a glance at Lucy and dropped my voice lower. "And we both know exactly *who* is responsible. I'm already involved, don't you see? I was involved since the day

the sailors pulled you out of the ocean and onto the *Curitiba*. You must agree to meet me and tell me everything. If you don't, I'll expose you. Lucy's other suitor is the detective leading the investigation of the Wolf of Whitechapel. I can have him here in minutes."

My heart pounded. I knew, on some deep level, that it was madness even to be talking to Edward. I also knew that, madness or not, Edward's and my fates were tied together. I was the one threatening to expose him now, but our roles could so easily be reversed.

He took out his gold pocket watch and flipped it open and shut in indecision. At last he closed it and said, "Where?"

We needed someplace public enough so that I would be safe alone with him, yet private enough to speak intimately. My mind went back to the island, he and I behind the waterfall, sharing secrets and even a stolen kiss.

"The Royal Botanical Gardens at Kensington," I whispered. "The greenhouse. We'll each leave separately and meet there within an hour."

He nodded.

The grandfather clock in the study chimed. Aunt Edith stood up and brushed the crumbs off her skirt, missing half of them. "Two o'clock already. I've got a dinner tonight at the club I must get ready for. Henry, dear, it's been a pleasure. Won't you walk me out?"

Edward's eyes met mine. We were accomplices in this lie now, for better or worse. "I'll be saying good-bye then,

Lucy. It was a pleasure to meet you, Miss Moreau."

I hesitated a breath, just long enough to remember his false name.

"And you, Mr. Jakyll."

TEN

THE PARLOR DOOR REMAINED open behind them, leaving only the sound of the ticking hallway clock. Henry Jakyll. Edward Prince. One and the same.

"I'm glad she's left," Lucy said, coming to stand next to me at the window. "I think Aunt Edith only ever comes to tea to chastise me for all the things I've done wrong." She hunted in the fruit bowl on the side table and selected a grape. "What did you think of Henry?" she asked slyly, popping the grape into her mouth. "He's just awful, isn't he? Didn't I tell you?"

"Yes, awful," I said carefully, glancing out the window to try to catch a glimpse of him as he left. "Not your type at all. Inspector Newcastle is more attractive anyway, don't you think?"

She frowned, but at that moment I glimpsed Edward and Lucy's aunt stepping out of the house below, where he helped her into a cabriolet and then started down the street at a fast pace, heading to the botanical gardens for our rendezvous. I looked at the sky, where the sun was already casting shadows. Maybe two hours before sunset. Damn these short winter days. I'd certainly not be able to meet Edward and still have time to rush back home for dinner at the professor's. He'd be beside himself with worry when I didn't show up.

Lucy plucked another grape, eyeing me strangely. She changed her mind and set it back down in the bowl. "The truth is, and I know this must sound absurd coming from me, but I actually think I might admire him. Not much, of course. Only a tiny bit. Perhaps it's just stuffy in here."

I shot her a look. I couldn't imagine anything that chilled my blood more than the idea of Lucy enamored of a boy with a monstrous other half who had already killed four people in London—for *me*. I clutched her hand suddenly. "He seems a bore to me. I think you should forget him. *Really*. Now I must go, Lucy. I'm so sorry."

Her eyes went wide. "You've only just arrived. I thought we might be able to talk, here, while we're alone. Didn't you want to speak to me privately?" She leaned in, her voice dropping. "I have things to tell you, too. I'm not certain Papa's been fair in his business dealings, and when I mentioned it to Mother, she didn't seem to care."

"Blast, I'm sorry, I really can't stay to hear about it right now. I'm a terrible friend, I know, but I really *must go*." I paused in the doorway. "Oh, and I forgot to tell you—Inspector Newcastle is going to propose. I thought you should know. And I really don't think he's that terrible; perhaps you should give him a chance."

I squeezed her hand and hurried from the room and down the stairs, waving to Clara as I ran out into the street.

Guilt gripped me for leaving her so suddenly, but part of this *was* for Lucy. I could hardly explain that her suitor—who she actually *fancied*—had a murderous other side to him, and it was either cure him, kill him, or have her end up dead.

A chill was settling into the shadows of buildings as late afternoon approached. I turned toward the sun in the west, in the direction of the Royal Botanical Gardens, where palm trees stood like ghosts within the captive heat of the greenhouse.

A thousand places to kill. A million reasons not to trust.

I started running toward Kensington.

My feet ached by the time I arrived. The tired-looking ticket collector glanced at his pocket watch.

"Palm House closes at sunset, the gardens at six. You haven't but a few hours."

"That's all right," I said breathlessly, shoving my coins at him. I dashed through the gardens to the bridge that stretched across the frozen lake. From there, I could see the greenhouse, where rays of light caught on the thousands of glass panels.

I felt as though I'd crossed some invisible boundary and was no longer in London. Gone were the city crowds, the smoke and the soot, the noise of carriages and yelling street vendors.

I took a deep breath and pushed open the Palm House's ironwork door. A flood of warmth escaped the crack, filling my lungs with steam as I entered the domed central atrium.

I slid out of my coat and left it hanging over a branch, then fumbled to open the top buttons of my dress. Sweat was already forming on my inner layers. Somewhere, the line between this world and another blurred.

I was back in the jungle.

The hiss of steam jets replaced the ocean tides. Machinery squealed like jungle birds. Steam filled my lungs with memories: Jaguar, with his flicking tail; the smell of burning refuse and unwashed animals in the islanders' village; the salt in the breeze. In a strange way I missed the island terribly, heartsick for a place I'd hated and a father I'd wanted to die.

No—a father I'd helped murder.

"Edward?" I called as loud as I dared, uncertain if it was an enormous mistake to have come here.

A chain rattled overhead. Iron catwalks spanned the ceiling so visitors could walk among the treetops. A well-dressed figure now descended the spiral staircase. Edward. He stopped a few feet from me, as quiet as the steam at our feet.

"Hello, Juliet."

Being here, in this place so reminiscent of the island, I felt beastly things stir inside of me, taking me back to the island where we had learned to move through the trees quiet as animals, where he'd kissed me behind the waterfall. My pulse quickened, hungry for those things again despite my better sense.

He stepped forward, toying with his gold pocket watch, and I stepped back. "I told you, for the time being I'm still stronger than him. I can fight him if I feel him coming on. I'm not going to hurt you."

"What about that thief girl, and Annie, and the others? You were quick enough to kill them."

"I'm sorry for them, truly. When the Beast takes over, I lose myself to him."

"Why only kill people who have done wrong to me?"

A flicker of confusion passed over his features. "You'll have to ask the Beast that question; he's the one who chose them."

"I don't understand," I said.

"He seems to know my memories, but I only share pieces of his. The next day I find newspaper headlines about three slashes to the chest, and I assume he was responsible. I knew the solicitor was an acquaintance of yours, but not the others. I had assumed they were random."

"Hardly. Each one of them committed a crime against me."

Edward's face softened. "That explains it, then. I hadn't realized why he was so intent on those particular kills. He's trying to protect you, in his own way."

"*Protect* me? Why?"

He regarded me strangely for the space of a few breaths, while I wondered if I was crazy to be here and not to try to kill him on sight. He said, "Because he's as much in love with you as I am."

My lips parted, though no words came. I paced over

a path between soft spring-green ferns, trying to process everything. Emotions had never come easy to me, and they now threaded themselves in knots I couldn't possibly unravel. "Killing is a choice. Can't he just stop?"

"You wouldn't ask that question if you understood how powerful he is. He'd like to kill everyone who crosses his path, but he's tried to restrain himself and, I suppose, kill only those who sought to harm you." He paused. "I try to keep him contained—look."

His wiry fingers went to his shirt cuff. I couldn't help but notice how his knuckles were swollen and knobby, so like my own when a bout of illness was coming on. He unbuttoned his cuff and rolled back his sleeve over his forearm, revealing dark bruises.

I gasped. The bruises ranged from dark blue to purple to a yellowing gray, a rainbow of pain. I could barely tear my eyes off their strange beauty when he reached for his shirt buttons. "I chain myself if I feel him coming out, but sometimes I'm not fast enough, or he breaks the lock." He opened his shirt to reveal his bare chest. Welts and bruises slashed his skin. I traced them with my eyes, entranced.

I swallowed. "Edward . . ."

He pulled his shirt back on and rolled down the sleeves. "I'm showing you because I want you to understand the lengths I'll go to in order to cure myself. I don't want to hurt anyone else, you least of all. I was as surprised as you were when you walked into Lucy's parlor today. I knew you two were very close, but if I had known you were coming by, I'd never have gone."

"What are you doing with her?" I asked. "You shouldn't ever have introduced yourself to her. And now she's practically ready to run away with you—what kind of madness is this?"

"An act, nothing more," he said, taking an uncertain step toward me. "She's a fine young woman, but I'm only posing as her suitor to get closer to her father. Juliet, I couldn't ever love anyone besides—"

"Stop," I said, throwing up a hand. "Please, Edward, don't talk like that." I took a deep breath. "Why do you want to get close to Mr. Radcliffe?"

He ran a hand through his hair. "It's part of the plan to cure myself. I have letters that I took from your father's laboratory before it burned. They contain correspondence with a former colleague of his, going back years to when he was first banished. All that time on the island, he maintained contact with someone, trading the secrets to his work in exchange for funding and supplies."

His words gave me pause. All those years when I'd thought Father dead, he was corresponding with someone back in London? I sank against the rough bark of a palm tree to steady myself. I'd once asked Father why he never wrote to me. He'd alluded to the fact that there was a warrant on him, and letters would have alerted the police to his whereabouts. And yet it seemed he hadn't hesitated to write to colleagues when it suited him.

I started to put everything together. "The letters were to Mr. *Radcliffe*? Lucy's father was his correspondent? But he isn't a scientist. Their money came from rail, and now he's doing something with the automobile industry, shipping engines all over Europe—"

Edward was quick to shake his head. "I don't know for sure if it's him. The letters aren't signed; whoever his colleague was, Moreau wished to keep it secret. The correspondent called himself a King's Man, nothing more. So I've been investigating all the members of the King's Club, starting with those closest to your father, such as Radcliffe. He's a hard man to get close to."

"The King's Club is wrapped up in this?" My mind ticked back to the grainy old photograph hanging in the hallways of King's College. Father's young face had seemed so hopeful then, brimming with ambition. I tried to remember the other faces. Hastings had been there, and Isambard Lessing . . . the rest of the names bled together in my head.

"So you used Lucy. Never mind that you would only end up breaking her heart, assuming you didn't first rip it out of her chest." I knew my words were laced with acid, but he didn't flinch. "Did you at least discover anything about her father?"

He shook his head. "Not yet. There are a dozen King's Men who fit the profile." A shadow passed through the golden flecks in his eyes. "Including your guardian."

My hand fell away from my collar. The professor? Words raced up my throat, ready to deny it, but they never made it to my lips. Doubts started to pull them back down— the professor *had* been in the photograph, standing right next to my father, of all places—but I gritted my teeth and ignored my doubts. "The professor was the one who turned

Father in. He'd never support his work."

But Edward didn't answer, and my blood went cold. Only the day before yesterday the professor had told me about how he'd met Father in the King's Club. He'd prodded me for information, asked me to talk about my time on the island. I thought he'd just been concerned. . . .

I shook my head fiercely. "No, I don't believe it. It's someone else. But it doesn't matter—whoever Father's secret colleague is, you can't contact him. It's too dangerous."

"I haven't a choice. If he knows Moreau's work, he might know how to cure me."

"He'll use you! On the island Montgomery and I swore we wouldn't let any of my father's research leave, in case the wrong people were to get ahold of it. That's the entire reason I destroyed his laboratory, the reason I wouldn't let Balthazar come back with me . . . the reason I helped kill my own father!"

My desperate words filled the artificial jungle around us, and I clenched my jaw as if I could take them back.

"I'm flesh and blood, not a diagram in a laboratory notebook," Edward said. "How could they possibly use me?"

"It wouldn't be impossible for someone with the right training. I saw a hybridized Bourgogne lily the other day and knew exactly what stock it had come from. If I'd been able to dissect it and further examine its various parts, I'd be able to tell even more." My voice fell to a whisper. "They could do the same to you, Edward. Cut you open and see how Father made you, and then re-create it. Think of what that would mean. How many animals would die on their operating tables. Humans, too, probably. And in the end, an army of beast-men not contained on a single small island."

His hand touched the scar under his eye absently and then fell away. "What other choice do I have? As long as the Beast is a part of me, he'll keep killing. That blood is on my hands too, Juliet. I've no one else to help me."

A thousand emotions warred in my chest. Some told me to run, some told me our goals were the same—finding a cure—and that we could help each other. Some told me to leave him to his fate. But it was my fate too, now. I'd had a hand in my own father's murder to keep this from happening. And I wasn't a fool. If Father's colleague got his hand on Edward, it would only be a matter of time before he found out I, too, was one of Father's experiments. If I wasn't careful, it might be me strapped to an operating table one day.

I cursed under my breath, wondering if I was making a huge mistake.

"Then I'll help you myself."

ELEVEN

LATER THAT EVENING, EDWARD and I stood on the landing of my lodging house in Shoreditch while I fumbled with the key. Sharkey had been waiting outside the front door, half-hidden in the bushes, having escaped Joyce again and come here, where he knew I'd give him whatever meat scraps I had left over from my experiments. I'd introduced the dog to Edward and he'd carried Sharkey up the stairs in his arms. Seeing him act so gentle with the little mutt stirred something inside me.

For months I'd thought Edward was dead, though that hadn't kept my mind from straying back to him. Edward had been a friend, possibly even something more, before I'd learned the terrible truth about the monster inside him. I think I would have felt more outrage if he hadn't died. But in death I had absolved him of his crimes, blaming my father instead for having created him, and I had absolved myself of blame, too, for not seeing through his lies earlier. But here he was, very much alive, responsible for a string of violent murders, and yet also very much just a boy learning what it meant to be human. Almost all he knew of the world he'd learned from books; the sights and smells of the city—even something as common as a street dog—must be a revelation to him.

I turned the lock and pushed open the door. This place was more than a workshop; it was my retreat from fine china and straight-backed chairs and weak tasteless tea. I liked coming here alone, where I could hide from the world, tucked under the patchwork quilt. I had worried that by bringing Edward here, that precious balance would be upset. But as I watched him rubbing Sharkey's head and leaning against the rough wood of the stairwell, he seemed to fit so naturally.

"Come inside," I said softly. "No one knows about this place. You'll be well hidden here."

It took a lot for me to say that—to invite a murderer into my one private space. But in a twist of fate, watching him shift the dog from one arm to the other and brush back a loose strand of hair, I felt strangely safe with him.

Safe with a murderer. With *Edward*. Perhaps this was how madness started.

Sharkey jumped out of his arms and curled up by the bricks around the woodstove. Edward came in hesitantly, scratching the back of his neck, looking uncomfortable in a lady's room. I lit the lamp and nodded toward the wood-stove. "Will you light the fire? I'll put the kettle on."

He bent to swing open the iron grate and add wood to the stove. While his back was turned, I chewed on a fingernail and tried not to steal glances at his frame, so much stronger than I'd remembered. Having him here triggered so many memories. A sun-scarred castaway on the *Curitiba*'s deck, clutching a crumpled photograph. A boy holding me close in a cave behind a waterfall. The one person in addition to me who wasn't afraid to stand up to my father, when even Montgomery wouldn't.

My left rib started to ache at the painful memories. Montgomery had the strength of a horse, and yet he'd been powerless in front of my father. I remembered being a little girl and listening through the laboratory keyhole as Father taught Montgomery how the circulatory system worked. It had hurt then, too, that Father was closer to a servant boy than to his own daughter. Perhaps I shouldn't have blamed Montgomery. He'd had no other family; his father was a Dutch sailor he'd never known, his mother died when he was barely five, no siblings, no other servants his age. Of course he'd fallen under the spell of Father's charms; any child that lonely would crave a connection wherever he could get it.

And yet I offered him love, I thought blackly. *I chose him, but he didn't choose me.*

Edward closed the grate and rubbed his hands together in front of the fire with a boyish grin. I didn't even consider trying to smile back. My heart was too shaken.

"Where did you get those clothes?" I asked. "They aren't cheap, and neither is that gold pocket watch."

He came to the cabinet, where the lantern tossed pools of light over his face. "The Beast keeps a room at a brothel in Soho—I wake there sometimes. He steals clothes and things from the wealthy patrons, always finds men close to my size . . . very thoughtful of the Beast." The hints of a smile played on his mouth.

"This isn't a joking matter."

He swallowed. "I'm sorry—I don't mean to make light of it. I've been staying in the Beast's room and selling the stolen goods. I know it's hardly proper, but a brothel's good cover—I don't know where else to go. People tend to overlook the screaming when I transform. . . ."

I shuddered at the thought. "You can't go back there," I said. "Sooner or later one of the patrons will report the thefts, and if Scotland Yard comes to investigate and catches you, it'll be all over the newspapers, and not long before Father's mystery colleague gets his hands on you." I nodded toward the bed, looking away before my cheeks warmed. "You can stay here."

He nodded, and silence fell around us. He took out his pocket watch, toying with it just to fill the quiet. He wandered to the worktable, where I'd left the laboratory equipment in perfect order, the boiler and beakers and glass vials arranged in descending order of height. It wasn't a vial he reached for, though, but one of the grafted rosebushes. I'd bound a single white rose to a bush of red, and he touched it as gently as a caress.

"You made these?"

I didn't answer, afraid he'd point out how similar the grafting and splicing was to Father's work, and how the placement of my laboratory equipment mirrored Father's exactly.

"Yes," I said at last.

"They're beautiful."

A surge of pride swelled in my heart. The kettle started whistling, and I nearly tripped over the dog to fetch it, along with my single mug. I poured a cup and handed it to him, trying not to think about his compliment. "I'm not used to guests here. I've only the one cup."

"Much obliged," he said, taking the tea, and only then acknowledged the medical equipment. "And all of this?"

"I have to have it," I said quickly. "The serum I take is failing. Father designed it for me when I was a baby, and as I get older, it's less effective. I'm trying to cure myself, just like you are." I let my hand fall over a crystal beaker. "That's why I offered to help you."

"Have you had any success?"

"Not yet," I said, though my voice caught as my eyes fell on the cupboard shelf. A book glowed there in the faint lantern light. It was one of many books I kept on anatomy, and botany, and philosophy, but this one was special. It stood out like a temptation, or maybe an accusation.

It was my father's journal.

I'd found it the day after Montgomery set me adrift from the island. He must have stowed it in the dinghy along with the water and food and other supplies. For a while, I had resisted opening it. And yet once I discovered that Father's serum was failing me, the temptation to look had been too strong. I had opened that leather cover and read his notes—some scrawled, most in his painstakingly precise handwriting. I'd flipped through the pages, desperate for some clues about how to cure myself. And yet the journal hadn't proven anything, half of it little more than lines of nonsense words and numbers strung together.

I touched the journal delicately, but didn't dare pull it out. "Father made most of his notations in here, before he transferred everything to the files he kept in his laboratory. There's a formula for my serum, and the one he used on the islanders, and I've been trying to adapt it to my current situation." I let my hand fall away from the book. "No luck so far. Much of what he says in there is nonsense, anyway. He must have used a personal shorthand when he was writing in a hurry, and I haven't been able to make sense of it."

Edward's eyes didn't leave the journal. When he spoke, his voice held a quiet sort of hope. "Does it say anything about me? He used cellular traits from human blood to make me. I never found out whose blood it was."

His fingers were still flipping the pocket watch over nervously, and I understood. To Edward it wasn't just blood in a test tube. That human blood was his only tie to another person—to a family, in a sense.

I shook my head. "It doesn't say. I'm sorry."

He turned to the chemistry set, looking through my beakers and vials of supplies. Science, math, literature—these were the things Edward was comfortable with, things easily learned from a book. He made a good show at social interaction, using lines and scenes from obscure plays no one knew, but I didn't think it ever came naturally to him.

"We can figure it out together," I said softly. "We'll cure both of us. It'll just take time."

"Time is something I don't have much of, I'm afraid," he said. "The longer I'm with the Beast, the more alike we become. I can feel him bleeding into me, trying to take over. I can still delay the transformations, but I'm not sure for how much longer. He could only hold his form minutes at first, a half hour at most. Now he can hold it for two hours." His eyes met mine over the flickering burner flame, and again I thought about how much darker they looked. "In another month, maybe less, I'm afraid he'll take over completely."

My lips parted. This was why he seemed bigger to me, and darker, and stronger. The Beast was melding with him. "Edward . . ."

"I can't let it get to that, Juliet. He'll terrorize everything. If he would let me take my own life, I would. I've tried a dozen times, but he prevents me." He paused. "Montgomery nearly killed me, once." He looked away from the flame. "You shouldn't have stopped him."

"Don't say that," I whispered.

His flickering eyes found mine. "You know it's the only possible end for me. I was never meant to exist."

"But you do exist, Edward. We'll find the missing ingredient, and we'll get rid of the Beast." I realized how desperate my voice sounded. Desperate for him, or desperate for me, now that I had someone in my life who shared my secrets?

"Juliet . . . ," he muttered, and brushed the back of his hand against my cheek.

Warmth bloomed where he touched me. For an instant I leaned into it, as starved for human contact as he was, and wicked temptations whispered in my head before I could twist away in shock at my own response. I was lonely, that was all, especially for someone I could talk to freely.

He killed Alice, I reminded myself, thinking of my father's sweet young maid. *He could kill you, if you get too close.*

"How did you survive the fire?" I asked, as though we could pretend that touch had never happened.

"The Beast is strong. He heals fast. I came to and was able to crawl out before the barn collapsed, and then I salvaged what I could from the house. The letters, for one."

"I want to see these letters."

He nodded. "I'll go back to the brothel and collect them. I must return anyway for the chains I use to bind myself and some changes of clothes."

I chewed on a fingernail, pacing. "I want to help you, Edward, truly, but not if . . ." I swallowed, thinking of those drained bodies. "Not if you keep killing people."

"I'll fetch the chains in the morning. He's weaker early in the day. If he has the choice, he prefers to emerge at nighttime."

"And tonight? Can you promise me no one else will die tonight?"

A flash of Annie Benton's face, Sir Danvers Carew, the red-haired thief girl.

Edward went to my worktable and searched through the vials, coming back with a heavy dose of sedative. "Give me this, then," he said.

"That much could kill you."

"You underestimate how strong I've gotten. It's only

for one night. Tomorrow I'll have the chains." He held it out to me, and I took it hesitantly. I'd gotten it from a veterinarian who had told me it was used to sedate animals for transportation. If it would stop a lion, it would stop Edward.

"Give me your arm," I said. "You'll fall asleep in ten minutes, twenty at most." He held it out to me and I inserted the needle into a vein, telling myself there was no choice, that I was doing this so we wouldn't wake up to any more bloody headlines in the newspaper. I rolled his sleeve back down gently. "One more thing. Promise me you won't see Lucy again. You're putting her in danger by being around her."

He nodded a little hesitantly. "I'll send her a note."

I felt the weight of the unfinished conversation and finally asked the question that kept circling in my thoughts.

"What happened to Montgomery?"

There was the pain again, sharp and quick, in my side, as though when Montgomery had shoved the dinghy away with his boot, he'd kicked my heart instead. I recapped the syringe, biting the inside of my cheek.

Edward didn't respond right away, and my mind filled with answers he wasn't saying. Perhaps he'd killed Montgomery, or one of the beast-men had. Or Montgomery was still there, on the island, content never to see me again.

"He's alive," Edward said at last, but I could tell he was holding something back. "He hunted me for weeks on the island. I left him notes, trying to get him to give me a chance to explain. . . . I thought maybe he could help me find a cure. But he was only interested in hunting me down, and I knew sooner or later he'd have his chance, and he wouldn't win. The Beast is too strong. So I left, to come here and find a cure before my other half killed him."

I toyed with one of the silver forks in the pile of stolen silverware, watching the glints from the lantern. He stepped closer, dropping his voice. "Forget him, Juliet. He abandoned you. He was keeping secrets from you."

I glanced up from the fork. "Secrets?"

"That he was helping your father, that he'd made some of the creatures himself, and worst of all . . ." He stopped and looked away.

"What secret?" I asked. When he didn't answer, I let the fork clatter to the floor and grabbed his suit lapel a little roughly. "What other secret was Montgomery keeping from me, Edward?"

"It doesn't matter. You loved him, and he left you. I'd never do that to you. I'd sooner cut off my own hand than do anything to cause you pain." My fingers were still coiled in the stiff fabric of his lapel, and he whispered, "If you'd only give me a chance . . ."

But I stepped back toward the cabinet, away from his promises and his offers. My breath was coming fast. The world was an upside-down place when Montgomery James was keeping secrets from me and Edward Prince telling me the truth.

But Edward was right—Montgomery *had* lied to me. He had left me.

I grabbed my coat before he could say another word, and said, "The professor will have half the city out looking for me. It's so late . . . I must get back. I'll leave Sharkey here with you; the drugs will put you to sleep in a few minutes, so lock the door behind me. If you aren't too groggy tomorrow, go through Father's journal—maybe you can make sense of it. I'll come back tomorrow night with fresh supplies." I squeezed the doorknob, afraid to let go. Terrified to leave him, terrified that I still might read of fresh murders tomorrow in the newspaper. Sedatives might not be enough. Chains might not be enough. I had seen what the Beast could do. I'd have to make something even stronger to contain him until we could find the cure.

As I slid into my coat, my eyes darted around the room. Edward, so handsome as he checked his pocket watch, stood amid the twisted rosebushes, with Sharkey curled on the woodstove's hearth and a warm fire churning away through the old iron door. Almost a sweet scene, if it hadn't been so terrible. I threw on my coat and shut the door, heart pounding.

I leaned my head back against the worn wood of the stairwell, eyes closed, uncertain if I was making the biggest mistake of my life by helping a murderer, or if I had found the one person in the world who understood me.

TWELVE

WHEN I'D LEFT THE house that morning, the professor had been so distracted by Isambard Lessing's visit that he hadn't asked when I'd be home. By now he must be worried sick, and I imagined every light in the house would be blazing, a search party gathered on the front steps.

But as I approached the brownstone on Dumbarton Street, not a single light shone in the windows. The professor's routine was predictable to a fault; brandy after dinner and a book until nine, then at the chime of the cuckoo clock, he retired to his bedroom on the third floor. But even as a man of habit, would he have dismissed Mary for the day and gone to bed without me home? Could he have been so distracted over his argument with Isambard Lessing that he'd forgotten to look into my room?

My mind turned back to that historian, and with a sharp stab I remembered that the professor had introduced Lessing as a King's Man. Could the professor have never left the King's Club at all? Could Edward have possibly been right, that my own guardian was the secret colleague?

Fears stirring, I slunk past the iron gate and tip-toed through the snow to climb the garden trellis. When I reached my bedroom window, shivering in the cold, I discovered that the window wouldn't budge. I shoved my weight against it, but it held fast. I squinted through the glass. The padlock had been substituted with a fresh one.

Blast. This didn't bode well.

I climbed back down and jumped into the garden, hesitant to knock on the door and wake the professor if it could at all be avoided. Fortunately, as I skirted the house, I found that Mary had left the kitchen window open a crack, and I silently thanked her forgetfulness. I gracelessly hoisted myself onto the window ledge and slid my stiff fingers into the crack, opening it as silently as I could.

The kitchen was dark, the icebox and basin nothing more than hulking shadows. I eased my head and shoulders in, kicking my feet to try to slide in further.

I had almost made it when two hands grabbed me under the arms and hauled me roughly the rest of the way.

I would have screamed if I'd found a voice. As it was, I fought and clawed, but the figure dropped me unceremoniously on the kitchen floor, where my knees banged on the hard stones and made stars flash in my eyes as I winced in pain. I reached for my knife, but my coat and skirts tangled around me as my hair spilled loose. I was able to push my hair back just in time to see a dark figure moving toward the kitchen table and striking a match.

The match flared to life, showing the face of a woman.

My hand paused above my boot, more in surprise than anything. *A stranger*, I thought at first, but no, that wasn't right—I recognized something in her long, loose blond hair, the fine set of her features only starting to show the first signs of wrinkles around her deep-set eyes, her Germanic ancestry evident in her face, just like the professor's, her uncle.

"Elizabeth," I said in a stunned whisper.

She lit the hurricane lantern calmly, as though it didn't trouble her in the least that I was collapsed in a bruised pile on the kitchen floor. She took a seat at the table and motioned to the opposite seat.

"Miss Moreau, a surprise to be meeting again like this. Though I imagine you won't mind if I call you Juliet, seeing as formality flew out the window when you crawled through it."

I scrambled into the seat, rubbing my elbow where I'd banged it. Ten years had passed since I'd last seen her, and yet little wear showed on her features. Her hair was just as beautiful as ever as it tumbled to her waist in soft waves that glowed in the lantern light. She was still dressed despite the late hour, in a pale red dress that was quite simple, though even a rag would look elegant on her. She gave me a smile that was slightly off balance, the only quirk in an otherwise perfectly proportioned face, and it looked so much like the professor's that I started.

"When did you arrive?" I stuttered.

"Shortly before lunch. The professor had fallen asleep in the library, and asked me to check on you in your bedroom and say hello. Imagine my surprise when I found the room empty and the window lock broken."

"I'm sorry about that." I swallowed thickly. "And about sneaking back in through the kitchen window. I didn't want to worry the professor."

"Nor did I, which is why I told him you weren't feeling well and were not to be disturbed for the remainder of the day."

"He doesn't know that I wasn't here?" I said, feeling a coil of hope.

"I kept your secret," she said, flashing those shrewd blue eyes at me. "For the time being, at least."

"Don't tell him, please. I was only—"

She held her hand up, silencing me. "Whatever you're going to tell me won't be the truth, but we're all entitled to our secrets. I remember what it meant to be a young woman in a city like this. In a *life* like this, where everyone is watching your every move. The professor told me you were clever, and that broken lock on your bedroom window seemed to support that theory, so I left the kitchen window cracked after he went to bed and hoped you would have the good sense to climb in through it. It's what I would have done." She leaned forward. "You'd be wise to never sneak out of this house again, or else you had better get far craftier at it, because if I catch you another time I won't hold my tongue again."

I nodded, unable to look her in the eye. I'd disappointed the professor's niece before I had barely met her. She stood and crossed to the still-open window, which let in slips of cold air that left me shivering, and slid it closed. When she took her seat at the table again, the sternness had eased from her face, and a deep concern knotted her brow in its place.

This is how a mother might look, I thought, and the idea filled me with a sense of loss and longing.

"Now that we've gotten that behind us, you aren't in trouble, are you?" Her eyes had a way of reaching somewhere deep inside me, beyond my past and my indiscretions and focusing instead only on my well-being. Such care from a stranger made my chest tight with an emotion I didn't know how to process.

I shook my head quickly. "No trouble. It was only a silly lark, sneaking out to see a friend."

She raised an eyebrow, uncertain whether to believe me, but then jerked her chin toward the top of the stairs, dismissing me. I gathered my skirt and hurried up, still shaken, and closed myself in my room.

I didn't know what I had been expecting from Elizabeth's arrival. Perhaps just one more person to lie to. I certainly hadn't expected a woman who thought like I thought, who anticipated my every move.

Who would lie *for* me.

THE NEXT DAY LUCY and I had an appointment at Weston's Dressmakers to be fitted for gowns for the masquerade ball. Elizabeth insisted that Ellis, the driver, take me in the carriage and wait outside the store, because of all the Wolf of Whitechapel panic in the city. As the carriage rolled down the Strand, I heard the call of at least a dozen newspaper boys yelling out headlines, all of them about the Wolf. I pushed back the curtain and watched the swarms around the boys, everyone hungry for news of the city's latest mass murderer. Signs had been pasted on the sides of buildings and alleyways with his nickname in thick red ink. I even saw two men and a portly older woman wearing metal breastplates not unlike Inspector Newcastle's, as though the murderer might leap out onto the busiest street in London in pure daylight and try to rip their hearts out right there. I let the curtain fall back, disgusted. This city hungered for violence nearly as much as the Beast did.

As I climbed out of the carriage, the sound of tense words caught my ear. A few paces from the dress shop doorway, Lucy and Inspector Newcastle stood arguing while his police carriage waited in the street with the door still open. My stomach tightened in fear, but I took a deep breath and tried to remember that he wouldn't arrest me. In fact, having a police officer close to Lucy while Edward was in the city might be the most fortunate thing that had happened to me in a while. As I approached them, I caught the tail end of the inspector's words.

"I'm only saying that your father knows best. No one's heard of this man's family. How can you be certain he isn't trying to take advantage of your father's money?"

"Of course no one knows him; he's from Finland!"

"Darling, Henry Jakyll is a complete stranger. You might think yourself infatuated with him, but your father has barely even met him, and—"

"Is Father the one who wants to keep me from Henry? Or is it *you*?"

As I approached, Inspector Newcastle caught sight of me. He straightened and smoothed his jacket over his breastplate. "Miss Moreau, a pleasure to see you again."

Lucy's head turned to me too, but her scowl didn't leave. "Good, you're here. John was just *leaving*."

"Lucy, darling—" he started, but stopped as the scowl on her face deepened. He leaned in and pressed a quick kiss to her cheek, but she pulled away and stormed into the dress shop with a wild clatter from the bell.

The inspector stared at the doorway, looking disheveled and lost.

"I've upset her, I'm afraid," he said, and then gave a sigh. "And not for the first time."

He looked crestfallen, and I searched for words but could only keep staring at his breastplate and thinking of the preposterous fervor I'd witnessed downtown. "You've started a fashion trend," I said. "It seems quite a few people have adopted your penchant for protective garments."

He gave a humble shrug. "They think because I'm leading the investigation, I must be a good example to follow. Well, it doesn't hurt anyone. Perhaps it might even save someone's life." I raised an eyebrow doubtfully, but he didn't seem to notice.

"You haven't reconsidered my offer, have you?" he asked. "I truly would like to close the case on your father. A promotion would help Lucy see me in a . . . more favorable light. Especially such a personal case. It might give you some peace of mind, too, Miss Moreau."

I pulled my hood higher. "I'm sorry. I appreciate your

concern, but I really can't help you."

He looked as though he might say something more, but then changed his mind and opened the door for me. I slipped past him into the dress shop.

A pair of seamstresses looked up as the bell chimed, as did Lucy, flipping a little angrily through a book of sewing patterns. I sat on a peach-colored chaise, while one of the seamstresses brought me a book of cloth swatches and a tray of biscuits. I halfheartedly felt the various samples of velvets, muslins, silks—they all felt itchy to me.

"John proposed," Lucy said at last.

"Oh my."

Her eyes flickered to the seamstresses, whose heads were cocked to eavesdrop, and she pulled me through the silk curtains into the privacy of a small dressing room that smelled of French perfume, with a screen and a stuffed ottoman, which she now flopped onto.

"He came around last night and told me he'd asked Papa for permission. I turned him down, and Aunt Edith spilled about Henry coming over for tea, and you should have heard the row." She shuddered at the memory.

"Lucy, I'm so sorry. Are you quite certain you don't care for him? He seems . . ." I fumbled for an appropriately pleasing word. "Responsible."

Drat. *Responsible* would never sway Lucy.

Her graceful fingers toyed with the ribbons on her gown. I took a deep breath, poised to tell her I also didn't trust Henry, and that she should stay away from him, when she stood up abruptly.

"Well. It doesn't matter. Henry sent me a letter early this morning, telling me he was leaving town and I wouldn't see him again." I heard the sting in her voice, though she tried to hide it. "So I couldn't have had him anyway, even if Papa had approved. That means it's either John or some fat vicar's son, I suppose." Her face grew serious, which didn't fit with the almost revoltingly cheerful atmosphere of the dressing room.

I hesitated. I'd intended to warn her away from Edward, but it seemed Edward had already kept his promise and done my work for me.

"That must have been hard for you, but perhaps it's for the best. You used to swear that Henry bored you as much as the others."

She flicked an impatient glance at me. "Yes, but you know me. I can't possibly admit when I actually *do* care. And Henry was different. I enjoyed his company, quite a lot."

I swallowed back my guilt for not telling her the truth that Henry—*Edward*—was right this moment in my attic chamber.

She turned on me a little abruptly. "We're like sisters, aren't we? We tell each other everything. You came to me with that awful business about Dr. Hastings, so it makes sense that I should reciprocate, if there was something bothering me as well. Something I wasn't certain how to handle."

There was something tense in her movements that I hadn't seen before. She kept toying with her ribbons, watching me carefully.

"Are we still talking about your suitors?" I asked

slowly. "Or is this about something else?"

She paced a little before the full-length mirror, which reflected the sharp angles of her face, her dark hair coiled intricately in pins atop her head. "It's . . ." She paused. "Well, it's nothing really. Just some business with my father, some investments he's made that I worry about. But what do I know about business?"

She was trying to turn her tone back to playfulness, but there was something in her eyes I rarely saw. Fear.

My voice dropped. "Lucy, what exactly is going on?"

But she silenced me with a curt wave as footsteps sounded outside the heavy curtain. One of the seamstresses drew back the fabric and asked us if everything was going all right, and if we'd like more biscuits.

After we'd dismissed her, Lucy smiled tightly and said, "Never mind, it's nothing. Papa's business isn't why we're here, is it? You listen to me rattling on about men so much, the least I can do is help you pick out a dress. Don't you dare try to come to the masquerade in one of those old-maid dresses the professor usually buys for you. Mother and Papa want you to be a guest of honor. Go on. Peel those clothes off."

I tried to conjure a smile to match her tone, but it wouldn't come.

"Don't just stand there," she said. "Take off that awful coat and throw it into the rubbish bin. Those stockings, too, while you're at it; they look like they're from the last decade. I've picked out a gown for you, behind the dressing screen."

The gown hung on a wooden hanger, red satin, low

lace collar, and sleeves that floated like clouds. I touched the fabric tentatively between thumb and forefinger, afraid my presence alone would stain it. I didn't deserve this—not the gown, and not her kindness.

I came out from behind the screen, frowning. "It's too fine for me."

"Goodness, how many times must I tell you that you aren't a maid any longer?"

"It's just that all this isn't really my world anymore."

"Of course it is!" She rested her hands on her hips, frowning, but then her face lit up. "I know what this is about. You've no one to take you to the masquerade. Well, I've refused John, and Henry's left me, so I haven't anyone either. *I'll* be your escort." She smiled so broadly that I hadn't a clue what to say. I couldn't help but feel her joviality masked the pain from Henry's rejection and the questions she had over her father's business.

"Lucy, don't be silly."

"I'm perfectly serious! Come on, you'd have half the men in London after you if you weren't so dour. That's why this masquerade is so perfect for you. The whole point is to be someone else."

Her lips curled, and this time I did manage to smile back. The idea of being someone else certainly had its appeal. Not daughter to a madman. Not jilted by Montgomery. Not a girl who found a flower laced with blood and kept it pressed in a heavy book.

Lucy slid her arm in mine and led me back around the dressing screen. I touched the lace trim of the red silk dress, imagining its feel against my skin.

"Try it on," she said. "And then decide."

I rolled my eyes but at the same time slid off my coat, then started with the long row of buttons down the back of my dress that followed the line of my scar. "Shall I have an alias, then?" I asked. "Perhaps an Italian heiress?"

Lucy's nose wrinkled. She helped me with the highest buttons, then together we peeled off my thin dress and layers of underskirts. "You'd never pass as an Italian. Your mother was French. How about a French baroness, fleeing the Radicals? Oh, the men will love it! They'll all want to save you."

I laughed for real this time. "Or swindle me out of my supposed fortune."

"Either way, it'll fill your dance card. What's more," she said, wiggling her eyebrows, "I hear Papa has invited a very eligible contract attorney."

"Oh, an attorney," I said, pretending to swoon. "What a dream. Do you think he has a friend for you? Maybe someone dashing, like a public registrar?"

As we laughed together, I stepped out of my final underskirt and stood in the dressing room in only my combination, like Lucy. My braid was loose and curly like hers. My smile not quite as wide—after all, my laughter hid pain, too.

The only other time I'd been so friendly with a girl had been Father's young maid, Alice. Days later she'd been murdered. I pictured Lucy in Alice's place, cold body dead on the tile floor, white feet dripping with blood.

That won't happen to Lucy. I won't let it.

But the thought conjured visions of bodies torn apart by razor-sharp claws, and flowers stained in blood, and a murderer hidden in my attic chamber.

Lucy gave me a devilish grin, banishing my troubled thoughts. "Don't worry, Juliet. This is going to be quite a memorable party."

I tried to smile back. Memorable was watching Alice's blood pool on the floor. Memorable was learning my father had betrayed me. Memorable was a white flower spotted with fresh red blood.

I wasn't looking for a memorable party. I'd have settled for a perfectly forgettable one, but ever since Edward had returned to London, I had the feeling nothing would be forgettable ever again.

THIRTEEN

THAT NIGHT I WAS sleepless with wracking pain. My knuckles popped in their sockets; my head ached in a low, dull way. I could feel each bone in my body as though it moved of its own accord. I had been taking my injections daily, and yet the fits were only getting worse. I lay in bed for an hour, sweating into the sheets, until at last the illness passed.

Elizabeth and the professor had long since retired, so I stood shakily and broke the new lock on my bedroom window with more hydrochloric acid, praying I could find another lock to match Elizabeth's so she wouldn't know it was gone. I eased the window up as quietly as I could. The snow fell in thick flakes, but the wind was mild for once—a small blessing. I crawled to the end of the overhang and then down the trellis into the garden with limbs that were still sore, and made my way along streets that grew noticeably more run-down until I arrived in Shoreditch.

I paused at the entrance to the lodging house. The fresh air and movement had eased my symptoms, and without the distraction of pain my mind could focus on bigger questions. Edward claimed he would never hurt me, but how much control did he really have over his other half?

My hand fell to the weight in my coat pocket. When I'd replaced my bedroom lock months ago, I'd ordered several extra padlocks from the blacksmith's, a few small ones to lock my serum and journal in private boxes, but also a heavy lock I'd intended to put on the attic door. Edward had said the Beast sometimes broke the lock on his chains—surely he couldn't break *this* one. But would a padlock really stop a monster? If only Montgomery were here. He was young too, unprepared too, but he'd always helped me figure out what to do. I felt at times as though his memory was fading around the edges like an old photograph.

"What should I do?" I whispered into the night.

Montgomery was far away, but I didn't need his voice in my ear to know that he would tell me to do everything I could to prevent Edward from hurting more people—and from hurting me.

I drew my knife and hid it in the folds of my coat, in case I needed it quickly. As I climbed the stairs to the fourth floor, a strange thrill plucked at my ribs, toying with my body like another symptom of my illness. The door was locked, so I knocked hesitantly.

Edward was quick to answer. The shock of the door suddenly opening and him standing there robbed me of any fears that he might hurt me. There was only concern in his dark brown eyes. I squeezed the knife harder to remind myself he was still dangerous.

"You should have asked who it was before answering," I managed to say.

The smell of roses and camphor spilled out around him. I could hear the woodstove crackling and the tea kettle rattling on top, beckoning me in. My stomach felt suddenly very hollow, and I was overwhelmed with the idea that the only place I truly belonged was this little room, with this boy who knew me so well when no one else did, and I was immediately ashamed of those thoughts. What would Montgomery have thought of *that*?

"I know your footsteps," he said. "Or rather, the Beast does. I don't share all his memories, but a few things bleed through. Information that relates to you, most of all."

He stood back to allow me entrance, and I came in almost feeling like a stranger in my own home. Edward seemed to fit so perfectly among the twisted rosebushes and frosted glass windows that it was hard to believe he had only been here a day.

I caught a glimpse of Sharkey curled on the hearth, fast asleep and dreaming, and that place in my stomach felt a little less empty and yet even more hollow at the same time.

"I've been working on the serum," Edward said, nodding toward the worktable. He picked up some yellowing pages that still had the earthy smell of the island. "These are your father's letters that I took from the compound before it burned. I doubt you'll find anything useful; he was careful to hide his tracks."

I devoured the letters in a matter of minutes. My father's handwriting felt so alive that it was hard to imagine

I'd never see him again. They discussed bank transfers and lists of surgical equipment, a few philosophical ramblings, but Edward was right—nothing concrete to tell me who Father had been working with here in London.

I set down the letters, and as if sensing my disappointment, Edward said, "I've gone through your father's journal and pieced together what I could. I performed two variations on the formula, but neither held longer than a few seconds. The phosphorous salts you're using are quite old. I thought I might go out and get a new batch."

"No!" It was my instincts speaking. "No, don't leave. I'll get the salts. You promised me you would stay here."

"Stay near the chains, you mean." There was a certain edge to his voice.

"Well, yes. Can you blame me? Edward, you're a *murderer*." I pulled the heavy padlock out of my pocket. "I had this made at the blacksmith's. It's created after one of Father's designs. Call him what you will, but he was a genius when it came to mechanical locks. No matter how strong the Beast gets, he won't be able to break through that."

I set it on the worktable with a thud. He picked it up quickly, as though its mere presence disturbed him, and stashed it in a drawer.

As I watched him, it struck me how truly handsome he was, despite the scar beneath his left eye. How could Lucy *not* have fallen in love with him? He was another creature entirely from her other stuffy suitors, who all dressed alike, spoke alike, made her the same tepid promises. Everything about Edward spoke of a different world, one richer in detail somehow, as though the waking world was merely a dream and he the only thing clear in it.

I cleared my throat and pulled out the worktable chair. He dragged over a stool, and together we started working on the serums. We spoke little, because little needed to be said. He and I had an understanding that didn't need words. I'd gesture to the salts and he'd hand them to me. He'd make a notation in the original formula and I'd take the pencil and tweak the amounts.

The chair had a rigid back, and I found myself constantly shifting so the stays of my corset didn't dig into my skin. After an hour of this, Edward glanced at me. "Is it the cold bothering you? I can add more wood to the fire."

I had another fork buried in the seams of my dress to scratch beneath the corset, and I paused. Edward watched me keenly, seemingly unaware that scratching oneself with dinnerware was frowned upon. That was one good thing about his limited past—he never seemed to know, or care, how strange my actions could be.

"The temperature's fine," I said, setting the fork aside and focusing instead on measuring the draught before me. "It's this awful corset. Be glad you're a man and don't have to deal with anything more constricting than a pair of socks."

I finished measuring the amounts, though from the corner of my eye I could still feel his attention on me. I shifted again.

"Why don't you take it off?" he asked. I turned to him in surprise, but his face was blank. "If it's bothering you, I mean. Take it off."

Take it off. As though removing such an intimate undergarment in a room alone with a young man was as commonplace as making a cup of tea.

"I can't," I stuttered. "There isn't even a changing screen."

He glanced around the room as though the impropriety of his proposal hadn't dawned on him, then turned back to his work with a shrug. The longer I sat there, barely able to breathe, the more I recognized that just because society said something was one way hardly meant it was right. Perhaps Edward's innocent comment made far more sense. This was my attic, after all. I could do what I liked here. *Be* who I liked.

"Dash it," I said. "You're right." I pushed myself up and reached for the buttons down the front of my dress, but paused when his eyes fell on the small triangle of exposed skin at the base of my throat. "Don't watch," I said. "Turn around."

His eyes darkened as a hint of desire flickered over his face, and it left me breathless despite myself. He turned back to his work, and as I stared at the back of his head, I undid the buttons with unsteady fingers down to my waist, and then turned my back and unhooked the corset. Air rushed into my lungs, though it was mixed with my fluttering nerves. I glanced over my shoulder to make certain he wasn't watching, then put my dress on again, which felt loose without the corset, and rejoined him at the table.

"I don't understand why women wear those," he muttered, keeping his eyes on his work. "It isn't natural. It's hiding who you are."

Now only the thin layers of my chemise and dress covered me, and it was both thrilling and unsettling all at once. "You *should* understand," I said. "Your whole life is about hiding who you are."

"*I'm* not hiding anything. This is who I am: these hands, this face. I might have named myself but that's still who I am—Edward Prince." He paused. "The Beast is something else entirely."

My eyes slid to him, curious. "You believe you've two souls in the same body? That you and the Beast have nothing in common?"

"I'm not certain," he said thoughtfully. "Not two souls, exactly. He and I are the same, and yet we're not. Two sides to the same coin, perhaps." His voice had wandered, and at my silence he cleared his throat. "You needn't fear me, though. Not you. The Beast loves you too much to hurt you."

My lips parted, as I found myself torn between ending this conversation and a desperate sort of fascination for it to continue. What did he mean when he said the Beast loved me? How could a monster love anything but destruction?

"What does it feel like when you become him?" I asked in a whisper.

His eyebrow raised, and his nervous fingers found his gold pocket watch. "It's painful. The physical transformation itself, I mean. Aside from that, it feels a little bit like drowning. Sinking into something that you can't come back from, and knowing you're still there, and still alive, but that there's something more powerful than you. I've no memory of what he does, only pieces like forgotten dreams, and sensations. Sometimes the sensations can be quite strong, depending on what he does."

"When he murders someone, you mean?" I whispered, riveted and horrified by the idea of it all. "Can you feel him doing it? Do you ever enjoy it too, just a tiny part of you, the part where the two of you meet? If you're the same person, I don't see how you can't." I stopped short, licking my dry lips, and found Edward watching me with a strange expression.

"No, I don't enjoy it," he said firmly. The edge to his voice had returned. "And you shouldn't ask me such things. Nor should you be interested in him, Juliet. He's a monster."

I blinked as though he'd shaken me, yet he hadn't laid a hand on me. I flushed deeply, mortified. I'd merely been curious, and curiosity was nothing harmful in and of itself, was it?

Edward slammed the book closed, still upset, and paced slightly as he replaced his pocket watch in his vest. "I'm going out for the phosphorous salts. You needn't worry about me killing anyone; I have him under control. I'll be back in a half hour."

I listened to his footsteps, followed by the door closing with a loud *thwack*. I thought about what he'd said, wondered why I *was* so fascinated by the Beast, told myself it was only because of my love for science, nothing more. I opened my journal, forcing myself to focus on the chemistry at hand and not our conversation.

I read over my formula once more:

- 1 DRAM .... CASTORIUM
- 80 MG .... GLYCOGEN EXTRACT
- 30 MG .... PHOSPHOROUS SALTS
- 30 MG .... EXTRACT OF HIBISCUS
- 10 MG EACH .... WHITE HOREHOUND, GOLDENSEAL,
  AND BITTER MELON

INSTRUCTIONS: *Heat over contained flame in spirits of nitre bath until separate oils combine; allow time for essential oils to evaporate. Note: Successful serum shall remain uniform in texture and color when allowed to cool below 40°C. If serum separates, THROW OUT.*

On the following pages Edward and I had scrawled our own notations: alterations to the dosage and ingredients, failed results, amended amounts.

The lantern flickered as a spool of air slipped in from the window cracks. I worked quickly, readying the extract, and finished the serum by distilling it over the burner flame and then transferring it into a glass vessel. Each minute that passed while I waited for it to cool was excruciating.

Five seconds passed, and still it held. My breath hitched with hope.

Ten seconds.

I took a thermometer, waiting at the edge of patience for the reading.

It reached 38° C, and still it held.

Still.

Then it split apart like oil in water.

"No!" I grabbed the vial full of separated liquid, shaking it, willing it to stay mixed. But it had failed, as all of them had. In a fit I threw the serum against the wall, where it shattered to the floor, making Sharkey jump up and bark in alarm. I doubled over in the chair and leaned my head on the table, barely holding myself together.

Failed again.

I listened to the wind push at the window, Sharkey's uneasy pacing on the floor before he curled up again on the hearth. Had Father had these same challenges? Everything had seemed so easy for him. I couldn't picture Father ever failing at anything.

Your father is still with you, a voice whispered in the back of my skull.

I tilted my head so one eye was free, and my gaze fell on Father's journal flickering in the lantern light. It wasn't exactly true that Father said nothing about serums. On one page near the back, I had found a detailed procedure he'd done on a cat.

Glycogen deposits are most potent when they are freshly collected, the entry said, *And in many cases, this means the difference between a serum's success and failure.*

"Freshly collected"—he meant from vivisecting a live animal.

I glanced toward the door to make sure there were no signs of Edward coming back soon and let my fingers creep toward the crooked shelf like a spider. The lantern cast a ghostly shadow as they moved closer and closer to the journal, until I could graze it with my index finger. The leather cover was soft, well worn, well loved.

The difference between success and failure.

I ran my finger along the top of the journal, testing its weight, how much pressure it would take to pull it from the shelf. I did so, just an inch, and then paused.

How desperate was I to cure myself? To cure Edward? Desperate enough for *vivisection*?

I glanced at Sharkey, curled on the rug by the wood-stove. His paws twitched as he dreamed he was chasing rabbits. I traced my eyes along his scrawny rib cage, where the bones stuck out like a map of his body. I'd seen enough of Father's diagrams to know where to cut to extract the pancreas. First I'd have to splay the stifles and make an incision from abdomen to sartorius, looking for the pink line of the diaphragm. The pancreas would be located between that thick wall of muscle and the spleen. It would take no more than four incisions to free it. A simple procedure, really.

A log cracked in the fire, and the dog twitched awake. I jerked out of my thoughts and slammed the journal back against the shelf like it was on fire. My head filled with the memory of watching Father at work in his laboratory, his poor victim twitching, screaming, dripping blood onto the floor. I stumbled to my feet, knocking the chair back, whole body shaking. Sharkey leaped up, worried for me, and scrambled to my side.

I looked down at his wet nose, his tiny claws. No,

I couldn't. I would never. God help me, I'd stop Edward some other way before *that*.

I pulled Sharkey into my arms.

"I won't do it," I whispered to him. "I couldn't."

But I could—that was the thing. If I wanted to, I could do it.

I didn't seem to feel any warmth from the fire anymore. All I felt was the sour taste of that journal's promise of a cure, but at a terrible price.

I couldn't get out of the workshop fast enough, though I knew Edward would be puzzled when he returned and I wasn't there. As I escaped back into the cold winter night, the moon was the only witness to that terrible flicker of temptation I'd managed to resist.

I should burn the journal, I thought, as the rest of Father's work had burned.

I pulled my coat tighter while I descended the lodging house's front steps. It was a quiet night, save for the wind that ruffled the strands of hair that had come loose from my braid. I could hardly focus on anything but the failed serum and Father's journal as I made my way back to Dumbarton Street, feeling naked without my corset, and exposed for all the world to see.

I knew, though I'd be damned for it, that I would never destroy that journal.

FOURTEEN

THE NEXT FEW DAYS were a precarious balance of secrets and truths, darkness and light. I snuck off to my attic chamber to work on the serums with Edward at night, and during the day I attempted to maintain a respectable life with the professor and Elizabeth as they hosted teas and took me ice-skating on the pond in Wimbledon and teased me about every young man who glanced my way.

The newspapers were blessedly silent. The Wolf of Whitechapel hadn't struck again, credited to Inspector Newcastle's prowess. Of course I knew it was *my* efforts that had kept Edward restrained, but I could hardly tell that to the *London Times*.

On a sunny morning the professor, Elizabeth, and I walked together in Covent Garden market, looking for Christmas presents for Mary and the other servants. By and large, Elizabeth was fiercely private, used to the solitude and quiet of the Scottish moors, and even days after her arrival I still had little indication as to the type of person she was. She stayed up late most nights, dressed in a housecoat in the library until all hours, wearing reading glasses not unlike the professor's wire spectacles, drinking licorice tea laced with gin—she didn't know that I knew—and staring out the window at the city lights.

"Have you heard of a man called John Newcastle?" I asked the professor as we passed a stall of silver dishware. "He's an inspector with Scotland Yard. I met him last week."

"Newcastle? Yes, a crackerjack, they're calling him. Trying to make a name for himself rather quickly. He puts on a show that he's from a good family, but his father owned a handful of shoe shops, nothing more. You haven't got your eye on him, have you? And here I thought you hated police officers." He gave his off-balance smile.

I laughed. "No, nothing like that. He's courting Lucy."

"Ah. Well, he's got ambition, and that would certainly please her father." The professor patted my hand as we followed Elizabeth to the flower market for mistletoe. "He wouldn't be good enough for you, anyway, my dear. You deserve at least an earl. Perhaps even a duke."

I laughed again until I saw the flower market stalls pressing in on us, and I was reminded of my twisted rosebushes and the attic where I sheltered the city's most terrifying murderer.

You're keeping him contained, I reminded myself. *He isn't hurting anyone.*

That evening, back at home, my feelings were still torn about Edward. The professor, Elizabeth, and I dined on *carré d'agneau*, and as I hid some of the meatiest pieces in my napkin to take to Sharkey later, my thoughts went from Edward to my father's letters. If Father indeed had maintained a correspondence with someone in London the entire time he was on the island, then Montgomery must have known about it, since he had been the one to travel to Brisbane and London for supplies, and deliver letters if there'd been any.

But Montgomery had said nothing. More secrets, just as Edward had said. It left the hurt of Montgomery's betrayal even more raw, as though perhaps I'd never known him at all.

"Well, we aren't much of a social bunch, are we?" the professor said. "Two weeks till Christmas, and the three of us sit home like lumps of coal."

I set down my soup spoon, then cleared my throat of my hesitation in bringing up a subject I knew they wouldn't like.

"I was thinking of Father."

The professor's good-natured smile wilted.

"The holidays," Elizabeth said tenderly. "They always make one think of family." She dipped her spoon into her soup as though that ended the conversation, but I couldn't let it go. I needed to discover who Father's colleague was—and prove that it wasn't the professor.

"What was he like before?" I asked.

Elizabeth exchanged a look with the professor, who leaned forward with his hands folded. "Yes, a girl should know what sort of man her own father was." He cleared his throat, thinking. "When I met him, he was quiet. Focused.

A lot like you, though considerably less pretty."

I smiled.

Elizabeth reached over and squeezed my hand. "Your mother was a lovely woman."

The professor had his head turned, almost as though listening for voices on the streets outside, or perhaps from his memory. "A brilliant man," he muttered, and then, almost as an afterthought, "A shame, the way it all happened."

It seemed he spoke of Father's banishment, but there was a far-off tone to his voice that tickled the back of my mind and made me wonder if his words weren't in reference to some other, darker memory instead.

"Did it happen quickly?" I asked, looking between them. "His madness, I mean."

The professor drew in a deep breath. "Oh, these things are difficult to know. There were times, early on, when he and I would share a cigar at the Hotel du Lac and talk of the possibilities of science. Grand conversations about experiments that would lead to saved lives and better medicine. Looking back, there were things he said that I should have taken note of. We had an argument once about using rabbits for medical trials—he didn't seem to think there was any morality involved at all. And he started keeping to himself more. Lying. He lied so easily. Only later did we discover he'd been slipping out nights, without even your mother being aware. Other nights he came home smelling of the butcher's. The dogs used to follow him around the city."

My hands beneath the table shook as I thought of

Sharkey following me because of the meat in my pocket. *Just like Father.* "When did you know for certain that he'd gone mad?"

The professor braced his arms on the table. "Are you quite positive you want to hear all this?" he asked. I nodded stiffly, as Elizabeth cleared her throat and stood to pour us more wine, and the professor leaned back in his chair, though his body never quite relaxed. "Our friendship had begun to drift apart by that point. I'd heard from colleagues—men I'd known in the King's Club—that his experimentation had gotten more severe, that he'd been reprimanded by the dean. Then my Helena had died, with little Thomas. Just six years old, he was. Your father didn't come to the funeral, and after all the lying and disappearing, I drank too much and got irate and went to confront him." He took a long draught of wine. "I found him in the laboratory with some poor animal. A dog, I believe it was, though so mangled you could hardly tell. He told me he was pioneering a new science, had been tinkering at it for years, and that it was going to change the world. The entire time the dog whined in terrible pain, and he didn't even seem to notice."

My heart clenched. Crusoe. That had been *my* dog. "And that was when you turned him in?" I asked, trying to keep my voice from shaking.

The professor rubbed his temple. "It was clear he'd gone mad. I'd no other choice. He fought me, and the dog managed to get away."

He sank deeper into his chair, as though speaking

the memories weighed him down. I felt the shape of them, too, like ghosts in the room, winding among the forest of candlesticks.

"And you never heard from him after that?" I asked.

He must have caught the strange note in my voice, because he looked up and said, with perfect frankness, "Heard from him? No, my dear. As I understand, no one heard from him ever again, until you stumbled upon that young assistant of his."

I met his eyes boldly, trying to read the truth there. He seemed so sincere, such a hero to the world for ridding it of a mad butcher and then taking in the orphan daughter. I had a hard time believing anything else could be the case. But I'd made the mistake of trusting my father, once. If the professor turned out to be lying, too, I didn't think I could take another betrayal.

Elizabeth blew out the candles one by one, then turned to me in the faint light from the tall windows.

"Come upstairs, Juliet. Enough of all these old memories. Let me draw you a bath, and after a good soak, you'll feel new again. I promise."

As SCALDING WATER TUMBLED into the claw-foot bath, Elizabeth poured in a handful of foaming salts that filled the room with the smell of roses. I balled myself up in the tub, naked beneath the foam but not self-conscious. Elizabeth had a motherly way about her, though she was childless. She took a comb to my hair and hummed a slow little tune while the water crept higher. The melody filled the room like steam, and at last I recognized it.

"The Holly and the Ivy," an ancient carol with pagan roots.

I closed my eyes and hugged my legs harder, laying my cheek on my knee. I liked how the sound of the water mixed with Elizabeth's carol singing to drown out my thoughts. My mother had never prepared a bath for me like this. We always had servants to do it when I was young, and then after the scandal we were lucky to clean ourselves in a neighbor's tepid bathwater.

"Don't you get lonely?" I asked. "Out there on the moors."

The comb drifted through my hair, pulling gently at the knots. "No," she said simply. "There are the servants, and a little village across the causeway, and Inverness is a day's journey if I'm desperate for a new dress."

"Desperate for a new dress?" I asked skeptically. Elizabeth's clothes were beautiful because she was beautiful, but no one would ever call them fashionable.

She gave a light laugh. "Well, I'd be far more likely to be desperate for some gin, but don't tell the professor that."

Rose-scented steam clouded around me, hiding my smile. But it faded quickly. Part of me wanted to confess everything to her, the real reason I snuck off at night and stayed out late, and how Sharkey followed me because of the smells from the butchers, just like the dogs had followed Father. I wanted her to kiss my forehead and tell me I wasn't anything like my father. But I knew I never would confess. I couldn't.

"I knew them both, you know," she said. Her tone was softer now. I opened an eye to look at her. "Your mother was six years older than me. I spent most of my life in Scotland, on my family's estate. All those fine old portraits hanging in the foyer—the figures in them look well groomed, don't they? Rich as they are, they're all illegitimate children." She laughed.

"The von Steins were from Switzerland but there was an affair, a Scottish lord's daughter, and that's how my grandparents came to own Balintore Manor. The professor doesn't like to talk about it, but the von Steins have as many skeletons in their closet as your own family, I'd wager. Each summer when I'd come back to London, your mother would take me for ice cream or chocolate biscuits, as though I was her baby sister. Our families were distant cousins, I believe, by marriage. I was sixteen when she married your father. Such a serious older man he seemed to me then, but handsome in his way. I remember one time your mother was ill, and he took me for ice cream instead, and told me about the work he was doing and how he wanted to save lives. I'll admit I had a bit of a schoolgirl infatuation with him. I suppose in part, that's why I went into medicine myself, though I had to teach myself nearly everything I know."

The comb caught on a tangle in my hair, and she paused to free it. "Whatever the professor has told you about your father, you must understand that he's biased. He felt as though one of his oldest friends betrayed him, which left more than a sour taste in his mouth. But as bad as your father's crimes were, there was good in him, too. When he was younger he laughed more, and he danced with your mother at all the finest balls, and if someone was ill in the middle of the night, he'd throw a housecoat over his pajamas and come running."

She finished combing my hair. The bath was nearly full, and she turned off the roaring water, plunging us into silence save for the soft crackling of bursting bubbles. She set a fresh towel on the side of the tub, and then leaned over and petted my head softly.

"Hate the part of him that gave in to madness. But don't hate your father, not all of him. There was a time when he loved you very much, and that's what you should remember."

She smiled a little sadly, and dried her hands on the towel in her lap, and then left me amid the smell of roses, where I stayed until the water grew as cold as the snow gently falling outside.

LATER THAT EVENING, AFTER the professor had gone to bed and Elizabeth retired to the library, I crept into the professor's study. It was a tidy place, with a cat curled in the desk chair, and letters paperweighted with the family crest, and a forgotten old stuffed bobcat perched on the upper shelves. I was looking for valerian, a distilled herb with sedative effects used to treat sleeplessness and restlessness, which Father had often used to calm his beast-men; but I also searched for any clue that would definitively rule out the professor as Father's correspondent. I flipped through the letters, all of them useless, and then opened his desk drawers and rooted through the assortment of papers and notebooks within. There was nothing to indicate he wasn't simply a retired academic from King's College, who volunteered at a clinic for the poor on Sundays and donated generously to foundations for medical scholarships.

I pushed aside a stack of boxes in front of the study's little closet, and coughed as dust poured out when I opened the door. If he'd been corresponding with Father within the last two years, then it certainly wasn't in here. Everything in the closet—his old medical bag, stacks of ancient journals with vellum pages—hadn't been touched in a decade. I carefully flipped through the journals' crisp, delicate pages, out of curiosity. Family heirlooms, it seemed, and most written in German. Then I opened his bag and found what I needed. Both distilled and powdered valerian, as well as quite a supply of castorium. I closed the closet and pushed the boxes back, telling myself that like the silverware, and the rest of the things I'd stolen, these drugs were things he didn't need nearly as much as I did.

I gave the sleeping cat a small pat and tiptoed back to my room, where I pulled on a coat borrowed from Elizabeth. It would be another sleepless night for me. But as I slid open the window and climbed outside, I thought about how at least I wasn't alone anymore. Edward would be waiting for me in that attic workshop, with Sharkey and the roses and a warm little fire going—and together we'd fix my father's wrongs.

FIFTEEN

EVERY NIGHT THAT WEEK, Edward and I worked on developing a serum amid the twisted rosebushes and howling wind outside my workshop, and every night we progressed a little more. On the fifth night, the compound held for nearly twenty seconds before splitting apart. On the sixth, it held long enough for me to prepare an injection, but separated only moments before I slid the needle into his skin. Without the missing ingredient, there was little we could do. I felt helpless, and frustrated, and mired in guilt. The Beast had stopped killing others—but he was still killing Edward from the inside.

On our seventh night together, eyes bleary with lack of sleep as I climbed out of the professor's window, I hurried through the streets with a new type of burner that would produce more even heat distribution. I raced up the lodging house stairs and threw open the door, the weight of the burner heavy in my satchel. Sharkey trotted over, tail thumping in his usual greeting, and I pushed my hood back and knelt to pick him up. He squirmed as he tried to lick my face, and I laughed and buried my face in his fur.

"Edward, I've a new piece of equipment," I said. Being here eased the tension from my bones in a wonderful way. "Edward, did you hear me?"

When there was no answer, I set Sharkey down. The attic was a small chamber, with only the worktable and bed and cabinet as furniture, and the alcove tucked away behind the woodstove, which was so dark that I only ever used it for storing grafting supplies. Now, though, I noticed one of Edward's thick iron chains running from the woodstove into the deep of the alcove. My breath caught.

Was the Beast there, chained in the shadows?

I'd seen the Beast only once, when Edward transformed on the island just moments before the fire started. I remembered his gleaming animal eyes, and how his whole body had seemed larger and hairier. The joints of his feet and hands had twisted together so he appeared to have only three fingers and three toes. Six-inch razor claws had emerged between his knuckles.

I remembered the Beast's voice, too, so shockingly human, and yet so different from Edward's.

We belong together, he had said.

"Edward?" I called. Sharkey darted into the alcove and I shrieked, bracing myself for a snarl as the Beast ripped him apart, but no sounds came except the thumping of Sharkey's tail.

I pulled on the chain, which rattled toward me—not attached to anything but air, which was a small relief. But where was Edward? He'd promised not to leave.

Behind me, the workshop door suddenly swung open hard enough to slam against the inside wall. I gasped and whirled, the chain falling from my hands with a terrible clatter that made Sharkey huddle behind my skirt.

"Edward!" I said.

He stood in the doorway, gold-flecked eyes heavy with surprise that I was there. His shirt was torn at the collar and sleeves, soaked with blood all the way to his elbows. His shoes were split at the seams, with jagged holes pushed through the top.

Holes for claws.

My hand went to my mouth, as Edward quickly shut the door and then rushed over, trying to calm me. "It's all right. I've control of myself now. It's me."

But as he came forward, all I could see was the blood on his shirt and arms that still smelled so fresh and ironlike. This wasn't supposed to happen. I'd planned everything to keep him contained. I stepped back with a strangled sound, bumping into the worktable hard enough to knock over one of the vials, which overturned and filled the room with the spicy smell of hibiscus extract.

"Don't come any closer!" I cried.

"I won't hurt you, I promise."

"You've killed someone."

He paused, eyes going to the stains on his clothes. He could hardly deny it—the evidence was soaked into the seams of his shirt. "Not me," he entreated. "The Beast."

"The padlock . . . the chains . . . my god, Edward, how

did this happen? We took precautions!"

"He came too fast; I didn't have time to lock the chains. The transformations are getting harder to control." He dragged a bloodstained hand through his hair, looking like that desperate castaway I'd met so many months ago. "You always knew this about me, Juliet. This is my curse—this is why we're here, what we're trying to stop." He took another step toward me, but I jerked away again. "You never come here before ten o'clock," he said. "I hadn't wanted you to ever see this—"

"Who did you kill this time?" I demanded.

His chest fell again in a deep exhale, and I saw how exhausted he was, how his muscles twitched and jumped, but I couldn't bring myself to feel sorry for him. He collapsed onto the bed, staining the sheets crimson, bracing his head in his hands like he was on the verge of fracturing. "You know I can't remember what he does. There are only hazy memories . . . following a doctor, but he let him live. And then I remember dark alleyways and the smell of blood. Whitechapel, most likely, which means another ruffian who would have died soon enough anyway, frozen to death drunk in some alleyway."

"And that makes it right?"

His eyes flashed with indignation. "Of course not!"

His outburst made Sharkey whine and hide behind my skirts again. A doctor, he had said. Could the Beast have been following Dr. Hastings? Hastings had wronged me . . . so why hadn't the Beast killed him yet?

He certainly deserves it, that awful man, I thought, and then caught myself. Judging who should live and die sounded too much like Father's arrogance.

Edward started tearing at his broken shoelaces until he could get kick both shoes off. His feet were knobby and caked in blood from where the claws had emerged between his joints. The claws were gone now, hidden once more between his bones. My own feet creaked with pain at the sight of them.

"Nothing's changed, Juliet. It's still me."

He looked at me with eyes that were all too innocent. A boy with a monster trapped inside, and nowhere to go but this dark attic, and no one to trust but me.

"I know." The crimson red spilled across his shirt was a terrible distraction, one I could scarcely look away from. "Although to see it so plainly . . ."

My left hand started shaking, and I clutched it to my chest before he could see the bones shifting on their own accord. He set his torn coat aside, looking so battered and beaten and hopeless that a small part of my heart twisted with sympathy for him.

"I know *you* aren't a monster, Edward. *You* aren't the one who wants to kill. It's just so difficult to understand where the line is between you and the Beast." I knit my fingers together and sat down next to him on the bed. "Before I knew about the Beast, I admired you greatly. You saved my life. You defended me against my father. I know that's still you . . . and yet *he's* in there as well."

Edward picked at his own fingernails, caked in blood. "If it wasn't for the Beast," he asked quietly, "would you have ever loved me?"

The bluntness of his question left me shocked. I didn't answer, because I didn't know how. Something had been stirring between him and me, feelings I had thought only belonged to Montgomery. But Montgomery had left me. For all I knew, I'd never see him again. Was I to live my whole life alone, then?

Edward reached over cautiously and took my hand. His hand was strong, so much larger than when I'd first known him—a testament to his beastly nature encroaching. Blood caked the beds of his fingernails and the lines of his palm, and it stained my own, too. That was fitting, in a way. His victim's blood was as much on my hands—my conscience—as his. If it hadn't been for me, Father would have never known the science to make him into the monster he was.

I felt hot tears on my cheeks, and then Edward wiped them away with the one clean patch of fabric on his cuff.

"It's my fault," I choked. "If only I was smarter, if I could have already cured you."

"You've done everything you can."

"Father would have figured it out by now."

He pushed back his shirt cuff and brushed my cheek with his thumb instead. "Your father had a lifetime of knowledge. You're only starting. And we're getting closer."

"But how many people must die first?"

"I'm trying," he murmured, smoothing my loose hair back with both hands as the fire in the woodstove cracked and sparked. "Don't you think that I would have stopped him if I could? I told you, I've tried to take his life by taking my own. He won't let me."

There was so much pain in his voice, so much self-hatred and guilt.

"That isn't what I want," I said, letting my fingers intertwine with his soaked fabric, holding him close so that he couldn't slip the chains of my hands. "I don't want you to die, Edward." My voice had a breathlessness I hadn't intended. His eyes found mine, asking a question, and I blinked.

"I mean . . ."

I started to clarify that I only meant he shouldn't die for Father's sins. Not that I wanted him to live because I cared for him, because I felt a strange sort of kinship to this boy torn apart by my father, just like me, just trying to find a place in the world between the dark shadows and the too-bright sunlight.

"I mean . . ." I started again, but my words faded. With the smell of roses around us, and his strong hands around my own, I wasn't sure what I meant. My life with the professor was so fortunate, so fragile, and half of it was a lie. I could only be that proper young lady during the day. But at night . . .

I let my fingertips trail over the folds and valleys of his shirt, coming away with another man's blood.

"In a way, I envy your other half," I whispered. "At least he's free to do what he wants."

Edward watched me staring at my fingertips. "No, he

isn't. He's as much a prisoner as I am, beholden to his own sick desires. The sooner he's gone from me, the better. I want to be just a man, that's all, who isn't marked with bruises, who can walk the streets without worry that he'll kill someone." He swallowed, as his hands again closed over mine. "Who can love you as you deserve to be loved."

My breath stilled. He'd made no secret of his feelings for me. Even on the island, behind the waterfall, he'd intimated that he'd loved me. I'd never given him any indication—not in words, at least—that I returned those feelings. Still, I couldn't deny that someplace deep, my thoughts had often wandered to him. Even in death, Edward Prince had been a difficult young man to forget about.

"Edward, don't talk like that," I whispered.

But he touched my cheek gently, turning my face back around to look at him. The blood on his shirt mingled with the smell of roses, making me dizzy in a way that had nothing to do with my illness. He was so close that his warm breath dusted my cold neck. It stirred something inside me, as though the animal within now sensed another creature like itself and was waking.

"I haven't been entirely honest with you," he whispered. "I told you I came back to London to find Moreau's colleague so I could cure myself, but that's not the only reason. Nor is it the only reason I befriended Lucy. I had to see you again. I had to hear news of you, even if only bits of gossip from your best friend. I tried to stay away from you—to keep you safe from the Beast—but I couldn't bear it. All I thought about was you." He leaned his forehead against my own, and this close to the window his breath fogged in the space between us, but I didn't feel cold.

"I came back to London for you, Juliet," he whispered.

Words I'd once wished to hear while staring at my bedroom ceiling, murmuring *he-loves-me, he-loves-me-not* into the silent air, but from someone else. In the small space of my workshop, tucked away amid the roses, it didn't seem to matter as much who said them, as long as they were said. Edward loved me. Edward had risked everything to come here, to be with me. Life in London had always been lacking some critical piece, like a piano missing a single key. And here was Edward, who knew my secrets and didn't judge me for them, desperate to fill that void in my life.

And I was desperate for him, too.

I tilted my head to look up at him, and our eyes met as my fingers coiled in his bloodstained clothing. I wasn't certain who moved first, after that. We were already so close, with his arms around me. Not a far change to press our lips together, to slide my hands around his neck and tangle them in his dark hair. He responded instantly, breath ragged as he kissed me.

He tasted of blood and bitter tea, and his kiss felt like something I had long wanted and only now realized.

Heart pounding, I slipped my fingers between the buttons of his shirt to pull away the bloody reminder of his recent crimes, but he held my hand. "Slowly, Juliet. I've wanted this a long time. We don't have to rush."

He kissed me again, achingly slow. But his breath was as ragged as mine, and his loneliness and desperation as deep as mine, and it wasn't hard to make him forget about childish desires like chaste little kisses. Once I whispered his name and pressed my body flush with his, he was broken.

We found our way to the wooden bed beside the woodstove, where warm flames splashed on both our faces. Our limbs tangled together, our lips found each other feverishly. The smell of blood was choking my lungs, and I helped Edward out of the stained clothes and threw them on the floor, and then my own, never wanting to think of the blood on them again. My bare skin slipped against his under the patchwork quilt, and without the barrier of my corset and skirts and chemise I felt a million miles away from London and all the propriety the city required, and I gave myself to Edward.

We fell asleep like that, tangled together, lips bruised, the worn old quilt thrown around my waist. I dreamed of a sea of blood, and Edward in a bobbing dinghy, and an island made of bones.

SIXTEEN

WHEN I WOKE, I was alone in the workshop's single bed. Edward was gone, though Sharkey was curled in a tight ball atop the quilt, stirring when I did, and blinking contentedly a few times.

I sat up, breathing hard, trying to sort through last night. What had been real, and what had been imaginary? The bedsheets were stained with blood from Edward's victim, as was my dress crumpled on the floor. I'd have to burn it, just like the coat.

My knuckles twitched, and I grasped my hands together as if it could hold off my illness, but the stiffness was already spreading to my arms. Soon all my joints would ache, and vertigo would set in. Already my head felt strangely light as I looked to the window. Traces of sunlight were coming through. Dawn. The professor would be up in another hour, and if I showed up drenched in blood with a wrinkled dress and bruised lips . . .

The doorknob twisted. For a brief instant a memory

from last night flashed in my head, Edward standing in the open doorway dressed in his victim's blood. It was Edward again this time, but he'd changed clothes and smoothed his hair back, and now he held a cone of newsprint in one hand that smelled of roasted chestnuts.

"I heard the vendor outside this morning," he said. "Dickens wrote about hot chestnuts so often that I've always wanted to try them. And I thought you might be hungry after . . ." He couldn't hide his smile. "Well, you know."

I stared at him as my mind still struggled to piece everything together. Edward and I had embraced last night with a wild recklessness I'd never known. But now, in the first rays of daylight, everything looked bleaker. I threw the covers back so hard that Sharkey yipped and jumped on the floor, and then I started stripping the bed of its sheets.

"I have to wash these," I said, then froze as the cold air bit my bare skin. Naked, not a stitch of clothing. I grabbed a sheet and pulled it around me as Edward set the chestnuts on the worktable and hurried over to stop my frantic movements.

"Juliet, wait. Calm down. What's the matter?"

"The matter?" I asked, wrapping the sheet tighter around me. "The matter? Edward, there's blood everywhere!"

"I'll handle it," he said. "Come here, to the fire. Sit down." He pulled me over to the chair by the woodstove and guided me into it. He took my hands in his, which were now washed clean of the evidence from last night.

Of the murder he committed.

I started to breathe faster. What was I doing, protecting him? I didn't even know who he had killed last night, and neither did he. He rubbed my shoulder, then touched my hair, trying to soothe me. "What we did last night was only improper if you think it is. I'll make it right. I've read about how these things happen. I need only find a minister, and we'll pay a fee for a license, and then once we're wed—"

"Wed?" My fingers dug into the wooden arm railings. "*Wed?*"

"Well, yes. I assumed that's what you would want. Isn't that what men and women do, after what happened last night? You could get . . . with child."

I pushed my way out of the chair, eyes wild, pacing a little in the strangling bedsheet. "No, I can't. I haven't had my cycles in months, not since Father's serum stopped working. And you . . . you . . ." I wanted to remind him he wasn't even human, he was a collection of animal parts made to speak and look and kiss like a boy. Oh god, what had we done?

I collapsed back into the chair, a hand over my mouth. I was hardly a prude when it came to such things. Half the girls who came to Lucy's teas probably had indiscretions with men they weren't engaged to, but this was different.

This was Edward. This was a *murderer.*

"No," I stuttered. "I don't want to get married. We can't."

He swallowed, though his eyes still gleamed with hope. "All right, then. Yes, you're right, we should wait until after we've cured ourselves. Then we'll have a lifetime together."

"No, Edward, you don't understand."

The light in his eyes flickered. "What do you mean?"

"It was a mistake," I said, though my voice broke. "I care about you, but I was lonely. I needed someone . . ."

"Juliet, shh," he started, shaking his head a little too quickly.

" . . . but I've never stopped loving Montgomery. I thought you understood that."

For a moment the entire room was still, no wind at the window, no cracking in the fire. Just me, and him, and Montgomery's name between us.

"Montgomery?" he repeated, barely above a whisper.

When I didn't answer, his hands curled on the wooden armchair rails so hard the wood splintered. I jumped at the reminder of how strong Edward could be, how quickly his moods could shift. He pushed himself up to pace before the fire. "Montgomery left you. He didn't come back for you. *I* did."

My heart started pounding. This was wrong—talking of Montgomery here, now.

"I must get home. It's nearly morning. I'll need to give myself an injection, and I haven't any here."

I crawled out of the chair and snatched my dress from the floor, shaking it out and struggling into fabric that was stiff with dried blood. I started to reach for my coat, but Edward grabbed my arm. "Wait."

I didn't dare look at him. "I'll come back tonight and we'll work on the serum."

But his hand held me with an unnatural strength.

Outside, the wind howled all the same warnings that my heart was whispering to me. My thoughts turned back to the broken chair rail and how easily that could be my bones splintered in two. I shivered, but not because of the cold.

Sharkey picked his head up and growled low in his throat.

"He'll never understand what's inside you," Edward whispered. "He wants Moreau's daughter, the girl he used to know, but that's not who you are now. You're no one's daughter anymore. You can think for yourself, take care of yourself. You're Juliet, and that's enough, and Montgomery will never fully understand that."

His other hand slid to touch the delicate skin above my rib cage but I twisted out of his grasp, not certain if I dared believe his words.

"The professor will worry," I stuttered.

"I don't care about the professor. I won't let anything, or anyone, come between us." He stepped close enough that I could feel his breath on my neck, warm and moist. I noted a different smell in the air—an animal smell. Not Sharkey's light musty scent, but something heavier, more primal. I felt like here, in this moment, I was seeing that tenuous line between man and Beast I had been so curious about.

And now my curiosity might get me killed.

"I love you, Juliet."

Sharkey stood up now, growling louder. I could tell by the deeper timbre in Edward's voice that the boy I knew was slipping. The Beast was used to getting his way, and I was refusing him what he wanted most—me. How far would he go to get what he wanted?

I had to be careful, now. Very careful.

"Edward, please . . ."

His fingers curled into mine nearly hard enough to bruise. When I met his gaze, my breath caught. His pupils were already starting to elongate. In moments the Beast would fully emerge. He leaned close enough that his lips grazed my earlobe. "I won't let you go."

It was the Beast talking. Not Edward. Edward would never scare me like this.

Sharkey barked now, twice, very loud.

"I *must* get home," I said, trying to keep my shaking voice under control. "If I don't, the professor will send half the police after me, and they'd soon trace me here. We can't let them find this place. Find *you*. I'll come back tonight, and we'll be together."

I forced myself to look him in his animal eyes. I ignored how broad his shoulders were growing, how dark the hair on his arms was becoming. I pulled my lips into a smile that I prayed would convince him. His tight grip eased a small degree, and I cautiously slid from his grasp. I reached for one of my boots, though the moment I picked it up, the knife slid from its holster and clattered to the floor.

Blast. I dove for it, but he was faster.

His hand clamped over my wrist. Sharkey exploded in barks that tore at my ears.

"Let me go!" I lunged for the knife again, but it only seemed to excite his predator instincts more. As he clutched my wrist, I could feel the bones in his hand shifting and popping as the transformation came faster.

A flurry of noise came charging across the room as Sharkey tore at Edward, growling. Edward gave him a single kick that sent him cringing under the bed.

"Don't you dare hurt him!" I cried, trying to pull him away from the dog. But my hands on his arm had the wrong effect, and he turned to me with a leer.

"Juliet," he muttered, his eyes dilated and glowing. The Beast was coming, fast. "How I missed you." He leaned in close, his forehead against my temple, breathing in the smell of my hair and skin. His lips grazed my cheek and I shivered, painfully aware of the coldness of his flesh.

"I can't help it," he said. "I am what I am. An animal. Can you blame me for that?"

He nuzzled my cheek again, breath cold against my skin, as the last traces of Edward's voice dissipated. That voice. That *humanity*. It was unnaturally deep in tone and yet spoken like a man, calculated, polite. The creature before me was larger, taller, stronger—the same body and yet such a different person. I couldn't control the shivers of fear that ran along my spine, nor the goose bumps on my bare skin.

Before I could think, he was kissing me. It wasn't Edward's gentle, slow kisses from last night. Now the animal was coming out and it was passionate—no, famished—and it started to awake something in me, too, a wildness, a reck- lessness, but I shoved that part of me away as my heart pounded frantically back to life. This is what had fascinated me about him—monster and man sharing the same breath— and now it terrified me.

Well, I could be a monster, too.

I just needed a weapon. *The knife* . . . it was too far away. My gaze darted around the room for anything within arm's reach that I could use. A jar of potassium powder sat on the table, and in my desperation I reached for it just as a terrible sound like bones sliding began, a sound I'd heard only once before, when the Beast had let loose its claws.

I shut my eyes as my hand closed over the potassium. I felt the tips of five sharp claws on my back, gentle at first, soon hard enough to tear my dress's fabric and press into my skin. I jerked, and his claws sliced into the front of my shoulder with a sting of pain.

"You can fight it if you like," he breathed. "It won't change anything." His kisses mixed with sharp pain from his claws, and I hurled the jar of potassium to the floor. The shatter of glass surprised him long enough for me to pull away and kick over the basin of water.

The instant the water hit the potassium powder, a chemical reaction began. The mixture hissed and sputtered, starting to gain heat. I braced my hands over my head just as the reaction exploded with a cloud of sparks and smoke.

He let out a furious growl as I pushed away from him. In the smoke it was impossible to see anything as I fumbled on the floor for the knife. I drove it into his side, pushing him back against my worktable.

Glass crashed as the Beast fell on my equipment. The sound of breaking tools mixed with his growls. Coughing, I fumbled along the floor until I found my boots, then called for Sharkey and threw the door open. Sharkey darted out ahead of me, racing down the stairs. I stumbled behind him, the hair on the back of my neck standing on end, certain the Beast was just a breath behind me.

We reached the lodging house's front door and I shoved it open, breathing in great gulps of cold winter air. And then I was running, Sharkey at my heels. It was all a blur, just flashes mixed with the smell of chemical smoke. The falling snow. A crack of ice. Blazing lanterns and Christmas wreaths. And then suddenly Sharkey wasn't there anymore, lost in the streets. I couldn't stop. I couldn't look for him.

I disappeared into the city of smoke and steel, not once looking back.

SEVENTEEN

I MADE IT OVER the garden trellis and back into my room only seconds before the cuckoo clock chimed seven in the morning. A minute later the floorboards overhead squeaked as the professor made his way down the stairs to the dining room on the first floor.

It was all I could do to strip off my bloody clothes, hide them under the bed, change into a fresh chemise, and crawl between the covers. I seemed to have forgotten how to speak, or stand, or do anything but sit amongst the hills of pillows with my knees clutched tightly against my chest.

My mind kept replaying Edward's transformation into the Beast. The slow elongation of his pupils, the splitting of his knuckles to let his claws emerge. I pulled my collar down and touched the angry red scratches on my shoulder. All those nights together in my workshop, comforted by the presence of someone else who shared my secrets, between the old wooden walls and the creaking woodstove. I had thought myself happy there.

I'd been a fool, and now I'd even lost Sharkey in the chaos.

A knock came at the door.

"Miss Juliet?" Mary's voice called through the door. "A letter was just delivered for you by messenger."

"Slide it under the door," I said in a hoarse voice.

There was a crinkle of paper as Mary did so. I waited for her footsteps to recede before pulling on a sweater to hide the cuts on my shoulder, and then I picked up the letter. It was sealed in wax still soft to the touch. I ripped the envelope open and drew out a single piece of paper, with but three words written upon them.

Please forgive me.

I crumpled the letter and threw it into the fire, watching the edges singe and curl inward. Edward wanted my forgiveness, but how could I give it? Part of me wanted to blame everything on the Beast. *He* was the guilty one, not Edward. And yet hadn't Edward said they were two sides of the same coin? The longer he lived, the more he and the Beast grew together.

I was certainly no physical match for the Beast. The only way I could stop him was to cure Edward—yet how could I even be in the same room with him again, after the Beast had nearly sliced me open?

And after what you and Edward did in that bed, a voice whispered.

I slumped to the floor. I was alone again. I could tell

the professor and Elizabeth, but they already thought my mind dangerously unstable. Without Edward, I had no one to trust.

I was lost in my thoughts all morning. Afraid to leave my room. Afraid to stay. After all, his note meant he could find me anywhere. Hours had passed when another knock sounded at the door, this time Elizabeth. "Are you ill again, Juliet? Would you like tea brought up? You know, if you've changed your mind about the masquerade tonight, I can send a note canceling."

The Radcliffe masquerade—it had been the last thing on my mind. What a terrible friend Lucy must think me, and she didn't even know what I'd done last night with the young man she loved. I doubled over, bracing my head with my hands. Edward's voice from this morning returned to me.

I won't let anything, or anyone, come between us.

I sat up, a tickle of worry at my spine. I had assumed he meant the professor, or Montgomery, but what would he stop at? Or rather, *who*? Lucy was between us, after all. He knew how strong willed she was, that she'd do anything to protect me. Would he hurt her just to keep me to himself?

I brushed back my hair with my fingers and then threw open the door. Elizabeth seemed surprised by my sudden energy, and she gave me a suspicious once-over.

"I haven't changed my mind," I said. "What time is it?"

Elizabeth glanced at the cuckoo clock. "Quarter past one."

"I'll get dressed at Lucy's—my gown and mask are

already there. Please have Ellis bring the carriage around at three."

She bit the inside of her lip, looking as though she didn't believe a word that came out of my mouth. Well, let her suspect something. Anything she imagined couldn't possibly be worse than the truth.

"I'll see you there tonight, then. The professor won't come, not even with the promise of Radcliffe's finest brandy." She paused. "It will be nice to have a bit of fun again."

THAT AFTERNOON, ELLIS LET me off in front of Lucy's house, where the iron gate hung wide open as though beckoning me in. A small fleet of workmen filled the front garden, sweeping the walk and securing candles among the trees that would be lit later tonight when guests arrived. I didn't want to get in their way, so I walked around back to the servants' entrance, where I used to sneak into the house to visit Lucy before her parents approved of me. It felt strange turning that corner, seeing the hedges trampled by too many workmen's boots, and dirty with street salt and all manner of muck. A flash of my former life—a life I never wanted to return to.

A delivery wagon waited in the alleyway, the horses' feet stamping impatiently. I could only imagine the extravagant purchases Lucy's father must have made for the party—lace tablecloths woven with red and green threads, white pillar candles of every height, champagne by the case. I knocked on the servants' door tentatively. It swung open to reveal Clara's tired face. Her mouth hung open to scold, but when she recognized me her face lit up.

"Miss Juliet! Why didn't you come to the front? Oh, never mind that. Hurry in, Miss Lucy's been expecting you." She waved me in and closed the door a little breathlessly as she wiped her hands on her apron. "Come—I'll take you upstairs before I'm missed. Goodness, you've no idea how many deliveries we've gotten today."

We both jumped as someone shouted in the kitchen, followed by the honking of a goose and a clatter of pans. Clara rushed me through the pantry and up a narrow set of stairs to the second floor, where I caught a glimpse of the sprawling ballroom with its enormous fir Christmas tree, a peek of polished floors, workmen on ladders, and house-maids carrying silver warming trays. Just as quickly, we were climbing up to the third-floor bedrooms.

It was blessedly quieter here, with the soft carpet and empty hallways, and I started to feel calmer until a curse came from a room to our left.

"Oh, stuff it, and this blasted ribbon, too!"

I sighed in relief. Only Lucy cursed like that and got away with it. Clara hurried me across the plush carpet runner to Lucy's room and stuck her head through the doorway.

"Clara, I've had an awful time with these curls. Won't you send Molly up?"

"Yes, miss. And Miss Juliet is here."

I heard a commotion like metal dropping to the floor, and then Lucy's disheveled head popped through the door-way. She was in her corset and a combination with lace trim, ribbons half untied in her curled hair, her blue eyes wide and beautiful.

She grabbed me with something like a growl and pulled me into the room. "You devil! I'd started to think you weren't coming."

I caught myself against a dressing table that was littered with ribbons and brushes and an overturned tin of face powder. It looked like a wild animal had been set loose in her room.

She picked up a mask from the table, a delicate thing of black and soft purple, made to cover just the eyes, with shimmering green feathers along the side like a bird taking wing. It was the most beautiful mask I'd ever seen, and she thrust it at me like a can of beans.

"Mother picked this one out. I detest it." She flopped into the dresser chair, tossing the mask to the side. "It's so boring. John will probably adore it."

I bent down to right the overturned powder tin. All the makeup, and ribbons, and the vase of lilies on her desk didn't fit with the words I'd come here to say. If only the masquerade wasn't tonight, and she and I could dance and drink champagne and have one last night together, before I had to shatter her world with my confession.

But Edward was out there, and she needed to know the truth about the man she claimed to love.

While she hummed a sweet little song and admired herself in the mirror, I went to her bedroom door and closed it softly. An array of brushes and powders and rouges was laid out in front of her as she debated which to apply first.

I took a deep breath. "Lucy . . ."

"If you don't start getting ready, we'll miss the masquerade altogether." She picked up a thick brush and started dusting powder on her cheeks. I remained by the door, not sure how to say the words warring in my throat. She threw me an exasperated glance and I crossed to her dresser, fiddling halfheartedly with a stick of rouge. The lilies on the table stole my attention. Flowers were subject to the laws of mathematics, a fact few people knew. You could see the repeating patterns if you looked hard enough. And I tried to look hard, but Lucy snapped her fingers.

She met my eyes in the mirror, giving me a questioning look. "Juliet, what's going through your head?"

Her voice had a softer timbre than normal. For everyone else she pitched her voice higher, exaggerating her words. But now, in the intimacy of the small room, she had dropped the act. The least I could do was show her the same courtesy.

I perched on the edge of the chair next to her. "Do you remember when you said we were like sisters, and we should tell each other everything?" She nodded slowly. "I lied to you about the island."

Her eyes went wide. She didn't speak right away; instead she set down the makeup brush and stood, then twisted the key in the door's lock before coming back and taking her seat again.

"I've always suspected it," she whispered, though there was no trace of hurt in her voice. "You were gone a *year.*

When you came back, showing up in that hospital looking thin as a twig and half crazed and utterly penniless, saying nothing more than you'd found your father and he'd died, I knew you weren't telling me something." She glanced at the door one final time. "Now tell me."

I wouldn't have thought it easy to reduce a year's worth of life to a short, whispered conversation in the quiet of Lucy's bedroom. But as soon as I told her about arriving on the island and discovering Father's secrets, the story started to roll out of me. I told her about Montgomery, and how we'd loved each other but he'd stayed behind instead of returning with me. I told her about the beast-men, who had been so gentle and childlike at the beginning, and witnessing Father create them in his blood-red laboratory, and then how they'd regressed into monsters. She didn't speak the entire time—her face was white, her voice stolen.

I was about to tell her the hardest part—Edward—but paused. She claimed to admire him. It wasn't so easy to reveal that he was one of Father's more gifted creations—as well as London's most notorious mass murderer.

"There's more, but . . ." I hesitated at her white face, fearing the news about Edward would shatter her. I swallowed and instead said, "Father was corresponding with someone here, one of the King's Men. There are letters. . . ."

But my words died at the look on her face. She'd been deathly silent throughout my explanation, but now a deep red color came to her cheeks.

"Letters?" she whispered. "*Letters?* Oh god, Juliet."

Before I could respond, she pulled me into a tight,

desperate embrace, her heart thumping nearly as fast as my own.

"I know it's all hard to believe," I said, squeezing her even harder.

"You don't understand," she said. "If you'd only told me sooner. If I'd only known . . ." Her fingers dug into my shoulders. "Juliet, there are things I haven't told you, either." She swallowed. "I know about the letters."

EIGHTEEN

My heart felt strangled. "Lucy, what do you mean?"

Footsteps sounded in the hallway, and I clamped my mouth shut until they passed—a maid, most likely, but it left me shaken. Downstairs, sounds of hammering and workmen arguing felt a million miles away. Inside Lucy's room there was only the small crackle of the fire, the ticking of the grandfather clock in the hallway.

"I wish you'd told me all this sooner, Juliet. So much makes sense now, and it's much worse than I'd imagined. I didn't realize all of this was related. . . ."

A creeping feeling spread through my body. "Lucy, I haven't a clue what you are talking about."

She took a deep breath, and when they came, her words were quiet and careful. "Remember at the seamstress's, when I told you about finding some disturbing documents about Papa's business? It was letters, Juliet, in a locked drawer of Papa's desk. There were no names used, only codes, but I recognized Papa's handwriting. I learned to forge his writing years ago to sign bank checks. I'm positive it was his."

Suddenly I knew exactly what she was referring to. Edward had come to London with a handful of letters written to Father from a colleague whose identity was secret. He'd suspected a dozen men—including Lucy's father.

"He was right," I muttered to myself, and then stood up so quickly, the flowers on the table quaked. "It's your father," I said, louder. "In the letters, your father calls himself a King's Man, doesn't he?"

"Yes," she said, looking confused. "How did you know that?"

My mind spun frantically to grasp what this all meant. I was relieved the secret colleague wasn't the professor, but Lucy's own father . . . If I knew anything, it was how terrible it was to fear and distrust your own father. "Because you're not the first person to tell me about the letters. What do they say?"

Her frown deepened. "Business transactions, mostly. Receipts and bank account numbers. A few things that made no sense, like a list of the books in the Bible. The letters mentioned experimentation in passing, and other details I didn't understand at the time. An assistant named Montgomery, and servants with strange names. Balthazar, I think, like from Shakespeare. The letters came from an alias called Paracelsus."

"Paracelsus," I repeated. "An old alchemist. Father had his book on the shelves in his study."

Memories came back to me of father's beast-men, the

strangely named servants Lucy was describing. Balthazar, Ajax, little Cymbeline. What a fool I'd been, thinking Father would limit his sights to a single island. He had been too arrogant for that. Of course he'd want the world to know of the science he'd uncovered.

"Were there any scientific papers with the letters? Diagrams, notations, that sort of thing?"

She shook her head. "No. The letters reference research he sent, but Papa must have kept those in a different place." She leaned against the dresser, stunned. "I . . . I thought our fathers only knew each other because our mothers had been friends," she stammered.

I thought of the photograph hanging in the hallway of King's College of Medical Research. "Your father and mine were old associates. They belonged to a professional association called the King's Club."

"I've heard Papa speak of it, but only vaguely. He isn't an academic. Most of his business is in rail and shipping and investing. . . ."

I could see her mind spinning as she tried to draw the connections, but I already had. All the supplies, and ships, and fine china—I'd assumed Father had a secret bank account somewhere to pay for it all, even though at the time he disappeared, our debtors told us Father was nearly bankrupt.

"He *was* investing," I said. "He was investing in my father's research. Have you told anyone about those letters? The police?"

She laughed bitterly. "With Inspector Newcastle as my

suitor? He'd never arrest the man he hoped would be his future father-in-law. Besides, the letters alone don't prove anything. I only thought them suspicious because of the large amounts of money sent overseas. Until you told me your story and I matched up the names and details, I didn't realize your father was the one receiving the letters."

Her hand fell on the green silk dress on the bed beside her. "If Papa was involved in the terrible things your father was doing, how do we know he isn't doing them too? Taking animals and cutting them open, teaching them to speak, combining them with human blood . . ." She looked as though she'd aged a year in the last ten minutes.

"Does he have a laboratory?" I asked.

"No—he's never shown an ounce of interest in science. But he's often gone for business for days at a time. I don't know where he goes or what he's doing."

Lucy stood, pacing, all of this information too much to handle. A knock came at the door, and then Molly's soft voice.

"Miss Lucy? Did you need help with your hair?"

I unlocked and opened the door a crack and told her we'd attend to our own hair. Guests would start arriving soon. We couldn't stop the masquerade from happening. The partygoers would come, and Edward might arrive among them, masked and dangerous, and pleading again for my forgiveness.

I ran my fingers down the red silk dress hanging on the screen. Could I really put it on and attend the ball as though nothing was the matter? *Everything* was the matter.

The very roof we were under sheltered my father's colleague—and there was no telling what he intended to do with
the information my father had sent him.

"I haven't told you the worst part yet," I whispered.

She stopped pacing. Her eyes were wide and scared,
and I hated that I had to be the one to tell her.

"Henry Jakyll isn't who you think he is," I said.

Her forehead wrinkled. "Henry? What does he have to
do with this?"

"He has everything to do with this." My fingers
twisted in the dress's fabric. "His name isn't Henry. It's
Edward Prince, and I'm well acquainted with him. We met
on Father's island, and he followed me back here." My hand
slipped on the smooth fabric and fell to my side. "He's one of
Father's creations, Lucy."

I'd expected her to cry out, or swoon. But she sank onto
the edge of the bed, careless of the silk dress she was wrin-
kling by sitting on it, and looked as deathly white as though
she'd seen a ghost. "I don't understand."

"I told you how Father made the beast-men. He used
surgery for most of them, resetting the joints of their bones
and grafting new skin so that they looked very nearly human
and could speak, though their mental faculties never progressed much further than a child's. But he had another
technique that didn't involve surgery at all. He combined
animal and human components through a chemical procedure that changed the animal flesh on a cellular level.
The creature he created surpassed all the others, might as
well have been an entirely new breed. It could think just as

rationally as any man, could read, could feel the entire range of emotions. It looked perfectly human, unlike the others." I paused, twisting my hands together nervously. "I didn't even know myself at first that Edward was this creation—"

"Stop!" she cried. "Stop—what you're saying is impossible!"

I heard the jingle of sleigh bells outside as the first guests arrived. Time was growing short, and I bit my lip and twisted my hands harder.

"It isn't. I've seen it with my own eyes. He looks human, and he does have a human side that's kind and generous, but he has a much darker side, too. There were murders on the island, hearts torn from bodies . . ."

My hands clenched together. I couldn't find the words to continue, but I could tell from Lucy's face that I didn't need to.

"It's Henry, isn't it?" she whispered. "Or rather Edward. He's the Wolf of Whitechapel." Her eyes locked to mine, wanting me to say it wasn't true.

But I couldn't tell her any more lies.

"I told him to stay away from you—that's why he sent you that letter. I didn't want him anywhere near you, in case he couldn't control his transformation and put you in danger. I'm sorry, Lucy. I was only looking out for your safety." Guilt pulsed like a broken rib in my side. I wasn't being entirely honest with her—I'd also shared a bed with him.

Her chin tipped in a small nod, an indication that she'd heard me. She chewed on a fingernail. "What are we going to do?"

A peal of laughter floated up the stairs as the front door slammed to let in more guests. I took a deep breath and then pushed off the bed and grabbed her green dress. "We're going to get dressed and go downstairs before we're missed. I want you to stay close to Inspector Newcastle all night. He's always armed, so you'll be safe with him. There's a chance Edward might show up . . . if you see him, promise me you won't talk to him."

She bit her lip. "But if Henry—I mean Edward—is wrapped up in all this too, couldn't he help us?"

The hopeful look in her eye told me her feelings for him hadn't dimmed despite the terrible truths I'd told her. I leaned forward, grabbing her arm. "Lucy, I said he's *dangerous*. You haven't seen him transform like I have. His muscles grow, his tendons pop. His eyes go dark and slitted like an animal's, and he has claws ready to spring from between his fingers."

"Stop!"

She covered her face with her hands. I realized that I was holding my hand like a gnarled claw in front of her face, ready to claw her like Edward had so recently done to me. Tears were coming down her face. She really did care about him. Was it my place to trample her affection? I had a responsibility to protect her from Edward; and yet if I found a cure and the Beast was gone, I supposed Edward wouldn't be a threat to her safety anymore. I'd have no reason to object to them going together.

So why did my heart falter and my anger stir just thinking about the two of them together?

As she cried softly into her hands, I sat back on the dresser chair, trying to understand my own feelings. Was it because of what had happened between us the previous night?

That was a mistake, I told myself. *A mistake you'll never make again.*

"He's too dangerous, Lucy," I said at last. "I know you care about him, but his dark half is gaining more power, and I don't even trust being around him myself. That's the reason I've told you all of this. To warn you."

"Even knowing the terrible things he's done, I can't bear to think of him alone out there. Being hunted down like an animal. No one to turn to. . . ." She leaned into her hands, sobbing gently.

From the hallway outside, the grandfather clock chimed again. Lucy looked toward the door. "Dash it, the party's starting." She dried her eyes. "They'll expect us. Help me into my dress. Quickly."

We picked up the green silk dress and pulled it over her head, and I hurried to do up the buttons on the back; then I dressed in my own. I had to turn my back on her while I adjusted the dropped neckline over my shoulder so it hid the Beast's scratches from sight.

"I don't see how it's helping him to leave him alone," she continued. "Surely he'd be able to control himself better if he had a proper shelter, and food, and medicine. . . ." She went to the mirror and started pinning up her hair with quick, well-practiced moves.

"He can take care of himself, I promise. The best thing

you can do to help Edward is to show me those letters. What floor is your father's study on?"

"Oh Juliet, surely not now, with everyone arriving!"

"Your father will be distracted. We might not have another chance soon."

She bit her lip, then went to the table and grabbed our masks. She shoved a handful of pins at me and said, "All right, but fix your hair, for the love of god; you look like some sort of savage with your hair down."

She twisted the key in the lock and peeked out. The hallway was quiet, with the only sounds coming from the party starting downstairs. I fumbled to pin my hair up as we darted across the hall. My dress shoes pinched my feet, but there was nothing I could do about that now. We climbed down the narrow servants' stairs quiet as mice in our elegant ball gowns, until they opened to a long hallway lined with doors. Lucy tiptoed to one and pressed her ear to it, then turned the doorknob.

Mr. Radcliffe's study was everything my father's wasn't. Father had been meticulous in his organization, so his desk was always cleared at the end of each day, save a single container for fountain pens and a ream of fresh paper for note taking. In contrast, Mr. Radcliffe's study was covered in a mess of crumpled papers in all manner of disorder, as well as boxes and deliveries stacked on the floor and in the single chair. Gilded framed portraits hung on the walls: the illustrious Radcliffe ancestors, no doubt.

"I found the letters in one of these piles," Lucy said, rushing toward the desk. "I remember what they look like.

If they're still here, I'll find them." She started combing through the piles with about as much disorder as her father. My heart thumped as the papers rustled. I dug through a few, but there was no order to them—useless pages of ledgers and accounts from his railroad business. Quite large orders for automobile engines by the French government and some research company in Holland and a private citizen in Germany who must have been richer than Midas. My hand fell upon a stiff leather folder stamped with the King's Club crest, and I drew in a quick breath.

Inside the folder, however, I found nothing of use. Only correspondence about the orphanage the King's Club sponsored, along with a roster of the association's current members and their charitable contributions for the year. The list contained twenty-four names. Radcliffe, Dr. Hastings, and Isambard Lessing, the German historian I'd caught the professor arguing with. Far more recognizable names too: Arthur Kenney, the *London Times* owner; Ambassador Claude Rochefort of France; a few lords and titled men; and several members of Parliament. A queasiness began in the pit of my stomach. I'd had no idea the King's Club's membership was so prominent, so far-reaching, with connections into France and Germany and beyond.

I finished sorting through several stacks but didn't find Father's letters, so I turned to the boxes instead, deliveries from an expensive tailor. I lifted the lids. A box full of crisp white shirts still smelling of tailor's chalk. A smaller box of handkerchiefs monogrammed with the Radcliffe crest. I moved those aside and opened a tall blue hatbox.

Just a single peek inside made me jump, silencing a scream. Lucy's head jerked up from the papers she was going through. I pointed a trembling finger to the hatbox, the urge to scream still rising in my throat.

"Inside that box," I said at last, breath strained. "It isn't a hat."

She stepped around the desk cautiously, starting to bend down to open the lid before I grabbed her hands away and started to pull her toward the door.

"But the letters . . . ," she started.

"Blast the letters, we'll come back for them later." When she still protested, I leaned forward. "It's a brain." I whispered.

Her eyes went wide as she backed away from the box. "Are you certain?"

"I know what a human brain preserved in a jar of formaldehyde looks like," I said. "We've got to get out of here. Go to the party, act as though nothing's happened. He can't suspect that we know."

"How can I act like Papa doesn't have a *brain in a hatbox*?"

"You must, Lucy. Come on."

I threw open the door, grabbing our masks on the way out, and we raced toward the spiral staircase. The music was louder here, as I put my own mask on and told Lucy to do the same. We hurried to the landing above the ballroom, where a tall man stood at the top of the stairs, presiding over his party.

The man turned his gaunt face to us.

Mr. Radcliffe.

Seeing his face turned my stomach. A man I'd known since childhood, yet a total stranger now. The entire time Mother and I were practically starving in the streets, he'd known Father was alive. He had corresponded with him. Sent him money. Even now he kept preserved organs in his study for who knew what purpose.

His eyes shifted to mine. They were a blue so light they were almost as white as the hair at his temples. It was all I could do to keep breathing beneath the mask. "There you are, Lucy. Your mother's been looking all over for you."

"Sorry, Papa," Lucy stuttered. "Juliet had a bit of a hairpin emergency."

He stood stiffly at the top of the stairs, still eyeing me.

"Is that you beneath that mask, Miss Moreau? Still causing trouble, are you?" His voice was light and teasing, but he didn't smile. He offered us each one hand. "If I may. My daughter and our guest of honor shouldn't enter a ball without an escort."

I dared a glance at Lucy. We had no choice but to obey.

I slid my arm around his, and Lucy did the same, and arm in arm with a monster we joined the masquerade.

NINETEEN

THE MASQUERADE WAS IN full swing as Mr. Radcliffe led us down the sprawling spiral staircase. The music swelled to meet us, bringing with it delicate notes of laughter and the smell of cinnamon and fir boughs. I stepped carefully, squinting through my mask's small eyeholes, trying not to step on my hem. Lucy was more practiced in these things and seemed to glide on air. No one would ever know she'd just learned that the young man she loved was a murderer, and that her father kept brains tucked away in hatboxes.

By the time we were halfway down the staircase, the full view of the ballroom swept out like a colorful sea. Masked couples in glittering gowns danced to the string quartet's waltz beside tiny glowing candles on the Christmas tree. The swarm of partygoers was so dense that my head spun.

My fist tightened on the handrail instinctively, as the joints in my hand stiffened. The vertigo, the joint pain . . . my illness was coming, induced by stress. I nervously bit the inside of my cheek, trying to overcome the symptoms through willpower, until I tasted blood. A sudden high note from the violin made me gasp.

Mr. Radcliffe turned to me, his unmasked eyes like two microscopes on my thoughts. I cleared my throat and let him finish leading us down the stairs. At the base he kissed Lucy on her masked cheek and gave me a gentlemanly nod. The moment I could take my fingers away from his, I grabbed Lucy's hand and dragged her into the chaos.

"Juliet, what will we do?" she whispered.

"Promise me you'll stay close to Inspector Newcastle," I whispered, searching the crowd for him. "I know you don't care for him, but he's an officer. You'll be safe with him. Don't leave his side for a moment, and then tomorrow come over to the professor's house. We'll figure out what to do when we can speak privately."

She nodded, and we plunged into the deep of the partygoers. Couples swept together in their waltzes, separating us. I tried to ignore the vertigo creeping into my head and spun, looking for Lucy, but all I saw were masks. My too-tight shoes slipped on the polished floor, and I had to catch myself against a window.

A beautiful masked girl stared directly at me.

I started—it was a mirror, not a window. The girl was me.

In the red silk dress and mask, I hadn't recognized myself. The girl in the mirror looked like a happier person, who belonged in this crowd. Her mask—*my* mask—was split down the middle, white on one side, a deep red to match my dress on the other. That was how I felt—half a person. The other half I'd left behind on the island. That was the stronger half, who knew how to move silently through jungle underbrush, who had fought a beast with six-inch-long claws, who had stood up to my father.

The other half would know what to do.

Behind the mask my lips were trembling. It was too much. I pushed into the crowd, my breath moist and hot beneath the papier-mâché mask. The flour paste and newsprint tasted thick in my mouth. Newsprint . . . headlines . . . my mask might be made out of reports of Edward's murders. I was suffocating. The lace around the edges of my mask irritated my skin and made me want to rip it off and fill my lungs with fresh air.

Where was Lucy? Was the crowd growing, or was it just in my head?

From the corner of the eyehole I saw the glass-paned balcony door and stumbled toward it. The handle was slick in my sweating palm. I twisted it and went out into the cold night and the solitude of the empty balcony. I caught myself against the railing and tore at my mask's ribbon until I could rip the thing off, gulping fresh air, making a mess of my hair.

The stars were out.

It was rare to see the stars in London, where the soot from coal chimneys and factory lights polluted the sky. I rubbed my shoulders for warmth. Snow covered the hedges and empty flowerbeds of the garden below. Lucy and I used to play hide-and-seek in those hedges, a lifetime ago.

I turned the mask over to look at it. The red paint had bled a little, and a few of the sequins had fallen off when I'd ripped the ribbon from my hair.

Is this how Edward feels too—half a person, split in two?

I heard the door open and footsteps behind me. I turned to find a tall man in a golden mask and instinctively stepped back, afraid my thoughts had manifested Edward into reality.

"Hello, Miss Moreau." The man removed his mask to reveal a familiar sweep of chestnut hair and white teeth. John Newcastle. Two weeks ago seeing a police officer would have terrified me; now I had far greater worries than an inspector besotted with my best friend.

"Inspector," I said.

He motioned to the party. "Needed some fresh air, did you? You're not the only one." He offered me his glass of champagne, but I shook my head. Intoxication meant lowering my guard, which I didn't dare do, especially now that he and I, the two people best suited to protect Lucy, weren't by her side.

"No, thank you," I said. "Shouldn't you be with Lucy? I think she was looking for you earlier."

"Truly?" He had been looking up at the stars but at my words faced me with surprise. "I thought she never cared to see me again. She told you about the proposal, no doubt."

I nodded. "You shouldn't lose hope," I said, looking for a glimpse of her green silk dress through the glass door. "Perhaps a proposal was too strong. Don't press so hard this early."

He leaned casually against the brick balustrades with the champagne flute in hand. "I must say, Miss Moreau, I had the distinct impression you didn't care for me. That makes your advice all the more surprising, but I'm grateful." He tipped the glass back and downed his drink in one swallow, then set it on the balustrade next to him. "Perhaps you've also changed your mind about helping to solve your father's case? I realize this isn't the proper place for such a conversation; you must forgive me. . . ."

I folded my arms tightly, suddenly very aware of the cold. "I'm afraid I haven't. Some things are best left in the past."

"It isn't wise to let something like this go unresolved. Until the case is closed, your father will be in your mind— and in the mind of the public. His death has never been more than a rumor. A dead cat was found in Cheshire six months ago, vivisected. A distasteful prank, we believe. But rumors could start so easily. Who's to say Henri Moreau isn't back in England, picking up where he left off—"

"He's dead," I said bluntly, unable to hear more. The thought of that cat, prank or not, filled me with malaise. I raised my hand to my aching head but it grazed the champagne flute, which slipped and fell to the ground below with a shattering of glass.

Inspector Newcastle didn't flinch. "How do you know that? Have you had contact with him? Am I to believe—"

"Believe what you like," I interrupted, angry with myself for the slip. I shouldn't have let a mere mention of Father get under my skin. I put my mask back on and headed for the door. "I assure you he's dead. You can close your case and stop asking me about it."

Perhaps I was too harsh, but I threw open the door into the warm ballroom and left him just the same. As I pushed through the thick crowd, something brushed by my head, nearly pulling my hair, and I stepped on a woman's trailing blue satin dress and mumbled an apology. I moved near the wall, away from the thick crowd.

With luck, Inspector Newcastle would ignore what I'd said about Father and react to my words about Lucy instead. He'd stay with her for the rest of the night, keeping her safe from Edward. *From Radcliffe, too*, I thought darkly, thinking of the brain. But as I headed for an empty chair, a woman dressed as a masked bandit grabbed my arm. I jerked away until she pulled her mask off and gave me a crooked smile. Elizabeth.

"I've been wondering where you've been all night," she said. "I thought I'd find you with Lucy."

I rested a hand against the tight bodice of my dress. "I stepped out onto the balcony for a breath of air."

She reached up to remove something caught in my hair, the same place where one of the partygoers had bumped into me.

A little white flower.

The room, with all its whirling commotion, stopped as though captured in a photograph.

"What a beautiful flower," Elizabeth said. "I don't recognize this one. Wherever did you get it?"

A gift from a monster.

I took the delicate flower, thinking of the matching one at home pressed between the pages of my journal. When I turned it over, this one too was tinged with blood. I crumpled it in my fist before Elizabeth could see.

Whose blood was it?

My throat went dry with the memory of the Beast's transformation.

"Lucy gave it to me," I lied, while my eyes darted among the crowd and my heart pounded harder. The flower meant the Beast was here, yet every face was covered in a mask. For a monster with his skills, this ball was a playground for his killing.

"I should find her." I balled my fist harder. "If you'll excuse me."

I stepped away, but Elizabeth held my arm. "Don't think I don't know what this is about," she whispered. I froze until a smile slowly worked across her face. She nodded across the ballroom. "That man in the black mask has been staring at you throughout our entire conversation. He's smitten, the poor fellow. You didn't tell me you'd an admirer."

I halfheartedly searched the crowd of faces. What use was an admirer, when a monster was in our midst? The masked partygoers swirled together in a gossiping tide, that made it impossible to single out just one face for long.

Except for one.

Amid the crowd one masked man stood still, eyes turned in my direction. He wasn't just looking at me. His every sense was trained on me in a way that made my heart race. This wasn't an admirer. This was a predator stalking his prey.

"Yes, that's the one," Elizabeth said, teasing me. "Who is he?"

His mask was black, covering his whole face, with two points like ears—or horns—and a sinister painted grin. It reminded me of an animal. A wolf. A *jackal*.

"He's no one. If you'll excuse me . . ." I stumbled away from Elizabeth, toward the twinkling Christmas tree filled with tiny wrapped presents and gold bows, and leaned against the wall. Apparently it didn't matter that I had hidden my face behind a mask.

The Beast was here, and he'd recognized me.

TWENTY

INSTINCTIVELY, I SCANNED FOR exits. There were only two—the grand spiral staircase and the balcony door to the gardens. Should I run? Or would it be safer in a crowd? Not even the Beast would attack a person amid all these witnesses. Then again, at some point the ball must end. The crowd would leave. I would have to leave too, with only Elizabeth to escort me into the dark streets.

A woman near us let out a laugh so shrill it sounded like a scream. The music was loud. The chatter louder. People were dancing out of order, tipsy from wine. The Beast stood so calmly among them, not taking his eyes off me.

I could ask Elizabeth for help, but she would think me mad. Inspector Newcastle was here with a dozen officers, but I didn't dare tell him that the very murderer he was hunting was here, just so Edward could fall into the hands of those who might cut him apart, *snip snip snip*, to learn my father's science.

"Are you feeling all right?" Elizabeth asked, the

teasing gone from her voice.

"I might have had too much champagne." I fanned my face, wanting her away from me, since close by was the most dangerous place for her to be. "I'm just going to rest here a moment, then I'll dance. Go on, really."

Her face relaxed. "You'd better," she said. "Or I'll make you dance with old Mr. Willowby, and he's all left feet."

The moment she left my side, the masked man started toward me. A dagger of fear twisted my insides. I had only the window behind me, no place to run. He moved so gracefully through the dancers, as if they parted to make way for him. In a few moments he'd be here, and what would he say? Would he threaten me? Attack me?

Or would he tell me, once more, that he loved me?

The mask choked me with the smell of newsprint. I tore it off and hurried toward the balcony door. Nothing mattered but luring him away from these warm, tempting bodies.

He'd come for me, after all, not them.

The man in the wolf mask cocked his head, dark eyes watching as I hurried across the dance floor. He paused for just a beat before changing his direction and following me. The doors to the balcony were still cracked from before, making the white drapes flutter. Men and women stood near the door talking, red glows to their cheeks, wineglasses in hand. I pushed my way into their midst and through the door.

The cold wrapped around my arms. I glanced back through the glass door at the candlelit ballroom, where a girl in a swan mask glided and laughed. Overhead, the stars and the moon shone as brightly as before, and I cursed them. Darkness was what I needed now. A place to hide.

The door opened again. The man in the wolf mask stepped onto the balcony. We might as well have been the only two at the party, alone outside under the stars, only a few feet of flagstone separating us.

I wouldn't let it end like this.

I ran down the staircase into the garden, knowing that the dark boughs of the hedges were the perfect place for a murder, but also my only chance of drawing him away from the crowd and escaping. At the end of the garden was a gate that led into the back alley, and from there I could lose him in the streets.

The man in the mask started down the stairs after me.

The garden hedges behind Lucy's house were as familiar to me as the basement hallways of King's College. So many memories here: Lucy and I exploring every inch of this garden, chasing fairies, playing Catch the Huntsman. That was my one advantage—I knew the maze of hedges, and the Beast did not.

I darted behind the closest hedge wall. It had thinned with age, and I could peek between the branches to see the man approaching. He stopped at the bottom of the stairs and looked back to make sure no one had followed us outside, then moved toward the hedges. I darted to the next row as snow soaked into my satin shoes. They'd be ruined. It hardly mattered. I just had to reach the back gate and pray I could climb over.

I froze and listened. The hedges were fuller here and blocked my view. He could be anywhere.

I took a deep breath and darted around the hedge wall, past another row until I reached the brick wall. The black gate loomed ahead. Just a few more paces . . .

A hand came out of the shadows and grabbed my wrist. I started to scream, but the man's other hand was over my mouth in a flash. I felt his chest against my back, all rigid muscle. I looked up at the lights shining onto the balcony, only a few dozen paces away from us, but it might as well have been another world.

"Shh," the man in the wolf mask whispered. "They'll hear you. They'll think this is a secret tryst and come to investigate."

I nearly choked with shock. That voice, so tender and yet so deep. It wasn't the Beast's.

It wasn't Edward's, either.

My wrist went slack in his hand.

"Montgomery," I breathed.

TWENTY-ONE

THE MAN REACHED UP and pulled off his mask, blond hair falling over his broad shoulders, but I already knew what face I'd find. There was no mistaking the voice that belonged to a young man I'd known forever, a voice that brought back memories of our hands intertwined, his lips on mine, my fingers tangled in his blond hair.

My head wouldn't let me believe it. Reason told me that he was just another hallucination, and yet my heart knew Montgomery was real.

The mask slipped from my hand into the snow.

His face had lost its sun-bronzed color, replaced by a few fading cuts. The angles of his features were sharper. He'd always been strong, but now he held himself differently: tenser, hardened. Seeing him again stirred those painful memories of that last night on the island, waiting in the dinghy as the compound burned in the distance. I still remember seeing the rope fall from his hands, the jolt from his boot as he shoved the dinghy away with no warning.

But I need you, I had yelled across the waves.

The island needs me more, he'd called back.

With those words, Montgomery had shipwrecked my heart.

The memory made my knees buckle, but he came forward and caught me in his arms before I fell into the snow. Still so quick. Still so strong.

Our eyes met.

Still so handsome.

He was close enough that I could feel the beating of his heart through our clothing. "Christ, I missed you," he said, his voice just a whisper as it grazed my lips. His tender words shook me from the sense that this was all a dream. All the pain of his betrayal rushed back like a reopened wound. I shoved hard against his shirt, stumbling away from him before he could kiss me.

If he thought I would forgive him so easily, he was wrong.

"What are you doing here?" I demanded. "You said you weren't ever coming back. You left me."

"I am sorry for that," he said, warm breath clouding the air between us. He stepped forward slowly as if I was a spooked horse. "I didn't want to leave you. I had no choice."

"You might have told me, instead of shoving me away in a dinghy with your boot!"

"I know," he said, glancing at the balcony overhead to make certain we were alone. "It was cowardly, but I didn't know how to tell you. I didn't think you'd understand, and I feared you would insist on staying behind with me. I needed to know I'd done everything I could to keep you safe."

"Safe? I nearly died in that dinghy."

He ran a hand over his face, searching for words. "If you'd stayed on the island, you would have died for certain."

The note of regret hanging in his voice gave me pause. He never would have abandoned the island, not unless something terrible had forced him to. What had happened on that burning piece of land after I'd left? I had tried not to think about it, though ever since that time, I'd been plagued by waking nightmares of reverted beast-men turning on one another, flesh ripping apart, and Montgomery like an ungodly prince amid the madness.

"If you're here," I said carefully, "does it mean all the islanders are dead?"

"Dead, or close enough to it." His words were flat, but his broken voice betrayed him.

"What happened?"

He glanced again at the balcony, then frowned at me shivering in the snow. "You're freezing out here. Let's go inside, and I shall explain everything."

"I'm not a fragile child who can't handle a little cold. Tell me."

He watched me through the darkness as though weighing whether or not to believe me. At last he removed his suit jacket and wrapped it around my shoulders, rubbing them through the fabric. The friction wasn't nearly as warming as his proximity. I'd forgotten his smell, fresh hay and sunlight even in the midst of the city.

"I had no choice but to leave," he began. "The

compound had burned. The islanders had reverted to feral creatures and taken to the jungle. They didn't know how to hunt for themselves or feed. I made my home in Jaguar's old cabin, thinking I could at least help them adjust by breeding the rabbits and feeding the beast-men myself. But their instincts took over, and it wasn't rabbits they wanted. They hungered for larger prey, and turned on each other instead. After a few months, they forgot I had ever been a friend to them. I was forced to hunt them down one by one, and kill them before they killed me."

His voice held steady, but the way he ran an anxious hand through his loose blond hair betrayed him. He had loved the creatures, even helped give life to many of them. When I'd first arrived on the island, the beast-men had been civilized, living in villages and eating only vegetables, even praying in a church of their own making. Yet once Father had taken away their treatments, they quickly regressed into the animals they were, and in the end all Montgomery's scientific genius and high morals were reduced to nothing more than the law of the jungle: kill or be killed.

"I'm sorry," I whispered.

He looked away, into the hedges. "You were right when you said they should never have been created. It was mad of him to do it, and folly for me to help him. Killing them mercifully was my penance." His voice dropped as he glanced at the balcony again and stepped closer. "But one escaped, Juliet. I went back to bury the bodies of those who died in the compound fire, and Edward wasn't there."

His words were low and thick with warning. Meant

to shock me, and yet how could I be shocked when just the night before I'd been in that very man's arms? The scratches on my shoulder burned beneath the piece of red silk so hot that I was certain Montgomery would feel them.

"He survived the fire," Montgomery continued, mistaking my silence for distress. "For weeks I hunted him. He left me notes, begging for a chance to cure himself, wanting me to help him. But I didn't—I couldn't. Because the monster inside him left me letters, too. They came from a Mr. Hide, addressed to a Mr. Seek. The quarry writing to his hunter."

The blood drained from my face. It made me uncomfortable to speak of the Beast like this, as a thinking creature. I preferred to picture him as a mindless animal, but I knew that wasn't true. He was sentient. He was clever.

"The handwriting was the same," Montgomery continued, "written by the same hand, I mean, though with more of a slant—yet it was the ramblings of a demon. He said he was going to leave the island and come to London. That he deserved to know all the pleasure and pains in life, and he would do whatever he must to experience them."

"You've been following him ever since?" I whispered into the night.

"Yes. He stowed away on the *Curitiba* when that damn Captain Claggan returned. He's left me notes across half the world, tucked in the pockets of his victims as though this is only a game to him." He rubbed some warmth into his face, or maybe he was trying to brush aside the memories. "He's in London now. I arrived last week and have been searching for signs of him. I came to the party thinking that with so many of your father's colleagues gathered in one place, he might try to seek some sort of retribution. When I saw you here—"

"How did you recognize me?"

"I made some inquiries when I first arrived and discovered you were living with Professor von Stein and his niece." The corner of his mouth twitched. "And I'd know you anywhere, mask be damned."

His hand grazed mine. I allowed myself this brush of contact. I hadn't forgiven him—it wouldn't be that easy. And yet as we stood with the snow soaking into our shoes, in this city where we'd grown up together, it was impossible to pretend I felt nothing.

"I already know about Edward," I whispered.

His hand fell away as a look of astonishment crossed his face. "You *know?* Have you seen him? Has he tried to contact you?" He held my arm roughly enough to shake me. In the blink of an eye the honest, hardworking boy I knew had been replaced by this single-minded hunter.

He has secrets, Edward had warned me. *Secrets you still don't know.*

My lips were trembling. I wasn't ready to have this conversation, inevitable as it was. Edward and I were connected in a deep way—a primal way—that Montgomery would never understand. It was the human in us fighting against the animal inside. It bound us, intertwining our fates, our desires.

"The murders," I stuttered. "I heard about the Wolf of Whitechapel's murders, and knew it must be Edward, back from the dead." I was about to tell him the rest, how I investigated the bodies and found Edward at Lucy's, and yet something held my voice. The look in Montgomery's eyes was one of pure determination.

He would kill Edward. Or Edward would kill him. Either way, one of them would die, unless I prevented it.

My hand drifted to the scratches hidden beneath my silk dress. Amid my unquiet thoughts, something else Montgomery had said came back to me. He'd been in London for a week already. He hadn't come to see me. If not for our accidental encounter tonight, would he have come for me at all?

I didn't get a chance to ask. The porch door opened above our heads, and footsteps came out onto the balcony. The fibers of my stomach shrank at the thought that it could be the Beast. Montgomery pressed a finger to his lips to tell me to remain silent and pulled me into the shadows beneath the balcony, where we couldn't be seen. I nodded, holding my breath, dreading the telltale clicks of claws upon stone that meant the Beast had found us.

But I heard only the hiss of a match springing to life, and then smelled tobacco on the breeze. There were footsteps of a few other men, three or four in all. A man's voice spoke, and relief rushed out of me.

"Did you see where she went?" the man said. His voice was the deep baritone of a lifelong smoker; I recognized it as Lucy's father, Mr. Radcliffe, and the vision of that brain came slamming back into me. Perhaps my relief had come too soon.

"So many damn masks in there, it's hard to keep straight," another man said.

"The masquerade is necessary for our purposes," Radcliffe answered. "Moreau's creation wouldn't have come unless he could disguise himself. You're certain no men tried to talk to her? I'd stake my life they've been in contact. That fool who brought Moreau's last letter—Captain Claggan, isn't it?—said the boy was quite taken with her."

My breath halted as I realized the girl they spoke of was me.

TWENTY-TWO

I JERKED MY HEAD toward Montgomery. Worse, they also spoke of "Moreau's creation," which meant they knew about Edward, too. Montgomery kept a finger to his lips and silently reached for a revolver holstered at his side.

"She got lost in the crowd," another man answered.

"Well, find her," Radcliffe said. "She's the best chance we have of hunting him down. If only Claggan could have given us a better description before he drank himself to death. Dark hair, not yet twenty—that could describe half the young men in there."

One of the men spat over the side of the balustrade and added, "That old blatherskite von Stein won't say a word. The moment he hears the name Moreau, he slams the door in my face. He practically threw Lessing out by the collar."

"Leave von Stein to me," Radcliffe said, and then added, "What of the preparations?"

"The specimens will be ready within two weeks, providing we can capture Moreau's creation. Then it'll be a simple matter of extracting what we need from him and finishing the preparations for New Year's Day."

"Rochefort is speaking to his contacts in Paris about the exact delivery date. They're threatening to change their minds, but once they see what we have planned, they'll double their current order."

"Excellent." Radcliffe snuffed out his cigar, and it fell to the garden at my feet. I drew in a gasp as it singed my slipper, but Montgomery pressed his hand to my mouth. It felt like an eternity while we waited until their footsteps receded and the balcony door swung closed, leaving us alone in the garden once more.

Montgomery let go of my mouth, and I gulped in air.

"They know about Edward!" I gasped. "Claggan must have learned on the ship about his two sides and somehow gotten in touch with the King's Club. This whole party is a trap. They knew I'd be here and thought it would lure him. That 'guest of honor' nonsense—I thought they were just trying to win favor with the professor, and all the while Radcliffe wanted me here as *bait*."

Montgomery ran a hand over his forehead. "They don't know what Edward looks like—that's good at least, so we can get to him first. Damn it all, how do they even know he *exists*?"

"Radcliffe is the one Father was writing to on the island—his secret colleague who went by the code name 'A King's Man.' Don't you know about the letters? You must have delivered them."

Montgomery shook his head. "I did, but all Radcliffe

ever did was pay the bills for my travel and the exotic animals and other supplies—chartering a ship to the island was exorbitantly expensive. There was never any science exchanged, or else I would have put an end to it."

"Did you ever actually read the letters?"

"Of course not—they were sealed. But your father swore. . . ." His voice trailed off as he realized Father had lied to him, as he'd lied to all of us. As much as Father had loved Montgomery, he wasn't above lying even to him.

I put a hand to my head as everything started to come together. "They *did* exchange science. They must have, because Lucy's read some of the letters that reference it, and you heard them talking about specimens. They said all they needed was to extract something from Edward. His blood, perhaps, or bone marrow, I can't imagine what else. They have to be attempting to replicate Father's creatures."

Montgomery's face hardened. He didn't disagree, and this worried me even more. I continued, "They said everything would be ready in two weeks, in time for New Year's Day. What are they planning?"

"I don't know," he said gruffly. "But we need to find out."

I paced in the snow. "Earlier tonight I found a human brain."

"A *brain*?"

"Yes, in Radcliffe's study, in a hatbox. He doesn't practice science himself—he must have been holding it for one of the others. Whatever they're doing, it involves humans, not just animals."

Montgomery jerked his chin toward the balcony. "I think there were four of them," he said. "Five maybe—one might have been small. It means . . ." He rubbed his face, letting it all settle in.

I finished his thought. "It means this isn't limited to Radcliffe. It's much larger than we ever imagined. That makes sense now—Radcliffe's a businessman, not a scientist. He's providing the funding while the others are handling the research, the specimens, the politics. There are several members of Parliament in the King's Club. They even mentioned Rochefort, the French ambassador. That means this goes beyond one man or even a group in London. They have connections in France, Germany . . . who knows how far this reaches?" I leaned against the wall, body numb but thoughts churning like a steam engine.

I pressed my hand against my chest. Men like that, with limitless resources and connections, could change the entire system. They could make vivisection and animal experimentation legal, if they chose to. They could establish entire colleges dedicated to Father's research. They could re-create his creatures. They could take everything Father had done on that isolated island and spread it throughout the globe.

"Montgomery, we can't let them—"

But I didn't get a chance to finish. A scream rang out from the ballroom.

MONTGOMERY AND I RACED up the balcony steps and through the glass-paned door. The crowd inside the ballroom was packed tightly, everyone murmuring and pushing forward to see what had happened.

The girl in the swan mask stood on tiptoe next to me, trying to see over everyone's heads.

"What happened?" I asked her.

"A woman screamed," she said. "I think it was Mrs. Radcliffe."

"That's Lucy's mother!" I gasped. I tugged Montgomery toward the grand spiral staircase, the swan girl forgotten. "Something might have happened to Lucy."

I tried to push through the crowd, but no one made room for me, so Montgomery took the lead instead. He had a way of moving among people as gracefully as he ducked trees and brambles in the jungle. I had to trip over my own feet to keep up with him. Soon we were at the front of the murmuring crowd.

"Lucy!" I yelled, spotting her by the stairs. She was leaning against the grand staircase banister, mask off, face white, looking shaken but unharmed. I wrapped my hand around hers.

"What happened?" I whispered.

Half dazed, she pointed to a clump of people on the stairs. "Mother screamed. There was a commotion on the landing, and then she tumbled down the stairs covered in blood."

Lucy's eyes were fixed on the bottom of the stairs, where Inspector Newcastle, Mr. Radcliffe, and several men were leaning over Lucy's mother. She was still screaming, though when I pushed closer I could tell with one glimpse that the wounds were only superficial. Just shallow cuts on her arm, though the three slash marks spilled a startling amount of blood onto her white gown.

Three slash marks.

I glanced at Montgomery and saw my fears confirmed in his face—three slash marks meant the Beast.

Apparently we weren't the only ones who noticed that particular detail, because once Mrs. Radcliffe's shock wore off, she started screaming, "The Wolf! It was the Wolf!"

"The Wolf is here!" a woman in the crowd yelled behind me. "Run!"

My imagination started churning. I pictured blood pouring out beneath torn flesh, pooling on the floor, staining everyone's fine dancing shoes. The blood just kept coming until the dance floor was covered, choking the quartet's instruments, spilling out in a waterfall over the balcony into the garden where Montgomery and I had stood.

Montgomery squeezed my hand, and the hallucination disappeared. I prayed a fit wasn't coming on, here in public and at such a terrible time, and massaged the joints of my knuckles. Everyone was screaming, grabbing their belongings, hurrying for the front door.

"He's toying with us," Montgomery said. "I've got to get you out of here."

The room churned with panic. In the turmoil someone smashed into the enormous Christmas tree at my side. Strong hands pulled me out of the way a second before it crashed to the ground, glass ornaments shattering, spurring another round of screams.

I turned to thank the person who'd pulled me out of the way. A massive man, and young, judging by his dark hair, though a red mask hid his face from me—all except for his eyes. My lips parted as I saw their deep yellow glow.

The Beast.

I screamed for Montgomery, but my voice was lost in the chaos as everyone ran for the door. I looked around frantically and caught a glimpse of him thirty feet away, helping a woman who'd been trapped under the enormous Christmas tree. But he didn't see me, and the Beast dug his knobby fingers into my arm and pulled me in the opposite direction from the one everyone else was running to.

I twisted, but I was powerless against him without a weapon. He pulled me into the doorway leading toward the rear halls, in the shadows where we'd be overlooked.

"I'll kill you for what you've done," I seethed.

"I think that quite unlikely," he said in that inhumanly deep voice. "You've had two chances to kill me and you haven't."

"Only because Edward inhabits this body too. Now let me go. If Montgomery sees you . . ."

A laugh came from deep in his throat, and I was glad for the mask that hid the face that was and wasn't Edward at the same time.

"You mean Moreau's hunting dog? He's certainly nothing I fear, and from what I saw in the garden, it seems he means nothing to you, either." He leaned in close enough that I could feel his unnatural heat, as though a powerful fever burned from within. "You spurned his advances, my love."

I twisted to look back to the crowd, but it was still chaotic, still filled with screams, and Montgomery nowhere.

"You didn't want his kisses, did you? You wanted mine," growled the Beast, low and seductive.

He leaned forward as though to kiss me, and I shoved him hard, but he only laughed, a game between two lovers, and pinned me against the wall. The corset ribbing stabbed into me, and I pressed a hand to my stomach. The Beast felt the stiff corset too, and whispered, "You don't belong like this, trussed up. Like me, you're too wild to be caged. Why don't you take it off?"

Hearing those same words Edward had once spoken, in his innocence, only made the pain sharper. I gritted my teeth. For the first time I noticed a small handful of mistletoe hung from a red ribbon over our heads.

"It's *my* lips you want to feel, isn't it?" he breathed.

I felt his breath closer, smelling of rum and meat, so unlike Edward.

"My love," he said, drawing the word out as though he could taste it, as though he yearned to swallow it whole.

Now.

I dug my elbow into the place beneath his rib where I'd stabbed him the night before. He howled in pain as I pulled away, restricted in my stiff clothes, frantically stumbling back into the ballroom. The fallen Christmas tree spanned the entire room, cutting me off from the doorway.

"Juliet!"

Montgomery stood on the stairs, searching the crowd for me. I raced toward him as he rushed down the stairs and climbed over the fallen fir tree in a few graceful movements.

"The Beast found me," I panted. "I wounded him, but it won't slow him down for long."

"Long enough, I hope." He grabbed my hands and helped to pull me over the Christmas tree, which smelled of rich sap from broken branches that pulled at my silk dress. I tore the skirts away, freeing myself, and once my feet were on the polished floor again, we raced toward the door. I caught a glimpse of Lucy's green satin dress bent over her mother, with Inspector Newcastle standing close to protect her.

"I can't leave Lucy here," I breathed.

"She'll be safe. He's not after her." Montgomery pulled at me, ready to drag me out despite my protests. Lucy turned at the last moment and saw me. Her frightened lips parted, and I thought of how I wished more than anything that she wasn't wrapped up in this.

But before I could call to her, Montgomery pulled me away toward the door. With his blond hair loose, he looked half wild, a savage amidst royalty. "Juliet, we must go now!"

I had only a second to look at Lucy. "Stay close to John," I yelled. "We'll talk tomorrow. I'm sorry—"

She was swallowed by the crowd. Montgomery's hand tightened over mine as he pushed through the partygoers toward the grand entrance.

"Did he hurt you?" Montgomery asked.

"He tried to kiss me."

Montgomery threw me an alarmed look as we raced up the staircase among the masked people. We moved so fast, I had to raise my skirts practically to my knees.

We reached the top of the stairs and hurried out with the rest of the finely dressed guests. The night was freezing. It was late enough that no carriages were out save the ones belonging to the attendees, too early for the bakers and early-morning vendors. Montgomery picked a direction and started down the street at a quick pace. I had to jog in my tight shoes to keep up with him.

As we were dashing away from Lucy's house, my slippers soaked and torn, I realized I still had pollen from the little white flower under my fingernails.

I wiped the pollen off on my dress. I'd been a fool to keep the first flower. Now Lucy—and Elizabeth, and everyone at that party—was in danger. Would I find one of their names in the newspapers the next morning, listed among the Wolf of Whitechapel's victims?

I had promised Edward I would help him.

But a promise to a murderer was a dangerous thing.

TWENTY-THREE

WE ONLY SLOWED WHEN we reached Piccadilly Circus, where the streets were filled with people no matter the hour. I tore my hand from Montgomery's and doubled over against a lamppost.

"I need to catch my breath," I gasped.

Montgomery paced along the curb, rubbing a hand on the back of his neck. His eyes went to every shadow as though Edward might be there.

"We have to go back for Lucy. She's in danger," I said.

"The Beast wouldn't kill in public. He's a devil, but he's no fool. All this is nothing more than a game to him."

I thought of the Beast dragging me beneath the mistletoe, wanting a stolen kiss. A game? Perhaps, but the deadliest game I'd ever known.

"What exactly did he say to you?" Montgomery asked.

"He saw you and me together in the garden. I think he was jealous."

"Damn it all." Montgomery kept pacing the length of

the curb, bristling whenever a carriage passed.

"If we aren't going back for Lucy, then I've got to go home. The professor and Elizabeth will wonder where I am," I said. "And I want to be certain Elizabeth made it home safely."

Montgomery considered this for the space of a few breaths. His forehead creased even deeper. "Are you certain we can trust the professor? He was once a King's Man."

It ruffled me to hear him suggest such a thing, just as Edward once had, though I knew he was only being careful. "You heard those men on the balcony—they've been after him for information and he's refused them each time. Perhaps he suspects what they're involved in. He might be able to help us."

"Have you told him anything about the island?"

"Only that I found Father there, and he died. Nothing more. I've told Elizabeth even less."

"I'd rather keep it that way for now. The fewer people involved, the better. I'm thankful for what the professor's done for you, but I'm not inclined to trust anyone right now. We don't know how far this conspiracy reaches."

I shivered. I'd lost his suit jacket in the chaos, and my bare arms were riddled with goose flesh. My thumb suddenly jerked of its own accord, and a dull ache spread to my left hand—a bout of illness coming, as I'd feared. I rested my head in my stiffening hands, trying to breathe, as a wave of vertigo engulfed me. Montgomery must have seen me swaying, because he crouched down and took hold of my hands to steady me.

"What is it? What is wrong?"

"My illness," I managed to whisper, though the sudden pain was so great, it even hurt to speak. "It comes to me in waves. It's gotten worse these last months. Father's serum is failing. I've been trying to create a new treatment, but I've had no success."

"You're burning up," Montgomery muttered, feeling my forehead. "We've got to get you out of this cold. Can you walk?"

I tried to push myself up, but dizziness sent me back to the cobblestones. "I just need another moment."

"We don't have another moment," he said. "You need medical care, and we need to get off the streets." He picked me up, and my protests were lost in the rustling of my red silk dress. "I've let a room at an inn in Camden Town, not far from here. I have medical supplies there."

"But the professor will worry."

"Blast and damn the professor," Montgomery said. "He shall have to worry a few hours longer. If I take you to his house in this state, he'll likely murder me."

By the time we reached Camden Town, the moon cast faint light over the street, where rats nosed through rubbish. The streets were even tighter here than in Whitechapel, where makeshift hovels of tin and loose brick crowded both sides of the road.

He stopped outside a public house on the corner. One shattered window had been hastily plugged with newspaper, but that didn't keep the smell of sour beer from coming out of it. There were chains above the door where a sign should have swung, but any sign had long since abandoned the place.

I convinced him I was well enough to stand, though he kept one arm around my waist for support. "I thought you said it was an inn," I muttered. "This looks more like the gutter."

"We left the island with only the shirts on our backs," he said. "I've earned a few crowns here and there doing medical work, but it isn't cheap tracking a murderer." He tilted his head toward an upper-floor window, put two fingers to his lips, and whistled a high, shrill note.

"*We*?" I said, trying to clear the fuzzy corners of my head. "Aren't you here alone?"

An upstairs window swung open and a hairy face shone in the moonlight, deformed and hideous, but cracked with a wide smile. Despite how ill I felt, I couldn't resist grinning back with a sudden giddy rush. Montgomery had brought Balthazar with him. It defied logic that he was even still alive, yet it was impossible not to delight at the sight of that ugly face that was so dear to me.

"Balthazar!" I called.

When I had met Balthazar for the first time, I'd been frightened by his sunken eyes and hunchback and enormous size, until I'd noticed the tray of tea and biscuits he held. He might have been one of Father's creations, but he was no demon.

"We're coming up," Montgomery called, and Balthazar's head disappeared. Though it was good to see Balthazar, I couldn't help but throw Montgomery a worried glance. Why had Montgomery brought him back to London? Wasn't it dangerous? We had sworn not to let any of Father's creatures off the island. The King's Club was already after Edward; what would happen if they learned of Balthazar's existence, too?

But Montgomery held the door open for me, and I resolved to ask him later, when my head wasn't spinning so fast. The ground floor was a run-down alehouse. Leering men of the sort to still be drinking long after midnight peered at us as Montgomery led me to the narrow back steps, where the frigid night wind blew straight through the chinks in the wall.

The stairs protested under our weight as Montgomery helped me shuffle up them. We reached the top and he fumbled with his keys, but the creaky door flung open and Balthazar threw his arms around me.

I stiffened at first, but quickly relaxed and hugged him back. Now I understood why they say smell can evoke the strongest memories. There were the smells of London on him—candle wax, greasy fried fish—but beneath that was *his* smell, like damp tweed and woodsmoke, and my gut pulled at the fierce recognition.

I squeezed him harder than I expected. With Balthazar life was simple. It didn't matter that he was a monster and I was a madman's daughter. We were just two friends, long parted.

I let him go and stepped back. "It's good to see you, Balthazar."

"Yes, miss." He shuffled his feet a little, grinning.

"All right, inside with you," Montgomery said. "She's unwell, Balthazar. Fetch my medical bag."

I stepped cautiously inside, where it was even darker than the hallway, with only the light from a few candles burning. The room was small. A single filmy window looked out onto an alleyway. There was a fireplace, but the fire had gone out and cold air blew down. The bed was unmade. A trunk was open, not fully unpacked even after a week. Montgomery hadn't been planning on staying long, I realized. Only long enough to hunt his quarry. If not for tonight, would he have come and gone without ever once seeing me?

I'd chosen him, after all. He hadn't chosen me in return.

Balthazar hurried to dig through the trunks, while Montgomery led me to a wooden chair at a table covered with stacks of newspapers. Headlines about the Wolf of Whitechapel's murders had been circled in dark red ink, with Montgomery's notes littering the margins. I had to shove my hands beneath the table to hide how they popped and shifted unnaturally.

"I'm sorry for the state of this place," Montgomery said, stacking the newspapers. "Without a woman's touch . . . well, you know. I've been scouring the papers for information about the murders. It seems to be all anyone is talking about, which means speculation and false leads are rampant."

Balthazar lumbered over with a black medical bag.

"Thank you, my friend," Montgomery said. "Now if you'd be so good, take this coin downstairs to the innkeeper and tell her we mightn't return for a few days." He fished in his pocket until he found a coin and gave it to Balthazar, who shuffled out.

The door shut, sealing us in the bedroom.

My face flushed. I hadn't been in a room alone with Montgomery since the island. I still felt a flutter of nervousness around him, as I had when I was a little girl infatuated with him, the quiet servant boy who helped Father in his laboratory and would sneak me biology books in secret.

Only now everything was different. I was no longer the master's daughter and he no longer a servant. Now I knew what it felt like to have his lips against mine. And now I was lying to him about having seen Edward. Having *made love* to Edward.

I looked away as if he could read my thoughts. The muscles in my arm started spasming and I rubbed them deeply, trying to work out the ever-present tension there. Montgomery walked to the hearth, where he knelt to rebuild the fire. I listened to the comforting sounds of wood being stacked, a match struck, a sizzle of flame.

Was I risking everything by keeping the truth from him? Wasn't he keeping secrets from me, too?

"I'm surprised to see Balthazar," I said slowly. "It's good to see him, of course, but I thought we agreed, on the island . . ." I didn't need to finish. He dusted the soot off his hands and came to sit across the table from me. The pained look on his face said enough.

"I know what we said," he answered. "But he's like family to me. It's childish, I know, but I've no father, no mother, no one. When I was young, I used to watch the boys play in the street and wish I had a brother, too. I know what Balthazar is, but it doesn't matter to me. He's the closest thing to a brother I'll ever have."

An urge overcame me to take his hand, kiss each of his knuckles. I'd been such a lonely child too. Children who had no family were the ones who cherished the idea of family the most. "It's just that you've come all this way to kill Edward, so that he won't keep murdering, but also so that no one will be able to deconstruct Father's work if they capture him. Balthazar was made with a cruder method, but if they catch him they could do the same."

"I know," he said, studying the lines of soot on his hands. "I know I shouldn't have brought him, shouldn't have even let him live. But I never claimed to be perfect. I have weaknesses. My affection for him." He looked up. "And for you."

The muscles twitched harder in my arms. I stood up, shaky and light-headed, and paced in part to ease the symptoms, in part to ease the pounding of my heart. All the while, Montgomery studied me with the keen eye of a surgeon.

"Tell me your symptoms," he said. "And how they've gotten worse."

As I explained the problem with the serum, he opened the medical bag, every bit the doctor. This was easier, more natural for both of us, to talk of such tangible things as bones and flesh, instead of matters of the heart.

He removed a corked glass vial filled with a cloudy-colored liquid. I expected him to draw it into a syringe, but to my surprise he handed it to me and said, "Drink this."

I took the small glass vial, but hesitated. "What is it?"

"A concoction I designed for Balthazar. It dulls the effects of his affliction between injections. It won't cure you, but it'll ease your symptoms long enough for us to get you to the professor's, where I can treat you properly."

"You're coming to the professor's too?"

"If you think I'm leaving you alone after what we heard tonight, you're mad. The King's Men run this city; if they're targeting you, you need me. I knew the professor, and with luck he'll recall me favorably as well. Now drink."

I uncorked the liquid and sniffed it tentatively. Astringent, with a hint of sulfur. "Valerian," I said, somewhat surprised. It was the same drug I'd given Edward to ease his affliction.

"That, and other ingredients," Montgomery said.

I swallowed it down and very nearly gagged. The taste was even worse than the smell.

"I would have flavored it with peppermint," he said. "But Balthazar never complains. Can you walk now without those tremors?"

He pulled the chair back for me, as he used to when he was a servant, and I braced myself on the table and stood shakily. "I'll manage."

The door opened behind me, and I heard Balthazar's distinctive shuffle. Montgomery patted him on the shoulder and said, "Balthazar here wouldn't mind carrying you all the way to Highbury, but I doubt the professor would enjoy seeing his ward in a torn dress in the arms of a man like him."

I glanced at Balthazar. "I daresay not."

Montgomery gave me one final look. "You're quite certain the professor can be trusted?"

"With my life."

"Christ, let's hope it doesn't come to that. Balthazar, throw some clothes into a bag for us. I'll have to devise some reason for why the professor should let Balthazar and me stay in his home to keep an eye on you."

Once he was quite certain I could walk, and Balthazar had packed a small bag for them, we descended the stairs. The moon was high, and I'd guess it was well past midnight. I hated to think of how frantic the professor and Elizabeth would be over my disappearance.

"How was your voyage?" I asked Balthazar, partly as a distraction and partly because seeing him again made me realize how much I had missed him. "Did you see much of the world?"

"Yes, miss. I rode a camel."

Montgomery leaned close and whispered playfully, "Nearly broke the poor thing's back."

We chatted on the way, and as much as it warmed my heart to see Balthazar, his presence in London unsettled me. Father's creatures were never meant to exist at all. On a forgotten island in the South Pacific they had been dangerous enough, but here, in the capital of the western world, where the most powerful organization in the world's greatest city was after my father's science . . .

But Montgomery loved Balthazar, and I didn't blame him for sparing his life and continuing to give him treatments. It wasn't so different from how I had risked so much to help Edward. But what fate was there for an ungodly creation like Balthazar, kind though he was?

At last we turned onto Dumbarton Street. The moon cast light over the wide street and sidewalks. My feet moved faster the nearer to the door—and safety—we grew. How strange it felt to have Montgomery real by my side, when for months he'd been nothing but a daydream.

I glanced at him sidelong. His body was here, but was his heart?

My feet slowed when the brownstone came into sight. Every light was blazing, which made it stand out unnaturally from its neighbors. I scanned the grounds, looking for Sharkey, hoping he'd returned after I'd lost him, but he was nowhere to be found. Montgomery's serum had helped, and I ran the rest of the way and pounded with the brass horsehead knocker.

The door flew open, with Elizabeth's worried face filling the space. At the sight of me she let out a strangled cry of relief and pulled me into her arms. I heard shuffling footsteps on the stairs and saw the professor descending, a dark red dressing gown over his pajamas.

"Thank god you're home," he said. "Elizabeth told me what happened at the Radcliffes'. We feared you'd disappeared in the panic and we'd never find you again."

His big hands kneaded my shoulder, as his eyes searched mine from behind his wire-rim spectacles.

"I'm quite all right, just a bit shaken," I said. "And I'm relieved to see you made it back safely, Elizabeth."

"I scoured every inch of the ballroom looking for you. I found Lucy, and she told me a young gentleman had practically dragged you to safety." Her eyes slid to Montgomery, taking him in with an analytical stare. "I assume we have you to thank for this, young man."

"This is an old friend," I said. "He is—"

"Montgomery James," he introduced himself with a cordial nod, and then took my hand in his own, which hardly seemed proper, and pulled me next to him so he could wrap one arm around my shoulders.

"I'm Juliet's fiancé."

TWENTY-FOUR

His HAND TIGHTENED OVER my shoulders. If I looked surprised by his words, it was nothing compared to the shock on the professor's and Elizabeth's faces.

The professor made as if to speak, but no words came out. Elizabeth's beautiful blue eyes scoured every inch of our hand-holding, my muddy dress, Montgomery's loose hair. Both of their mouths were folded hard, their deep-set eyes peering at us like a pair of birds from the cuckoo clock.

"It seems this evening's surprises just keep coming," she said. "Perhaps you should come inside, Mr. James."

"There is one other thing," Montgomery said, and looked over his shoulder to where Balthazar stood half hidden in the shadows. The moonlight had a way of highlighting the deformity of his back and darkening the shadows under his eyes, so he looked the very picture of a monster.

"I have a friend with me," Montgomery continued. "We've been traveling together for some time, and I'd be much obliged if he could warm himself by your fire."

As Balthazar lumbered up to join us on the front stoop, Elizabeth's eyes went even wider. The professor seemed ready to slam the door in his face.

"Good evening," Balthazar said with his lopsided grin.

The professor remained speechless. It was only after Elizabeth cleared her throat and mumbled something about good manners that he let us inside.

Though the cuckoo clock sounded one in the morning, we soon found ourselves sitting in the library around a pot of tea Elizabeth had insisted on making. Montgomery sat next to me on the loveseat, his hand tightly around mine. He hadn't let go for a moment since making the announcement.

"Play along," he'd whispered as we'd settled on the sofa. "I have my reasons."

The cuckoo clock ticked, and the steam rose from the pot. I think as shocked as they were by Montgomery's announcement, it was Balthazar's presence that had truly rendered them speechless. Now he sat awkwardly on a too-small stool near the fireplace, half cast in shadows, so quiet he might very well have fallen asleep.

"Well. The tea." Elizabeth broke the silence and stood to pour. She eyed Montgomery carefully. "You'll imagine our surprise to see you, Mr. James. Juliet neglected to tell us you were in London, nor did she give us news of any engagement." Her eyes slid to mine, and I shifted uncomfortably.

"I'm afraid I worried what you'd say. Montgomery is the one who took me to Father's island last year."

"A servant!" the professor said suddenly, but there was no disdain in his voice. "That's where I recognize you from, yes, of course. You were a servant for the Moreau family."

Montgomery nodded.

The professor settled back into his chair. "I recall you as a quiet boy. Loyal. Hardworking. Though I can't say I approve of your proposing to my ward without first seeking my permission."

"I apologize for that, sir," Montgomery said. "I proposed the moment I returned to London. I'm afraid in my haste Juliet's opinion was the only one I could think of."

"Is this why you've been so cagey and slipping away?" Elizabeth said suddenly, twisting her head at me so that she nearly spilled the tea. Equal amounts admonishment and relief mixed in her voice. She had been so worried the night I'd climbed through the kitchen window. To know I was just meeting a secret fiancé must have come as a considerable relief.

"Yes," I lied. Now would have been the time to give Montgomery an adoring look, or playfully apologize for worrying them, and yet I couldn't bring myself to do it. Acting the part of Montgomery's sweetheart now, when I'd only just seen him again and still had the feel of Edward on my skin, was a role I wasn't ready to play.

It didn't seem to matter. The others took my stiff reaction as nothing more than lingering tension from the masquerade, perhaps.

"And what are your intentions, Mr. James?" the professor asked.

"I have some medical skill. I'd like to apprentice myself to a doctor, perhaps in a rural village, and have

Juliet join me there as my wife."

I glanced at him, wondering if this was the truth or just some story to appease the professor. Montgomery was normally so painfully easy to read, and yet none of his usual tells were showing, which left me feeling deeply curious and even a little suspicious. He'd broken my heart once; I wouldn't give it so easily to him again.

He's keeping secrets from you, Edward had said.

Montgomery glanced at me and smiled.

The cuckoo clock sounded that another hour had passed, and Elizabeth glanced at the professor's drooping eyelids. "It's a pleasure to meet you, Mr. James, but you understand our shock at this news. I think we'd all like more sleep, and tomorrow you can explain more."

The professor roused himself. "Yes, and in the meantime, you and your companion—if he wakes from that chair—may sleep in the guest room on the third floor."

His words had an obvious edge to them, as his pointed stare went between the two of us. Engaged we might be, but not married yet. There would be at least one floor separating us until that day.

We bade him and Elizabeth good night. She paused at my bedroom door, a candle in hand, as the others continued upstairs.

"Why didn't you tell us?" she whispered.

"I wasn't certain you would approve of his former position, nor his association with my father."

"We were all associated with your father, Juliet. By that logic each of us is guilty."

I looked at my hands and nodded.

"Do you love him?" she asked.

I felt that pressure to play the part again. And yet as I struggled to sort out my feelings and provide Elizabeth with a satisfactory answer, I found it wasn't that easy.

"He's a good man," I said.

I left out the hundreds of reasons why love between Montgomery and me wasn't simple. How he'd abandoned me, and had helped my father, and how I'd made love with another man. I could still feel the tangle of all those things choking me like summer vines.

She gave me a somewhat pitying smile. Elizabeth had never married, and I'd overheard her telling the professor that she thought marriage was a trap meant to keep women in the bedroom and kitchen. If she pitied me that fate, she didn't know me very well. I couldn't be a sweet, obedient wife if I wanted to.

She left, and without her presence the room took on a cavernous, lonely feel. I changed out of the stiff silk ball gown with the mud on the hem into a shift. I closed my eyes and listened for the sounds of the house settling. Everything was silent except for the wind pushing at the windows.

I pulled on my house slippers and padded silently to the door. Montgomery's room was on the same floor as the professor's, but the old man slept as though in death, and I'd learned how to be silent on the island.

I twisted the doorknob, ready to sneak out. To my surprise, Montgomery was already waiting on the other side. He'd beaten me to it.

His eyes met mine, and they were the deep blue of a flame.

"May I come in?" he asked.

MONTGOMERY ADDED ANOTHER PIECE of wood to the small fireplace in my bedroom. I watched him working, remembering how he'd laid my fires for me when I was a little girl. He'd been so quiet back then. He was still quiet, and yet impossible not to notice. It wasn't just how he'd grown into a powerful young man, but also a certain stillness to the air around him, as though even the fire springing to life in his hands knew he could be trusted.

He brought the fire to a roar, spilling flickering light over the bedroom's soft curtains and thick duvets bursting with goose-feather down. I wondered if I looked the same to him, against such an elegant backdrop, when he had fallen in love with me amid jungle vines and the crashing sea.

"It was a rash decision," he said. "But it was the best I could think of in the moment. If I'd shown up at your door after midnight, with your dress torn and muddied, they'd have thought me a villain at worst. If they'd allowed me time to explain I'd rescued you from the masquerade and escorted you home, I'd be a polite stranger, and they'd have thanked me profusely and dismissed me. Telling them we were engaged gives us the ability to be alone, to travel together, to explain why we sometimes sneak off just the two of us."

"I understand. It only came as a considerable shock. I haven't seen you in months. For all I knew you were dead.

And I've already lied enough to the professor, when he's done nothing but show me kindness."

He tucked back a loose strand of blond hair. "Is it that far from the truth?" he asked quietly.

I let the roaring fire fill the silence. On the island, I'd never wanted to be apart from him. But now there was a rift between us wide as the ocean I'd crossed, alone and wounded. He'd shown up at the masquerade amid the swirling masks and looked at me as if nothing had changed.

But everything had changed.

I'd shared a bed with Edward the night before. I'd made love to a *murderer*, while I'd blindly thought I was safe in his company. I'd been worse than a fool.

"Why didn't you come for me sooner?" My whispered words blended with the crackling of the fire.

He settled on the bed next to me, amid the silk sheets and sea of pillows that were a million miles away from the sparse simplicity of the island where we'd fallen in love. Then he took my small hand in his much bigger one and ever so slowly brought it to his lips.

My heart roared to life just like the fire. The memories of him pushing me away in that dinghy were still so tender, and I wasn't certain I was ready for this again. Such deep wounds didn't patch over in a day.

"It was complicated," he said, keeping his voice low. "When I followed Edward here, of course I thought of you. I wanted to come find you every day, and apologize for parting the way we did, and say that I've thought of you constantly." His hand tightened around mine, not letting me drift away like that dinghy's rope had so many months ago. "And yet every time I thought of a life together, there was too much in the way. At first it was the fate of the beast-men; if I had left them there alone, I would never have forgiven myself."

"The beast-men are gone now," I whispered.

"Yes, but now Edward stands between us. I want a simple life, Juliet. No monsters in our closets, no jumping at shadows. Before I could have that life with you, I wanted to resolve the question of Edward. Then I planned on finding you and having that life." He'd moved quite close on the bed now, as my pounding heart was all too aware. He reached up and cupped my chin in his hand. "I never stopped loving you. I never will."

In the quiet intimacy of my bedroom, logic seemed to have left me. He'd wounded me so deeply, and yet he was still the young man I'd fallen in love with. Could I throw away a lifelong friendship over an old wound?

"I missed you," he muttered.

His lips brushed against my cheek. I asked myself if I could forgive him so easily. But the answer was simple, as we sat on my satin duvet. Yes, yes, *yes*. I'd forgive him anything.

I leaned in to him, and he kissed me. I had dreamed of seeing him again for so long that it hardly felt real. I pressed my lips to his again and again, dizzy in the moonlight streaming in from the high windows.

"Juliet." He whispered my name against my cheek like a caress. The feel of his warm skin woke me as if from a dream, as if I'd merely been sleepwalking through life since leaving the island.

I pulled his head down, kissing him again. Not softly this time. My breath started coming fast, my pulse pounding. He returned the kiss just as passionately. I wanted to kiss him forever, never let him leave me again.

His thumb found my shift's neckline, running along the place where the fabric ended and skin began. As he trailed kisses down the length of my neck, he pulled the fabric over my shoulder, replacing it with his lips.

I leaned back, hands coiled in his hair, thinking of how making love to Edward had been a mistake. I should have saved myself for Montgomery, the man I truly loved.

What would he do if he found out?

Montgomery stopped and sat abruptly. His gaze fell to the bare skin of my shoulder. I parted my lips, confused, and touched the tender place where he'd just kissed me.

My fingers found the rough scratches from where the Beast had clawed me.

"Where did you get those scratches?" he said. There was an odd inflection in his voice, and I remembered that he'd seen the Beast's scratches on countless bodies. He knew exactly how the claws cut through skin, how far apart the spacing was. Of course he would recognize them.

"Montgomery . . . ," I said in a rush. I could feel the intimacy of the moment slipping out of my hands, and I grabbed his arm to keep it there.

He pulled out of my grasp and stood, pacing by the fire. "You said you hadn't seen Edward before tonight."

"Stop pacing, and I shall explain."

"You said you hadn't seen him. You lied to me."

"I never actually said as much—you just assumed. I didn't know how to tell you."

"He could have killed you!"

"You think I don't know that?" I snapped, standing to face him. I chewed on my lip, trying to focus my thoughts. "Of course I know he's dangerous. I think about that every minute, every second! Each one of his victims died because of me—each one had wronged me. One was a girl I used to know from the boardinghouse, who stole Mother's ring. One was a member of Parliament who beat Mother and me, many years ago. Another was the solicitor who commandeered our fortune on behalf of the courts. None of them angels, though none of them deserved *death*. I've been living in a prison of fear ever since Edward came back, so don't you dare try to tell me I'm ignoring how dangerous he is."

My words ended short, and I took a few breaths. "But there's good in him too, and it's worth saving. He's as desperate to stop the Beast as the rest of us. He's trying to cure himself, and he asked for my help. Perhaps if you'd shown the same compassion—"

"Compassion?" he hissed. "Why would you have sympathy for a monster?"

"Because we're not so different! I know what it means to be experimented on. I'm in need of a cure just as much as Edward. He and I were working together. We were making progress, until . . ." My hand went to the scratches on my shoulder. "It's getting harder for him to control himself. The Beast gets stronger each day."

"You should have told me," he said. He went to the

windows, pushing aside the curtains to look down on the world below.

"Well, I'm not the only one keeping secrets," I said.

His head jerked up, eyes fixed with the intensity of a hunter. "What do you mean?"

"Edward said there are things you haven't told me."

He crossed the room to stand beside me. "What did he tell you?" The quick, almost desperate quality to his movements proved Edward right. Montgomery was hiding something.

"The letters, for one."

"I told you, I never read them. Moreau told me they were just business transactions. Funding for the supplies he needed."

"And you never thought that his financial backers expected something in return for their payments?"

He ran a hand over his face. "I made mistakes, Juliet. I admired your father. I loved him. I didn't question things that I should have. But it would be a mistake now to let Edward live."

"Just as it's a mistake to let Balthazar live? Why an exception for one and not the other?" I snapped. He threw me an annoyed look, which I returned. "Balthazar's a good creature, but so is Edward. You've just never understood him. Not like I do."

There was a tenderness to my voice I hadn't intended, and it made Montgomery stop his prowling. "How is that? As a friend?" His eyes drifted to the bare skin of my shoulder. "Or as something more?"

My jaw clenched. "Don't you dare throw accusations."

But jealousy had gotten its fingers deep within him, and he wasn't about to stop. "Did he tell you lies about how he loves you, how he'd do anything for you? Did he kiss you? Did you kiss him *back*?"

Instinct brought my hand toward his face to slap him, never mind that he was dangerously close to the truth. But he caught my wrist before it made contact. His breath was coming fast; mine was faster.

I said in a rush, "You were right. Edward did try to kiss me, and I let him. I let him do more than that too, because *he* came back for me. He truly loves me."

Montgomery's eyes went wide. I'd gone too far, I realized. He'd hurt me, and so I had hurt him. But love wasn't about swapping wounds, tearing each other apart. We weren't animals. I bit my lip, wishing I could take those words back. Wishing they'd been a lie instead of the truth.

"I'm sorry," I said. "You were gone. I thought I'd never see you again."

I reached toward him, but he jerked away. "You think I don't truly love you?" he said, and then muttered something under his breath and stormed toward the door.

"Where are you going?" I demanded.

"To find Edward and put a bullet in his head." He vanished through the door, letting it fall closed behind him. I heard the stairs groan and the front door slam as he disappeared somewhere out in the cold night.

I threw on my coat and slippers and opened the door to run after him but tripped over a gigantic mass asleep a few feet outside my bedroom door. I would have landed against the hard wood loud enough to wake the entire household if Balthazar's sleeping bulk hadn't broken my fall.

"Balthazar," I whispered, scrambling to sit up as his hand found my arm. "What are you doing out here?"

But he didn't take his hands off me. He pushed to his feet and lifted me up with him, then dusted off my coat, gently picked me up, and set me back down in my bedroom.

"Montgomery says to keep you here. To make sure you don't leave."

I glared at him, but he didn't flinch. Balthazar was nothing if not loyal. If Montgomery told him to eat a pint of arsenic, he'd do it without question.

Balthazar smiled as he closed the door in my face. "Sweet dreams, miss."

Sweet dreams indeed, I thought, as I raced to the window and fumbled to get the lock open. It would be waking nightmares, not dreams, if I didn't get to Edward before Montgomery did.

TWENTY-FIVE

I HADN'T TAKEN THE time to change out of my shift, but by the time I ran all the way to Shoreditch, sweat was pooling beneath my heavy coat. I paused outside my lodging house. A lantern was on in the attic chamber, flickering calm and bright.

The Beast, with his animal eyes, wouldn't need a lantern. Edward had to be up there.

Just the same, I was cautious going up the stairs. I held the knife in my hand, ready to strike if needed. I reached the landing and pressed my ear to the door. I could hear the old building settling and creaking, then a gentle clink of glass from within, and the scrape of chair legs on the floorboards as someone stood.

I adjusted my grip on the knife before quietly twisting the knob just enough to peer within. There was a shadow of movement on the wall, looking inhumanly large before I realized it was just the lantern casting too-long shadows, and that the figure was just a young man bent over a tin can of ham, scooping it into an old china dish for the little black dog who wagged his tail impatiently.

A floorboard creaked under my foot, and Edward looked up. He stood when he saw me, the spoon and tin can clattering to the floor. Sharkey nosed through them, oblivious to the tension between Edward and me.

"Juliet," Edward said. He still wore his clothes from the masquerade, though they hung slightly looser on him without the Beast's swollen muscles. The suit jacket was tossed on the bed, and he was only in shirt and vest, the gold chain of the pocket watch dangling from his pocket.

He shook his head, coming forward. "You shouldn't be here."

"This is my flat."

"It's too dangerous. *I'm* too dangerous."

"You said the Beast can't last more than two hours, and the party ended long ago." I came in and closed the door behind me. He didn't look happy about it, but he didn't protest. He stooped down to finish feeding Sharkey.

"That was true a week ago, but I've been so worried about you that he's taking advantage of my distracted mind. He can last three, four hours now. He could have still had control over me."

"Well, he didn't," I said, standing in the center of the room, hoping I sounded bolder than I felt. I stared at the tips of my slippers. "Do you remember what happened at the party tonight?"

Edward paused. "I have a few memories, but they're foggy. I remember mistletoe and red ribbon." He dropped his voice. "I remember your face."

It's my lips you want to feel, isn't it?

I paced in front of the window, pulling at the itchy lace of my shift. "The Beast attacked Mrs. Radcliffe."

He nodded. "I remember that, too, slightly. The smell of blood . . . well, it's very evocative."

"Why her?"

"The Beast is very protective of you," he said. "Lucy mentioned to me once how her mother snubbed you after your family lost their fortune, and the Beast must have kept it in mind." He paused. "It's my fault he was even able to emerge. I thought I had him under control, until I saw you with Montgomery in the garden. I'd gone to the party to apologize for what happened here the other day. But seeing you with him made me jealous, and it gave the Beast the weakness he was looking for."

His words stirred all manner of feelings within me. My chest felt tight with warring emotions, to see him here so handsome among the roses, and pity for Mrs. Radcliffe, and among it all, though I would certainly be damned for even thinking it, the faintest twinges of flattery that the Beast would go to such lengths for me.

I cleared my throat. "I came to tell you that Montgomery is hunting you tonight, but he doesn't know about this place. I didn't tell him."

He nodded. "Thank you."

"I did it as much for him as for you. If the two of you met right now, I fear someone would end up dead, perhaps you both. In any case, Montgomery isn't the worst of your worries. We overheard several members of the King's Club discussing you tonight. Father was corresponding with Mr. Radcliffe, but it seems the entire organization is involved. They know about you. Captain Claggan told them you were in London."

Edward looked away. "It was impossible to hide the Beast for that long at sea. He emerged on Claggan's ship and killed a few sailors. Claggan knew about Moreau's work—he must have deduced that I was a creation."

"Well, they're trying to catch you. I'm not certain what their plans are yet, but they mentioned specimens, and I found a brain, of all things, in Mr. Radcliffe's study. They said they needed to extract something from you. You can't let yourself be caught."

As he stepped closer, the golden flecks in his eyes caught in the light and almost glowed. He was Edward, but the Beast was bleeding through even now.

"Why are you warning me?" he asked.

A thousand reasons sprang to mind. That Edward and I weren't so different. That I was at least in part responsible for his existence and thus his crimes. Guilt that I'd made love to him and then turned to Montgomery.

"We can't afford for them to catch you," I said at last, because it was the one reason that stood out from the tangled knot of my emotions. "They want to use you to re-create Father's work."

My voice faded, and the only sounds were Sharkey eating the canned ham and the wood in the small stove cracking. The chair by the hearth still bore the shape of my body. This place was an extension of myself. A place where I could have my secrets, like the boy looking at me now with simmering desire in his eyes.

"Is that the only reason?" he asked. His words were heavy with an implied question: Was this about Father's research—or the undeniable bond between us?

"Juliet, I can't apologize enough."

"Then don't try," I said quickly. "It wasn't you anyway; it was the Beast." I heard myself saying the words, and they sounded true enough, yet part of me still wondered where the line between the two of them truly lay. "Now that Montgomery is back, I shall try to convince him to help, though lord knows it won't be an easy argument. He assisted Father with all the serums, so among the three of us, we'll discover the missing ingredient. But you must give me time. Right now, he's ready to sever your head if he sees you."

I turned to go but paused in the doorway and felt for a packet in my coat pocket. Sharkey barked, and Edward crouched down to rub his head. While his back was turned, I poured the packet of powdered valerian into his tea canister. I wished drugging him wasn't my only option; and yet the Beast had taken over twice before Edward could chain him, and at least one person was dead because of it. Could I forgive myself if the Beast got free and hurt someone else?

I turned to go.

"Wait!" He picked up Sharkey and held him out to me. "Take him. He won't leave my side, and I'm afraid one day soon I'll transform before he can get away. The last thing I want is more innocent blood on my hands." He paused. "I've grown quite fond of him."

I LEFT SHARKEY IN the professor's garden overnight with a bowl of beef stew. He was a street dog, so he was used to foraging, and I knew he could find his way back to Joyce in the market if he needed to. As soon as I'd crawled back into my own bed, my knuckles started to swell and stiffen, heralding the fit that had been threatening for days. My whole body seemed to lock up, wracked with chills, as a headache behind my left eye sent shooting pain throughout my head. It was worse than any fit I'd ever had. Amid hallucinations of three-toed footprints on my ceiling, I saw flashes of Montgomery injecting me with serums, and the professor's worried eyes peering at me over his spectacles, and even Lucy's face. But I couldn't be certain which of those were real, and which were figments of my troubled sleep. In my grogginess, my mind kept going back to Father's journal, the page that said fresh glycogen extracts were the most effective. But that meant animal vivisection, and the thought of strapping down Sharkey—or any living creature—made bitter bile crawl up my throat.

When I finally awoke, drenched in sweat and ignorant of what time it was or even the day of the week, Montgomery told me I'd been in and out of consciousness for three days. Over his shoulder I saw a fire burning in my bedroom's fireplace, stacked in his signature way. Our argument from the night my illness struck had left a rift between us, but not one so deep it couldn't be bridged in the face of desperate times. We loved each other, but he was right. Until Edward was no longer between us, we could never be together.

He commandeered the professor's dining room and spent the morning testing various serums in an effort to cure my illness, much to the perplexity of Elizabeth and the professor, who ate at the kitchen table instead. By afternoon tea my tongue was raw from swallowing pills, both arms were riddled with needle holes, and I felt decidedly uncured.

I rested my head on the dining room table, his make-shift examination space. "I told you, I've already tried all of Father's various formulas. They're practically the only things that make any sense in his journal, but none of them work."

The front door slammed, followed by a commotion in the hall. Montgomery and I hurried to the hallway, where a strange sight met us. Balthazar, cringing, held Lucy by one hand while she pummeled him with her handbag.

"Let go of me, you devil!" she cried, smashing the handbag against his ear.

"What on earth is going on?" I exclaimed.

"Found a girl snooping around the garden," Balthazar said.

"Oh, for heaven's sake, I was hardly snooping around," Lucy said. "I came to see if you had recovered yet, and this devil accosted me."

"Let her go, Balthazar," Montgomery said.

"You hear that?" Lucy snapped. "Unhand me!"

Balthazar's mouth folded in a frown, but he released her. She dusted off her jacket and cast an angry stare at him over her shoulder.

"You still look like death, Juliet," she observed. "But at least you're no longer raving about cutting dogs open. Now you can tell me why the devil I heard you're engaged. Elizabeth told Aunt Edith, and everyone is talking about it." She glanced pointedly at Montgomery, who backed away slowly and returned to his medical notations at the dining room table. I pulled Lucy into the foyer, but she kept straining to look back at Montgomery.

"That's him, isn't it?" She peeked back around the doorway. "Oh my, Juliet, he's quite handsome."

"The engagement isn't true. That's Montgomery James, the assistant I told you about. He followed Edward back to London and made up the engagement as justification for being alone with me while we figure out what the King's Club is planning."

Her face wrinkled in confusion and I paused, realizing she had no idea the danger spread beyond her father. I pulled her into the dining room, where Montgomery looked up from his work.

"Lucy knows everything, except what we learned the other night." I explained to her what we'd overheard her father and the other King's Men saying on the balcony.

"But why do they need Edward?" she asked, sounding worried.

"We aren't certain," Montgomery said.

"They spoke of extracting something from him to complete the rest of the specimens," I said, then paused, forgetting I was talking about slicing open the man she loved. "Whatever they're planning, it seems to culminate on New Year's Day."

Lucy sat straight up at this. "New Year's Day? And the King's Club is involved?"

I nodded, filled with an unsettling premonition. "Why, do you know something?"

"Papa's on the planning committee for the club's charitable activities. This year they're planning a paupers' ball for the city's poor. They're distributing warm meals and secondhand clothes. The crowd will fill Parliament Square." She paused. "It's scheduled for New Year's Day."

I exchanged an alarmed glance with Montgomery, who stood and paced to the window, deep in thought.

"What does it mean?" Lucy asked. "Is it a coincidence?"

"We don't know," I said. "At least not yet."

Lucy pulled over her handbag and drew out a thick set of keys, which she threw on the table. "Then let's find out. I stole these from Papa. I thought they might come in handy."

My eyes went big. "Lucy, if he finds out . . ."

"That's why we have to be fast. One of those unlocks the smoking room at King's College of Medical Research, where the King's Club holds their meetings. It should be empty tonight, since Papa left on business first thing this morning. I'll need to have the keys back in his desk by the time he comes home tomorrow, or he'll be furious."

"You want to investigate *tonight*?" I said.

"Juliet, this is my father. You have the luxury of knowing yours was insane. I can't sleep until I find out what the devil mine is up to."

I shook my head, reluctant to involve her. "How would we even get to the college? The professor watches me like a hawk now, especially after the attack at the masquerade."

"There's a lecture there this evening on women's role in household management," she said. "It's being held upstairs in the same building. Tell the professor we're attending. Montgomery can go as our driver."

Her idea wasn't a bad one, and I drummed my fingers, thinking. "I suppose I could feign a fainting spell halfway through the lecture. You could run and fetch Montgomery under the guise of taking me home . . ."

" . . . but we'd really sneak into the King's Club smoking room," Lucy finished.

"Absolutely not," Montgomery said, interrupting our scheming. He reached out and grabbed the keys. "It's far too dangerous. I'll go alone."

"To a *ladies'* lecture?" Lucy asked. "You might stand out, don't you think? Anyway, you haven't a clue what to look for once we're there. I'm the only one who's read the letters."

They stared each other down until at last Montgomery cursed under his breath and threw the keys back on the table.

"Very well. We go together." He glanced at me. "Now I understand why you're friends. I thought you were the most impossible woman in the world, but now I see there are two of you."

TWENTY-SIX

PRETENDING TO FEEL FAINT during the women's-role lecture wasn't difficult, especially in light of my recent illness. We sat in the university's mahogany-paneled lecture room amid a sea of straight-backed chairs filled with bored-looking ladies. The lecturer's drone might have put me to sleep, if I wasn't so jumpy from the knowledge of what we were planning to do. As he went on about tending to household tasks, it seemed perfectly natural to swoon and clutch the back of the chair in front of me and complain about the vapors. Lucy made a show of saying she'd fetch the driver, and soon returned with Montgomery. His handsome presence woke up a few nodding heads in the audience, but we were gone before the lecturer had even started in on the proper way to attend to a sick husband.

We raced down the marble staircase to the main floor. Lucy led us past the long line of framed photographs, including the one from 1875 where Father's young face watched me. She stopped at a locked door and pulled out her jangling key ring, but I held her back.

A finger to my lips, I pressed my ear to the door and listened for the sounds of voices within. Just because Lucy's father was out of town didn't mean the rest of the King's Club wasn't meeting, but the room behind the door was silent, and I gave her a nod.

She inserted a key emblazoned with the King's Club crest into the brass lock and opened the door cautiously. It was pitch-black inside save for the light from a few windows on the east wall. The scent of cigars was heavy in the room, though beneath it I detected a lingering trace of men's cologne, and another more earthy scent that made me think of Sharkey when I buried my face in his fur. I swallowed. Why would a smoking room smell like *animals*?

We entered cautiously, and Montgomery found a switch on the wall and flipped on the electric lights. I shaded my eyes from the sudden brightness.

Lucy let out a cry and I whirled around. A beast hovered on the wall next to her, tusks bared, black eyes glinting. She ducked behind a sofa as I let out a deep breath. It was a taxidermied boar, and it wasn't the only trophy. At least twenty mounted heads hung on the walls: bucks with nine-point antlers, lions with snarls frozen in time, bodiless zebras, and stuffed owls perched atop the upper bookcases.

"This can't be a good sign," Lucy muttered, backing away from the boar.

"Not necessarily," I said, studying the unblinking eyes of a stuffed squirrel on the table nearest me. "Plenty of people like taxidermy, and it doesn't mean anything. Even the professor keeps a stuffed bobcat in his study. A gift from some relative, I think."

"Well, I don't like it," Lucy said, shivering.

Montgomery had already gone to the bookshelves, and was now riffling through the leather-bound titles. Lucy occupied herself by inspecting the framed awards and diplomas on the walls. There were no cabinets, no desks or boxes where notes might be stored. The room was exactly as it appeared—an elegant, masculine space filled with leather club chairs and cigar humidors for a dozen or more men to lounge in while they bragged about their accomplishments.

I ran my hands along the seams of the walls and the grand fireplace for hidden compartments, but found nothing. There were more framed photographs on the walls, documenting the King's Club's history of charitable works. Photographs of the construction of the orphanage, and a framed royal decree dated 1855 thanking the members for their efforts to stop the cholera outbreak. Seeing their supposed good deeds hanging on the wall only turned my stomach. There was no telling what their *real* motives were. For all I knew, those poor orphans were destined for a terrible fate. After all, that brain in the hatbox had to come from somewhere.

After twenty minutes, we had searched every inch of the room and found nothing about the plans for the New Year's paupers' ball, or references to any kind of scientific experimentation they were funding.

"They must store their records elsewhere," Lucy said, flouncing onto a leather sofa.

I nodded. "Perhaps if we could get a copy made of the key, and come back to spy on them when they've a meeting in progress—"

But Montgomery cut me off with a quick signal. "Someone's coming," he whispered. "Into the hallway, quick." He flipped off the light, plunging us into darkness.

I found Lucy's hand, and we hurried through the doorway. I could hear footsteps coming but the hallways were like a maze, and the echoes of sound fooled the ear. Lucy had just enough time to slip the key into the lock before someone rounded the corner. It was a pair of men with a bull's-eye torch that shone directly onto us.

"Who's there?" one yelled.

I felt like a deer blinded by a hunter's lamp. Montgomery grabbed our hands and we raced away from them, but Montgomery didn't know these hallways. I did.

"This way," I said, rounding a corner that led to a staircase into the basement. The professors often left one of the exterior doors down here unlocked from the inside. We hurried down the stairs, but the men pursued us. A shrill night guard's whistle echoed through the dark halls.

"Over here!" I whispered as loud as I dared to Montgomery and Lucy. The cadaver storage room was just around the corner, and from there it wasn't far to the exterior door. There were no windows here to break the darkness, and the only light came from our pursuers' torch as it flashed on the walls behind us.

At last we reached the exterior door. I threw myself against it, but it didn't budge. "Blast!" I said. "The one night they lock it from the outside."

Our pursuers were nearly upon us, so I felt the grooves and blocks of the wall until my hand connected with a doorknob. I threw it open, heedless of where it led.

The three of us stumbled down a narrow flight of stairs, black as death, which led even deeper to a level I hadn't known existed. The air was thick with mildew and an earthy smell not unlike the jungle. We huddled together at the base of the stairs, listening. The sounds of footsteps came overhead, but no one approached the door. We waited for what must have been ten minutes, though it felt like an eternity. My fingers felt the wall, but there were no electric light switches, nor gas lines, either.

"They must not have fitted this level with electric lights," I whispered.

The air sizzled as Lucy struck a match, throwing a dim light on the corridors. They were older than I even imagined, part of the original stone foundation. The ground was littered with the husks of dead insects and refuse, and I wasn't certain anyone had been down here in years until Lucy lowered the candle to reveal fresh footprints in the dust.

Montgomery bent down to pick up a broken candle, and while he and Lucy struggled to light the ancient thing, I wandered to a doorway at the end of the hall. I tugged on it—locked. I stooped to my knees to peek through the keyhole, but it was very dark within, not a single window. Yet in the pitch-black my ears caught a hint of a strange yet familiar sound, almost like rippling water. I leaned closer to the keyhole and nearly choked from the thick chemical smell.

"Over here," I called. "Someone's been here recently."

Montgomery tugged on the door. "Locked."

"Try your keys, Lucy," I said.

"These are Father's personal keys. The only one with the King's College crest is for the smoking room upstairs."

"We haven't many options."

To our surprise, the fourth key twisted in the lock. My stomach knotted with foreboding worries about why the King's Club would need a secret room so deep in the belly of the university.

Montgomery drew his pistol. "Stay behind me, just in case."

The door creaked open. We stepped inside, at first seeing only worktables and rows of cupboards in the flickering candlelight. But on the far wall, Lucy's candle reflected in what looked like mirrors. The smell grew stronger. In the faint light I began to make out the shapes of a half dozen identical glass tanks, which upon closer inspection were filled with a clear fluid. We exchanged uneasy glances. Lucy hung back, but I took a step closer to peer into the murky liquid.

"Juliet." Montgomery's voice came with a warning. "Not too close."

Something roughly the size of a large cat was suspended, unmoving and silent, in the liquid. As my eyes adjusted to the low light, I could make out the vague shape of a half-formed creature not unlike a large rodent with only a hint of limbs. It was hairless from the tip of its jaw to the suggestion of a curling tail. The mouth was further developed than the rest of the body, powerful and wide like a reptile with a gleaming set of teeth.

Recognition dawned on me. "They're the creatures from the island. Father's ratlike creatures, only much bigger."

Montgomery came to peer within the murky liquid. "It's your father's design, for certain," he confirmed. "Although I've never seen one created in this fashion. They haven't been stitched together. It's as though they're growing them here, made from various animal components, using these tanks as artificial wombs. Rat and opossum, I would guess, given their physical traits, with something to account for their large size."

Memories returned to me of a glass jar in Father's laboratory, a strange living thing pulsing in the liquid. Was that what Father had been doing with those glass jars I'd smashed on the island? Could this be how he'd created *Edward*? My stomach shrank to think of Edward in a tank like this; he was too real for such things, too much a person like me.

"There's more!" Lucy said. She shone the candle against the opposite wall, which had a dozen more half-formed creatures in tanks.

"What *are* these things?" she asked.

"Experiments," I said, glancing at Montgomery. "This is where the King's Club does their experiments. They've already begun." The horror of it crashed into me, and I leaned against the wall, afraid I'd be sick. Lucy's face had gone white as the walls.

Desperate to know why, I grabbed the candle from

Lucy's hand and went to the cabinets lining the walls. A stack of journals sat on one end with a bundle of loose notes. Flipping through the pages, I recognized Father's precise handwriting. *This* was the research he'd sent, in exchange for them funding his expenses and supplies. I pored over it quickly, but as well trained in anatomy and physiology as I was, I understood little of it. Highly detailed explanations of cellular replacement and something Father kept referring to as "hereditary transmutational factors," with complex pen-and-ink blueprints of the water tanks and creatures within.

"See if you can make some sense of this," I said, handing the pages to Montgomery, who took them and pored over them with careful attention. I started in on the notebooks, which were all in the same hand, but not Father's. I called Lucy over, who said it wasn't her father's handwriting, either. The notebooks contained dated records of the writer's experimentation. The most recent was on top, the latest entry just this morning. I read it with stilled breath.

DECEMBER 22, 1895, 7:10 AM.

Provided the specimens with a nutrient-rich compound. Rate of growth is 29/38, even faster than we had anticipated. By all projections, specimens will be full-grown within one week of receiving the cerebrospinal fluid replacement. With an estimated 200 ml of cerebrospinal fluid from the host, we will have enough for a minimum of 100 cellular replacement therapy procedures.

I let the notebook tumble from my fingers as I turned to study the half-formed creatures in the water tanks. This wasn't the vivisection I had witnessed in Father's laboratory. This was something new, the procedure he'd designed to create Edward. And now they just needed Edward's spinal fluid—the host—to finalize their development and bring them to awareness.

I turned to the others. "Father's letters outline blueprints for these tanks and the fluids to use and how to grow the creatures. But his letters can only take them so far. It's one thing to build a body, quite another to give it life. For that they need Edward and the transmutational code in his spinal fluid. If they can insert that code into the host bodies, they'll replicate and make life possible."

Lucy put a hand over her mouth.

I flipped back through the notebook and saw that the attending biochemist came twice a day, morning and evening. All the evening entries were dated between eight o'clock and eight-thirty at night.

"Montgomery, what time is it?" I asked quickly.

He drew a watch from his vest pocket. "Ten till eight."

"The King's Club's medical officer will be back soon. He can't find us here." I replaced the notebook in a hurry and arranged the stacks to give no sign that we'd been there. "It's time we told the professor about this. He knows these men. He can give us information."

We locked the door behind us and climbed the stairs back to the basement level. Whoever had been pursuing us was long gone, and only silence echoed in the hallways.

We climbed up yet another flight of stairs to the main floor, where the lecture hall was just emptying of sleepy-eyed ladies, and we joined the crowd headed back out into the dark evening. Montgomery helped us into the carriage before climbing into the driver's seat outside.

Once we were safely alone in the carriage, Lucy leaned forward. "You said they need something within Edward's body," she whispered in a trembling voice. "Does that mean they'll have to kill him?"

I was glad the carriage was dark enough to hide her face. "I believe so, yes."

We were silent the rest of the way to Lucy's house, where we dropped her off with plans to meet tomorrow. Alone in the carriage, I worked through what I'd tell the professor. Perhaps it had been a mistake not to tell him sooner; he'd exposed my father's crimes because it had been the right thing to do, and I knew he would do what was right now, too. He was a quiet old dog, but he could bite when provoked. Elizabeth would make us her licorice tea, and the professor would dig up some cold meats from supper, and we'd come up with a plan and have a good night's sleep for once.

At the professor's street, Montgomery stopped the carriage up short in front of the neighbor's house. I didn't understand why until I climbed out and saw another carriage already blocking the professor's front gate.

A heavyset horse with a cropped dark mane stamped its feet beside a constable. I caught sight of Elizabeth on the front steps, talking to another police officer. The front door was open, spilling warm light into the night shadows and over her face and hair. At the sound of my footsteps, she turned.

Tears streaked her face. She wore her housedress with an old coat of the professor's hastily pulled over it. The lecture had only run a little late, so I couldn't imagine we'd worried her. When she caught sight of me, she pressed a hand to her chest and stumbled down the steps.

"Juliet," she breathed. "Thank God you're home."

"I didn't mean to worry you."

Her hands pulled at my hair, reassuring herself that I was safe.

"Is the professor still awake?" I asked, swallowing back a feeling of foreboding. "I'd like to talk to him."

At the sound of his name, she sobbed harder and pulled me close. Over her shoulder, I saw the policemen shifting nervously, then noticed several more people inside the house.

All these men just because we were a little late?

"Oh, Juliet. The professor . . ."

My eyes fell on the broad side of the police carriage. It had bright white lettering painted over blackened wood, two words that seemed to sear themselves into my soul.

Police Morgue.

"The professor is dead," came her strangled voice. "He's been murdered."

TWENTY-SEVEN

THE POLICE HAD NOT yet moved the body. Dimly, I was aware of them explaining about a "crime scene" and a "murder investigation." Words that reduced the professor's life to pages in a report. It wasn't a crime scene; it was the professor's tidy little study where the cat liked to nap in the worn depression of his chair. He wasn't just another victim, as the police kept referring to him—he'd given me a life again. In time, he could have been the father I should have had.

As they explained the murder, Montgomery kept his arms tightly around me, as though he feared the news would make me slip away into nothing. Elizabeth shivered in the professor's oversized coat, despite the warmth in the house.

"I want to see him," I said.

"Oh, Juliet. I don't think that's a good idea," Elizabeth said. "I wish I hadn't seen. Coming home from supper at the ladies' club and walking into that study to find . . ." She turned away before her voice broke.

"I have to," I said.

Montgomery said nothing, just took my hand and exchanged a few words with the police, who followed us into the study. I recognized the shape of the professor's head, sitting like he always did in that chair. He was as cold and silent as the rest of the room.

Beneath the chair was a pool of blood.

I stumbled forward, one shaky step at a time, until I could see him. His wire-rim spectacles were missing, his eyes still open. His murderer hadn't touched his face, only left three deep slashes across his chest.

I turned away with a cry.

I thought of how the professor had made me tea once when I'd been ill, and how he loved to tinker over that old cuckoo clock with a plate of Mary's gingerbread.

"Don't look," Montgomery said. "It's better if you don't." Even his voice, normally so calm in the face of any crisis, sounded hollow.

"He's dead," I said, coiling my fists in Montgomery's rough shirt, anger sparking through the nerves of my muscles.

"I'm so sorry."

"He's *dead*, Montgomery! Heart clawed out, just like the rest . . ." I choked on the thought of the bodies in the morgue. I thought the Beast killed only those who had wronged me, but the professor had done nothing but provide for me, believe in my chance for a future, treat me as a father should treat a daughter. Those thoughts turned to the Beast's snarling lips as he'd held me down in my workshop, twisting Edward into a fiend before my very eyes.

I never should have forgotten what he really was.

"You *know* who did this," I hissed.

Footsteps sounded in the doorway. I looked up to find Inspector Newcastle, dressed in finery as though he'd been called away from a state supper. His copper breastplate was gone now, as was the revolver at his hip, and it made him look younger somehow. He paused in the doorway, exchanging a few low words with Elizabeth before taking in the body with the calm eyes of an inspector who had seen this sort of thing countless times.

"Miss Moreau. How sorry I am for your loss, and in such a manner . . ." He swallowed, looking for once unprepared. I doubted he'd had much practice speaking to ladies on Highbury Street about murder.

"I don't believe we've met," he said, stepping forward and extending his hand to Montgomery.

Montgomery introduced himself and added, "I'm Juliet's fiancé from Portsmouth. I've been staying here a few days."

Elizabeth cleared her throat and excused herself, though as she left the room she gave Montgomery a careful glance, her eyes settling on the bulge at his side where his revolver was holstered. She was a shrewd woman. Before the night was out, she'd want an explanation for why my supposed fiancé was carrying a pistol.

"I'll have to examine the body before we move it," Inspector Newcastle said. "Terribly sorry. It would be best if you weren't here for that, Miss Moreau." He raised his hand as though he might give my shoulder a reassuring pat, but Montgomery cleared his throat, and the inspector let his hand fall. "Perhaps you might stay, Mr. James, for a few questions."

Montgomery turned to me, a question in his eye. I nodded.

"I'll be in the kitchen," I said, and started to leave.

"You'll have to be questioned as well, I'm afraid, Miss Moreau," Newcastle said. "They've already taken Elizabeth's statement." But he must have seen the look on my face, because he quickly added, "I'll get what I need now from Mr. James, and you and I can speak later, at a more appropriate time."

I didn't answer, just slunk into the hallway. I heard the cuckoo clock squawk on the landing, then squawk twice more in quick succession, and looked up to find Elizabeth standing before the clock, winding it again and again to make the little wooden bird pop out so she could pet it as the professor used to do. It made my heart clench to see her so lonely, so lost, capturing this echo of his habits.

My dress shoes clacked too loud in the quiet room, so I kicked them off and walked in my stockings to the kitchen. I'd always felt comfortable there, between the roaring fire and Mary's herb box in the windowsill. But I stopped in the doorway. The two chairs at the kitchen table were already taken.

Balthazar sat in one. I'd been so distraught over the professor's death that I'd scarcely given him a thought since we came home. He kneaded his big hands together, mumbling soft reassurances.

In the other chair sat Sharkey. He must have slipped inside during the commotion. I realized that Balthazar wasn't just mumbling to himself; he was assuring the little dog that everything would be all right.

"Balthazar," I said, though my voice cracked.

He jumped up, lips moving as he awkwardly searched for words. "So sorry, miss," he said. "So sad, what happened." He gestured to Sharkey and added, "I'll put him out again, miss, if you like. Only he looked so cold outside those windows, I thought I'd just let him warm up a bit."

"It's fine." I stepped into the kitchen, where the stone floor froze my stocking feet. I picked up Sharkey and held him in my lap. I scratched the scruff of his neck and stared into the dying kitchen fire.

"His name is Sharkey," I said. It felt good to talk about anything other than the body upstairs. "He belongs to me, in a way. I never told the professor about him because I feared what he'd say. But now . . ." My voice trailed off. "Well, I can't imagine Elizabeth would deny me a comfort after what's happened, even if he does bring fleas into the house."

Balthazar nodded his agreement. "That's good, miss. No one should be alone. Not a girl. Not a dog, either."

At last I set Sharkey down and went upstairs to my room, where I locked the door and climbed onto my silk bedcover, then opened my journal to the page with the pressed white flower. I picked it up by the stem, afraid to touch the delicate dried petals. Edward had warned me that his transformations were coming more frequently and unpredictably. I had been so arrogant as to think I could cure him of an illness so insidious.

I replaced the flower and closed the journal angrily. If only I'd just told the professor everything, this might not have happened. He might not have been home alone, or opened the door for a stranger.

But it was too late.

I feared it was too late for Edward as well. Montgomery and I would find him. If we couldn't strangle the Beast out of him, if there was no way to separate the two, then I'd kill him myself.

The only thing I was certain of, as I went back downstairs, was that the beast inside Edward Prince would not have another chance to kill anyone I loved.

I WAS USED TO long, sleepless nights, but that was one of the longest of my life. The police removed the professor's body, and Mary came to clean the bloodstains on the floor, crying soft tears onto the parquet floor. It wasn't until the cuckoo clock sounded midnight that the house was ours again. Elizabeth made us a pot of licorice tea and we retired to the library—none of us wanted to be anywhere near the study with the reminder of the professor's unblinking eyes.

Elizabeth had changed into a simple white lace dress with a housecoat, elegant as always. The only clue to the night's horror was her hair, which now hung limp down her back, instead of in its usual curls. I thought of her petting the wooden cuckoo bird, and my heart clenched all over again.

"Well, drink," she said, as none of us took our cups.

"The man loved a good licorice tea. You're doing his memory a disservice by letting it go cold."

Montgomery cleared his throat and took a cup with the awkward manners of a former servant who wasn't used to being served himself. "Very grateful, madam." He'd pulled his hair back and unbuttoned his shirt a few buttons, and he looked quite possibly like the most handsome man I'd ever seen.

"Now that the professor is gone, your guardianship falls to me, Juliet." Elizabeth paused, as though there was something more she wished to say. But her eyes flashed to Balthazar in the corner, and she shook her head, changing her mind. "It's been a long night. We should all get as much sleep as we can."

She pressed her lips to my forehead and whispered a prayer I couldn't quite make out.

As soon as she was gone, I slumped in the chair, exhausted. Montgomery asked Balthazar to take Sharkey into the kitchen for a bowl of water, with a mind to sparing his friend the conversation I knew we were fated to have.

The fire crackled, and the room smelled like licorice, and all I could picture was blood.

"It was the Beast," I whispered.

Montgomery ran a hand over his face. "I know."

"He killed the *professor*, Montgomery. He has to be stopped."

"I've been scouring the city. He hasn't left a single track."

I swallowed. The Beast hadn't left a track because I'd

told Edward his previous room at the brothel wasn't safe and then warned him about Montgomery following him, and this was what my warning had gotten us—the professor, murdered.

"He was staying in a lodging house in Shoreditch, the attic room, for a time," I said softly. "Though you'll never find him there now; he wouldn't dare return after this, nor to the room he kept before. But I know how we can find him. Wait here." I ran upstairs and retrieved the pressed white flower from within my journal, then returned and set it on the tea table. "He leaves these flowers at his crime scenes. They're very rare; he must be getting them from somewhere."

Montgomery took the flower from the table, and my stomach cringed to see such a delicate thing in his big hands, afraid he'd crush it. My anguished heart didn't know what to make of all this. Edward had never betrayed me, and yet now I forsook him in cold blood. But what choice did we have?

I became aware of Montgomery watching me. His blue eyes held a strange sort of look, almost as though I was a stranger to him. He had only looked at me that way once before, when I had frantically climbed into the wagon on the island as the compound had burned—only seconds after I had helped kill my father. To this day, I still didn't know if he had seen how I'd helped Jaguar enter the laboratory.

That's when I realized the look in his eye was fear. He was afraid of the things I was capable of. He was afraid of *me*. My heart surged again in worry, and I bit my lip nearly hard enough to taste blood. Did he know my greatest secret? Had he seen what I'd done that night on the island?

Would he still love me if he did?

"We'll find out where the flower's from," he said carefully. "And then we'll do what needs to be done."

TWENTY-EIGHT

THE FLOWER SHOP WHERE I sold my grafted rosebushes was one of London's finest, owned by a Middle Eastern couple who imported their flowers from countries I'd scarcely even heard of. As I made my way toward Narayan Flowers & Wholesalers, I clutched my satchel with the journal inside. It had taken some time to convince Montgomery that instead of coming with me, he would better spend his time eavesdropping on the King's Club members.

I entered the flower shop, jumping as the bell tinkled above the glass door. A dark-skinned middle-aged woman in a bright orange scarf leaned over the counter. She held a broom in her hand as elegantly as a parasol's handle.

"Ah, Miss Moreau. How are those roses coming?" She set the broom aside and brushed clippings off the countertop, sending dancing pollen into the hazy morning sunlight. It smelled of summertime here, amid the flowers that watched from every corner with perfect and still attention.

"I hope to have a few more finished before New Year's,

Mrs. Narayan, but I actually came today to ask you a question. Do you know anything about tropical flowers?"

She gave me half a smile. "Where do you think we import most of these from?"

I took a hesitant step forward, clutching my journal through the satchel's stiff leather. I dared a glance at the street outside, nervous about revealing the flower, which by all rights should have been logged into Scotland Yard's evidence file.

"Would you take a look at a flower to see if you can identify it?" I asked.

"Of course. Let's see it," she said, nodding to the counter.

I slid the flower from my journal's pages and set it on the counter. "I'd like to know where one can buy them in town. It's quite important."

She stooped down, eyeing the flower closely. A tiny, feathered white seedpod drifted across the room to settle on my coat sleeve. I pressed it between my fingers as if it might grant a wish.

To find Edward, I wished on impulse. *To be wrong about him, and learn the professor's death was caused by something else, someone else. . . .*

It was a silly wish, and I let the seedpod fall on the floor.

Her drumming fingers stopped suddenly. When her eyes shot to mine, they no longer looked cheerful. "Where did you get this flower?" she asked.

I swallowed a lump in my throat. "I found it on the

street. I . . . thought it quite lovely and wanted to buy more."

She thrust the flower back at me. "It's called *Plumeria selva*. You won't find this flower for sale in any shop, not even the most exotic stores. It wouldn't last long enough out of water to import it, and it isn't valuable enough to grow in a commercial greenhouse." She spoke her next words very carefully. "Which is exactly what I told Scotland Yard, when they came around asking if we sold them."

She leaned forward, dropping her voice to a whisper. "You've read the newspapers, haven't you? That flower is the calling card of the Wolf of Whitechapel. If you found one in the street, it might be important to their investigation. You must turn it in to the police."

I stowed the flower back in my book. "Oh my. I'll head there straightaway," I lied. I slid the journal into my bag, but hesitated. "Just out of curiosity, if the murderer didn't purchase them from any shops in London, where do you think they came from?"

Mrs. Narayan picked up her broom again, fingers drumming on the handle, reluctant to dwell on such grisly topics. "He must grow them himself, though I have no idea why. Perhaps he lives outside the city with enough space for a hothouse or a winter garden. It would have to be someplace warm and humid, and even then he would have to be a master gardener to grow tropical flowers in England."

Edward certainly had no private hothouse, nor was he any type of gardener. *Somewhere hot and humid*, I thought, mind turning back to the island. It struck me then—the one place that always made me feel as though I was back on that sun-drenched slip of land.

The Royal Botanical greenhouse.

"Well." I gave her an unsteady nod. "I suppose I'd best be off to Scotland Yard."

I hurried from the store with my heart clanging as loud as the bell.

I rushed back to the professor's house, heart thumping at what I'd learned. The morning sky was clouding over with a threatening storm, and shoppers hurried past, anxious to be out of the weather and tucked near a warm fire with their loved ones, singing "Silent Night" and "We Three Kings."

When I arrived, I found Montgomery gone but Balthazar home, making licorice tea for Elizabeth, who sat in the library with an open book and those reading glasses that made her look so like her uncle. I stood in the doorway and observed her; she didn't turn a single page, just stared at the professor's old decanter.

"A man came by today," she said, surprising me, somehow sensing that I was there. "A historian by the name of Isambard Lessing."

I sat on the brocade sofa opposite her. "Was he after your family's journals again?" I asked.

Her head cocked as she regarded me strangely. "Journals?"

"He came to visit the professor several weeks ago, asking about the heirlooms and things."

Elizabeth raised an eyebrow. "Is that what the professor told you? No, my dear, that's not what Lessing was after at all. He was asking about *you*. I told him nothing, of course. Any interest an old man like him would have in a young girl can't be good."

I swallowed, uncertain what to make of this information. "What did he ask, exactly?"

"He wished to speak to you. Some nonsense about a trust the college had established in your father's name . . . not a word of it true, I'm sure. I can smell a liar. I don't even think history is his true profession." Her forehead wrinkled in worry. "You must be careful, Juliet."

The professor had lied to me, then. Lessing had come asking questions about me—on King's Club's orders, no doubt—and the professor had argued with him and then made up a lie about heirlooms so I wouldn't worry. One more thing the professor had done to improve my life, perhaps even save it, that I'd never be able to thank him for.

"Elizabeth—" I started, wanting to offer my condolences, but she cut me off.

"The funeral will be Thursday at Saint Paul's. That's where his grave plot is. He was well-known in this city; it'll be a grand affair." She wiped a thin hand over her face. "I wish I didn't have to attend. I know that sounds terrible, but all those people, all offering their condolences when they hardly knew him. . . . I don't know how I'll get through it."

From the corner of my eye I saw ghosts of movement in the doorway, and looked up to find Montgomery returned from his errand. His face was deeply lined.

I gave Elizabeth's hand a good squeeze, and then kissed her on the cheek just as tenderly as she'd kissed me the night before. "You won't be alone. I'll be with you."

She gave me the ghost of a smile.

I met Montgomery in the hallway, where he motioned for me to follow him into my bedroom and close the door.

"What did you discover?" I asked.

The heavy set to his features told me whatever he'd found wasn't good. He glanced toward the door and said, "Crates."

"Crates?"

"Railroad shipping crates. You recall that we overheard the King's Men mention Rochefort, the French ambassador, at the masquerade? I followed his carriage to Southhampton train station, where he met with Radcliffe and the stationmaster about constructing several dozen crates reinforced with steel beams. For automobile parts, they said, on a shipment to the French Ministry of Defense that Rochefort was negotiating for one week after New Year's Day."

I frowned. "That doesn't prove anything."

"They were drilling air holes in the crates, Juliet."

The realization hit me hard enough that I sank against the wall. "They're going to ship the creatures," I whispered, since the words were too terrible to voice aloud. "They're going to make the creatures and ship them to France—to the Ministry of Defense. . . ."

Montgomery nodded gravely. "All they need is Edward."

"We have to find him first," I said, fumbling in my satchel for the journal. "I showed the flower to Mrs. Narayan. I know where he's been getting the *Plumeria*—the Royal

Botanical greenhouse; it's the only place with the right climate. The professor used to take me to flower shows there on the weekends; the Beast must have followed me, and it reminded him of the island. It'll be closed now for Christmas week. The perfect place for Edward to hide out."

Church bells chimed, and I looked through the window to see the snow had started, soft flakes that fell over the holly branches, as a governess on the sidewalk struggled to get her three charges to stop catching them on their tongues.

"I'll go tonight," Montgomery said. "Balthazar and I."

"The Beast will never come if he knows you're there. We need some sort of enticement, while you observe from afar."

"What do you propose, a raw hunk of meat?" Montgomery asked wryly.

"Not meat." I hesitated. "Me."

Montgomery shook his head forcefully. "Absolutely not. You sound like Radcliffe, proposing to use yourself as bait."

"You know it's our best chance," I said. "We know he's been following me. We know he wants me; and there, where it's so much like the island, he won't be able to resist."

"But there's no guarantee Edward will show up as himself. There's a good chance he'll have transformed into the Beast."

"Then we'll be ready for either."

Montgomery paced, considering this, but shook his head. "He'll sense it's a trap. He'll smell Balthazar and me there."

"Not if you stand downwind, outside the glass. You can see right through the walls. I'll leave a door propped open, so you can rush in and capture him." For an instant I felt as though I were giving him orders in the same way Father used to, as though he were still a servant.

It's not like with Father, I thought. *Montgomery and I are partners in this.*

"And take him where?" Montgomery asked.

"Here. There's a stone cellar in the basement that is quite soundproof."

"What do we tell Elizabeth?"

"Whatever we must. It doesn't matter nearly as much as capturing Edward before they do. She's a strong woman. She'll be able to handle it."

"I still don't like it," Montgomery said.

I rubbed the delicate bones on the back of my hand, which had started to grind together of their own accord. It was a terrible time for my illness to be setting in, so soon after the last bout, which had laid me out for three days. "We don't have any other choices."

Montgomery paced, back and forth, and at last gave a curse. "When?"

I swallowed. "Tonight."

TWENTY-NINE

AT NIGHT, THE ROYAL Botanical greenhouse had lost its splendor. Sunlight no longer reflected off the thousands of glass panes. No glow of lanterns came from within. It was a fragile castle of shadows and frost, and it was the last place in the world I wanted to be.

I scaled the fence with my skirt hitched around my waist, as Montgomery and Balthazar circled the garden in the carriage to climb over from the opposite side. The row of stone gargoyles glowed white in the moonlight, sentry to the secrets within, as I raced through the gardens and pulled open the heavy door.

The warmth eased the stiffness from my joints. Boilers churned beneath my feet, pumping steam that obscured palms into dark lurking shapes. I heard nothing but the rustle of leaves, the babbling of the stream. I slid out the knife as sweat dripped down my temple.

The spiral staircase to the catwalk looked skeletal at night, a twisting iron hand reaching to the domed ceiling. I gripped the railing and started up the stairs, which swayed as I moved, and climbed onto the high catwalk that allowed me to see the entire greenhouse at once.

It was even warmer here, where the heat had risen. This high, I could look through the glass roof to see the lights of London. Somewhere out there Lucy dined with her parents, trying to hide the fact that she knew her father was a conspirator. Elizabeth slept soundly, unaware we'd snuck out of the house. Thousands of people who didn't deserve to die did thousands of normal things.

I kept walking until a splash of white far below caught my eye, and I paused. It was a grotto, tucked behind a spray of ground palms, hidden from view among the pathways.

I gripped the catwalk railing and peered closer. The grotto was blanketed with little white flowers—*Plumeria selva.*

I ran back down the spiral stairs, footsteps echoing in the cavernous glass room. I hurried along the stone paths and pushed through the colorful sprays of birds-of-paradise until the grotto opened before me. My breath caught.

I was standing in the middle of a bed of *Plumeria selva*, the source of all the blood-tinged flowers that had been the murderer's grisly calling card.

I had found the den of the Beast.

A twig snapped behind me. When I turned, Edward stood amid the palms.

THE EDWARD I KNEW was gone—slipping away like a fallen leaf taken by the babbling brook. But neither was the man in front of me the snarling monster who had clawed my shoulder. His eyes were cast with a yellowish tint, the hair on his arms darker. He was trapped somewhere between man and Beast, just as I was caught in my illness's icy grip.

"Edward," I whispered.

I glanced toward the glass wall, hoping for a glimpse of Montgomery. With luck he'd already be rushing for the door, ready to tackle Edward to the ground. Muscles rippling, Edward bent over to pick up heavy iron chains that made my stomach twist. I'd dreamed once of Edward freeing me from chains; now he was poised to trap me with them.

I raised the knife, but he shook his head.

"Don't," he said. "It's hard enough to keep him at bay, with him whispering in my ear. The transformations are quick now. If you threaten me, I won't be able to contain him."

"This is a trap, Edward," I whispered. "Montgomery will be here any moment."

"I know," he said calmly, to my surprise, and threw the chains across the brook, where they clattered at my feet. "The chains aren't for you. They're for me. I read the headlines about the professor's murder." He paused, seeming to war within himself. "When the Beast was killing people who had wronged you, it was easier to forgive his crimes. But I know now that he's grown too strong. I can't contain him myself any longer. Now hurry and chain me to that tree. I can't hold him off for long."

I stared at him, wondering if he could be believed. I

shrieked as he leaped over the brook with unnatural grace, afraid he was attacking, but he only pressed his back up against a palm tree.

"Hurry," he said.

I scrambled to my feet, fumbling to wrap the chain around him as tightly as I dared, though each time around he grunted, "Pull it tighter," until the links tore at his clothing. I secured the chains in place with the thick padlock I'd given him and looked into his eyes.

They shone with an ungodly glow.

"Now back away from me," he said, as his voice grew deeper. "And whatever you do, no matter what he tells you, don't unlock these chains."

I scrambled back to the grotto, falling among the flowers. Where was Montgomery? He should have been here by now. I had seen Edward transform before, once in Father's barn, and once in my attic, but this time, amid the palm trees and vines, it seemed even more savage. I looked on in horror as pain wracked him, as his swelling muscles strained to split the seams on his shirt. His nails turned black. His hair turned darker, grew longer.

I crawled backward, heart throbbing.

Edward's head hung, and for a moment all I could hear was him breathing, breathing.

Why didn't he speak?

"Edward?" I whispered. "Can you still hear me?"

The chains groaned under the restricted movements of his chest. I could smell him now, a mixture of sweat, the iron chains, and a deep earthy scent like tobacco smoke.

His head tilted up to reveal a pair of insidious yellow eyes.

"No, my love. Not Edward."

THIRTY

I JERKED MY HAND up, holding the knife as though it was an extension of my hand. I braced for him to lunge and tear at me with claws, but as my panic stretched and still no horror came, just the soft sound of his breath against the chains, I exhaled slowly.

I took a few cautious steps until I was within feet of him.

"You can't hurt me," I said. "You're chained, and I have a knife."

"How endearing that you think a knife can stop me."

It was the same voice from the masquerade, when he'd trapped me beneath the mistletoe and spoken from behind the red mask. A voice too human for such a devil, and yet it evoked the smell of the island, the feel of caves hidden behind waterfalls and beasts crawling through jungle leaves, and a little part of me longed to hear him speak again.

"If you could free yourself of those chains, you would

have by now," I said. "That padlock was designed to withstand a force far stronger than you."

I could almost feel his sinister grin. The boilers let out another burst of steam as sweat dripped down my face and soaked into my dress. At first his silence felt as though I had triumphed—I had the power here, the freedom, and he was trapped. Yet as the silence stretched, so did my uneasiness.

Where was Montgomery?

I went to the window and pressed my face against the frosted glass. Only darkness outside, not even the ring of lanterns around the frozen lake to give me comfort in the desolate night.

"Loosen these chains, my love. Only an inch. I can't breathe."

I winced at the memory of the bruises cut into Edward's chest and arms in such intricate patterns that they were almost beautiful. He'd have more bruises before the night was out, because of me this time.

I tightened my hold on the knife. "I can't."

"It's killing me."

"I don't care."

"It's killing him, too."

His gaze was keenly focused. I knew it was a trick, and a transparent one at that. But the body was still Edward's. The voice—certain words, certain expressions—rang as slightly familiar.

"I'm sorry," I stuttered. "You know I can't. Montgomery will be here any moment. Until then, it's better if you don't speak to me." I felt my cheeks burning and prayed he couldn't see in the dark. "Especially don't call me . . . by that name you use."

"What, *my love*?" I heard a strained bark of laughter. "But that's what you are. We're more alike than you want to admit."

"I hate everything about you."

"What you hate is what you are. An animal, just like me. Don't pretend like you've never imagined it—the thrill of the hunt. No chaperones, no silk stockings, nothing holding you back. Tearing through the city like we were back on that island, feeling your blood boil, your pulse race. You're jealous of my freedom. You said it yourself once."

"I've no desire to *kill*."

"I did you a favor. Don't tell me some part of you didn't delight to find them dead: Penderwick, Sir Danvers. You fantasized about hurting them after what they did to your family, didn't you?"

"Stop it," I snapped. "You can't pretend that what you're doing is for me. You *enjoy* murder." I shook my head. "There's no justification for that."

A sinister smile crossed his face. "Not even for your own father's murder?"

I drew in a quick breath, realizing I'd fallen into the trap of his words. When I had opened the door for Jaguar to kill Father, I had assumed Edward dead at the time. It had never occurred to me that he would know about what I'd done.

"Ah, seeing things differently now, are you, love? I know exactly what happened that night on the island. You thought me dead, but I was very much alive. I saw it with my own eyes. A girl aiding a monster to kill her own father. You did it to stop a greater evil from spreading. How is that any different from what I do?"

I could only stare at him, at a loss for words. I didn't like what he was suggesting—that he and I were the same. I hadn't killed my father because I'd hungered for blood, and yet the results were the same. What did motivation matter, when death was the result?

It was true that I hadn't regretted it for a moment.

My mind scrambled to piece together an argument, a justification, a rationale for why we were different, yet the only words I could manage were "What about the professor? He never did anything but help me!"

The Beast watched me closely, silent as the boilers let out another burst of steam. I saw a flicker in his otherwise penetrating eyes. "That one was not me, love."

"Of course it was you," I snapped. "I saw the body. I saw the wounds."

He cocked his head, still eyeing me with that strange, too-human look. He was lying to me. He had to be. He would say anything to get what he wanted.

"You killed him," I seethed. "Because you're out of control."

He raised an eyebrow at this. "Out of control? Yes, perhaps you are right. Nevertheless I didn't kill him. I wasn't anywhere near Highbury last night. Believe me or not, it's the truth."

I didn't dignify him with an answer. Instead I paced

among the ferns, mind fractured like a broken pane of glass, terrible memories of the professor's dead body coming back to me. I pulled at my itchy collar.

"You know it's unnatural," he said softly, his insidious voice working its way into my ear. "Dressing up in stiff clothes and pinching shoes that one can barely walk in. Making small talk about holiday decorations when terrible things are happening in the city. You've never felt a part of this world, have you? We weren't meant to live like this. We're a different breed. I've watched you working away in that secret room you call a workshop, though we both know what it really is—a laboratory, laid out exactly like your father's. I've seen you reading your father's journal for hours on end, barely stopping to breathe. What do you tell yourself—that you have no choice but to read it? That you don't enjoy reading through the scientific marvels he uncovered, how he revolutionized the world? Admit it. You *loved* reading it."

"I was looking for a cure," I whispered, though my lips were dry.

"Ah yes, the fabled cure. Don't you realize why you haven't cured yourself yet? Not because you can't—because you don't want to. You've always had that animal inside you, stirring, since you were an infant. It's been more of a friend to you than any of those girls who titter behind their fans in church. You're afraid that if you rid yourself of it, you'll be hollow. A shell of a person content to let the days pass in boredom and chores, never really feeling, never truly living. Not like how *I* live."

I could only stare at him. I wanted to tell myself there was no truth in what he was saying. I *desperately* wanted a cure—I'd die without one. Even now a stiffness spread up my arms to the pit of my elbow, and my head throbbed behind my left eye.

"Without a cure I'll go into a coma."

"Will you? You really have no idea what will happen, do you? All you have is your father's speculation, and we both know his arrogance was far greater than his actual talent." He grinned. "You're dying of curiosity—that's why some deep part of you is sabotaging any attempts for a cure. You're desperate to know what you'll become, and as far as Edward goes, let's just come out with the truth, shall we? You don't want to cure him, either, not deep down, because the one who fascinates you is *me*."

I tried to shake my head, but my neck had gone stiff.

"Montgomery," I whispered. "Montgomery will be here any moment."

"I even saw you eyeing that hideous little dog," he whispered as though I hadn't even spoken. "You were thinking about it, weren't you? Cutting him open, seeing what lay within."

"No!" I shook my head violently. "I would never."

"I'd wager your father made that same magnanimous claim a long time ago. You'll change your mind just as he did. Haven't you wondered why that fool Dr. Hastings isn't dead yet? I've saved him for you, my love. You've dreamed about repaying his cruelty for months, and I couldn't rob you of that joy. Consider him a gift."

I remembered Hastings accusing those two students at King's College of following him as a prank, and Edward telling me later the Beast had been stalking a doctor. It *had* been Hastings—and this is why the Beast hadn't killed him.

For me.

"Nothing you're saying is true," I spat. "We aren't anything alike, and the sooner Edward is rid of you, the better." I slapped my hand across his face, but he barely flinched. The chains rustled as he strained against them, jingling and clanking. To my horror, he pulled an arm free.

He grabbed my wrist before I could run.

The Beast smiled in the moonlight and dislocated his shoulder.

HIS BODY CONTORTED AS one by one the chains fell to the ground, unbroken. He didn't let go of my wrist for a moment.

I'd been wrong. I'd been so, so wrong.

"No!" I said, trying to pull away. "I put valerian in your tea only days ago; it should have lasted. And the padlock—you can't break it."

"Come, come, my love. You think I didn't know about the tea?" He leaned closer until I could feel his warm breath. "And the chains, well. I've always been able to free myself of the chains."

My hand went slack with shock. "But in the attic . . . you were contained. You didn't kill for days."

"Of course I did. I slipped my chains and hid the bodies so you wouldn't find out. Don't you see? It's all been for you."

"I didn't ask for any of this!" I pulled the knife from my boot and slashed across his arm with all my force. He barely flinched, nearly impossible to hurt, but I was able to pull away. I scrambled over rocks, splashing into the creek, but a hand closed over my ankle. I clawed at the dirt, grabbed for the plants, but it was useless. The Beast's hands found my calf, then my thigh, then my waist, and he spun me around, pinning me to the earth, laughing. *Laughing*, like this was a game.

Where was Montgomery?

His eyes glowed yellow. Edward's face, Edward's body, though it no longer belonged to him.

"Let me go!" I cried, but he dragged me to the center of the flowers with superhuman strength.

"You think we're not the same?" he said. "You think we don't belong together? I could have caught you a thousand times. I could have killed you, tasted your blood—and how badly I wanted to. I'm done being patient with you." He dug a knee against my thigh, and I cried out with pain. "Doesn't a monster deserve a chance at redemption?" he continued. "Doesn't a monster deserve a mate? You were so quick to help Edward, but what about me?"

I flexed my fingers behind my back, which were even now starting to pop and shift, triggered by his own transformation. "You're the monster, not Edward!"

"But you're a little monster too, aren't you?" His breath came hot on my face as he leaned closer to whisper. "If I'm to be punished, love, so should you."

"You're insane," I hissed. He'd crossed into madness,

into savagery. My only chance was the knife, but where was it? With my head pressed into the dirt, all I could see were the flowers, with their cloying aroma, their soft petals grating against my skin.

He ripped my dress along the shoulder seam, pulling it down over my arm. I could feel the bones in his hands shifting to make room for the claws that lay buried in his flesh, as my own body responded with its familiar symptoms and aches. It was his lips that found my skin first, kissing my neck, running his teeth over my shoulder as though he wanted to take a bite out of me. I tried to twist away, but he growled and pinned me harder.

"You taste so sweet," he whispered in my ear. "All the sweeter when you struggle."

He kissed me hard while one hand found the hem of my dress, drawing it up over my thigh. His fingers grazed the soft skin by my knee. Bones popped in the socket.

A sound like metal against metal came, and I realized his claws were emerging.

Sweat rolled off his forehead and onto mine. "One last chance, love. Say the word and I shall bring Hastings to you, and we can end him together, the pair of us as we are meant to be."

For a second an image flashed in my head of Hastings's dead body, blood trickling from a slit in his throat, and I was glad of it. *Hungry* for it. He'd caused me such misery, and what of the other girls he'd abused? Because I knew there must be others.

I was tempted, but I wasn't a fool. My hand closed over

a rock, my sweating fingers slick on its surface, as I gritted my teeth. Only one chance. Aim for the temple, aim to disorient.

I squeezed the rock as the Beast ran his claw down my cheek, drawing a line of blood, stinging me with pain.

"Well, love?"

Wind pushed against the windows, making the entire structure sway and creak. The Beast glanced up, which gave me just enough time to slam the rock into his temple, knocking him off me as his blood spilled on my dress.

At the same time, the world shattered in an explosion of glass.

THIRTY-ONE

I SCREAMED AND COVERED my head with my arms. Showers of glass rained onto the bed of flowers, clinking in the brook like terrifying music, just as a burst of steam formed a thick cloud around us.

Beside me, the Beast groaned and clutched his head. I glanced over just long enough to see the claws were gone; he was shrinking in size slowly, shifting back into human form.

An icy gust of wind ruffled my dress. I managed to sit, shaking, as frigid winter air poured in through a shattered glass panel next to the grotto. A man crouched in the middle of the glass, half hidden in fog, white shirt latticed with cuts on his arms and shoulders that already seeped blood.

"Montgomery!" I choked, crawling toward him over broken glass, heedless of the sharp pain in my palms and knees. He'd thrown *himself* through the glass.

"Juliet," he breathed, straining with the weight of his wounds. One hand held a pistol and the other a hunting knife, but he threw his bloody arms around me. "We were held up. A fire on Eastwick and all the roads shut down, blocked by police. We couldn't get the carriage through, so I came on foot as fast as I could. I feared I'd be too late."

"My God, you're bleeding everywhere."

"Did he hurt you?"

"No—I dazed him, at least for now." I pulled away, gasping at the sight of blood dripping down the crown of his head, glass still tangled in his hair. "We've got to get you to a doctor."

Montgomery shook his head. "Not before we finish with Edward."

"There are chains attached to that palm tree. He can't break through them, but he can dislocate his joints and free himself, so we'll have to take care."

I tripped on my torn skirt as we hurried with the chains. The Beast was fading back into what was left of Edward, though he moaned in pain.

"Let me handle him," Montgomery said. "Run outside and fetch Balthazar. By now he'll have found his way to the gate with the carriage. I can't carry the Beast by myself."

I started to turn toward the broken glass panel but paused. A cold blast of air pushed through my thin dress.

"Juliet, what are you waiting for? We must hurry."

I had once sworn that Edward Prince would not have another chance to kill anyone else I loved. I'd been so drunk on anger, right after the professor's death.

And yet.

I couldn't shake the Beast's words. *That one was not me,*

love. There had been no mirth on his face when he'd denied killing the professor.

It was madness, surely—but I actually almost believed him.

"You'll kill him once I go," I whispered.

Montgomery raised an eyebrow. When he didn't deny it, I grabbed a handful of his torn shirt. "Promise me you won't," I said.

"He was about to *kill* you. This is what we agreed to."

"Maybe he deserves to die, maybe he doesn't. Edward knew this was a trap but came anyway to turn himself in. He assumed his darker half had killed the professor, but the Beast swore he didn't do it. I know it's probably a lie, but I don't want it to end like this. I want to take him back to the professor's house and decide his fate there." At Montgomery's silence, I shook him again. "Promise me!"

"All right!" Montgomery dragged me toward the broken panel, one hand on his pistol. "You have my word." His eyes were angry, but they were honest.

I climbed over the tangling ferns and away from that terrible grotto of *Plumeria selva*. My skirt was in tatters; I'd lost a boot somewhere. As I ducked through the broken pane, my bare toes didn't even feel the cold—every sensation I had was fixated on the urgency of the moment. I darted across the bridge to where Balthazar waited by the gate.

"Come quickly," I said. "We need your help!"

Balthazar hitched the horses to a post and climbed the fence with surprising agility for a man of his size, and we raced back to the greenhouse. I smelled the traces of chloroform in the air and saw a rag tucked into Montgomery's pocket. One glance at Edward's slowly rising chest told me he was unconscious but still alive. Montgomery had managed to wind the chains in a pattern around his limbs so that no matter of shifting bones could set him free.

"Can you carry him?" Montgomery asked Balthazar, who nodded and slung Edward over his shoulder as though he was a sack of oats. All together we raced to the carriage, back into a city I'd never felt I belonged in, but that I greeted now as an old friend.

Balthazar climbed the fence and helped lift Edward's body over. Montgomery made a stirrup of his blood-soaked hands to help me scale the fence, and we both landed on the other side and climbed into the back of the carriage while Balthazar took the driver's seat. With a crack of the whip, we were off.

I looked around the carriage for some scrap of fabric and settled on one of the curtains, which I ripped down to stanch the bleeding on Montgomery's face.

"We don't have much time," I said. "You need medical attention, and there's no telling how long the chloroform will keep Edward sedated."

My own bleeding hands shook uncontrollably as I let out a single sob. Montgomery took the torn curtains from my hand. "It's all right," he said. "We got Edward before he could kill anyone else, and before the King's Club could get their hands on him. It's over."

I ran a hand over my face. "It's not over! They're

negotiating with the French military. Spending a fortune on shipping crates for the creatures. They aren't going to just give up."

His big hand smoothed my hair back. "For tonight, at least, it's over."

Before I knew it, his lips found mine. He tasted of blood and sweat, and it twisted my insides into sharp angles. Tears started down my face but he kissed them away, cupping my cheek, trailing rough fingers along the smooth skin of my neck.

"I was so afraid I'd be too late," he whispered into my hair. "I would have torn him apart if he'd hurt you."

I let my eyes sink closed so I could exist in this single instant. I'd had few moments in my life that felt so right. The last time I'd felt this way had been on the island, before I knew of Father's gruesome crimes, and I had thought we could be a family again. I'd been wrong then, naive. Surely I wasn't wrong now, too. . . .

I kissed him again, silencing those thoughts. I didn't want to think about Father, or Edward, or what would become of him. For months I'd dreamed of Montgomery, and he was here now, wrapping an arm around me as we rode in an exhausted silence. Every bone in my body ached, reminding me that I was just as cursed as Edward—though my affliction stayed buried deep beneath my skin.

It's a part of you now, the Beast had said. *What will you be without it?*

I pushed aside the curtain, focusing on the city outside, rows of storefronts with holiday wreaths, quiet streets spotted with snow, until at last we arrived at the professor's. I stumbled out of the carriage and pounded on the front door, while Balthazar and Montgomery dragged Edward, unconscious and chained, out of the back. I tried to run my stiff fingers through my hair, but it was useless. My dress was torn and covered in bloodstains; Elizabeth would instantly know we were in trouble.

And yet Elizabeth didn't answer. I pounded again, called her name, peered in the front window.

"She must be asleep," I called back to Montgomery. "I'll climb in through my window."

Once I was up the trellis and into the house, however, there was no sign of Elizabeth, only an eerie silence in the big dark rooms, and her keys missing from the front door.

I opened the door from the inside to allow them entrance. "She isn't home. She must have gone out."

"Fortunate for us," Montgomery said. He and Balthazar carried Edward into the foyer, then through the dining room, still set with silver finery, and into the kitchen. The basement doorway was low, the stairs narrow, and Balthazar had to step carefully not to miss a stair. At the bottom I twisted open the rusted cellar door. Balthazar carried Edward inside and I followed him, fumbling to unlock the chains.

"Are you mad?" Montgomery said. "Leave him chained."

"The chains will serve us better wrapped through those door handles to keep it closed," I said. "The only thing the professor ever imprisoned in here was vegetables, and they hardly required a lock." I handed the heavy chains back to Montgomery.

Edward's sleep was troubled. His head tilted to the side as his eyes fluttered behind his lids. A dried patch of blood clung to his temple from where I'd hit him. I brushed it off with the pad of my thumb. His skin burned with a deep fever.

"Juliet?" Montgomery asked.

I blinked and pulled my hand back. Montgomery helped me out and locked the root cellar behind me, testing the chains. I tossed one final glance through the barred window in the cellar door at Edward's bruised body, and something hitched in my chest.

Maybe I *was* fascinated by Father's research. Maybe I *did* think some of it brilliant. But the Beast was wrong when he said I didn't want to be cured and didn't want Edward cured. There was nothing in the world I wanted more than for both of us to be free of Father's curse.

Father had won in life; he wouldn't win in death.

THIRTY-TWO

WE CLIMBED THE STAIRS to the kitchen just as the cuckoo clock squawked that it was midnight. I looked around the quiet house, shivering at how empty it felt.

"We should try to find Elizabeth," I said. "She might have gone looking for me."

"It's a big city," Montgomery answered. "We'd have no hope of finding her. Best to stay here and wait for her to return." He stumbled slightly, and my eyes went to the glass still embedded in his skin, the web of cuts across his arms.

"First things first," I said. "You need sutures before you pass out on the floor. Come with me." I led him up the stairs to the professor's study and turned on the lamp. For a moment I expected to see the professor's body still there, the blood dripping onto the floor below, but it was empty now, save the cat. With my knee I gently nudged the cat out of the chair so Montgomery could sit. I sat on the edge of the desk, examining his wounds.

I found the professor's medical bag in the dusty old

cabinet, stacked atop the ancient journals and boxes, and placed it on the desk. With the soft lamplight and the cat winding between my feet, I felt safe for once—if only for a little while.

"You'll have to unbutton your shirt," I said softly.

He started at the cuffs, taking care with a glass shard embedded in the fabric, and then undid the buttons down the front of his chest. Wincing, he let me help him peel it away from his blood-soaked skin.

My breath caught at the sight of his chest—bloody, slashed, bruised. Not so very unlike Edward's bruises, in fact. I touched his shoulder softly, studying the cuts with a surgeon's eye, then grabbed a bottle of whiskey from the bookshelves. "You might want a swig of this before I start."

He took it gratefully as I arranged the handful of medical supplies I'd dug out of the professor's bag. Forceps. Sterile needle and thread. Tin pan.

As I picked up the forceps, I couldn't resist studying the pattern of his cuts. Wounds had always fascinated me. These were so smooth, perfectly sliced. A shame, really—straight cuts like these never healed as well as jagged ones.

He flinched as I touched the cold forceps to his forearm.

"Sorry," I said.

He brushed back a strand of blond hair. "It's fine. I just wish you'd let me clean that cut on your face first."

I touched my cheek, surprised to come away with my own blood on my fingertips. I'd felt so numb that I could hardly feel the scratch the Beast's claw had made.

"*I* didn't crash through a glass wall. My cheek can survive a few hours without soap and water." I examined the glass in his forearm and then carefully extracted it with the forceps.

Tactile work like this gave me pleasure. I could get lost in the routine and give my head a rest. I worked in silence, filling the tin tray, and then, once I was certain all the glass was removed, mopped the blood from his skin before coming back with thread to stitch the worst wounds.

It wasn't until I was nearly finished and a web of black stitch marks crisscrossed his arms that his unsteady voice, threatening to shatter, broke our silence. "I feared he would kill you, Juliet. I saw him through the glass attacking you, and it was like he was ripping out my own heart."

I shifted, needle and thread poised above the last cut. "I'm thankful you were there."

"I should have been there sooner. You took care of the Beast on your own. You're stronger than you realize."

I wasn't sure how to answer such tender words that made knots of my veins, so I punctured his skin with the needle. He didn't flinch. I made the stitch quickly, then another, then another. I blinked furiously with my head ducked, but a tear still found its way onto his skin.

Montgomery tilted my chin up gently, forehead creased in concern. "Why are you crying?"

I turned away, running the back of my hand over my wet cheeks. His chair creaked as he leaned closer, but I shrugged away from him and paced in the small space between the desk and the bookshelves, my emotions pulling me in too many directions.

"Tonight, before you came," I started, "I had the Beast chained against a tree. We spoke. The things he said about my father, and who I was . . . A part of me thinks he was right. There *is* something unnatural about me. I can feel it, deep inside. I don't care for the things other girls do. I'm curious about things I shouldn't be. I'm so fascinated by Father's research that I can hardly stop thinking about it. I feel like a monster for thinking that."

I squeezed my lips together as if that would help me hold in tears.

"It's your illness," Montgomery said after a pause. "It's getting worse, and your mind doesn't know how to handle it. It's causing these unnatural urges. Once you're cured, there'll be nothing abnormal about you."

I thought of the spasms, the dizzy spells, the hallucinations of beasts crawling through tall jungle grass. "Do you think so?"

"Of course I do. Do you truly believe I could love a monster?"

A sob caught in my throat. "That's just it. There are things you don't know about that last night on the island. Terrible things I've done."

"Shh," he said, running a hand through my hair. "The island is long behind us. I've made my peace with it, and so should you."

"You don't understand. That night, while you were packing the wagon, I lied to you. I said I was going back for my treatment, but I went to the laboratory instead. Father had locked himself inside. Jaguar was there—"

"Juliet," his soft voice came. "Let go of these night-mares."

I shook my head as memories came back faster: of blood-red paint bubbling under a burning door, Jaguar's tail flicking in the darkness.

"I killed him," I choked, turning toward the windows. "I opened the door for Jaguar. He might have been the one to do it, but I was just as responsible."

I faced Montgomery and the terrible penance I was due. He'd paid for his sins by staying behind for the beast-men he'd helped create. *This* was my due—admitting my guilt, telling him everything and resigning myself to what-ever fate he decided.

"Well?" I asked. "Do you still think me not a monster?"

He tucked a loose strand of my hair back tenderly. When I dared to look into his eyes, I was surprised to find them absent of any judgment. "I already knew, Juliet."

I swallowed. "What?"

"I saw what you did that night. It took me a long time to understand how you could do such a thing, and it frightened me, too, for a while. But I know you. I *love* you. You did it for the greater good. You see a chance for redemption in even the darkest beast." He tilted my chin up. "You're brilliant like your father, but you've none of his cruelty. I thought I might have lost you tonight, and I discovered there's noth-ing in the world that frightens me more. I want to always be with you."

He touched his lips to mine. "Marry me," he whispered.

My heart stopped. The world stopped.

I hadn't words. My thoughts seemed to diffuse through the room like the lamp's soft light.

Marry me.

I sank onto the windowsill before I could fall. I'd been half in love with Montgomery ever since I was a little girl and used to daydream about our quiet servant. But so much had changed. There'd been Edward, and Father, and an ocean between us.

At my stunned silence, he cleared his throat in a rare moment of shyness. "I had hoped to find some mistletoe, wait until Christmas, do this properly. . . ." He swallowed hard, fumbling in his pocket until his hand came out with a silver ring. "I know I said I wanted everything resolved about Edward, but it can't wait. My entire life I've wanted a family. My father's the only relation who might still be alive, and I'll never find him; I know that. But I can have this. You and me, our own family." His blue eyes, soft as the early-morning sky, found me. "I want to marry you."

My heart wrenched. Who was the man I loved, exactly: The childhood servant? The brilliant surgeon? The single-minded hunter? He was still so young, still unsure of his path in this world, just as I was.

"Juliet?"

My stomach felt hollow. I loved Montgomery, but we had both changed since the island. He'd been forced to slaughter all the beasts he'd once called friends, which had hardened him. Would marriage bring a little of his softness back? And would I make a good wife? I hadn't any domestic skills; I could barely sew a button. It was more than that, though. A wife had to surrender all her property and wages to her husband, had to seek his legal permission to sign a contract or, in some cases, even to travel alone. I trusted Montgomery, but I'd been wrong about men before. . . .

"Juliet, did you hear me?" His voice was heavy with concern.

I gave a jerk of a nod. It was all I could manage.

"Is that a yes?" he asked, as his face broke into a smile.

My lips parted as I started to contradict him. I had nodded to mean I'd heard him, nothing more. The question of marriage was something I couldn't answer so easily. Elizabeth had once told the professor marriage was a cage, and I wasn't certain I entirely disagreed.

I felt something cold on my finger and looked down to find him slipping the silver ring on my hand. My voice caught, still speechless, and he drew me into his arms and kissed my temple, my forehead, my cheek.

"I love you," he breathed.

I stared at the ring. Good lord, how could I contradict him now? Did I even want to? Marriage was logical for us. I loved him. I wanted him. I thought of him constantly. So why did a part of me feel like I was a runaway train headed for broken tracks?

I pressed a hand to my corset, wishing I could ease it just an inch. Maybe my fear was only because this had come so suddenly; I'd never doubted my feelings about him before, except for when he'd left me in the dinghy, but we'd put that behind us.

"I'm happy too," I said. His question had caught me by surprise, but I could make it work. Just because my own parents had been failures in marriage didn't mean I was doomed to repeat their mistakes. When I smiled, it was genuine. "Yes, I'll marry you."

My voice only trembled slightly, and it was easy to pass it off as girlish nerves.

His hand tentatively found mine, his thumb absently tracing circles around the silver ring.

"The easiest decision of my life," I whispered.

Though was it?

Montgomery's fingers intertwined with mine, still flexing restlessly. Slowly I realized that the source of his agitation no longer had anything to do with Edward; his eyes were drifting over my neckline, gliding over my curves. I had the wild notion that he wanted his hands to be touching all the places his eyes were.

He leaned in to brush his lips across my cheekbone. My pulse sped at his touch, as my mind drifted to being married and everything it meant . . . especially the things that married couples did, alone, things that I'd done in a heady rush with Edward but that I'd take my time about with Montgomery.

My pulse fluttered, a bird without wings. Why was I suddenly so shy around him? It wasn't as though we hadn't kissed, hadn't ever touched each other, and I was hardly innocent when it came to being with men. The house creaked and settled, reminding me that it was empty of servants and Elizabeth. Save for Edward locked in the basement and

Balthazar guarding him, it was just us.

I crossed to the door and shut it. Engaged to Montgomery James, with his heartbreaking blue eyes . . .

Montgomery pulled me to him and kissed me so hard the stitches reopened on his arms, and I had to set him down and stitch them up again, but he kept smiling and eventually I laughed too, despite my sins, despite his, despite knowing the King's Club would be coming for us soon, and he kept kissing me, and time ebbed away before the work was done.

"My future wife," he whispered against my cheek.

His smile only faded at the sound of footsteps on the stairs outside, followed by the sound of the study door thrown open. Elizabeth stood there, snow still caught in the web of her hair.

I gasped, wiping my face of his kisses.

"I was out looking for you," she said as she took in the scene with a deeply wrinkled brow. "Now please tell me where you have been, and why Mr. James is covered in stitches, and most importantly, who the young man is locked in my cellar."

THIRTY-THREE

ELIZABETH WAS THE CLOSEST thing to a mother I had.

The night that she had combed my hair and told me her memories of my parents had cemented a bond between us. A part of me longed to tell her about the proposal, yet Elizabeth already thought we *were* engaged, and judging by her face, she was far more concerned with immediate matters.

We followed her to the library, where she hung her coat by the door while Montgomery and I took our places uneasily on the sofa. My thoughts churned between the ring on my finger, the boy locked downstairs, and how we would possibly explain everything so that she wouldn't immediately send for the police.

"Mr. Balthazar retired for the evening," she said. "I found him guarding the basement door when I came home. You can imagine my surprise to find a man locked in the root cellar. I tried to question Mr. Balthazar, but the poor fellow was quite flummoxed by the whole thing, so I gave him one of the professor's sleep shirts and showed him to an upstairs bedroom." She knelt by the cold hearth, a strange expression on her face. "He changed his shirt in front of me. Not a modest one, your friend." Her eyes slid to mine. "And not like any human I've ever seen."

I hesitated. Elizabeth was clever—of course she would have realized, with her medical training, that there was something more than odd about Balthazar's deformities. But did she suspect his true nature? Like her uncle, she had been staunchly against Father's work, so I couldn't imagine what she would do if she knew we'd brought one of Father's walking experiments into her house and had another far more dangerous one locked in the basement.

"Balthazar's a good man. He's no risk to you, I promise," I said.

"And the man in the cellar?"

My silence was its own answer. She raised an eyebrow as she reached for a log for the fireplace. Montgomery protested and offered to build it for her, but she shot him a withering look.

"I'm quite capable of stacking firewood, Mr. James," she said, striking a match. "Now, I shall dismiss Mary and Ellis for the rest of the week. I think it best, given the fact you've kidnapped someone." She dusted her soot-blackened hands, then took her seat in a leather chair. "Which one of you would like to explain to me what's truly going on?"

Montgomery and I exchanged a glance. He shifted uncomfortably, never having been at ease around Elizabeth.

"Tell her as much as you see fit," he said to me. "I should check on Edward, anyway." He kissed my cheek before leaving us alone.

I knew I should speak, but there were too many things to say, and not enough words to convey them. From somewhere outside came the sound of harness bells as a carriage passed, and my head jerked toward the window. Such merriment didn't belong in this room, not now, with the conversation we faced.

In the end, Elizabeth spoke first. "My father—the professor's brother—enjoyed taxidermy. A foul hobby, for sure, but as a girl I idolized him. So I'd plug my nose against the smell and help him with the pelts. I know the difference between animal fur and human hair, Juliet, and your friend upstairs falls into the former category."

I swallowed. "Yes. I know."

Her voice dropped low, like the hearth's warmest flames. "He's one of your father's experiments, isn't he? You found your father on that island, and he hadn't stopped his work at all."

To hear it spoken aloud made it true all over again. My secret was out, but perhaps this was for the best. I'd regretted not telling the professor everything. I couldn't bear to have Elizabeth's death on my conscience, too. "I thought you would think it impossible."

Elizabeth reclined into the leather chair. "Unfortunately, I am all too familiar with the strange things in this world. I told you my family had skeletons in our closet, but I'm afraid it's more than just our illegitimate lineage. Our ancestors were half mad, and not all of them scrupulous. I've read accounts of their travels, and it's chilling." She leaned so close to the fire that I was surprised it didn't burn her face. "All along I suspected your father might succeed, which is why I turned him in."

Suddenly the small fire seemed to throw off far too much heat. I was on my feet without thinking. "*You* started the rumors?"

"Yes."

"I thought the professor had turned him in."

"The professor was the one to alert the police, yes," she said calmly. "But I was the one to start the rumors. You forget that I was friends with your mother. She was a sweet woman, but none too bright. She hadn't a clue what he was doing down there in the laboratory, but I figured it out rather quickly." She paused. "I apologize for what happened to you and your mother—it wasn't my intention that you would be left without resources."

I ran a broken fingernail along my lips, thinking. For so many years I'd thought I hated the men who had brought scandal upon my family, and yet all along it had been this one woman, who wasn't so different from me, who had betrayed him for the good of the world.

The same reason I'd helped kill him.

I went to the window. It was still dark of night, and the street below was quiet save for the wind ruffling the garlands. A light turned on in a downstairs window across the street, and I caught a glimpse of a man in a stocking cap heating milk on the stove. My stomach rumbled with more than just hunger.

"Before my father's blade, Balthazar began life as a bear and a dog," I said.

"And now you call him a man?" she asked.

Next door, the kitchen light extinguished. "I call him a friend," I said.

"And the young man downstairs? Is he a friend as well?"

"He was, once. Now I can't say *what* he is. Father developed a new procedure to change a creature's composition on a cellular level. He created Edward from a collection of animal parts and human blood, but the results were unpredictable. Edward is a man, but he's also a monster. It lives within his skin, quite literally." I paused. "He's the Wolf of Whitechapel."

Elizabeth sat straight up, eyes aflame. "The professor's *murderer*? Is that why you've brought him here, instead of to the police?" Her voice dropped. "Do you intend to murder him as some sort of revenge?"

I bit my lip. "I'll not deny he's a murderer. He admits to killing many of the Wolf's victims, but he claims he didn't kill the professor. It sounds mad, but I'm tempted to believe him."

The wind whistled down the chimney and made the fire flicker, and she didn't take her keen eyes off of me.

"We can't turn him over to the police," I continued. "There's an organization searching for him, and their plans are worse than anything Father ever imagined. They want to use him to create more creatures like him, which we think are destined for France's Ministry of Defense. I can only imagine what the military would want with those things. They're vicious, Elizabeth. Bloodthirsty."

Her eyes flickered in that cold way that told me nothing. "What organization?" she asked.

"They're called the King's Club. You've heard of them, I'm sure—the professor was a member, though briefly. They want to continue my father's experimentations, and they've already begun. We found a laboratory."

She leaned back, thinking. "The King's Club, involved in all this . . ."

"I know it's difficult to believe," I said.

"Oh, I never said that," she said dryly. "I never trusted a single one of those men, and neither did the professor, which is precisely why he left their ranks. Do you recall hearing about the cholera epidemic of 1854?"

I nodded, thinking back to the royal decree framed in the King's Club's smoking room. "The King's Men were involved in stopping it, if I recall," I said. "Part of their charitable work."

Elizabeth let out a harsh burst of laughter. "Charitable work? I hardly think so. If anyone benefited from the epidemic, it was the King's Men's own bank accounts. The city invested in a new system of waterworks and sewers for the city, and their companies produced all the granite and piping for that project. And I know for a fact that one of their members was a doctor of epidemiology."

I leaned closer. "Are you saying they *started* the epidemic for their own monetary gain?"

She shrugged a little stiffly. "There's no evidence, of course, but that's what the professor suspected." She leaned back, picking anxiously at her fingernails. "For the last few years they've sent representatives around to visit the professor, trying to get him to rejoin, pestering him about our ancestors' journals. I'm sure that's what the professor thought Isambard Lessing was after. He must have been shocked when Lessing mentioned your name instead."

I tilted my head, thinking of those journals stacked upstairs in the professor's study. "What's in those journals that they want so badly?" I asked.

Elizabeth followed my gaze. "The ones up there collecting dust are nothing but genealogical records. I have the rest of our family's history at the manor in Scotland, well hidden." She stood to stir the fire. Her movements had a practiced calm to them that suggested she wasn't a stranger to midnight surprises such as this. I wondered what exactly her life was like, in the wilds so far north. I suppose a woman living all alone had to be prepared for anything.

"We need your help," I said. "Your silence, nothing more. As long as Edward is locked in that cellar, he can't hurt anyone. We just have to develop a cure for his condition before the King's Club finds him."

"I can certainly offer you my silence," she said slowly. "And more than that. I've developed treatments before. I can help you cure him."

The look in her cold blue eyes had softened. I remembered her pressing her lips to my forehead like a mother to a child, and my heart clenched.

"You'd do that for us?" I whispered.

She came and sat beside me, touching my hand. "You're my ward now, Juliet. That means we're family. My uncle used to say nothing is more important than family."

I wasn't certain what to do with her words. Both my parents had been absent most of my life. I hadn't any siblings. All my relatives had cast me out. In the last year the word *family* had come only to mean betrayal, at least until Montgomery's marriage proposal. Now he would be my family, and I his. But a husband wasn't the same as a mother, or a father, or a brother. Elizabeth's words gave me hope for a bond like that again.

Tentatively, I squeezed her hand.

THE SKY WAS A thin, hazy gray as we trudged the short few blocks to the funeral at St. Matthew's Church. Thinking of all those strangers' faces and whispered rumors caused wracking tremors in my wrists, but I pulled on gloves and ignored the pain. I had promised Elizabeth.

The professor had been well-known, so I wasn't surprised to see a long line of fine carriages waiting to drop off attendees. I hadn't expected, however, the sprawling crowd pressed against the churchyard gates, sailors and vendors and all manner of people dressed in shabby winter coats, whispering hushed rumors into the cold morning air. Two or three wore cheap metal breastplates and clutched smeared newspapers.

They weren't there to mourn the professor, I realized with a sickening lurch. They had come to ogle the Wolf's latest violence. This was a circus to them. A heartless game.

Montgomery's hand tightened in mine.

"How could they?" I whispered fiercely as my joints twisted, angry as my heart. I would have cursed much louder if the crowd hadn't caught sight of us in our church finery and badgered us with probing questions. *Did you see the body, miss? Was there blood? Did ya see the flower?*

I felt at the point of screaming before Montgomery shoved past them to escort Elizabeth and me through the gate. She was the type to go quiet with rage, a dangerous sort. It wasn't until we were inside the palatial church with the doors firmly closed that color returned to her face.

"A travesty," she spat. "If it's the Wolf they want, it's the Wolf they deserve."

Inside, the crowd wasn't much better. Hundreds of faces turned at our entrance, all harshly kind, pitying smiles mixed with flickers of scandal in their eyes. *Whispers, whispers, whispers.* How they must have reveled in the fact that the madman's daughter was caught up in yet another horrific scandal.

At least one friendly face caught mine in the crowd: Lucy. She waved to me quietly from a pew near the front, where she sat with her parents and Inspector Newcastle. He nodded to me solemnly and then whispered something to Lucy, who looked at him in surprise and shook her head.

My heart twisted. Surely *they* weren't trading rumors too, were they?

Seats had been saved for the family of the victim in the front row, but I couldn't bear to sit that close to the casket.

Montgomery sat with me in the last row instead, where the preacher's voice was nothing but a hum, and curious faces kept twisting to look back at me, pretending they were adjusting their fine winter hats.

Those stolen looks ate away at me until I could no longer bear it. After half an hour, I mumbled something to Montgomery and made my way to a side door, twisting it open to a cloistered courtyard where I gulped fresh air. I stumbled into the snow in my Sunday shoes, weaving between the headstones of the church's graveyard.

No faces here, no whispering. Only a freshly dug plot.

My feet led me to it on their own, knees slumping in the dirt at the foot of his grave. The headstone was plain, unlike most of the others. A testament to his simple life.

Victor von Stein, it read, *1841–1895. Beloved father and friend.*

I supposed Elizabeth had come up with that phrasing, though if she was referring to me or the professor's son who had died long ago, I wasn't sure. The gaping hole awaited the casket. I dug my fingers into the freezing soil, wishing I could hold the professor's wrinkled old hands instead.

I'm sorry, Professor, I thought.

"My condolences, miss," a voice said behind me.

I whirled, having thought I was alone. A spindle-thin man wearing a canvas work jacket and a few days' unshaven beard leaned on a shovel, nodding toward the gravesite. "You must be family," he said. "You'd be surprised how often family comes out 'ere, needing a moment o' peace. Reckon he was a great man. Never seen a crowd like this."

He removed his cap in a stiff gesture.

"He was," I whispered. "Will you be the one to bury him?"

He nodded, the cap pressed to his chest, wisps of graying hair dancing in the wind.

I opened my purse and fished out a few coins. "Thank you, then," I said, holding out the coins.

He took them almost reluctantly. "Won't be nothing. The empty ones are easy."

"*Empty* ones?"

"Empty caskets, I mean. Cremated ones. Don't weigh an ounce, really." He paused. "Didn't you know, miss?"

Cremated? It made no sense that the professor's body had been burned. As next of kin, Elizabeth would have been the one to make that request, and though she had modern beliefs, there was no reason for her to have done something so blasphemous.

"Who gave that order?" I asked.

He scratched his ear. "Came straight from the police."

The *police*? My blood went cold. There was something very odd about this situation. Cremations were only done in rare cases, such as if the body had been plagued with disease. The professor's death had been violent, but his body was still intact and certainly not diseased. Why on earth would the police have ordered him cremated?

I mumbled my thanks to the gravedigger, who tipped his hat before shuffling through the snow.

The Beast's words returned to me: *I didn't kill him. Believe me or not, it's the truth.*

It was true that the professor's murder went against the Beast's twisted desire to protect me. And thinking back, where had the Wolf of Whitechapel's telltale flower been? A strange tingle began at the back of my spine.

If the Beast hadn't done it, who had?

"Juliet," Montgomery called.

I turned, watching him cross the courtyard toward me. Behind him Balthazar stood in the cloister with a constable in a police uniform. I dug my fingers into the earth to steady myself.

"Are you feeling well?" Montgomery asked. "You've been out here half an hour. The service is over."

I nodded, thoughts on the empty grave site.

Montgomery's voice dropped. "Inspector Newcastle wishes to speak with you. I tried to put him off—said you've been feeling unwell, and today of all days, right after the funeral . . . But he says he can't wait any longer for your statement. He's already stretched the law as much as he can."

I wet my parched lips. Scotland Yard was the last place I wanted to be right now. And yet, as the tickle grew up my spine, I realized Inspector Newcastle would have details of the professor's murder. He'd have the autopsy reports, investigation reports. He might be able to tell me why the professor had been cremated, and confirm that no flower had been left by the murderer.

"It's all right," I said. "I'll go."

"I'll come with you," he said. He led me past the professor's freshly dug grave, toward the waiting constable.

THIRTY-FOUR

Stepping through the front doors of Scotland Yard with the constable at one side reminded me of the last time I was here, months ago, handcuffed and sick and seething with anger at Dr. Hastings and a society that would let him accuse me when *he* was to blame.

"This way, miss," the constable said, motioning to a staircase. "I'm to take you to the inspector's office. The gentleman will have to wait here, I'm afraid."

Montgomery touched my back. "Will you be all right?"

"This is a police station. If I'm not safe here, god help us." I motioned him to the bench lining the chilly entryway hall. "I'm sure it won't take long; he only needs my statement." I didn't say how I wanted to feel out Newcastle cautiously, perhaps discover some new information about the professor's murder.

The staircase of Scotland Yard was made of marble that might once have been grand, but years of dragging feet had worn it through. The constable led me up three stories, where the freshly polished floor contrasted with the rest of the worn-out building. These must be the officers' offices, high above the riffraff.

The constable knocked on the last door, which swung open to reveal Newcastle in his copper breastplate and the black silk cravat he'd worn to the funeral. He dismissed the constable and gestured me in.

"Miss Moreau, I do apologize for this unforgivable inconvenience. I know you're grieving, and Elizabeth told me you've been unwell recently." He shepherded me into his office. "Some tea, perhaps? One of the constables swears by an herbal remedy for getting over illness. I could have some sent up."

I put a hand to my head, wishing he didn't speak so fast. "I'll be fine, but thank you." I sank into the wooden chair across from his desk.

His office was a bastion of academic learning. Bookshelves with stately tomes spanned the length, and two paintings hung on either side of his desk, one of London in the rain, the other of a Middle Eastern bazaar. I supposed the son of a shoe seller didn't have portraits of illustrious ancestors to hang on his walls.

I reminded myself that I would have to be very cautious. Newcastle wanted what was best for the city, but the King's Club was powerful, and an orphan girl making accusations against them would seem preposterous. It might even stir questions about my *own* background.

He took his place at the desk. "You're certain about the tea?"

"Yes, thank you."

He smiled sympathetically, drumming his fingers on the edge of his desk. I folded my arms self-consciously, waiting for him to start, so I could ask my own questions. My eyes fell on a daguerreotype of Lucy on his desk, in a silver frame that must be the most expensive item in the room. It made me smile, despite everything. At least she had someone who loved her, who would keep her safe.

"I didn't get a chance at the funeral to offer my condolences on the professor's passing," he said at last, easing back in his chair. "I understand he was quite gracious to take you in, with no living parents of your own. I found it curious that you insisted at the masquerade that your father had passed away, and yet there's been no obituary, no court records. . . ."

"I'd rather discuss the professor's murder. I'm sure you understand."

"Indeed," he said. He moved to the edge of his chair, producing a handkerchief from his coat pocket in case I needed to dab my eyes. I didn't take it. "I imagine his death affected you very much. I'm sorry for that. Especially at the hands of that monster."

I didn't answer, wondering if I dared to share my doubts with him. A glance at his desk revealed a thick brown file labeled WOLF OF WHITECHAPEL.

"Why don't you tell me what happened the night of the professor's murder," he said gently. "If you can manage."

I tried not to keep staring at the file I so desperately wanted to look into. "Montgomery James is an old friend—and my fiancé, though we haven't made a public announcement. He escorted Lucy and me to a lecture at the university. When he brought me home, that's when I saw the morgue carriage and learned of the murder."

He scribbled some notes on a pad, nodding solemnly. "Very good. Terribly sorry to make you come all this way today, of all days. But we've policies, you know."

I started. "You mean that's all you need from me?"

He nodded, setting down his pen. "Unless you wanted that tea?"

"No," I stuttered. Now was the time I was supposed to leave, and yet I still couldn't shake the feeling something about the professor's murder wasn't right.

"I wonder, Inspector," I asked slowly. "Do you have other leads on the case?"

"Oh, I'm quite certain the murderer is the Wolf of Whitechapel. The wounds were identical." He cocked his head. "Why, do you have cause to believe someone else might be responsible?"

I balled his handkerchief in my hand, thinking of the Beast chained in the greenhouse.

That one wasn't me, love.

"It struck me that there wasn't a flower left in the professor's study the night he was murdered. Strange, don't you think?"

He nodded, leaning back in his chair. "We've been looking into that, but it means nothing in and of itself. Perhaps the murderer ran out of flowers. Perhaps they all froze." He rubbed his chin. "You're very observant to have noticed."

"Well, it didn't occur to me until later." I hesitated. I might not like the police, but Inspector Newcastle had proven quite different from those constables who had arrested me so long ago at the hospital. He'd made his way to the top at such a young age through hard work and ambition. He had every reason to want to solve this case—a promotion, gratitude from an entire city, perhaps even a more favorable chance with Lucy.

My eyes traced over the books lining the shelves. Philosophy, journalism, forensics. If I told him that I suspected there might be another murderer, a monster even, would such a rational man believe me? The Beast had said he was innocent, but there was no way to verify that claim except by proving the identity of a second killer.

I tapped my boot against the floor, debating. Inspector Newcastle might think me mad. Or perhaps he might have the tools to help. . . .

"There might be another possibility," I said slowly.

Newcastle raised an eyebrow. I stood and paced in front of his bookshelf to help ease my nerves. "I'm afraid it will sound a bit far-fetched," I said.

He smiled. "You've no idea how many far-fetched theories I've heard of the Wolf's identity. A girl as observant as you, however, I am inclined to take a bit more seriously, unlike all those other blatherskites."

I froze at the word. *Blatherskite.* Not a common term, yet I'd heard it before. I remembered standing with Montgomery in Lucy's garden the night of the masquerade, eavesdropping on the King's Club members overhead. One of them had used that word.

I peered keenly at Newcastle. Perhaps it was a coincidence. Like the missing flower, it proved nothing. We had seen the roster of King's Club members, and Newcastle wasn't on it.

"Your theory, Miss Moreau?" he prompted kindly.

I gave him a second glance. He said he trusted my opinion, but what inspector would take seriously anything said by a seventeen-year-old girl? I bit my lip. Perhaps he was only humoring me because I was a friend of Lucy's. I sat down slowly, trying to make sense of it.

"Yes, my theory," I started. "It has to do with the missing flower, and why the professor was so unlike the other victims." My mouth felt dry, and I swallowed hard. Newcastle was watching me intently, seemingly patiently, though his fingers were drumming on his desk rather quickly.

Why would someone merely humoring a young woman listen so anxiously?

My eyes fell on the brown folder, and I looked closer. Unless I was mistaken, I had seen that handwriting before. I scooted closer, clearing my throat, using my illness as a reason to lean on his desk.

The particular slope to the l's, the flourish of the p's. Yes, it was quite familiar. I had seen it only days ago and remarked on it, but where?

The hidden laboratory in King's College, I realized. *The journals.*

My insides shrank. The handwriting was the same as that in the journals kept by the King's Club's scientist who monitored the water tanks. Inspector Newcastle was that scientist; he had to be. But how had he learned so much about biochemistry? I clenched my fist to keep it from shaking as I looked around the room, at the books, the paintings. The plaque over his desk said he majored in forensics. Forensics was the study both of criminal investigation *and* medicine. He wasn't just an inspector, then.

He was also a scientist.

The air in the room started to feel too thin. I did the calculations in my head as fast as I could—Inspector Newcastle was the right age to have been one of Father's students.

All of it came together in one terrible suspicion.

Was John Newcastle *one of them*?

I thought back to what I knew of him. When he'd caught me searching the cadaver room . . . hadn't the door he'd emerged from been the same one that led to the subbasement laboratory?

Newcastle regarded my silence strangely. I grabbed his handkerchief and dabbed at my eyes to cover my shock. Was this why he had asked me so many questions about Father? Why he was so ingratiating to me?

This entire time, he'd played me for a fool.

"I wonder if I might have a cup of that tea after all," I stuttered. "Thinking of the professor, I find myself quite weak all of a sudden."

I forced a few tears, which looked all the more convincing given how hard I was shaking.

"Certainly." Newcastle jumped up, thrown by the sight of a woman crying in his office. He opened the door.

"Marlowe? Where the devil did that man get to . . . One moment, Miss Moreau." His footsteps echoed in the hallway as he disappeared.

The minute he was gone, I practically crawled over his desk. I opened the folder and found pages of notes and letters, but nothing out of the ordinary. I searched through Newcastle's drawers frantically, finding more letters and journals, but none in Father's handwriting, none that spoke of an island or experimentation.

I heard a door closing downstairs and was about to return to my seat when my eyes settled on a familiar emblem printed on one of Newcastle's envelopes. An image of Prometheus bringing fire to mankind, writing in Latin encircling it.

Ex scientia vera. From knowledge, truth.

The motto of the King's Club—I recognized it from the old photograph hanging in the King's College hallways.

With trembling fingers I opened the letter, read the contents. An induction letter into the King's Club, pending certain unspecified achievements, to be announced and enacted upon in the new year.

I dropped the letter, stunned. It fell on a tin of tobacco and a handful of personal trinkets. Cuff links, a cigar clipper, an old pair of spectacles.

Trembling, I lifted the spectacles to the light. They were simple, well-worn, with wire rims that curved around the ear. There was a scratch on the left lens and a single drop of blood on the right.

They belonged to the professor.

I dropped them back into the drawer and slammed it shut, backing away from the desk as though it had singed my flesh.

There was only one reason Inspector Newcastle would have the professor's missing spectacles among his personal effects, not carefully catalogued in the evidence room as they should be: The Beast had been telling the truth. He hadn't killed the professor. Inspector Newcastle must have arranged for the professor's murder—or killed him himself, though I couldn't imagine it.

Either way, I was in the den of the enemy.

I flung open the office door, racing down the polished-wood floor. I nearly tripped on the stairs in my hurry to get back to Montgomery and tell him everything—that Newcastle was a King's Man, was Father's protégé, had framed Edward in what must have been a bid to get me to cooperate—but I ran into Newcastle himself coming up the stairs.

"Miss Moreau," he said, shocked to see me. "The tea will be up momentarily. Why are you—"

"I'm nauseous, I'm afraid," I stuttered. "It came upon me all of a sudden. We can continue this conversation later."

"You were going to tell me a theory."

"Oh, it was nothing. Excuse me." I pushed past him and stumbled down the rest of the stairs.

Montgomery rushed over when he saw the state I was in. I slipped my hand into his and stood on tiptoe to reach his ear.

"I was wrong about being safe here," I whispered. "We need to get out. *Now.*"

THIRTY-FIVE

I DIDN'T DARE EXPLAIN what had happened until we were safely within the walls of the professor's house. Elizabeth gave us a questioning glance when we entered, but I walked straight past her to the kitchen, where I threw open the door to the basement stairs and hurried down.

"Edward," I whispered. Through the bars in the cellar door I saw hints of a figure pacing back and forth. "Edward, I must speak with you."

The shadowy form moved closer until the light from the stairs spilled over the edges of his face. The eyes that met mine glowed unnaturally, like cats' eyes. I drew in a quick breath.

"Come to visit me, love?" the Beast asked.

"I need to speak to Edward."

"You'll be waiting a long time, then." From behind me came the sound of Montgomery's boots on the wooden stairs as he joined me by the cellar door. The Beast smiled slowly. "Ah, Moreau's hunting dog. I thought you would have gotten yourself killed by now. No bother; I'll remedy that soon enough. Now, why have you come to see me?"

My heart clanked in my chest like the rattling of chains. "It's about the professor's murder."

His eyes glowed brighter. "I told you already I wasn't responsible, and if you're here asking me more about the murder, it's because you know I was telling the truth." He cocked his head. "Let me guess. There was no flower left with the body, was there?"

"How did you know that?" I gasped.

The Beast threw his head back and laughed. "Those fools at Scotland Yard never did figure out where I got the flowers from. I know *I* didn't kill him, so whoever did wouldn't have left a flower." He studied us again, cold and calculating. "Let me out, and I'll help you find his real murderer."

"We don't need your help," Montgomery said. His words were so cold. I understood his anger, but where was that boy I had known, who knew the world wasn't black and white, who believed in second chances even for a man as ruthless as my father?

But the Beast wasn't focused on Montgomery. "Let me free, my love," he whispered. "I'll do what you cannot. I'll rip the true killer's heart out and get you your justice."

There was a purr to his voice, both alluring and dangerous, and it spoke to the parts of me that were like him: restless, prowling. He was close enough to reach through the bars, but he didn't. I had the sudden urge to touch his face instead, rough features that were so like Edward's but weren't.

Montgomery pulled me away from the door. "Come on. We'll get only lies from him."

I let him lead me up the stairs into the kitchen, though I couldn't quite tear my mind away from the haunted face behind that door.

The Beast was many things, but I didn't think a liar was one of them.

ELIZABETH WAS WAITING ANXIOUSLY for us in the kitchen. Balthazar had gone to bed, so we made tea and moved to the salon and I told her about what I'd discovered at Scotland Yard.

"Newcastle is part of the King's Club," I said. "He knew I was protecting Edward, so he framed him in hopes I'd turn against him and help the police catch him. I nearly did."

"The King's Club already used Juliet as bait at the masquerade," Montgomery added. "Now they're willing to commit murder. They aren't going to stop at anything until they have Edward. There's only one thing to do."

He meant kill Edward.

I studied his face to gauge how serious he was. I didn't like this side of him—the hardened hunter—yet at the same time I feared *I* had been the one to make him into this. I'd shattered his faith in my father, I'd brought about the regression of the beast-men, I'd made him face the terrible things he'd been doing with his own hands.

"No," I breathed. "We can't."

Elizabeth paced behind the sofa. Her jaw was clenched tight, but her hands were surprisingly steady. "Perhaps he's right, Juliet."

"It would be murder!"

"He's killed a dozen people!" Montgomery countered. "And twice that on the island. The fact that he didn't kill the professor hardly makes him innocent. Why are you so desperate to protect him?"

Because he protected me, I thought. *Because you weren't here, and he came back for me and in his own way tried to save me. Because the Beast was right when he said we weren't so different.*

"The professor gave me a second chance," I said. "He gave me a life when everyone else thought I was suitable only for prison. My hands aren't clean either, nor are yours. We owe it to Edward."

"If we open that cellar door, the Beast will go on a rampage."

"I'm not talking about setting him loose. I'm talking about curing him."

"We've tried—"

"And we'll keep trying!" I snapped. "There's a piece of Edward still in that body. I can feel it. We still have time. Father did this to him, don't you see? If Edward dies, Father wins."

Montgomery was looking at me strangely. "Is this about saving Edward?" he asked, voice suddenly dangerously quiet. "Or about besting your father at his own work?"

A strange feeling crept up my spine. Elizabeth's

eyes flickered to mine. Besting Father at his own work? I wanted to shake my head. To deny it. This was about giving Edward another chance. Giving *me* another chance. I'd always felt that our fates were intertwined, the beast in him not so unlike the animal in me. Both headed toward our own destruction; him lost to the Beast, me lost to my illness.

If there was no hope for Edward, what did that mean for me?

"This isn't about besting Father," I said in a tightly controlled voice. "This is about doing what is right. Give up if you want, but as long as there's still good in Edward, I will keep trying. If you kill him, know that you're killing a part of me, too."

I turned and hurried upstairs to my bedroom. I heard Montgomery calling my name, and Elizabeth's voice telling him to let me have some peace. I changed into my shift but couldn't stop pacing. I didn't want to be alone now, in that empty bedroom with a cold fireplace and stiff pillows. I wanted something simple, something that wouldn't twist and stab at me, a single moment of peace in this crashing time.

I went into the hall and looked toward the attic. My feet took me there, to the little bedroom Elizabeth had given Balthazar. I knocked softly, but no answer came. When I pushed open the door, I realized the room was a nursery, filled with small furniture and toys. I remember Mother having talked about the professor's wife, who had died years ago, not long after their young son.

In the little bed, Balthazar was curled like an infant with his long feet hanging off the end, a stiff doll on the floor by his side. He slept soundly; I didn't want to wake him. I pulled up a rocking chair and sat next to him, picking up the old doll. It must have been a hundred years old, well loved, stitched back together in the places where it had begun to fall apart over the years. I ran my finger down the perfect row of stitches, clearly made by a surgeon's hand. I could picture the professor lovingly patching the old doll for his son. I tucked it at the foot of the bed from where it had fallen.

The darkened room was eerie now with moonlight streaming through a gauzy curtain, landing on one of the old family portraits. This one of a boy, the nameplate lost, and I remembered the professor telling me that his son had died at the same age as one of their ancestors.

I rocked in the chair, in the room that had been left exactly as when the professor's son died, the ghosts of toys long covered in dust. A rocking horse, a wooden puppet theater, a set of blocks. I ran my fingers lightly over the roof of an old dollhouse, feeling sad for everything the professor had lost, sadder still that I could never tell him how much I'd cared. Montgomery wasn't the only one who longed for family.

I hadn't intended to stay long, but my body was heavy with exhaustion, and at some point I must have fallen asleep there by Balthazar's bedside. I dreamed I was standing in an island creek stained with blood, grass rustling as beast-men surrounded me on all sides.

When I woke, it was to a heavy arm shaking my shoulder. I jerked with a start and found Balthazar's face very close to mine.

"Something outside, miss," he said.

I pushed back the curtain in a hurry. It was snowing fast, as hard pellets clattered against the glass. I could barely make out a carriage on the street below, with a swinging lantern at the driver's seat.

Suddenly a pounding upon the front door shook the house. I let the curtain fall. It must be one of the small hours of the night, caught between midnight and dawn. Why would someone come at such an hour?

Balthazar gripped onto my arm. "Best to stay quiet, miss."

I heard someone on the stairs heading for the front door—Montgomery, from the heavy sound of the steps. The pounding came harder, along with voices I couldn't make out. I turned back to the window, squinting through the snow, to read the thick block letters on the side of the carriage.

Scotland Yard.

"Oh no. This can't be good," I muttered. "Come downstairs with me."

But he held my arm. "Wait, miss."

"Montgomery's down there," I whispered. "It might be Newcastle for all we know. He might try to arrest him."

But Balthazar's face was deeply wrinkled as he cocked his head, listening. His hearing was keen, but could he truly make out words from three stories down?

At last his lips folded in.

"It's you they've come for, miss."

More footsteps came from below, inside the house now, amid the sounds of arguments. My heartbeat sped. Five men at least, and then came a crash, and lighter footsteps on the stairs as Elizabeth must have rushed down to investigate.

I fumbled with the window, but this wasn't my bedroom with the broken lock. This one held fast. "I need your help, Balthazar!" I cried. He picked up the lock in his meaty hand, examined it, then fumbled through the dusty collection of toys until he found a stick horse, which he rammed against the lock until it broke. I pushed open the window as bitter-cold snow stung my face.

"Go downstairs," I urged him. "Help Montgomery and Elizabeth. I'll hide somewhere outside and come back when it's safe."

"Please take care, miss," he said, and pointed to my feet. "You haven't any shoes."

"I'll manage." I climbed out of the attic window, stomach shrinking at the four-story fall to the garden. A copper drain spout, ancient and corroded, clung to the exterior wall. I made my way down it carefully, freezing in only my shift. I slipped near the end and tumbled to the garden, landing in a pile of snow that broke my fall but left me with a terrible scrape on my shin. When I looked up, the lights were on in my bedroom. If I'd spent the night there instead of the nursery, they would have already caught me.

Cold bit at my bare limbs. Pain would come soon, and

then terrible numbness.

I scrambled to my feet. I would freeze in minutes without coat or boots, not enough time to race across town to my attic in Shoreditch. Perhaps not even time to make it to Lucy's in Cavendish Square, but I had no choice. I stamped through the snow toward the garden gate, eyes blinded by flurries.

Someone was waiting for me.

I felt his hands on me before I saw his face. The shock of it made me scramble and claw, but he had another man with him wearing leather driving gloves, and the two of them together were too strong. It wasn't until the lights from the house shone on his white hair that I recognized his terrible visage.

"You won't get away from me this time," Dr. Hastings said.

THIRTY-SIX

ANGER SEETHED IN ME. I had overpowered him once, and I could have done it again if not for the driver holding me. He had twelve inches on me, and I had no knife, no mortar scraper, nothing to give me an advantage.

"Put her in the carriage," Hastings said with no little relish. "And notify Newcastle that I've got her."

The driver shoved me in, despite how I scratched at his face and kicked at the soft parts of his body. I winced, shivering in nothing more than my shift, as I landed in the carriage. It rocked as Dr. Hastings climbed in after me and locked the door.

I scrambled to the opposite door—locked as well. Trapped. I pressed my back into the furthest corner, eyes wide. Dr. Hastings clutched a pistol.

"You know, I always detested von Stein, thinking himself so much smarter than the rest of us," he said. "Pity he isn't here to protect you anymore."

"Were you the one who sliced him apart?" I hissed.

"That honor wasn't mine, but no matter. Seeing you locked away for the rest of your life will please me well enough." He held the pistol unsteadily in his left hand, the one I had maimed. I couldn't see the scars in the dark carriage, but I knew they were there.

"Newcastle promised me a chance to dole out my *own* punishment. The courts can be so lenient sometimes. I'm a biblical man myself. An eye for an eye, isn't that how the expression goes?"

Anger seeped up my spine, vertebra by vertebra. I'd be damned before Dr. Hastings laid a hand on me again. I wished the Beast had clawed his heart out when he'd had the chance. Some people didn't deserve to live, and if that made me a monster, so be it.

He smiled in that thin-lipped way that showed the tip of his tongue.

"Now, now, Miss Moreau. *I've* the blade this time." He flicked open a knife, sliding closer until I could smell his spoiled-milk stench. The pistol's cold metal barrel pressed against the gooseflesh of my arm.

"Hold out that wrist of yours like a good girl. It's either a slice through the tendons of your hand, just as you did to me, or a bullet in the head. Your choice."

I could kick him, throw myself at him, yet he held the two weapons. As he reached the knife toward my wrist, there came the sound of a key turning hastily in the lock.

The carriage door swung open, and my hopes surged

until I recognized the familiar outline of Inspector Newcastle, his copper breastplate glinting in the moonlight.

"Another few moments, Inspector," Dr. Hastings said, "and I'll be done with her."

"You're done with her now," he said. He grabbed the doctor by his collar and dragged him onto the hard street. I could only stare, stunned and numb. Newcastle coming to my rescue was the last thing I'd anticipated.

He said a few words to the driver in reference to Dr. Hastings moaning on the sidewalk, then climbed in and shut the door. With a rumble, the carriage started moving.

"My apologies for exposing you to that vile man," Newcastle said, adjusting his shirt cuffs. "He was a necessary evil, I'm afraid. Without his statement we had no grounds to request a warrant." He paused. "Were you truly the one who mangled his hand like that? Quite impressive."

I tore at the door handle, trying to break the lock, but he hauled me away, pushing me onto the plush seat cushions across from him.

"Miss Moreau, calm yourself. I've no wish to hurt you. I desire only to speak."

"Is that why you've abducted me?"

"This isn't an abduction. It's an arrest, and I'm fully within my legal grounds. The case against you was dropped last year, but not the formal charges." He adjusted his copper breastplate. "With luck, we'll be able to reach an agreement that will keep you out of prison. In fact, I think you'll find that what I shall propose is exceedingly beneficial for both of us."

When I didn't respond, he smiled in an almost sad way and added, "I know you saw the spectacles. You left your fingerprint on one of the lenses. We have a copy of your fingerprints on file from your former arrest."

The carriage jostled as we left Belgravia's smooth pavement and moved onto a cobblestone street. Stately Street, perhaps, or the north end of Highbury. The heavy curtains hid the outside world.

"Who killed him?" I asked, deathly quiet.

Newcastle reached up to turn on the lantern as though he hadn't heard my question. He sat below the flame, hidden by its own flickering shadow, so all it accomplished was blinding me whenever I looked at it.

"You must be freezing. Take my coat." He shrugged out of his wool coat and extended it to me. As much as I wanted to throw the coat back in his face and demand an answer, my bare, damp limbs were shivering beyond my control. I wrapped the coat around me, hating having the smell of him so close.

"You haven't involved Lucy in this, have you?" I asked.

"It wasn't I who involved her, Miss Moreau, but you. I would never have put Lucy in any sort of danger."

"You can't expect me to believe you actually care about her." A man like him, so deceptive, was not the type to care about anything.

But he frowned in a sincere way. "I care about her a great deal. I'm in a business where I hear lies all day, Miss Moreau. You've no idea how I admire a young woman who says what she truly thinks, even if more often than not it's to express her poor opinion of me. It only makes me care for her all the more. If she suffers because of all this, it's on *your* hands."

"I had to warn her. Her own father is wrapped up in this."

"Miss Moreau, the entire *King's Club* is wrapped up in this." He smiled, teeth glinting in the shadows. "But you already suspected that, didn't you? When I heard you were back in London, I was curious to meet you. After we received word from Claggan that your father had died, all our hopes fell on you. I guessed you'd be clever. I'm delighted to find it's true."

He settled back into the seat and took out a pipe and tobacco from his breast pocket, which he packed delicately, as though we'd all the time in the world.

"You saw the laboratory, didn't you?" His exhale of pipe smoke filled the carriage. "The night guard caught a glimpse of a girl in the hallways. I found footprints the next day that were decidedly dainty for any of our members."

I considered lying. I considered not saying anything. I considered many things, including lunging for his throat. But in the end, my curiosity got the best of me.

"Yes, I saw it."

"I'm terribly interested to know how it compares to your father's laboratory, since you are one of the few people to have seen it."

"Father kept his things tidier."

He laughed at this, deep and rich. "Clever. You're a rare woman, Miss Moreau." The carriage jostled again as we returned to smooth pavement. He took another long, thoughtful puff on his pipe. "I was a student of his, you know. Forensics. He took me under his wing but never extended an invitation for anything social. He was a difficult man to get to know."

"Did you hire someone to kill the professor?" I interrupted. "Or was it one of your own?"

He reclined farther into the plump cushions, moving easily as the carriage swayed from side to side, more than content to let my question go unanswered. "A pity, to be certain, but the professor was an old man. His death was necessary; we knew you were sheltering Moreau's creation, and we thought the only way to flush him out was for you to turn on him—if, for example, you thought he'd murdered someone close to you."

"Yet your ruse didn't work, and now you've blood on your hands."

"Another necessary evil, I'm afraid."

"You have no idea what will happen if you bring those creatures in the tanks to life," I said. "You've seen what the Wolf can do. You think you will be able to control them, but you won't. They'll destroy this city."

When he only flicked the ashes of his pipe onto the carriage floor, the terrible truth suddenly dawned on me, all their plans for New Year's Day and the paupers' ball in Parliament Square.

"That's what you want, isn't it?" I whispered. "You *intend* to wreak havoc throughout the city. But why? For what possible purpose?"

"This isn't about creating chaos, Miss Moreau. It's about building something. Your father might have been a madman, but I assure you, I am quite sane. I've always seen the practical uses for your father's research, and I'm not alone."

"The French Ministry of Defense, you mean," I spat. "They're going to use them as biological weaponry, aren't they?"

He shrugged. "Weaponry is one possible application for Moreau's research, yes, and certainly what the French government is most interested in. This isn't limited to the French, though. We have an American research hospital that wants the technology for experimental procedures on baboon-kidney transplants. And a Dutch weaponry development company that wants to give its soldiers better eyesight and hearing with animal biological grafting. They've even discussed using it for communications—talking dogs that can sneak behind enemy lines, though that seems a bit fantastical to me. We even have a private individual in Germany, a baron, dying of heart failure. He's willing to pay half his fortune if we can prove pig-heart transplants are possible. Your father's science will revolutionize the world, Miss Moreau."

"You expect me to believe the King's Club is building monsters and murdering people out of *altruism*? So an old man can get a fresh heart?"

He raised an eyebrow. "Believe what you like. We aren't interested in the final ramifications, only in developing the mechanisms to make it possible. What the world chooses to do with the technology is its own business. Our plan is merely to perfect Moreau's science and then do what we do best: profit off it." He took another long draught from his pipe and let the smoke cloud between us. "Unfortunately, our potential buyers are skeptical. We need to demonstrate the technology's efficacy."

"The paupers' ball," I said. "You're going to let the beasts loose in a crowded square—" I did some calculations quickly. "Hundreds of people might die! Just so you can prove your point to some *buyers*? How are you going to explain it to the newspapers? You can hardly tell them what you've done."

He took another puff calmly. "Haven't you heard of the wild dog epidemic? Rumor is it's been such a harsh winter that they're coming into the city at night by the pack, looking for scraps or whatever they can sink their teeth into."

I stared at him speechlessly. *Wild dogs?* Would the public believe such a ridiculous story? But the King's Club controlled the *London Times*, among many other businesses, and Newcastle had influence over the police. They could publish whatever story they wanted.

"Montgomery found the shipping crates," I said, almost to myself as I thought through their plan. "You'll let the beasts loose on New Year's Day, let the blood flow for your awful demonstration, and then ship them to France."

He gave a casual shrug. "As I said, France is only the first. We've already started planning a second demonstration for the Dutch weaponry company. That one's more difficult. Involves human test subjects. Lessing's coordinating the planning stages, since he oversees the orphanage. All those children with no one to care what happens to them, you know."

I dug my fingers harder into the plush seat, squeezing my eyes closed. Elizabeth had guessed that Lessing wasn't truly a historian, and she'd been right.

"You're going to murder *children*," I said.

"No, no. We aren't totally heartless. They won't be killed, unless something goes wrong. In fact, I imagine those orphans will love having sharper hearing and better eyesight. The scars will heal, in time."

For a moment the carriage rumbled as we each silently assessed the other. He didn't look like the monster he was. He had the easy air of someone used to getting his way, but there was nothing of the dandy about him, as I'd first thought. Beneath the metal vest the sleeves of his cream-colored shirt showed hard lines of the muscles that took discipline to develop. And his eyes—as they searched me, looking for clues as well—had a fire to them.

"I arrested you tonight so that we might speak as equals," he said.

"*Equals?* A teenaged girl and Scotland Yard's finest detective?"

"We in the King's Club are modern thinkers. A woman could gain great power in our midst. The daughter of Henri Moreau would be highly respected. I'll even get rid of that fool Dr. Hastings for you. There aren't many places that can offer you all that."

I studied the lines of his face carefully. His mouth didn't twitch. Hand didn't scratch his nose. He was telling the truth—or at least one aspect of the truth.

He continued, "If you wish to influence our decisions regarding the future of your father's research, then join us. We would listen to what you have to say. And in turn, we might be able to convince you of some of the positive implications of your father's work. Don't be so quick to judge without first considering all the information. We've convinced many doubting men of the validity of what we're trying to accomplish."

He was quite serious. A Scotland Yard inspector offering me an official role in determining the fate of my father's research, amid the most powerful men in the greatest country in the world.

I couldn't deny there was something appealing about the offer. Women were relegated to the bedroom or the tea salon in this city. No positions of power, authority, influence. Elizabeth's fate told me that. A clever woman like her, interested in medicine, had been forced to live at the edges of the world to rule her own life.

But Newcastle was a fool if he thought I might ever be able to see the positive ramifications of Father's work. I knew the results of Father's work all too well, chained in the root cellar of the professor's house.

"The devil take you and your offer," I said.

His left eyebrow arched. "I must ask you to reconsider. The future of scientific achievement hangs in the balance."

The carriage hit another rut and we both jostled. One thing I was certain of: his words might be polite, but they were still a threat. Side with him or face a prison cell.

"My answer is the same," I said.

Newcastle rubbed his chin, considering my words. "I'm afraid I can't take no for an answer. All your talents would be lost behind bars, talents that are very useful to us. We're a partnership, you see; each of us has a role. The members of Parliament keep the government in support of our businesses. Men like Radcliffe fund operations and provide discreet transportation for our products. Arthur Kenney tailors the newspaper headlines to read just the way we want them to read."

"And your role in all of this?"

"To control the police force, of course. To hunt down Moreau's creation under the guise of an investigation for a mass murderer." He took one final puff of his pipe. "And some of the more distasteful tasks, I'm afraid. I'm the newest member—it was part of initiation."

"What was?"

He set his pipe down. "Murdering your guardian."

I cried out, lunging for his pipe with the intention to bash it through his nose into his brain. But he'd anticipated that, and held me back against the soft velvet seat.

"I admire your bravery, but I will need you to

reconsider. I would hate to kill such a pretty young thing. Lucy would be inconsolable."

I dug my nails into his fine velvet seat, ripping the fabric. "You're as mad as my father was!"

"I'm determined. There's a difference."

With a panicked whinny from one of the horses, the carriage jerked to a sudden halt.

I heard a scuffle outside, followed by a quick yell from the driver. The cab jolted, then rocked back and forth, the lantern flickered wildly. Newcastle was thrown against the opposite bench.

The door flew open.

"Balthazar!" I cried as his hulking figure filled the doorway. Newcastle's eyes went wide at the sight of him. That pause was all I needed for Balthazar to haul me, still wrapped in Newcastle's coat, out of the carriage. My bare feet touched frozen pavement, where Sharkey yipped with his tail wagging. Newcastle reached after me, but Balthazar caught his arm and wrenched him from the carriage, knocking his head cleanly against the door. The inspector slumped to the pavement next to the equally unconscious driver.

Balthazar pointed a meaty finger to Sharkey. "He followed you, then came back to the house. Montgomery didn't understand what he wanted, but I did."

"He led you to us."

"Yes," Balthazar said, bending down to pat the little bug-eyed dog. "Good dog."

"Indeed. I owe you both my thanks, but now we must

run," I said. "I've a place in Shoreditch that Newcastle doesn't know about. Will you take me there?"

Balthazar picked me up in Newcastle's thick coat, since I could hardly walk the frozen streets barefoot, and, with Sharkey trotting alongside us, carried me through the snow.

THIRTY-SEVEN

I HADN'T RETURNED TO my attic chamber since the night I warned Edward about the King's Club. Once there, I sent Balthazar back with Sharkey to tell Montgomery what had happened. I was left alone in the quiet room, only my memories for company. I used to long for solitude like this.

Without Edward or me here to care for them, the roses had wilted, filling the room with an earthy scent of sweet decay. The threadbare quilt was pooled on the dusty floor, and I knelt to shake it out and draw it around my frozen shoulders, then crawled into the bed still dressed in my shift, where for once I slept a dreamless sleep.

It couldn't have been more than an hour or two before a frantic knock woke me with a jolt. I was terrified until I heard Montgomery's voice. I threw open the door, and he pulled me into his arms.

"Balthazar told me what happened," he said. "I came immediately, and Balthazar, too. He's going to sleep on the landing downstairs, keeping guard." His cheek nuzzled my own. "I'll murder that bastard Newcastle myself."

I pulled him inside and closed the door. "It won't do any good. He isn't working alone. If you killed him, you'd have half the police force in London after you." I sat on the bed again, amid the traces of lingering warmth.

"Newcastle will likely send more officers to arrest you," Montgomery said. "Elizabeth has a plan to set it up so it appears you've fled. We'll sneak you back into the professor's house once it gets light."

"And Edward?"

"He was unconscious when I left. Exhausted from the transformations."

His eyes fell to the bed. With the sheets twisted in knots, it was all I could do not to think about that passionate night Edward and I had spent together. From the way Montgomery's hand balled into a fist, it seemed he was thinking the same.

"How long was he staying here?" he asked.

I fumbled with the corners of the quilt. "A week or two. It was before the masquerade." *Before you.* "He had better control of himself then." My fingers drifted to my shoulder, where the scratches had all but faded.

"I'd rather not think about that. Or about him." He sat on the bed, rubbing my shoulders through the quilt. "All I want is to be with you." He drew my hand to his lips and kissed the silver ring, sending my heart pounding.

It struck me that he and I would be alone the rest of the night, a time when anything could happen. We were engaged, after all. I knew that proper young ladies didn't sit in bed with brooding young men, even those they were engaged to, yet I had long ago stopped caring about society's opinion regarding my chastity.

I stood and went to the door, needing a moment to breathe, and double-checked the lock. I lingered there, resting my forehead against the door as I tried to get my trembling nerves under control.

When I turned around, Montgomery was bent over to unlace his heavy boots. His strong hands worked fast. His blond hair had strayed from its tie and fell over his eyes. By the time he finished and looked up at me through those fair strands, I was helpless.

I had made love to Edward in a rush and now regretted it. I didn't want the same to happen with Montgomery.

Blast regret, I thought.

I would have stumbled across the room to him if he hadn't stood first and dragged me back to the bed. My lips found his as I shrugged the quilt to the floor.

"Take off this shift," he whispered. "It smells of Newcastle's tobacco."

My hands fluttered to the lace tie. Was I supposed to act a certain way? Try to entice him? From the look of it, he didn't need any enticement. He looked ready to tear my shift off himself if my hands moved any slower.

I paused. As much as I wanted him, it still felt wrong like this. Too sudden. This was no desperate act of loneliness, not like before.

"Montgomery, I think . . ." But my words faded, breathless.

He circled my hips with his hands and pulled me onto the bed. I thought of all the things we should say to one another—asking permission to touch here or there, crawling under the sheet for modesty's sake, discuss the lengths we intended to take this. But as soon as his lips were on mine, those thoughts vanished. Words? I could barely think. All I could do was feel, and each one of my senses was so flooded that I doubted I could even manage that for much longer.

"I know what you're thinking," he whispered, surprising me. "We can wait until we are properly wed. I won't rush you. But I don't want to be away from you, Juliet, not now. Please."

I wasn't certain if I was relieved or not. Part of me longed to feel him; another part of me felt it was best to wait. As we kissed in my old wooden bed, I thought of how society said intimacy was supposed to be gentle, and quiet, and tender. There was nothing tender about the way Montgomery had his lips all over mine.

And yet he was true to his word; and so was I. I fell asleep in his arms, still dressed in my shift and he in his trousers, and for those few hours it didn't matter that I was being hunted by Scotland Yard; it didn't matter that my fate was as uncertain as Edward's; it didn't matter that I was parentless once more.

Montgomery and I had each other, and our love could survive anything.

WHEN I WOKE IN the morning, Montgomery was already packing my collection of scientific equipment into a crate to take back with us. "We should be able to sneak back into the professor's now," he said. "Balthazar's waiting outside."

I untangled my limbs from the old quilt and dressed slowly in a gown I'd left behind here, taking my time to notice all the little details of my attic I'd taken for granted: how the window let in warm rays of light, and how the woodstove looked like a squat old gnome.

"I'll never return here, I imagine," I said.

I let my fingers run over the bedpost, worn though it was, and trail along the cabinet where I'd stored the mint tea that had warmed my bones after many a long night's walk to get here. If I closed my eyes, I could pretend nothing had changed: Sharkey curled by the warm stove, pot of water ready to boil for tea, the old chair waiting for me.

The professor had given me everything a girl could desire—a sea of pillows, forests of silver candlesticks, mountains of books. So why did my heart clench at the thought of leaving this broken-down little room?

I glanced over my shoulder at Montgomery, who knew nothing of the war raging in my heart. He had told me that these odd tendencies were a symptom of my illness. Once I was cured, no longer would I have such strange sentiments.

I went to the worktable, where Montgomery tucked my canisters of phosphorous salts into the crate. My finger ran along the spine of Father's journal.

"That was your father's," Montgomery said in surprise.

The book found its way into my palm. I flipped open the cover carefully, tracing my hand down the worn paper. "I found it on the dinghy, among the other supplies. I assumed you'd put it there."

"If I did, it was by mistake. I was in such a rush to pack that night. May I see it?"

I surrendered it to him hesitantly. He handled it more roughly than I had, flipping through the pages haphazardly.

"Half of it doesn't make any sense," I said. "He used a personal shorthand I could never decipher."

"Yes, I recall. Although it wasn't shorthand; it was a code he'd developed. Blast if I could ever figure it out."

"If we could decipher it, it might say something about a cure for Edward." I paused. "Or for me."

The idea seemed to energize him. He flipped through pages of nonsensical letters and numbers strung together, smiling almost fondly. "Your father used to curse like the devil when he was writing in code. Rambling on about church and religion. He would curse the books in order. 'Goddamn Psalms! Blasted Proverbs! Cursed Ecclesiastes!'" He shook his head and closed the book, then stowed it in the crate and started to pack my burners.

I frowned and picked back up the book. "I don't recall Father being religious in the slightest. I can't imagine he would even spare a few words to curse it."

"He was insane, Juliet. Don't try to find logic in him."

But the words nagged at me. I flipped open the journal to the coded letters and numbers, imagining Father writing them, thinking of the books of the Bible. His interest hadn't been of a religious nature, so what use did he have for it?

A thought ruffled my mind like wind through dried leaves. "My god," I said, as my heart began to thump. "That's it. The Bible! He used a Bible cipher based on the books in the Bible because it's the one volume every King's Man would have in his home."

"A Bible cipher?"

"Yes—look at these letters and numbers. They're code for chapters and verses."

Montgomery squinted at the writing in Father's journal. "You may be right, but without a written key we'd have no place to start. It would take us ages to go through the books one by one and try to determine where he began."

"What would a key look like?"

"A grid of some fashion. A chart with the sixty-six books of the Bible and the corresponding—"

He stopped when he saw the look on my face.

"Lucy," I murmured. "Lucy's seen it. She read all the letters Father sent to Radcliffe, and she mentioned references to the books of the Bible. Father must have put his key in his letters." I couldn't hide my thrill at the prospect of decoding Father's secret journal pages.

"We can hardly just walk up to her front door," Montgomery said. "Newcastle knows we're on to him, and he'll have alerted the rest of the King's Club."

"Then we'll have to be a little more creative," I said, and peered through the window at the clock on Saint Paul's Church spire, which told me it was nearly ten in the morning. Balthazar was sitting on an old stone wall on the street below, tossing crumbs from his iced bun to the pigeons. I glanced at Montgomery. "How fast can we get to Grosvenor Square?"

THIRTY-EIGHT

ONCE MONTGOMERY AND I finished packing everything we needed for the serums, I locked the attic and left a note to my landlady that I wouldn't return, then let my fingers run one last time over the rough wood door that I'd never see again. Downstairs, we gathered Balthazar and hailed a cabriolet to take us to Grosvenor Square, one of the wealthier neighborhoods north of the Strand. I had the driver let us off by an ancient church's ivy-covered archway, where we could hide unnoticed.

I leaned close to Montgomery. "Lucy takes lessons three mornings a week at the Académie de Musique across the street. She finishes at half past ten and takes a carriage home from Lincoln Park. She'll have to pass this way. I was thinking Balthazar could help. . . ."

Montgomery gaped. "You mean to *abduct* her?"

"He's very gentle. I know from experience." I straightened and spoke louder. "Balthazar, we're picking up a friend of mine. You remember Lucy Radcliffe, don't you? I want to surprise her, so I'm going to need you to bring her here without making a sound. Can you do that and be very gentle?"

His head nodded enthusiastically.

We waited a few moments longer until a young woman in a dark green cloak with long dark curls emerged from the academy, violin case in hand.

"There she is," I said to Balthazar.

"Yes, miss." He faded into the shadows with surprising stealth. For a few moments Montgomery and I waited, watching from the ancient archway. Lucy sauntered along the sidewalk toward Lincoln Park, hardly suspecting a man was lying in wait for her behind the bushes.

I heard a muffled cry, followed by a rustling of branches. Montgomery and I darted to the far side of the churchyard just as they emerged from the snowy boughs. Balthazar's fist pressed hard around her mouth. She tore at his hand with her fingernails until she caught sight of me, and then her eyes went wide.

I waved Balthazar away. "That's good work. You can let her go now."

He stepped back and she gulped air, making angry little hisses. "Juliet, are you behind this abduction? My god—bravo, I suppose. I didn't think you had it in you." Her face fell. "I've been worried about you since the professor's death. Such a tragedy . . ."

The mention of his death brought a lump to my throat. "Thank you, truly. I'm sorry for abducting you like this, but I didn't dare come to your house, and I needed to make certain no one was following you." I bit my lip, dreading to tell her the rest. "I went to give my statement to Inspector Newcastle. I found a letter from the King's Club in his office."

Her lips parted. "The King's Club? In *John's* office?"

"I take it you didn't know he was a member."

She pressed a hand to her chest. "Of course I didn't!"

"It gets worse. I found the professor's spectacles in his desk, too." I took a deep breath. "Edward didn't kill the professor—Newcastle did, and framed Edward for it."

Her face went even whiter. She slumped against the wall in shock. "Good lord, are you certain?"

"He admitted as much to me."

"I always thought him a bit strange—but a *murderer*? I suppose if my own father could be wrapped up in this, anyone could be." Her jaw tightened, not pitying herself for a moment. "Did you abduct me to warn me of this?"

"Only in part. We have Father's journal, which might help us develop a cure for Edward, but it's written in code. The key is hidden in the letters he sent your father. We need you to find the letters and steal them."

I glanced at Balthazar, who was sitting calmly on the crooked back steps of the church, nudging a sluggish moth with his big forefinger toward a sugar cube he'd taken from his vest pocket.

"Papa's out of town for the rest of the week," she said. "And Mother hasn't gotten out of bed since the attack at the masquerade. Have your man flag us down a carriage, and I'll have the letters for you in a half hour."

* * *

LUCY WAS TRUE TO her word. We hadn't waited in the cabriolet more than twenty minutes before she reappeared at her
front door, walking briskly with a leather satchel tucked
under one arm. As soon as she was safely in the carriage and
Montgomery signaled to the driver to go, she let out a deep
sigh and tossed the satchel to me.

"I daresay I'm not cut out for all this," she said. "It's
one thing to sneak about when it's for a gentleman's kiss,
but letters from a madman, and my father caught up in all of
it . . . and that bloody brain is still in the hatbox!"

She rested a hand on her forehead as though she might
be faint.

"You've done incredibly well," I said.

"You have no idea what it's been like living in that
house, knowing what Papa is doing. Thank god he's gone for
the week. I wouldn't be able to face him without my stomach
turning. Whatever you all are planning, I hope it resolves
this. I suppose it will be prison for him, or banishment just
like your father. Mother will be crushed."

Balthazar leaned over and patted her hand reassur-
ingly. The color rose to her cheeks at this kind gesture. She
adjusted the cuffs of her dress and was silent for the rest of
the trip.

We arrived at the professor's around noon, and I
knew something was wrong the moment we crossed the
threshold. Elizabeth sat at the dining room table, polishing an ancient musket that must have been from the
sixteenth century. A bottle of gin sat beside her along with

a half-empty glass. Sharkey sat trembling at her feet.

I paused in the doorway. "Why do you have that musket, Elizabeth?" I asked.

She looked at us with half-wild eyes, then glanced toward the kitchen, where from this angle I could just make out the cellar door, closed now, with the buffet table pushed against it.

"Did something happen while we were away?" I asked hesitantly.

A second after I spoke a great crash came from downstairs strong enough to shake the house. Lucy shrieked, and I grabbed the table to steady myself.

Under the table, Sharkey trembled harder.

"He's been making a din like that all morning," Elizabeth said, throwing back the rest of her gin. "Raising the dead with his prowling about. I went down there earlier to check. . . ." Her face drained of color, and she returned to cleaning the old musket with renewed vigor. "Well, see for yourself, but I'd advise you to take a pistol just in case. And you needn't worry about Inspector Newcastle or the police. I gave them quite a story, and they'll be halfway to Dublin by now looking for you. It'll be at least a few days before they figure out the truth."

I set down the satchel. "I hope that will be enough time. We found a way to solve a code that Father used in his journals, and it might help us cure Edward."

Another loud crash sounded from downstairs, and Elizabeth started to refill her glass.

I glanced at Montgomery. "We'd better check on him."

He gave a single nod, and told Balthazar to help Elizabeth. Balthazar took a seat across from her happily, pulling a rag from his vest pocket with a flourish.

"Stay here too, Lucy," I said.

She shook her head violently. "I want to see him."

Montgomery turned to her before I could speak. "Miss Radcliffe, I've spent the better part of a year tracking the Beast. It isn't Edward down there now, I can assure you. His alternate personality won't care that you had him over for a lovely tea at your home. To him you'll be blood ready to be spilled. Nothing more."

Lucy's face paled, but she still stood tall. "I said I'm coming with you. I'm not afraid."

Montgomery stared at her until at last he sighed. "I did warn you, Miss Radcliffe."

With straining muscles, he pulled the buffet away from the cellar door. Old townhouses like the professor's had been built before gas lighting, so a system of makeshift pipes ran down the length of stairs, ending in a single gas bulb at the bottom. Its flame reflected on the heavy metal chains on the cellar door.

Footsteps sounded from within the cellar. *Tap-tap-tap.* A familiar sound that took me back to the island: claws on a stone floor.

"I'll go first," I said, though my voice came out thin. "He might turn wild with rage if he sees you, Montgomery. And Lucy, you stay back too."

Hesitantly, I took a step onto the creaking stairs. Montgomery and Lucy followed a few steps behind, treading as quietly as they dared. Halfway down Lucy stumbled and landed on a creaky stair that squealed like a wounded animal.

The footsteps behind the cellar door froze. I was only one step away and could peer within the barred window if I stood on my tiptoes. I leaned closer, breath half frozen in the abnormal silence.

"Edward?" I whispered. "Are you still there?"

There was nothing but silence, and then the scraping sound of claws on the stone floor. I stood higher on tiptoe.

Suddenly a jerk of the rug at my feet hurled me to the floor with a painful *crack*. I cried out as gnarled fingers reached from the inch-wide gap under the door to grasp my feet, pulling me closer. Montgomery slammed his boot into the Beast's hand, and I scrambled away.

A great howl came from within as the Beast hurled himself against the door, again and again, beating himself to a bloody mess. Was Edward still in that body, fighting against him?

"Lucy, fetch a candle," I gasped.

Lucy raced up the stairs as Montgomery helped me to my feet. The Beast's writhing made a terrible sound. I wanted to cover my ears. Lucy returned with one of the grand silver candlesticks from the dining room, but her fingers were shaking too much to light the match. I fumbled to do it while Montgomery rechecked the lock on the chains. I held the candle to the window, peering within.

A gasp came from my lips.

The Beast writhed on the floor, caught somewhere between man and creature in the midst of a transformation. He was doubled over in pain as claws slid into his bloody joints and then out again. His back buckled and strained as the two sides of him fought for control. In one instant he was the Beast, snarling and furious; in the next he was Edward, reaching out a hand toward me and trying to form words, and then back again.

"Montgomery, get a sedative!" I said. "And as much valerian as we have. He's going to rip himself apart unless we stop him."

Montgomery took the stairs two at a time, and I turned to Lucy, who was breathing so rapidly I thought she might burst.

"It'll be all right," I said.

"It won't be!" she cried. She ran upstairs, tripping on her skirt, tears streaking down her cheeks.

I'd been a fool to let her down here. Hearing about it was one thing, but watching the transformation happen was another. Lucy was infatuated with a different boy every week—why had I thought her love for Edward would stand up to seeing the truth of what he was?

Montgomery soon returned with a glass jar of chloroform and syringe of valerian. "We'll have to be quick," he said.

The growls from within the cellar came louder. Montgomery removed the chains from the door and handed me the syringe. "I'll hold him. You go for the neck."

I nodded, and he threw the door open.

The creature on the floor—Edward or the Beast, I knew not what to call it—was so tortured in its rapid transitions that it seemed hardly aware we were there. Montgomery threw himself upon it, pressing a chloroform-soaked rag to its mouth.

"Now, Juliet!" he cried.

I aimed for the neck, but the transformation made Edward's body shift and twist. At last I threw myself upon him, plunging the needle deep. His body shook like a death rattle; then he slumped unconscious, smelling thickly of blood and fever sweat.

"He'll be out for at least a few hours," Montgomery said, wiping his brow. He helped me up and his hand lingered on my waist, as though afraid to let me go. When we made our way back to the kitchen, Lucy wasn't there. I found her at last on the second floor landing, sitting on the top stair. She'd stopped crying, but the dazed look in her eye frightened me even more.

"He's all right now. We sedated him. Come into my room and let me clean your face," I said, pulling her up gently. My bedroom fire had gone out, but the air still held its lingering warmth. I sat her on the bed, wiping the dried tears from her cheeks, petting her head as gently as if she were a frightened little creature like Sharkey.

"Shh now," I soothed. "I know it's terrible to see."

She squeezed her eyes closed. "Oh, Juliet . . ."

"I won't let him hurt you, I swear."

"Hurt me?" she whispered. Her green eyes snapped to

mine. "It isn't me I'm worried about. It's *him* who's suffering. My god, to hear him cry out like that! He's in such pain. I can't bear it."

The soothing words I was poised to say next disappeared. I had assumed Lucy's tears came from fear of what she'd just seen. I wasn't sure how to understand what she was saying.

She was crying *for* him?

"Father's science made him into that monster," I said. "Montgomery and I are going to stop anyone from doing it ever again."

She let out a frustrated breath. "Don't you see, Juliet? Your father's science isn't the problem. Because of it Edward exists, and he has just as much humanity in him as any of us. You've had it all wrong. It's just like what you said at the flower show: 'It isn't about the sharpness of the blade, but the hand that holds it.' Science doesn't do good or ill by itself—it's the intention behind it. And your father's intention to create Edward was good." She stood up, brushing a hand over her dripping nose. "Blame your father for failing to rid Edward of his darkness, if you must. But don't blame him for *creating* Edward. Edward isn't a mistake."

I could only stare at her, at a loss for words.

So much of my life had been about rejecting Father's work and castigating myself for my curiosity. And yet here was my best friend telling me that Edward's existence was a gift. Could there be a grain of truth to that? Perhaps not entirely a gift—but not a curse, either?

I went to the window, struggling with my thoughts.

I'd never allowed myself to fully think about it that way—science as neither good nor bad, merely a tool. Father had used it in cruel ways, for certain, but had he been wrong to explore its depths?

Or had he been a revolutionary?

"I need to go downstairs," I said, filled with confusion. "I need to check on Montgomery."

I stumbled from the room, thoughts churning. My feet caught on the oriental rug and I leaned on the doorframe leading into the dining room, where Balthazar and Elizabeth sat next to each other, heads close, the old musket forgotten as they pored over Father's journals.

A board creaked under my feet, and Elizabeth looked up.

"Juliet, you must look at this," she said, voice brimming with excitement. "I think we've decoded a section of your father's journal."

In my exhaustion, my body mustered one last surge of hope. "Please tell me you've found the cure for Edward."

She shook her head. "For you."

THIRTY-NINE

PERHAPS I SHOULD HAVE felt a thrill at her words. After all, a cure was what I'd been searching for these past few months. Yet Lucy's assertion—that Father's science had been just as good as cruel—had given me so much to think about. Hadn't Newcastle tried to argue the same thing? It was true that Edward was a phenomenal triumph of scientific achievement. Father had given animals the gift of speech. He'd created Balthazar, such a kind soul. Father's science had even saved my life as a baby.

Had I misjudged his work this entire time?

What will you be without it? the Beast had asked.

Montgomery hurried in, wiping his hands on a rag. "Did you say a cure?" he asked, hope in his voice. He picked up the loose pages to pore over the decoded text. "Juliet, look at this. Phosphorous salts—we were right there. But we were lacking something to stanch the cellules . . . my god, it's so simple. We've been going about it all wrong." His face, when he looked up from the page, was more handsome than I'd ever seen. "We can do it," he said.

I forced a smile, and the motion alone started to give me hope. Yes—this was what I wanted. To be whole, to be pure, not to be plagued by these wracking spasms and hallucinations. I wanted to be just as honest a person as Montgomery, all the darkness caused by my affliction banished.

"What about for Edward?" Lucy asked. I turned to find her standing behind me, eyes still spotted with red, but cheeks dry.

Elizabeth exchanged a doubtful glance with Balthazar. "We haven't finished decoding the journal entries," she said. "There might still be something that can help him."

"Then I'll help you," Lucy said, dragging out a chair. "What can I do?"

"Start with these," Elizabeth said, handing her a stack of torn pages. "Compare the entries on these pages against this list of Bible passages Balthazar is compiling. He can help you find the verse and line they reference."

While they set to work, Montgomery snatched up the rest of the decoded pages and pulled me into the kitchen. He cleared the leftover dishes and set the crate from my workshop on the table. It still held the sweet-decay smell of the roses in my attic chamber, searing me with memories.

"It should be a relatively simple procedure," he said. "We just need to include a binding agent to trick your body into thinking the animal organs are your own."

I glanced back into the dining room, where Elizabeth and Lucy pored over the journal, while Balthazar flipped through the Bible chapters with big fumbling fingers. On the island he'd developed a fondness for religion, even daring to stand up to my father over reading a prayer at Alice's funeral. It was a strange world when Balthazar was religious and my father the nonbeliever.

Could Lucy be right? Was Balthazar's existence, like Edward's, a blessing?

Some evils are necessary, Newcastle had said.

I felt a nuzzle at my ankle and looked down to find Sharkey wagging his short tail. I bent to scratch his bony head, thinking of how much the little dog loved Edward. Dogs had a way of sensing if people were good.

"Juliet?" Montgomery asked. "I could use your assistance."

"Of course," I said, brushing my hands off. He handed me a beaker while he read through Father's notes. My attention kept trailing to the cellar door, wondering if Edward also felt conflicted feelings over the prospect of the cure. Would he feel incomplete without the Beast? Would some deep part of him miss it?

Montgomery and I worked through the afternoon and into the evening, not stopping even for tea. In the next room Elizabeth and Lucy exchanging frustrated words as they decoded page after page of useless observations. The first two serum batches failed, but Montgomery adjusted the ingredients, and as darkness fell outside on Christmas Eve, he held up a vial.

"This one has held steady for three minutes. I think it might work." His blue eyes met mine. "Are you ready to try it?"

"Yes," I said. "But let's not tell the others yet. If it doesn't work, I don't want them to lose hope for Edward."

A corner of his mouth pulled into a bittersweet smile. He went to the table and readied the syringe. I rolled up my sleeve, touching the soft skin on the inside of my elbow where I'd injected myself daily for my entire life. Soon, if this worked, I would never need to hold a syringe again.

"Are you ready?" came Montgomery's gentle words.

I nodded, and he pressed the tip of the needle against my skin, sliding it expertly beneath the surface until he found the vein. I winced as the hot liquid spread. First came warmth. Then pain. My arm jerked suddenly as a white-hot light seared me and I knocked the syringe from Montgomery's arm, heard the glass crunch under my bare foot, and felt a sting of pain as I stumbled toward the window.

"Juliet?" I was vaguely aware of his arms around me, keeping me from falling, but it felt like my body belonged to someone else.

"The window," I rasped. "Air."

He threw open the pane behind the herb garden, and I gasped cold evening air that still smelled of rosemary and thyme. The lights of the city beyond were too bright. I squeezed my eyes closed, covering them with my hand, but they still burned behind my eyelids. All the sounds of the city—coal plants churning, rumbling carriages, people snoring—were magnified a thousand times.

The pain diffused through me, steady and throbbing. The sensation of my bones separating themselves from flesh had never been so great. My fingers curled against the open window, reaching for something that wasn't there. Wanting to hold myself together but finding nothing more than air. My body started to shake uncontrollably, though of its own accord or by Montgomery shaking me out of some kind of fit, I wasn't certain.

"Juliet," he called. "Juliet!"

And then my vision telescoped back into focus, my hearing sharpened, my bones crunched together as the various parts of my body pulled back together. Bones along bones, muscles quiet beneath skin, like all the disparate notes of an orchestra tuning up in a concert hall, coming together with a single jerk of the conductor's baton.

I blinked, returning to my senses. Montgomery's hands on mine no longer felt rough as sandpaper. I rediscovered my own legs.

"How are you feeling?" he asked. I blinked again, taking in the room with eyes that no longer burned. A fire roared in the stove. Sharkey wagged his tail at my feet. I stretched my fingers out, studying them, waiting for the telltale pops and clicks.

They were beautifully silent.

"Well." My voice was rusty, but I wet my dry lips. "I feel well."

Montgomery smoothed the sweat-soaked hair off my face. "It near enough killed you."

I couldn't stop looking at my hands. Moving them, flexing the fingers. Something was missing, and when I realized what it was, I nearly laughed. The stiff, lingering pain I'd lived with forever was gone.

This is what life was meant to feel like.

"Have some water," Montgomery said. I clutched the glass, drinking it greedily, then thrust the empty glass back at him. I wanted to cry with relief. I had been so worried and conflicted over nothing; the Beast was wrong when he said that I would miss that twisted, ill part of me. I didn't miss it at all. Even better, if Father's journals held the secret to my cure, surely they would hold the secret to Edward's, too.

I steadied myself against the door, no longer dizzy, but head reeling with our success. From the dining room came sounds of Lucy and Elizabeth arguing, but I couldn't focus on anything except this feeling.

Montgomery held my chin to study my eyes, checking for illness, but I could *feel* it, deep inside.

I was cured.

I had the urge to laugh. I was whole now, just like I'd always wanted.

Montgomery had told me once that my unnatural curiosity about my father's work was a symptom of my illness, just the same as the popping knuckles and pain behind my left eye. At the time I'd doubted him, wondering if it was truly possible to cure a dark heart, but now . . .

"You were right," I said, kneading the fabric of his shirt, wanting to never let go. We'd be married now, live the type of normal life that normal people did, church on Sundays and dancing on Saturdays and maybe, years from now, even pushing a baby pram through the park.

He smiled, and I matched it, and I had never felt such sweet relief in my life.

If only Edward could feel this way too . . .

Sharp voices came from the dining room, rupturing the perfect stillness between Montgomery and me. Lucy and Elizabeth were arguing in heated voices, and Montgomery frowned and headed for the doorway. I started to hold him back, to savor a few more precious seconds of this calm I'd never known. But just because the world had turned right side up for me didn't mean it had for everyone else.

"No!" came Lucy's voice.

I stood in the doorway with Montgomery, watching as she balled her fists in the papers as Elizabeth tried to calm her. "It's not true! It can't be. . . ."

"There's no other way," Elizabeth said.

Lucy looked up suddenly and, through the layer of tears, her eyes met mine. Blinded by her own panic, she didn't see how changed I was since the cure. She rushed over and grabbed me by the shoulders. "It's all there, in the journal. The unknown ingredient. And it's impossible to replicate. Juliet, there's no hope for him!"

Her hands dug into me like claws. I pried them from my shoulders and rubbed them gently. "Don't say that, Lucy. We won't give up. We found a cure for me—we'll find it for him, too."

But Lucy couldn't stop sobbing. She shook her head and then stumbled off to the kitchen for a rag to wipe her face. Balthazar pushed up from the table clumsily and went after her, offering her his handkerchief.

Outside, the church on the corner chimed six o'clock mass. I glanced at the window, where the family across the street appeared at their door with rosy faces as they made their way to the Christmas Eve service at St. Paul's.

Elizabeth squeezed my hand. "I'm so relieved to hear your cure worked, Juliet, truly. But I'm afraid Lucy was right. We can't do the same for Edward."

"Why not?" I asked, baffled. My hands were still now. My heart cured of darkness.

"It came down to the unknown ingredient," Elizabeth explained, clutching the letters.

I bit my lip. "What is it?"

To my surprise, her eyes shifted from me to Montgomery. She took a deep breath. "Montgomery, did Dr. Moreau ever draw your blood?"

FORTY

THE SOUND OF LUCY'S sobbing in the kitchen faded as the beating of my own heart grew. Beside me, Montgomery was tense as wrought iron.

"What are you suggesting?" he said.

"Did he, or didn't he?" Elizabeth asked.

Montgomery glanced at me as he dragged a hand through his hair. "Yes—all the time. There were few illnesses on the island, but malaria was a threat. Only to us, not to the islanders. I caught it a few times, and he drew my blood to study the disease before giving me a treatment to cure it, the same as his own."

I recalled the conversation I'd had with Edward when he first told me what he truly was.

Whose blood did my father use to make you? I had asked.

I don't know. I've never known, Edward had said.

My god, it was all so clear now.

Elizabeth continued, "When we decoded the journal, we discovered that the unknown ingredient was human blood. Moreau hadn't wanted to use his own because of his advanced age. He wanted strong, young blood, and there was only one source to get it from." She paused. "Edward was made from your blood, Montgomery."

"Mine?" His head shook in denial, even in anger, but I knew him better than that. There was an uncertainty to the way his hand hovered anxiously over his mouth, the same move he'd made a year ago when I'd found him again. That move betrayed tender emotions that he was afraid to admit. All his life he'd wanted a family. It was why he'd been so loyal to my father. It was why he'd kept Balthazar alive. *When I was young,* he had told me once, *I used to watch the other boys play in the street and wish I had a brother.*

What a terrible twist of fate: Edward shared his blood—a brother of sorts. It meant if there was still some way to cure Edward, that Montgomery would have the family he'd so desperately wanted. Edward would, too.

Montgomery paced by the windows, and it struck me that this information might be far more welcomed by Edward than by Montgomery. Over the past year Montgomery's sense of mercy had given way to a harsh desire for justice. Would this information soften him at all? Give me back the boy I'd fallen in love with? Or would it only make him more determined to kill Edward?

"I don't understand," I said to Elizabeth. "If we only need Montgomery's blood to cure Edward, it should be a relatively simple procedure."

"That's the problem, I'm afraid," Elizabeth said. "Montgomery's blood was tainted with malaria at the time. The malaria played some role in the composition of Edward's genetic material, but when Moreau treated it, the malaria was cleaned from his body. Without that strain, we won't be able to replicate it. It's winter in London. The closest mosquito is halfway around the world."

"It's true, then," I muttered. "There really is no hope for him." Even spoken aloud, I couldn't bring myself to believe it. I had always thought Edward's and my fate were intertwined, and yet here I was cured, meant to live a long, healthy, wholesome life—yet for Edward there was no future but melding with the Beast.

"How much time do you think he has left before the Beast takes over completely?" Elizabeth asked.

"A few days. A week, at most," Montgomery said shakily.

"As it is, he can barely keep himself in one form or the other," Elizabeth said. "I know you don't wish to hear this, Juliet, but if we can't cure him, the kindest course of action might be to put him out of his misery."

Put him out of his misery.

I remembered a rabbit, long ago, laid out on an operating table being dissected alive by medical students. I'd taken an ax to the rabbit to put it out of its misery. But Edward wasn't a rabbit. However he was created, he was a person now. How could I do the same to him?

I looked at Montgomery. He had wanted Edward dead all along, but could he truly learn he had a blood relation, only to kill him?

"You can't kill him," a voice said. Lucy stood in the

kitchen doorway, tears dried and a hard resolve on her face. "I've just been downstairs talking to him—" She silenced me when I tried to object. "Balthazar went with me. I was safe. Edward had a right to know all of this, since it's his life we're talking about. He's woken and is back to himself, for now, though the Beast is just beneath the surface." A look of tenderness crossed her face. "You can't kill him for crimes that monster inside him committed. It isn't fair."

Lucy was right—here we stood discussing Edward's fate, when he should have some say. Montgomery called after me, but I ran into the kitchen that still smelled of rosemary, and descended the stairs.

The basement was quiet. *Put him out of his misery*, Elizabeth's voice echoed. No, no, no. I *knew* I could find a way to cure him, too. I wasn't my father's daughter for nothing. We could replicate the malaria somehow, send Montgomery south to the tropics. . . .

At the bottom of the stairs, I wrapped my hands around the cellar door bars. "I know Lucy told you it's hopeless," I said. "But I'm better now, Edward, and soon you will be too. . . ."

My voice trailed off when I caught sight of the body crouched in the corner. Signs of the Beast were all over him—the way his fingers twitched, the powerful curve of his muscles. Lucy had been down here only moment before, but it didn't take long for the Beast to transform.

He looked at me with gold-colored eyes. I should have been afraid. I should have been *terrified*. Such beastly eyes, such a cruel-looking face didn't belong in this world. Yet as he stood and sauntered toward the door, never taking his eyes off mine, it wasn't fear I felt. It was a strange thrill, those old tinges of curiosity that had always drawn me to him despite my horror. I had thought all that banished when I'd been cured.

And yet I still felt it. That shouldn't have been possible, should it? Not now. Not cured. An uneasiness grew in my stomach, tasting of bile and mistakes.

"Cured, are you, love?" he said. There was almost a flicker of humanity in those yellow eyes, before it burned away. "No, I don't think so."

I KNIT MY FINGERS together, rubbing the smooth joints, reminding myself that they no longer cracked and ached. They *were* cured. The Beast was merely toying with me, working doubt into my head as he loved to do.

"Yes, I am," I said, trying to sound brave. "Montgomery and I made the serum, and it held. I can feel the difference in my body."

"I'm not talking about your lovely little fingers and toes," he said. "Flesh, blood, bone—the body is only a container for who we truly are inside. Maybe the serum cured your physical afflictions, but it didn't cure the illness of your soul." There was a tenderness in his voice, a truth in his gaze . . . he could capture me, a wolf stalking a deer, if I wasn't careful. I stepped back, shaking my head.

My heart started to thump harder, in time with his

fingers tap-tap-tapping on the cellar bars. "You don't under-stand," I said. "I'm a different person now, body *and* soul."

But a coldness crept from the old stone foundation, weaving among my skirts to my bare legs. It was quiet down here, a million miles from London, from the island, even from the others arguing upstairs. In a way, it felt *right* to be down here.

The Beast's eyes fell to the chained handle of the cellar door. "There was a different door once," he said quietly. "A red door on a jungle island."

I took another step back, frightened by the memory. A red laboratory, paint bubbling beneath my fingertips as a fire raged in the compound, my father trapped inside. And most memorable of all, Jaguar waiting for me to open the door—just a crack—so he could slip inside and kill my father.

I had done it. I'd helped him kill my father. And yet that had been the *old* me, sick of body and soul.

"You say you're cured. You say all that darkness is behind you. But would you change what you did?" the Beast asked quietly.

One would have to be sick to be capable of killing her own father. The new, cured me could never have done some-thing so ruthless. And yet. My eyes sank closed, as my heart beat harder, painfully, wrenchingly.

"No."

His voice was softer now. "Would you still have opened that door?"

And this is what it came down to: surely a normal girl,

that girl I'd imagined pushing a baby pram through a garden and dancing on Saturdays, couldn't be the same girl who helped kill her father. But I *was* still that girl, still my father's daughter, still the one who, even now, would open that door if faced with it again.

"Yes."

He smiled grimly, though there was no glee in it, as though for once he understood how heartbreaking this was for me. "No serum can change who you are. Nor should you change. Genius or madness—it all depends on who's telling the story." His hand stopped tapping, and that humanity flickered again in his eye. "You're perfect as you are, my love."

I took another shaky step away from him, fearful and confused, and hurried up the stairs. It didn't matter. I couldn't get away from his words.

He was right. No serum could cure who I *really* was—a Moreau, through and through.

It was late when I rejoined the others. I told them I was exhausted and wanted to be alone, then picked up Sharkey and climbed to the attic nursery. I liked the quiet here, the stillness of the unused toys, Sharkey's grainy fur beneath my fingers.

I sat in the rocking chair and leaned my head back, watching the moon beyond the city's skyline. It was so easy now to move my neck, my hands. Their former stiffness was nothing but a fleeting memory.

But the Beast was right. A coldness lingered in my heart and always would, no matter how much I lied to myself.

I shouldn't have been so single-minded in the way I viewed Father's research. Elizabeth had told me Father was more than just a madman, but I hadn't listened. The Beast had seen the truth on me, plain as day, among the jungle vines of the greenhouse. Even Lucy—even *Newcastle*—had known that science in and of itself wasn't good or bad.

Sometimes, even, it was a necessary evil.

As I petted Sharkey, I watched the tendons on the back of my hand plucking like piano strings. I had tried to deny the darkness inside me, but all this time, perhaps I should have embraced it for the potential good it could wield.

Sharkey jumped out of my lap, stretching on the rug so that half his body was thrown into moonlight, half still cast in shadows. I sat straighter as an idea tickled the back of my head.

Enough with the secrets.

Enough with hidden horrors.

There was only one way to protect Edward from the King's Club's machinations and also ensure that no one would replicate or condone what they were trying to do ever again.

Outside, church bells chimed midnight. I thought of the family across the street, tucked into warm beds, the children dreaming of waking in the morning to toys wrapped in big red bows. All over the city, families like theirs slumbered. Families that wouldn't sleep nearly so deeply if they knew what was happening in those basement laboratories of King's College.

I swallowed. My plan was a cruel one, dangerous, yet I couldn't deny that the curious corners of my soul curled at the thought: Maybe the best way to prevent the King's Club from enacting their plan was to enact it *for* them, and show them—and the world—exactly what would happen if my father's science was unleashed.

FORTY-ONE

I woke to the sounds of Saint Paul's bells ringing in Christmas Day.

I had stayed up half the night going through the details of my plan. Lucy slept over after sending a note home to her mother and was now fast asleep in the sea of pillows on my bed. I made a list of three King's Men—Inspector John Newcastle, Dr. Hastings, and Isambard Lessing—and when she woke, told her to write an urgent message to each one in her father's forged handwriting, calling for an emergency meeting at precisely nine o'clock in the evening and not to be a moment late. When she asked to what purpose, I refused to say. Still half asleep, with the trust of a lifelong friend, she did as I asked regardless.

In the meanwhile, I gave Edward another injection of valerian to keep him sedated, then pored over every word in Father's journal and letters, studying his procedures, focusing on the science the King's Club was trying to duplicate. For the first time I allowed myself to truly delve into it, guiltlessly, and the genius of his work made my whole body feel alive.

Elizabeth paced around the house like an unquiet ghost, throwing wide-eyed glances at the cellar door, never far from the musket and bottle of gin. In the afternoon Lucy left with Balthazar to deliver each of the letters personally, with instructions for her to meet back at the professor's house in the evening. The final step in my preparations involved Montgomery, but when I asked him to get his medical bag and come with me to King's College, he didn't obey as unquestioningly as Lucy had.

"You must tell me what this is all about," he said. "I'm to be your husband. You must trust me."

I bristled at the word *husband*, still unused to the idea despite how much I loved him.

"That trust goes both ways," I said. "Once we're there, I promise to make everything clear. You said once that before we are wed, you want no more shadows in our lives. Tonight I can end all our fears about the King's Men and Edward falling into dangerous hands." I held his hand, squeezing hard. "But I can't do it alone."

He leaned in, resting his forehead against mine, and the feel of him so close kindled the coldest parts of my body.

"Come with me," I whispered. "I need you."

The tensed muscles in his back eased. "You know I'd follow you anywhere. Though I fear we'll both end up damned."

We left Elizabeth to keep an eye on Edward and slipped out the back alleyway under cover of darkness. As we darted down the lanes, I peeked into open windows. Each one showed a different vignette of city life. A stout family shared a feast of ham and bread pudding amid the twinkling lights of a Christmas tree. A wife baked a meat pie for her husband. A young woman tucked a baby into a bassinet under a sprig of mistletoe.

We're doing this for them, I told myself. *To keep power out of the hands of the King's Club.*

At last we reached the imposing brick archway of King's College. On Christmas Day the place was deathly quiet, no horses or harness bells or students tromping around. We climbed the main stairs and I used a poured-tin copy I'd made of Radcliffe's key to allow us entry. As I'd anticipated, not even Mrs. Bell and her cleaning crew were working. Only faint moonlight filled the long hallways, even the dust having long settled.

I jerked my head for Montgomery to follow me.

The halls threw loud echoes of our footsteps as we hurried down the marble floor. He headed for the King's Club smoking room, but I grabbed his hand.

"Wait. Come with me to the basement first."

His face hardened. He knew, as I did, what those subterranean hallways held. But he followed me without argument, trusting me, and we took the stairs into the basement that smelled of sawdust, where the windowless halls held a darkness thick as fogged breath, and then we climbed even lower to the subbasement level where the stone walls smelled of ancient times. I felt along the wall until my fingers brushed the doorknob of the King's Club's secret laboratory, but Montgomery stopped me.

"Wait, Juliet." In the darkness, his voice was disembodied. "Tell me what you are planning, first."

"Come inside, and I will." I pushed open the door and lit a match to illuminate the various lanterns, which threw circles of light onto the tanks of liquid and the ungodly beasts suspended within. With one glance, I could tell they had grown in the week since we'd been here. They now had inch-long claws and powerful jaws that could snap a man's bone in one bite.

It was better than I had hoped.

"This is what I wanted to show you," I said. "These creatures. All this time we've tried so hard to keep the King's Club from catching Edward, but they'll never stop. So we're going to finish the King's Club's work for them." I curled my hands into fists, my fingernails digging into my own skin. "They wanted a monster. Let's give it to them."

"ARE YOU MAD?" MONTGOMERY asked, closing the laboratory door behind him as though afraid someone would overhear us. "That is exactly what we've been trying to *prevent* from happening."

"Yes, trying to prevent by keeping things secret. But don't you see—secrets are their ally. The moment rumors spread about Father's research was the moment his work in London ended. If the public knew the truth about what the King's Club was endeavoring to accomplish, they'd never stand for it. Imagine the newspaper headlines. So many illustrious men, captains of industry, even Scotland Yard's most promising detective—all in on this conspiracy. They'd be banished. Arrested. Even if some of them escaped the courts, they'd never dare pick up a scalpel again."

"Your father did." Montgomery stepped closer. "Say they're banished, or let off with a light sentence. What's to stop them from fleeing to an island of their own?"

"Don't flatter them," I answered, perhaps too harshly. "My father was a genius. Half of the King's Club members are only pawns. Radcliffe was never a man of science; he just saw this as another investment. They don't have the brilliance, nor the drive. If we expose them, their families will be shamed. They'll lose their social standing, their credit. They'll move on to some other, respectable scheme—investing in agriculture, promoting some new politician—and curse themselves for ever getting involved in my father's work."

I glanced at the water tanks before continuing. "The ones who are truly dangerous are the few who aren't doing this for financial advantage but for sheer scientific hubris. There are twenty-four King's Men, but I gave Lucy a list of only three names: Inspector Newcastle, Dr. Hastings, and Isambard Lessing. The ones who are scientists, the ones who might dare to consider dabbling in Father's realm again, the ones who would murder to get what they want, or experiment on humans—those are the ones who can't be allowed to continue at any cost. Without those three, the others will scatter."

Montgomery studied me very carefully. "What do you intend to do to those three?"

When I turned toward the water tanks as an answer, he grabbed my arm a little roughly. Ever since learning that Edward was his own blood relation, he'd seemed to stop thinking in such stark terms. In a way it was as though we had swapped places, he now more concerned with the gray parts of life, and me with the black and the white.

"You're going to kill those men, aren't you?" he asked.

"Not necessarily," I said, drawing a vial out of my pocket. "I only want to show them the dangers of what they're doing. I extracted this from Edward this morning while I gave him a shot of sedative. It's twenty milligrams of his spinal fluid. Not enough to harm him, but enough to bring five of these creatures to awareness. We'll lock the men and the creatures together in the smoking room upstairs."

Montgomery's jaw went very hard. "They'll die."

I tried to keep my voice steady, though my heart was fluttering with a dangerous kind of excitement. "Perhaps they will—that's what they deserve. Or perhaps the King's Men will be able to defend themselves. We have no idea what will happen, and that's the beauty of it. Leave it up to nature. Survival of the fittest."

Montgomery drew a hand over his face. "It'll be a bloodbath."

"All the better if it is." I whispered the words, because such words were never meant to be spoken. "Imagine the spectacle in the newspaper. You know how the public hungers for blood—it's why they've gone into such a fervor over the Wolf. The King's Men control the *London Times*, but not the other newspapers. They'll call it the Christmas Massacre at King's College, or something with an equally macabre ring. Everyone in the city—the entire country—will know the truth about what they were trying to do."

The blood had drained from Montgomery's face, and yet he hadn't left, nor had he called me mad and broken off the engagement. "And the creatures?" he asked.

I rested my hand on the nearest glass tank. "We kill them after it's done. We haven't a choice. We both know any creature of my father's is fated to die either way."

I tried hard not to think about Edward. Or Balthazar. Or myself.

Montgomery let out a weary sigh. "Hunting them down, just like on the island. I thought all that was behind me."

"We'll inject them with a large dose of stimulant that will stop their hearts after ten minutes. No hunting, no shooting. They'll die quietly. That's more mercy than the King's Club would have shown them."

He leaned on the worktable. "You have it all figured out, don't you?" There was an edge to his voice. He looked over the creatures in the tanks, his blond hair slipping loose and veiling his face. "There must be some other way. If we just destroyed the specimens . . ."

"They'd make more."

"We could warn the authorities about their plans for the paupers' ball."

"They *are* the authorities. Newcastle controls the police, and the members of Parliament have control over the military."

He sighed, still unwilling to accept that my plan was the only option. "It makes me think of Edward, how I was so certain he had to die. Then I learned that we share the same blood, and it changed something. I'm tired of killing, Juliet. Man or creature."

I placed my hands over his. "I wish there was another way too," I said. "But I've thought it through. It has to be this."

"You've never operated on one of these things. You've only seen it happen, and as I recall it was enough to send you running into the jungle in horror."

"I won't run this time," I said quietly.

I could still see the hesitation written in the tense muscles of his neck. I walked over to the wall and took down two leather aprons. I slid one over my head and cinched it at the waist, then handed Montgomery the other.

"I swore I'd never touch a scalpel again," he whispered.

"You don't have to touch a scalpel," I said. "I've studied Father's journal. I know every word he wrote about the procedures." I held out the vial of Edward's spinal fluid. "All we have to do is inject them with this material, and then stress the bodies with an electric shock. No cutting. No slicing. The electric current will weaken the cells to allow the material to permeate, which will bring them to life. We'll awaken five and poison the rest, then throw all the journals and instructions into the tank with them. The chemicals will destroy the writing."

Montgomery leaned on the counter, studying the blood-red liquid in the vial. I would have paid dearly to know what was going through his mind. Did he think I was lying to myself? If he did, he was wrong. This had nothing to do with besting Father's work, or even giving the King's Men the cruel justice they deserved. This was about that family next door on Dumbarton Street, and the girls at Lucy's teas, and Mrs. Bell and her cleaning crew. There was still beauty in the world, still innocence.

I squeezed Montgomery's arm. "We can't let them win. We're to be married, and we've Edward, who's practically your *brother*, and Elizabeth, who's my guardian now. If you won't do it for the good of the city, do it for them."

His hand took mine, circled the silver ring. He spun it a few times, thinking, and then let my hand fall. He tied the loose strands of his hair back and glanced at the chemistry equipment. "Go through the cabinets and look for a neural stimulant. We'll need at least a hundred milligrams per creature to ensure their heart rates increase enough to give out after ten minutes." His voice was flat, unemotional. He paused. "How exactly do you intend to transport five ravenous creatures with claws and sharp teeth to the upstairs smoking room?"

I swallowed. "I have a plan for that. It sounds a bit mad, but hear me out. The entire upstairs was fitted with electricity within the last two years. They had to run the electric wires in external casings along the walls. It won't be hard to expose a bit of wire. Enough to provide an electric shock if attached to living flesh." I paused. "The King's Men won't notice a few more animal bodies among all that taxidermy. Once they go in and flip on the lights . . ."

Montgomery looked torn between sickness over what I was proposing and a strange sort of admiration. I swallowed back the part of me that was secretly thrilled by my plan.

Montgomery selected five of the healthiest-looking specimens, while I searched through the cabinets for a neural stimulant strong enough to kill the creatures after ten minutes. He handed me a needle.

Together, we brought to fruition the terrible plans of the King's Club.

FORTY-TWO

Even without surgery, the work was a grisly task.

The creatures in the tanks might have been created in an ungodly way, but their little bodies were warm with life. Each weighed perhaps twenty-five pounds, not so different from holding Sharkey in my arms. The liquid within the tanks wasn't water, but rather a viscous chemical bath that clung to my leather apron and dress. As we laid the creatures out on the table, fluid dripping off their drenched fur and onto the floor, my heart twisted.

Sometimes you have to embrace the darkness to stop it, I reminded myself.

On the island, Father's ratlike creatures had been hairless, but these had a line of fur down the spine thick as quills. The creatures' eyelids were nearly translucent, showing a web of threading veins above eyes that would soon open for the first time. I dried the creatures with a towel as tenderly as if I was giving Sharkey a bath. Damned though they were, I couldn't bear to abuse them any more than they already had been.

As soon as I'd finished, Montgomery showed me where to inject them at the base of their spines, explaining how the central blood system was separated from the brain and spinal column by a membrane.

The syringe trembled in my hand.

It was I—not Father—giving life now.

I set the needle at the base of the first creature's spine, counting the vertebrae. The tank's fluid had kept their skin soft and thin, revealing rivers of purple veins beneath the surface. I pierced the skin gently and worked the needle until it hit the spinal sac. It was thicker than I'd imagined, and I had to thrust my hand to puncture it. Then I depressed the lever, breathing life into the thing on the table.

"The next one," Montgomery called over his shoulder, while he gathered all the notes and journals and plunged them into the viscous tank liquid to destroy them. "Hurry, before the stimulant starts to wear off."

I finished the injections. The creatures looked so strange, caught in this half-life. Bodies so perfect and yet breathless, pulseless, waiting in stasis for that one spark to set off the reaction that would start their hearts.

We carried them up two flights of stairs to the King's Club smoking room, where we worked by candlelight. Amid the taxidermied wildlife, a few more motionless bodies wouldn't be noticed. I set the last one on top of the mantel, the focal point of the room, where I hoped Newcastle would be standing when the creatures first woke.

This is for the professor, I thought with grim satisfaction.

Montgomery used his knife to pull away the electric wiring from the walls. He knew a thing or two about electrical systems and showed me how to make certain both the positive and negative wires touched the creatures' flesh.

We worked in silence, so when I heard a rustle of clothing behind me I nearly jumped.

Lucy stood in the doorway, Balthazar behind her, the two of them silhouettes in the dark hallway. Lucy's hand reached for the electric light switch.

"Don't!" I cried.

Her hand hovered above the switch. "It's dark as night in here with just those candles. What on earth are you doing?"

I rushed over to her. "My god, don't touch the lights! What are you doing here, Lucy? We were supposed to meet back at the professor's."

"I had to know what you were planning," she said, as she looked around the room, not yet noticing the few extra animal bodies among the rest. "I'm involved in this too. My father—"

"Is out of town," I interrupted. "He won't be affected by what we're doing, at least not immediately. Once he returns and learns that the King's Club has been exposed, he'll be the first to denounce his association with them."

"You're exposing them? How?"

She tried to see what Montgomery was doing on the mantel, but I pulled her into the hallway. "What time is it?" I asked.

"Around a quarter till nine," she said. "I delivered the letters. Those three men should be here shortly."

"We'll need to clear out." I peered back into the room. "Montgomery?"

"Twenty seconds and I'll be finished," he answered.

I pulled Lucy to the storage room directly across the hall, empty now save a stack of chairs. "We can hide in here," I said. "Balthazar, come."

Montgomery finished and locked the smoking room, and then we piled into the storage room and closed the door.

"Juliet . . . ," Lucy started.

"Shh. If they hear us, this will all be over."

A few painfully long minutes passed. Balthazar's chest was at my back, and the feel of his solid strength gave me relief. Lucy pressed closely to my side.

"What the devil is that smell?" she hissed, sniffing the wet spots on my dress that were soaked in the creatures' tank fluid. At the same time, I heard the groaning hinges of the main courtyard door and whispered for her to be quiet. We all held our breaths.

It wasn't long before footsteps sounded in the hall, then the low voices of two men talking. From the slips of conversation I could make out, they weren't happy about being called upon on Christmas Day. I heard them rattle the doorknob of the smoking room across the hall, but neither had a key.

After another few minutes more footsteps came, brisker than the rest, and Inspector Newcastle's familiar voice said, "Isn't Radcliffe here with the key? He's the one who called this bloody meeting. Never mind, I have mine somewhere."

My gut wrenched. I squeezed Lucy's hand, wishing she hadn't come. The sound of a key turning in the smoking room door came, followed by footsteps filing into the room.

I stared at the crack of light beneath the storage room door. It suddenly glowed brighter as someone within the smoking room must have flipped on the electric light.

For a few seconds, the four of us waited, breathless. We were pressed together so closely, I couldn't tell whose hand was brushing mine, whose elbow was in my back.

I closed my eyes and thought of a jungle far away, a father I'd once idolized.

"What the devil?" a sharp voice came from outside.

"Now!" I yelled.

Montgomery threw the door open, and he and I raced across the marble hall. The smoking room door had been left cracked, and as I reached for the knob to pull it closed I saw flutters of movement within: the startled face of Dr. Hastings, Isambard Lessing twisting to look behind him. My eyes met those of Inspector Newcastle—his blue, cold, calculating eyes—an instant before I slammed the door.

One of the King's Men threw himself against the door, but Montgomery had already twisted the key. Balthazar slid his rifle through the handles to blockade them in. For an instant, there was only the sound of someone desperately twisting the doorknob, back and forth, back and forth, and then a sudden silence.

A high-pitched animal squeal erupted, ungodly and terrible. I bit my lip hard enough to draw blood.

Lucy twisted her neck to stare at me in horror. "Juliet, what have you done?"

"They would have brought this upon the city," I said, desperate to convince her what I'd done was right. "They would have killed Edward to do it."

Someone pounded the door hard enough to nearly split the hinges. A lamp crashed. It was terrible, listening to those sounds. Terrible and satisfying, in a cruel way. I could only imagine the King's Men's shock at seeing their creatures suddenly animated. The confusion. Then the horror. Another wail came, though from beast or man, I couldn't be sure.

Lucy screamed as blood trickled beneath the door.

"Make it end!" she cried. "It's killing them!" She threw herself against the door, pulling at Balthazar's rifle.

"No, Lucy, don't!"

Both Montgomery and I rushed forward, but it was too late to stop her. The rifle clattered and her hand twisted the key. She didn't even have time to turn the doorknob before it was flung open by Isambard Lessing, blood dripping from his eye sockets, his chest already stained crimson. He collapsed in the doorway, dead.

None of us was prepared for the carnage inside.

FORTY-THREE

WHAT STRUCK ME FIRST wasn't the dead man at my feet, nor the scrambling chaos within.

It was the smell.

A King's Man—or perhaps one of the creatures—must have knocked over the liquor cabinet, because now the sticky-sweet smell of rum clogged the air, mixing with the odor of fresh blood, laboratory fluid, and the musk of wild things on the hunt.

I gagged as I reached to slam the door shut, but Isambard Lessing's body was in the way. Balthazar stooped over to move the body, but it was too late; one of the creatures was already hurling itself toward us, all glowing eyes and scrambling claws and a body that moved more like snake than rodent.

Lucy screamed again, diving to the blood-soaked floor. I grabbed the rifle and tossed it to Montgomery, but we hadn't time. The creature was three feet away, two, and then it was on him. It let out a hideous cry and sank its long claws into his arm. I screamed and stumbled toward him, wrapping my fingers around the thing's furry back to rip it off. Balthazar picked up the fallen rifle and slammed it into the creature's head, cracking the skull again and again, until cranial fluid seeped onto my dress.

I dropped the dead creature, heart pounding, and stumbled backward until I collided with the sofa. Blood poured from the wounds on Montgomery's arm.

"God help me!" a male voice called, though I couldn't tell if it came from Dr. Hastings or Newcastle. I looked around as though in a dream—a nightmare—but there were too many bodies crawling on the floor, stumbling around the room, too many flashes of furry creatures scrambling with glistening claws and teeth.

I'd had no idea what chaos five freshly awakened creatures could cause. For a moment, time was frozen. Lucy was pressed in a corner with arms braced over her head. Montgomery and Balthazar each fought with a creature, blood dripping from their arms, inhuman screeches filling the sticky-sweet air.

"My god," I muttered.

I stumbled toward Lucy, over Isambard Lessing's dead body. Dr. Hastings fell onto the leather club chair next to me, moaning as blood spilled from a deep gash on the side of his neck that turned his white shirt crimson, before tumbling off the chair and landing near the fireplace.

I threw myself on the ground in front of Lucy, wrapping my arms around her, dragging her deeper into the corner. A broken bottle lay on its side that I grabbed as a weapon, heedless of how it cut into my palm. Across the room, Montgomery aimed the rifle at a creature he'd cornered in the fireplace. Balthazar gave another a sharp kick. The sounds of bullets filled the air, the dying cries of little creatures that should have never existed.

I had done this. I'd killed these men, I'd spilled this blood, just as a year ago I'd spilled Father's. I tried to tell myself this was just as necessary, yet I hadn't *seen* Father's death. I hadn't witnessed the carnage of his body torn apart, seeping blood like the dying body of Dr. Hastings by the fireplace.

Montgomery let out a final gunshot that echoed in the room. For a few moments there was the sound of moaning and wheezing little animal breaths, but no movement. Wherever the remaining creatures were, they were hiding. Montgomery raised a finger to his lips and started to crouch on the rug, but Lucy screamed suddenly as two creatures flew out from under the sofa. One went for the fireplace, and Montgomery leaped up and fired his pistol, again and again. The other skittered on the ground toward us. Balthazar lifted a heavy foot and stomped on it, smashing it dead with a crunch of bone.

"Your rifle!" Montgomery yelled to Balthazar. "One's still alive on the other side of that chair!"

The sound of squealing beasts and gunshots was terrible, and I threw my hands over my ears. God help me, something about the chaos was thrilling, too. I could almost taste it, like the shock of first frost. Balthazar lumbered behind the cabinets, rifle in hand. I pulled Lucy deeper into the corner, brandishing the broken bottle, ready to slice a creature apart if one lunged for us. Montgomery fired again and his pistol clicked—empty.

"Damn!" he yelled, drawing his knife.

Lucy kept screaming, and the dying men moaned in pain, and the room filled with swirling smells. I caught sight of a letter opener that would make a much better weapon and staggered forward, when from out of nowhere Balthazar slammed into me and knocked me against the table. I cried out, and at the same time another gunshot went off. Balthazar collapsed behind the sofa, letting out an anguished cry.

"Balthazar!" Montgomery yelled.

Pain burst in my shoulder from where I'd collided with the table, making my vision spark, but I crawled to my knees and tried to find Balthazar. I saw glimpses of his back and meaty arms in the midst of a brawl behind the leather sofa, but by my count all the five creatures were dead. I must have forgotten one, missed one . . . I stumbled toward him with the letter opener in hand, ready to plunge it into the living flesh of a creature, but when I looked around the sofa, I froze. Balthazar struggled with not a creature, but a man. A copper breastplate gleamed on his chest.

Inspector Newcastle was still alive.

It all made sense to me in flashes. He'd shot at Balthazar. No—he'd shot at *me*, but Balthazar had shoved me aside. He'd taken the bullet in my place.

My insides wrung like a washrag, and all I could think

was *Balthazar, Balthazar, Balthazar*, that he'd taken a bullet for me, a rifle blast no less, a shot that would have killed me instantly.

"Montgomery, help!" I cried.

I stumbled forward on hands and knees, skirts tangled around my legs, as Montgomery leaped over a couch to reach us. Dr. Hastings's body lay in my way, the life draining out of him, and I had to drag my skirts to crawl over his bloody chest. With his dying strength he grabbed my ankle, but I kicked free, shrieking, and toppled onto the rug. In a way, the Beast *had* left him for me to kill—what terrible irony.

Newcastle lurched for the door just as I collapsed against Balthazar.

"Where are you hurt?" I cried.

He peeled back a meaty hand clutched against his rib cage to reveal a pulpy wound seeping blood. I gasped as Montgomery rushed to my side.

"He's shot," I said. "Newcastle aimed for me but Balthazar pushed me aside." My stomach clenched. If Balthazar didn't survive . . .

Lucy rushed over. "You can stop the bleeding, can't you?"

"Perhaps," Montgomery said, hurrying to remove his coat. "Newcastle's a good shot. How did he even survive?"

"It's the copper breastplate he wears," I muttered, glancing at the door, dragging a bloodstained hand through my tangled hair. "That blasted armor protected him."

Fury seethed in me as Balthazar lay bleeding, just as the professor had bled to death. A man as ambitious and highly connected as Newcastle wouldn't stop because we'd exposed him. If he escaped, he'd concoct some new scheme, move to a new country and invent a new name, involve new patrons—there was certainly no shortage of wealthy, unscrupulous men in this world—and anyone who stood in his way would be murdered. Worse, he was the sole witness to the massacre tonight. He might tell Scotland Yard what we'd done, turn this around to blame it on us, absolve himself of any involvement. Montgomery and Balthazar and Lucy and I would hang for what we'd done.

No, not Lucy. He loved her enough to spare her the noose, but what would he demand in return? A lifetime of marriage under threat of prison if she ever left him?

Men like John Newcastle stopped at nothing.

It was up to me, then, to stop *him*.

My fingers went to Balthazar's bloodstained coat pocket, digging for the sugar cubes he always kept there to feed insects. "Stay with him, Montgomery," I choked. "I'm going after Newcastle."

I raced for the door before he could answer. I skidded out into the hall, following the sounds of Newcastle's footsteps. It was a maze in these hallways, but one I knew well. The exterior door on this level was always kept locked, so if he was headed north as his footsteps indicated, he'd have to circle around.

I could intercept him.

I hurried to search each of the rooms until I found a small supply closet filled with bottles and powders, and

I located a glass jar of nitric acid and another of standard ether, staples of any laboratory. I crushed the sugar cubes in one hand, turning them into a dissolvable powder, and then took a deep breath.

Did I truly want to do this?

On their own nitric acid and ether caused minor burns, but when mixed with a metal alloy and a reactive agent—the sugar—they would create an exothermic reaction strong enough to melt copper.

Dash it. I hadn't a choice. As I ran to intercept Newcastle, I unscrewed the lid of the acid and added the sugar, then shook the mixture. It was dark in these hallways, with only the moonlight, and I was able to hide myself in the shadowy alcove of a doorway. I heard his footsteps approaching as he doubled back, each step as loud as the thumping of my heart.

I squeezed my eyes closed.

He killed the professor, I reminded myself. *He shot Balthazar. He was aiming for you.*

He turned the corner and his face fell into a beam of moonlight just as he saw me.

I rushed him. I didn't think, I didn't listen, for fear that I'd lose my courage. I hurled my body against him, kicking and tearing. His rifle skidded down the marble hall as we tumbled to the hard floor.

"Get off me!" he yelled.

"Are you going to kill me?" I hurled back. "Like you killed the professor? Like you nearly killed *Balthazar*?"

He managed to pin my shoulder to the ground. "Like

you just killed those men?" he hissed back at me. "Your father would be proud of your resolve, Miss Moreau. There can't be too many girls as ruthlessly determined as you. He was the same way."

I let out an angry cry and pushed away from the floor. I couldn't let this man escape—he'd have us arrested, only to continue his schemes. He was much stronger than me, but in his wounded state, we were equally matched. As we tussled together, I managed to free my left hand and slam the glass jar of nitrate across his breastplate. Acid ran down his chest but Newcastle ignored it, knowing the copper armor protected him, and let out a harsh laugh.

The acid was only the beginning, though.

I took the glass bottle of ether from my pocket and, with more curses than prayers, aimed for the same place on his armor. He threw up an arm to deflect me, and the bottle smashed against the edge of his shoulder instead, spilling down over his chest. The dizzying fumes made me choke.

Newcastle coughed too, as I skittered back against the far wall. He whirled his head around, wondering why I suddenly looked so frightened. It wasn't until the reaction began, the volatile gas igniting the acid and reactive agent binding to the copper, which began to glow a faint red, then a molten yellow and white hot, searing into his skin, burning his flesh, that he began to howl.

He tore at the copper breastplate, trying to get it off, but it had already begun to fuse to his flesh as it glowed bright as the sun.

I shaded my eyes from the light. By the time it faded,

Newcastle had stopped howling. He lay on the stone floor, the smell of burned flesh in the air mixing with the sugar-sweet aroma of chemicals.

It only took one look to know that if he wasn't dead, he would be soon.

My legs gave out. I sank against the wall, sliding to the floor. Behind me came footsteps, and I saw Lucy standing in the hall.

For a moment we only stared at each other. There were no words for what I had done; no words to forgive me, nor to condemn. I'd just killed one of her suitors, a man who despite all his terrible crimes had truly loved her.

"We've stopped the bleeding," she choked at last. "But we've got to get Balthazar back to the professor's house so Montgomery can remove the bullet."

I stood on shaky legs. My body was weary with exhaustion, and yet despite everything there was a small, terrible thrill of pride. It burned in the dark part of my heart as brightly as gleaming copper.

"Take me to Balthazar," I said.

FORTY-FOUR

WE LEFT INSPECTOR NEWCASTLE'S body smoldering in the shadows. The copper armor still glowed a deep red and smelled of burned flesh, an odor I wished to live my entire life without smelling again. By the time we returned to the smoking room, Balthazar was sitting upright with a makeshift bandage across his chest. He smiled when he saw me. I stumbled to my knees next to him.

"You saved my life," I said.

"You're so small," he said. "One bullet would kill you."

Love for this big man swelled in my throat as Montgomery patted him on the shoulder. "His pulse is strong. I've never known a man who could take a bullet to the chest and walk away from it. What do you say, my friend, can you stand?" With our help Balthazar lumbered to his feet, wheezing only slightly.

I led them as fast as Balthazar could hobble through the maze of hallways to an exterior door. Snow blew in, making wind eddies in the hallway corners, replacing the miasma of singed flesh.

The empty carriage waited in the alley, tethered to horses that stamped impatiently in the cold. We helped Balthazar into the back, and Lucy and I climbed in with him as Montgomery mounted the driver's seat and cracked the whip. The steady rumble of horse hooves was eerily soothing, and by the time we reached the professor's townhouse, my wild determination had drained away and left me with only the cold reality of what we'd done.

What *I'd* done.

Outside the carriage, church bells rang eleven at night. *Christmas is almost over*, I thought. *A supposed day of joy.* At the university I'd felt such an arrogant swell of pride to know I'd defeated Newcastle and Hastings and Lessing, and that the rest of the King's Men would scatter. Such pride sickened me now.

Elizabeth was waiting for us anxiously when we arrived. Sharkey came running down the stairs, sniffing the air and our clothes, tail low as he wound circles between our feet while we helped Balthazar shuffle into the dining room. Elizabeth cleared the table and set out her medical supplies, and now directed us while trying to keep Sharkey from tripping us with his frantic whining. I laid a hand on Balthazar's swollen shoulder, wishing I knew how to give him my thanks. All I had were words, and words were poor payment for a saved life.

His big fingers drifted to his shirt's nape, where he fumbled with the small buttons.

"Let me help you," I said, undoing them for him. He groaned in pain as I slid the shirt off his hunched shoulders. I tried to look away to protect his modesty, but I couldn't help glancing at the bullet wound.

My stomach lurched. The wound was bad enough—it certainly would have killed me—but it was his deformities that stole my breath. His rib cage was swollen on one side, shrunken on the other, his shoulders lopsided but powerful, dark hair covering every inch of skin. These deformities weren't the results of an injury—they were the results of Father playing God.

I closed my eyes, his shirt clutched tightly in my hand. *Never again.*

Montgomery came from the kitchen with some fresh bandages, and I stepped back to give him room. He pulled away the rest of Balthazar's shirt, examining the wound, not flinching at the deformities. "I don't know how you are still standing, my friend. You must have the strength of an ox."

While Montgomery stitched him up, I stared out the window, too stunned to think. I could still feel Dr. Hastings's hand on my ankle. See Isambard Lessing's eyes gouged out. Smell Newcastle's flesh burning.

Mrs. Bell's cleaning crew would find them in the morning. I could imagine the thin cleaning girl frozen in the doorway at the sight of such carnage. The police would eventually find the laboratory on the subbasement level. Even though we'd destroyed the journals, it would be easy enough for the police to deduce that the King's Club had been practicing illegal scientific experimentation. The newspapers would love the scandal. The entire *city* would love it. And with Newcastle dead, no one would ever know of our hand in it.

I vaguely heard Elizabeth and Lucy talking, though in my exhaustion their voices were only bits of words like *carriage* and *manor* and one repeated only in hushed tones: *murder*.

They were talking about me. They were talking about fleeing the city. Another word found its way to my ear.

Edward.

I looked down at my hands, still coated with chemical residue and blood. Some of it was Newcastle's. Some was the creatures'. Some belonged to Balthazar.

My gaze turned to the cellar door.

We both know any creature of my father's is fated to die, I had said in the laboratory, about the water tank creatures. But did that mean Edward, too?

I felt Lucy's hands on me, followed by a warm cloth wiping my face and hands. "They'll soon find that scene in the smoking room and raise the alarm. You have to leave, Juliet, in case there's any way they can trace it to you."

"I want you to go to my estate in Scotland," Elizabeth said. "It's listed under a cousin's name who resides on the Continent, so they won't be able to trace it back to either of us. I'll ride with you tonight just as far as Derby to make sure you leave the city without trouble, then we'll part ways and I'll return here to do what I can to cover our tracks. I'll meet you at the manor in a fortnight."

Her words were a distant echo. I kept staring at that cellar door, thinking of the boy chained below. He had few days left before the Beast consumed his humanity. Not much time.

"You must leave tonight," Elizabeth insisted. "You'll have to change clothes. It's a three-day journey, if the weather holds."

My eyes shifted to Montgomery, then to the little dog curled by the cellar door, tail thumping, knowing his master was trapped below. For a few seconds we all stared at the cellar door, each alone with our secret fears and thoughts.

"Elizabeth was right before," Montgomery said at last, though hesitation filled his voice. "The humane thing to do would be to kill him mercifully."

Lucy let out a sob.

I grabbed Montgomery's arm, pulling him to the window, where we could speak privately. "You've wanted a family for so long. A brother. I know it isn't the same, but—"

"That *is* why I'm doing this," he answered in a whisper. "I'd feel no regret killing an enemy; only a brother I could bear to put out of his misery mercifully, given the alternative of watching him turn into a monster."

"You aren't thinking through this. We still have a few days; there's still time to work on a cure. There must be ways to synthetically replicate the effects of malaria in the bloodstream. Elizabeth will have medical supplies at her estate." I squeezed his hand. "Don't give up on him, not after what we've learned."

It was as much for Montgomery's soul that I pleaded.

If Montgomery did this—killed the closest thing he had to a brother, after killing all the island's beast-men—that kind little boy I'd once known might be gone for good.

"I don't know what else to do." His voice broke. He had just stitched up his best friend, and now we were debating the fate of a young man who shared his own blood.

I eased my grip.

"We can give him the rest of the valerian all in one dose," I said. "And sedate him if the Beast starts to emerge. We'll bind his hands as a precaution. The professor had an old set of shackles in the closet upstairs."

He sighed, and I knew I had won him over.

When we told the others our plan, Elizabeth looked apprehensive, but she didn't argue. Lucy wrung her hands in relief.

Montgomery rubbed his forehead as he turned to me. "Balthazar won't be able to drive the carriage the entire time, not with his wounds. I'll need to be up front most of the time. When I am, you must keep a pistol aimed at Edward every second of the trip."

I nodded. My head was racing with the thoughts of draughts, serums, elixirs I would try. What I felt for Edward wasn't love, not like with Montgomery. But in a way Edward was also dear to me, because he and I weren't so different at heart.

"I'm coming too," Lucy announced.

My head jerked to her. "You can't. You've a life here."

"A life? My father was one of those men. He knew what they were doing, and he supported it. You wouldn't go home after that, so you can't tell me *I* should." She was standing very close to the cellar door, throwing it little glances, and I had a feeling her decision had as much to do with the boy in the cellar as anything else.

I turned to Montgomery for help, but to my surprise he just wiped his tired face with a cloth. "You know better than anyone what it is to have an immoral father," he said to me. "Let her come."

The room still felt unnaturally cold, or maybe it was the chill in my blood. I looked at each of them, settling last on Montgomery. My heart clenched. Even if I turned out to be a terrible wife, he would still love me, always forgive me, always be the boy who had pushed a sullen little girl around in a wheelbarrow to make her smile. There was good in each of them, good still in this harsh world, and it blew a small bit of warmth into my limbs.

"Tonight, then," I said. "All of us."

FORTY-FIVE

MONTGOMERY GAVE THE HORSES fresh feed and water before the journey, work that was second nature to him. Lucy packed as many extra blankets and coats as she could find. Had she always had this practical side to her, and I'd never noticed? It wasn't until everything was packed, the horses' harnesses checked one last time, that I slipped down the basement steps to the cellar with shackles in hand.

Edward was awake, in his human state, though his muscles twitched under his skin like eels beneath water. He fingered his pocket watch anxiously, running his nails along the seam as though he would open it, but he never did. He wouldn't meet my gaze.

"We're leaving, Edward." His gave no indication of having heard, and I felt for the syringe of valerian in my pocket. "You don't have to worry about the King's Club any longer. We made certain that the entire city will know what they've done, once the police . . ." I cleared my throat. "Once the police find the bodies."

His head jerked up at this. "What did you do?" he asked.

I hesitated. "It doesn't matter, but the police might trace it to us, so we're headed north to Elizabeth's estate. We're taking you with us."

He laughed, cold and harsh. "Ah, Juliet, you'd best leave me here."

My hands curled against the bars. "You wouldn't have abandoned me, and I'm not going to abandon you."

He didn't answer, and I unchained the door and cracked it open. He'd used all his strength to fight against the Beast these final few days, and it showed in the sag of his limbs and the lines of his face. I didn't dare step closer, not yet.

He shook his head. "It will be finished for me soon. The Beast will take me over completely, and he'll do terrible things. You'd do better to kill me now."

"Don't give up, Edward, please." I stepped forward hesitantly and reached out a hand to touch his shoulder, but his eyes went to my silver ring. For a painfully silent moment, the ring was the loudest thing in the room.

"Lucy told me about the engagement," he said at last, bitterly. "I suppose congratulations are in order."

"You always knew I loved him. I never lied about that."

"Yes, but it isn't *you* he loves in return. It's the idea of you. A fantasy."

"How is that any different from you? You claim to have fallen in love with me from a photograph. But I'm not a fantasy, Edward—I can be heartless and cold and stubborn, just like my father. Montgomery will come to accept that, in time." I swallowed, covering the ring with my other hand. "Lucy adores you. She knows what you are and still loves you. If you'd only spare a thought for her . . ."

"Has Montgomery told you the truth yet?"

The secrets. In all the chaos, it had been easy to disregard what Edward had told me about Montgomery keeping secrets. With the engagement, I had assumed everything was right between him and me, or at least would be once we were out of London. But now a thorn of doubt dug itself into my palm.

Edward coughed a humorless laugh. "He hasn't. I didn't think so, or else you wouldn't be so quick to marry him." He leaned closer, jaw set hard. "Ask him about Moreau's laboratory files on the island. About the ones you *didn't* see."

I felt caught between desperate curiosity and fear. "If you know something," I started, "then you must tell me—"

"Juliet?" Elizabeth's worried voice, coming from the top of the stairs, interrupted me. "Are you down there alone with him?"

My fist tightened over the shackles. I leaned out of the cellar door and called up to her, "There's no cause for alarm. He has control of himself for the moment."

Elizabeth stood at the top of the stairs, musket in hand, silhouetted by the kitchen light. "I have something for you." She started down the stairs and I climbed up to meet her halfway, where she extended me a sealed letter. "Since I'm only going with you tonight as far as Derby, I've written you a letter of introduction to Mrs. McKenna, the housekeeper, and explained I'll be joining you in a few weeks. I should warn you, it's a large manor, quite remote. There's a village five miles away, but it can be difficult to reach when the moors flood. The servants are all a bit out of practice with polite society. You'll find some of them rather strange, I think."

"I'll be quite at home then." I tucked the sealed letter into my bodice. "I'll bring Edward up in a few moments."

She nodded, and I returned to the cellar. Edward was being strangely quiet. A small metal object gleamed on the floor next to his hand.

I crouched down to pick up the pocket watch he was always fiddling with, open now, only where the clockwork should have been was only empty space.

"There's no clock—" I started.

He took it from me and closed it in one snap. "You wish me to join you? Very well. Let us be gone from this place."

His voice was heavy, almost a mockery of himself, as he held his wrists out. I closed the shackles around his hands guiltily, wishing we didn't have to treat him as a prisoner, angry at the Beast for making it necessary. I uncapped the syringe of valerian and injected it into his arm. He winced as the drug wove its way through his system, causing his body to shudder. I was relieved that his eyes, when they met mine, had cleared at least briefly.

I helped him to his feet, but he paused at the door. "It isn't that I don't care for Lucy," he said. "There is much to admire. But Juliet . . ." He paused. "Ah well, it doesn't matter anymore."

I twisted the ring on my finger anxiously as we made our way up the stairs, through the kitchen, and toward the waiting carriage. He was being strangely quiet again, and a premonition that something was wrong itched at the back of my neck and made me throw sidelong glances at him in the gas-lit courtyard.

His face was the same; no sign of the Beast. What was it about him that had changed? He came with me too easily, as though he'd given up, content to be a puppet pulled along at my feet.

Montgomery locked the townhouse behind us, then climbed into the driver's seat with a bandaged Balthazar. Elizabeth was already inside the carriage with the professor's cuckoo clock in her lap, the best thing she had to remember him by. Lucy sat next to her with Sharkey, a bit of twine tied around his neck as a leash. His tail thumped at the sight of Edward. We climbed inside and, after our tap on the roof, Montgomery started the carriage.

He drove the horses with haste. Elizabeth clutched the clock, lost in her own thoughts. I marveled that she was so willing to help us, until I remembered that without the professor she had no family save me, her new ward, and that family meant much to her. Neither she nor the professor had spoken at length about their deceased relatives. Only that they'd been Swiss by ancestry but Scottish by birth, descendants of an illegitimate line of unscrupulous scientists not so unlike my own father. Maybe for this reason, Elizabeth saw a younger version of herself in me as well.

Edward coughed, pulling his coat tighter the best he

could with his wrists bound. Lucy rested a hand on his knee but then frowned and slid closer to touch his forehead.

"Edward, you're burning up."

"A fever. That's all."

I studied him in the faint light as we bounced over the streets. Sweat poured down his brow despite the cold night. He doubled over, coughing harder, a deep rattling that came from too far down in his chest. Even Elizabeth seemed unsettled.

"Edward . . . ," I started.

He squeezed his pocket watch and coughed more, starting to shake. I inched forward and took his hand in mine, feeling for his temperature. He was sweating all over.

"My god, Edward, what have you done?" I whispered.

His fist tightened over the watch and I ripped it from his weak fingers, inserting my fingernail into the seam to open it. What had he been keeping in here, in the space meant for a clock? All those times he'd toyed with it, I'd thought it nothing but a bauble.

I lifted it to my nose—odorless. On closer inspection, I found a faint trace of white powder. The watch fell from my hands and clattered on the floor.

Arsenic.

My heart stopped. My breath stilled.

The horses were moving faster now; we must have left the city center for the open roads of the country. It didn't matter how fast they moved, or if we turned around and rushed to a hospital. There was no antidote for this poison.

"Why?" I whispered. Neither Elizabeth nor Lucy had

seen the powder, and for a few moments the poison was a secret only Edward and I shared.

He doubled over again. "You know why. Someday soon, the Beast would take control. He'd kill one of you. You've protected this city tonight in your way; now let me protect it in mine. I've tried to end my life a dozen times, but he was always too strong—until now. I'm becoming him, but he's becoming me, too—he can no longer prevent me from taking both our lives."

I fell back against the cushions, stunned. I wanted to argue. I wanted to scream. I wanted to do anything but sit on this soft carriage seat in my fine coat and watch him die.

Lucy gasped as she realized what had happened. "Stop the carriage!" she cried.

But neither Montgomery nor Balthazar, outside in the wind, heard her. Lucy screamed as Edward convulsed and fell onto the bottom of the carriage.

"Now it's done," he coughed. "The worst of your father's creations, finished."

"Edward, no!" I collapsed next to him. "It didn't have to be this way. I would have found a cure."

He convulsed again, pressing a hand to his head as though it ached, the skin around his eyes and mouth turning dark.

"Elizabeth, help him!" I pleaded.

She set the clock aside and felt his pulse, brow furrowed. The carriage hit a rut and the cuckoo clock tumbled to the floor with a crash of gears and squawk of the wooden bird. Squawking and squawking, each time the carriage jostled. Furious, I reached over and ripped the back panel off, clawing at the gears until they came loose in a terrible mess and the squawking stopped.

"There's no cure for as much as he's taken," Elizabeth said, releasing Edward's wrist. For the first time since I'd known her, she looked lost. "He'll be dead before we reach Derby."

Lucy wailed everything that I wanted to but couldn't express. I slumped to the bottom of the carriage amid the wreckage of the clock. I picked up the little wooden bird, thinking of the professor, how I'd failed him, too. There was an inscription I'd never noticed before, written on the underside of the bird in German.

Für meine Lieblingskusine Elisabeth, VF.

To my favorite cousin Elizabeth, VF.

The clock was an heirloom, the inscription a century old. It wasn't *this* Elizabeth then, and the V must stand for a different Victor. I started to toss the bird back into the wreckage of the clock, yet at the last minute paused and looked at the inscription again.

I turned to Elizabeth as a strange sensation grew in the corners of my mind. Elizabeth and Victor von Stein—they must have been named after ancestors of the same names. I pieced together everything I knew of the von Stein family, from those nameless portraits, the journals in German, even the ancient doll in the nursery stitched together by the hands of a long-ago surgeon.

There was only one conclusion to draw, only one dark science that must be detailed in their ancestors' journals, only one explanation for their names.

"But that's not the end, is it, Elizabeth?" My own hands trembled at the thought. "Death, I mean. It isn't the end."

She regarded me as one might a madwoman. "What are you saying?"

"Your family was from Switzerland. They were illegitimate. They changed their name, didn't they?"

She didn't respond with even as much as a nod. She was clever, perhaps far cleverer than me, and yet I had figured out the von Stein secret.

"What was their name, Elizabeth?" I demanded.

"Frankenstein!" she cried. "Their name was Frankenstein before they changed it. Is that what you wished to hear?"

Lucy gaped. "But that's just an old story!"

I had heard the tales too, like most children. But I also remembered Father mentioning the name Frankenstein in his study with his colleagues. At the time I'd thought they were swapping ghost stories, until I realized that grown men didn't sit around at night telling stories.

"Victor Frankenstein was my great-great-uncle," she admitted quietly. "He died in 1794. He'd traveled to the Orkney Islands and fathered a bastard son with a Scottish lord's daughter—that son was the professor's grandfather. What you've heard are only rumors. But all rumors, Victor Frankenstein's tale especially, are rooted in truth."

"That's why the King's Club wanted your family journals, isn't it?" I asked. "They knew. They wanted Victor Frankenstein's research."

"Yes," she said, her voice revealing nothing. "They wanted those journals. My great-great-uncle was very precise in his notes. And I've helped you because thus far, you've been merely victims to dangerous science like his. But what you are suggesting crosses that line. It's a hard line to come back from. My uncle dabbled when he was younger, but he saw the errors of his ways before it was too late. Your father wasn't as fortunate. If you cross that line, Juliet, you'll be in danger of becoming just like him."

Unconscious at our feet, Edward moaned; his fingertips had already turned black.

"Edward's not just anyone," I said. "He's Montgomery's blood relation. He sacrificed himself to protect all of us." My voice dropped. "If he hadn't poisoned himself, I know I could have cured him in time."

Elizabeth leaned closer. "Think hard, Juliet. It's only a handful of scientists who are ever even faced with this decision. The smart ones turn back. Only the mad push forward."

Edward would be dead within hours. He *was* like kin to me, my father his creator as much as mine. Was Edward worth more than my soul? My sanity?

I was already a murderer, after all. Already damned.

As Edward lay dying and my thoughts turned as fast as the carriage wheels, the horses whisked us away, far north, where the heath grew and wind twisted the trees, to a place where people were forgotten.

To a place we'd never be found.

To a place where I might lose myself to the same dark madness that had claimed my father.

ACKNOWLEDGMENTS

To MY EDITOR, KRISTIN Rens: You know exactly what to say to inspire me to take my drafts to the next level. Taking this book from the spark of an idea to the finished version has been a wonderful and challenging journey, and I'm so lucky to have had you as my guide.

To my agent, Josh Adams, and Tracey and Quinlan Lee at Adams Literary: Any author would be fortunate to be on your team. You guys are the whole package!

My thanks to the Balzer + Bray and HarperCollins team: associate editor Sara Sargent, publicist/miracle worker Caroline Sun, designers Alison Klapthor and Alison Donalty, copy editors Renée Cafiero and Anne Dunn, marketing mavens Emilie Polster, Stephanie Hoffman, Margot Wood, and Aubry Parks-Fried. I owe my book's beautiful design, marketing savvy, and book shimmies to you guys.

To my critique partners and writing support team: Megan Miranda, Ellen Oh, Carrie Ryan, Constance Lombardo, Andrea Jacobsen, Melissa Koosmann, the Bat

Cave superheroes, Friday the Thirteeners, and Lucky 13s. This book is a thousand times better for your insight.

To my wonderful family: Peggy & Tim for reading my drafts and being my biggest cheerleaders; Lena for being a constant inspiration and for talking me down from the ledge when I'm ready to abandon tough drafts; and Nancy, Gene, Marilyn, & the Shepherd clan for your enthusiasm and accepting me into your family, weird book ideas and all.

And lastly, to my husband, Jesse: I can't possibly put into words everything you mean to me. Because of your encouragement, I became a writer. Because of your support, I became an author. With you life is an adventure, and I can't wait to see where it takes us next.

Megan Shepherd grew up in her family's independent bookstore in the Blue Ridge Mountains. The travel bug took her from London to Timbuktu and many places in between, though she ended up back in North Carolina with her husband and two cats, and she wouldn't want to live anywhere else. *The Madman's Daughter* and *Her Dark Curiosity* are her first novels. Visit her online at www.meganshepherd.com.